Coming Home

A novel by Charles Russell

For Dorothy V. Russell
My mother

Who continues to inspire us all

And

James T. Russell
my late dad

Acknowledgements

This is the fifth book I have published in five years. Without the assistance and encouragement of my wife, Patricia, none of them would have gone to press. She has been my loyal companion, friend, and love for over 50 years.

A special thanks, again, to Glenda Watts, whose patience with my illiteracy is amazing, for editing the book.

Appreciation to Rose Mary Jones Delane, who was a Flying Queen, for the information she provided about this amazing group of ladies whose accomplishments will probably never be equaled.

Author's Note

In this story, I included areas that have not received the attention they deserved. The work is fiction, but that the Korean War is known as the 'Forgotten War', is fact. The brave men who fought in that war, with almost 40,000 giving their lives is real, as is the final outcome, which resulted in no peace treaty and the line separating the countries almost the same as it was when the war began. No one could argue with the fact that the war was extremely bloody and fought in terrible conditions or that politics played a major role from the beginning until the end of the war.

On a lighter side, the story revisits the inspirational girl's basketball team from Wayland Baptist College, who became known as the Flying Queens. They complied a record, from 1953-1958, of 131 wins and no defeats. One could almost call them the Forgotten Dynasty, since many have never heard of them.

The story takes place in the 50's during the seven-year drought, which affected everyone who lived in this part of the country during that era.

I wove the facts of these three events into the fictional lives of the two main characters to create, what I hope to be, an interesting and yet informative novel.

"It's a thing to see
when a boy comes home"

-John Steinbeck, *The Grapes of Wrath*

Chapter 1

Sam

October 20, 1953

When I stepped off the bus, there was no one to meet me. I hadn't really expected anyone, but it was depressing. I'd been discharged three days earlier in California, and after countless bus changes and delays had arrived at home. My last two years had been spent in Korea trying to stay alive. Somehow, I was successful, even though some of my friends were not as fortunate. Loneliness swept over me as I found a bench and sat down. I lit a Camel and inhaled deeply. I hadn't smoked before going into the service, but combat will make you do a lot of things you hadn't done.

I was home or would be when I could get a ride to the ranch which was located 20 miles south of town. No one would meet me there either. That wasn't true. Our loyal hired hand, Jose Samaniego, would be there. He had been with us as long as I could remember. My mother had passed two years ago and that was the last time I had been home. My dad had died when I was ten and it had been me and Mother even though I did have an older brother and sister. When I say older I mean 20 years. I had come along when my mother and dad were in their 40s. My brother and sister had left years ago. My sister lived in Oregon and my brother lived in Maine. As far as I knew, they had only been home one time in years and that was for my mother's funeral. Both had said they wanted nothing to do with the ranch. The ranch was actually small by Texas standards, including two and a half sections which translated into a mere 1640 acres. In this part of the country that was not much land. The grass was not good most years due to lack of rain and we had struggled to make a living. The ranch had been in the family for several generations and was paid for, which enabled us to get by.

I was drafted right out of high school and the army had been my family since then. I had made good friends and already missed them. Of course, after being gone three years, most of my friends here would have left the area.

It was still an hour before daylight. I would have a better chance of finding a ride to the ranch later. I walked down the street to Woozys' Cafe and ordered coffee. I didn't know the waitress who was talkative. I was still wearing my uniform.

"Would you like something to eat, solider? You look like a gutted snowbird."

"No, thank you. Just coffee."

"You sure? Our specialty this morning is two eggs with pancakes and sausage. I bet you haven't had a decent meal in a long time."

"No thanks." What I wanted was to be left alone to enjoy my coffee.

"Did you just get out of the service?" she asked.

"Yeah. Three days ago."

"Where were you stationed?"

"Korea."

"Korea. Are they still fighting over there?"

I just looked at her. Her stupidity should come as no surprise. The war was unpopular and not in the news much. I noticed she said 'they' and not 'we'.

"No. The war ended in July."

"Did you kill anybody?"

I didn't bother to answer this time, looking down at my coffee. She took the hint and moved to the one other customer present. I couldn't believe people would be that rude to ask such a question. I finished my coffee, put a dime on the counter and left before she could return with more questions. I began walking west for five minutes before crossing the railroad tracks and turning south on farm-to-market road 126. I passed the school and continued walking for an hour. The sun was up and I began to think no one was going to come along that recognized me. I heard a vehicle behind me, and turning saw it was a school bus. It slowed to a stop and the door swung open with the driver saying, "Sam Colter, is that you?"

"Yes sir."

"Well, bless my soul! You look like a skeleton. I like not to have recognized you. You've been in the army, haven't you?"

"Yeah, for the past three years. You've been driving this route since I was in junior high."

"That's right. Now get in and you can ride it again. I still go right by your place at the end of my route."

"Thank you. I'd about given up on getting a ride."

We talked briefly on the half hour drive, mostly about his family. He didn't ask me any questions about the war, which I appreciated. When I climbed down out of the bus at the ranch and he drove off, a deep sadness came over me. I was home... but to what? My mother was gone. I did have some relatives but not within several hundred miles. My $66 a month had allowed me to save $1500, which is all I had to my name. The sign over the gate that was hanging by one nail read, COLTER.

I started the quarter mile walk that lead to the house, thinking, at least I'm alive, that's more than a lot of the men I served with. Then I saw him coming at a dead run. Reaching me, he never slowed down, jumping into my arms, nearly knocking me down, and giving me kisses. "Hablo, you're glad to see me." Hablo was my black and white, little bit of everything dog. His left eye was brown and his right eye was blue. He barked constantly so the name fit. It had been two years since he had seen me. I immediately felt better, and after getting him calmed down, we moved on to the house. It was built of stones from the surrounding hills with an arch protecting the front porch. Mother's yellow roses framed the steps. They were still living, I imagine, due to Jose's care.

I heard him before I saw him. "Little Bit, you home!" he hollered, coming around the house. He met me with a handshake and huge smile.

"How are you, Jose?"

"Good! You home! It's lonely out here. Let's go inside, and I fix you something to eat. You skinny."

Inside, was a one-room house he lived in just behind ours. I had encouraged him to move into our house when I came back for Mother's funeral but that hadn't happened. He had beans and mutton with peppers which was delicious. I'd eaten so much bad food, forgetting what home cooking tasted like. Jose was short, just a little over five feet and slender. I had no idea how old he was. He was one of my first memories. He was the reason I could speak Spanish. Even before my dad died, I spent more time with him than anyone. He had a limp caused by a horse falling with him and breaking his leg, which was not set properly.

"Jose, that meat and beans was delicious. I forgot what a great cook you are. Now how much do I owe you? I know you've been working without a salary since Mom passed."

"No worry. I have a place to live. A home. I have enough to eat. I day work some for other ranchers. I get by. Maybe now, we get this ranch going again. Then we talk about pay for me. You my family, Little Bit. Family don't pay each other."

A lump came up in my throat and I couldn't speak for a minute. "Thank you, friend. Now, is that old pickup running?"

A big smile broke out when he said, "Sí, I got 'er going."

"Good. I'm going to change into some civilian clothes and go into town for supplies."

Opening the door, the musty smell hit me. Of course, dust was everywhere, and whatever positive thoughts had occurred with Jose, were gone immediately. The sadness returned with a vengeance. I sat down in the first chair available and memories came flooding back. My mother and I had become close after Dad passed. We never had a cross word in the eight years after his death. She was there for me and me for her. I could feel her presence in the room and it overwhelmed me. Suddenly, I could hear her voice, "*Sam, you have to move on. Nothing good comes from dwelling on the past.*"

I moved into my bedroom, opened my closet and took out a pair of Levis and a long sleeved shirt. I took off my uniform, folded it, put it in a drawer and for the first time in three years, put on a pair of jeans. They were at least two sizes too big. I had played high school football at 170 and when I was discharged, I weighed 138. No wonder the pants were too big and wouldn't stay up without a belt or suspenders. I smiled at how ridiculous and even scary the image of me appeared in the full length mirror on the back of the door. The shirt was not as bad, but was too large. I was thin, 'gutted snowbird' was a fitting description. My eyes were sunken back and the short haircut only added to an image that would have passed for a patient in the final stage of a terminal illness.

Before the service, I had a full head of black hair, a face that was considered attractive by the girls even with the crooked nose that had been broken twice and the oversized ears. Now, a child seeing me for the first time would probably run. I turned away from the image, saying to myself; *quit complaining, you're home and in one piece, be thankful.* I found a belt in the closet, put it on, and had to take it off and put another hole in it to tighten it enough to hold up my pants. I put on my Justin work boots and hat for the first time since leaving for the service. That was going to be the best I could do for the trip to town. I took forty dollars from my stash and hid the remainder in a drawer. Now I was ready to begin my civilian life again.

Jose was waiting for me outside, and we walked over to the garage behind his house. It was on the verge of collapse, and would soon, if something wasn't done. The green 1948 three-quarter ton Chevy pickup had little wear, having limited use the last several years. It was actually the newest thing we had on the place. Due to high livestock prices, 1947 was a good year and we bought the pickup new. I remember how excited I was, driving it to school that first day.

We discussed how we should begin stocking the ranch again. "How many sheep do we have currently?" I asked.

"Maybe 50. Drought terrible since you left," he answered.

"Do you think we should buy cattle or more sheep?"

"Not much. Grass not good. Maybe few cows and 200 more sheep. No more."

"We need to find out about the market. I have no idea what the price of livestock is today."

"I listen to market on radio. Cows $110 to $150. Little cows cheaper. Still have good calves with good bull."

"That's going to be a lot of money. I'll have to visit the bank," I said, taking out a cigarette.

"Your momma not like that," Jose said, frowning.

I didn't respond, knowing he was right. "Do you want to go with me into town?"

"No, Little Bit. I stay home and start working on fences. They in bad shape."

The pickup kicked right off and I enjoyed the drive into town. Our place was located at the bottom of a hill and the trees on both sides of the road were beginning to change. There were live oaks and red oaks with the red and yellow leaves announcing that winter would be here soon.

I passed the city limit sign which read population 2124 and pulled into the first filling station. An attendant appeared, and getting out, I told him, "Ten gallons." I bought a Coke and paid the man, who I didn't recognize, the $2.10.

My first stop in town was the dry goods store where I bought two pairs of Levis. I could do with the oversized shirts, but I had to have pants that fit. The store was owned and operated by a Jewish family who had been in business since right after the turn of the century. They were friendly and well liked in the community. The clerk wrapped up one of them and my old ones with brown paper and tied them with a string. I wore the other pair, feeling better immediately. After paying the $12, I left, headed for the grocery store. Several people came up to me while I was shopping and told me they were glad to see me home safe. A lady even hugged me and said she would like to see me in church Sunday. It felt good to have people greet me and welcome me back. I filled my grocery list with staples, including milk, potatoes, cereal, bread, eggs, bacon, hamburger meat, canned vegetables, and two packages of cigarettes. I was determined to begin limiting my smoking. My bill came to $8.68 and I left the store with three bags of groceries that would last a week and maybe more.

My next stop was the bank. It had been owned for years by the same family. The owner was the only one who approved loans so he was the person to see. I approached his secretary, asking if I could talk to him.

"Yes. What's your name?" she asked.

"Sam Colter."

"Sam! Goodness, I didn't recognize you. It's been several years and you've changed. How're you doing?"

"Good, Mrs. Donovan. I knew you didn't recognize me. I've lost a lot of weight since you've seen me. I just returned from the service."

"It's good to have you home. I'm so sorry about your mother. She was a nice lady."

"Thank you," I said, wishing she would cut the small talk and get me in to talk to him.

"How long have you been back?" she asked.

"Just came in this morning."

"It's good to have you home," she repeated. "I'll tell Mr. Warren you're here."

She came back shortly saying, "He'll see you now."

I was nervous going into his office. I had taken out loans while in high school to buy a few cows and knew that Mr. Warren was all business. I had removed my hat when I entered the bank knowing how he felt about that. We exchanged greetings and shook hands before I sat down.

"You've been in the service?" he stated, in the form of a question.

"Yes. For the past three years."

"Were you in Korea?"

"For the past two years," I answered, hoping questions about the war wouldn't continue.

"The football team has missed you. You were a tough kid. I enjoyed watching you play."

"Thank you. Those were good times," I answered.

"Now, what can I do for you?" he asked.

"I need to restock the ranch. After Mom passed, I sold nearly everything to pay bills and the funeral expenses. I only have $1500 to my name."

"Cattle market skyrocketed during the war but after it ended in July it's gone down. Now might be a good time to stock. How many head were you thinking about? The drought has been terrible the past couple of years."

"I've only had a few sheep on the place. I have some grass but not enough to run many cattle for long unless it rains. Maybe 20 or 30 cows and a few hundred sheep," I explained.

"Sounds reasonable. I tell you what, Sam; some of the ranchers in the Canyon bank with me. Several of them have known your family for years. In fact, I believe you're named after one of the pioneer ranchers in the Canyon. They generally run a good many cattle and sheep on their ranches. Let me talk to the first one that comes in about selling you some heifers. I think you'll get a better deal than you can find at the auction. Plus, you'll save on delivery expenses."

"I appreciate that."

"I appreciate your service, Sam, to our country. I know you had it tough besides this being an unpopular war. I'll see what I can work out for you. Whatever the cost, I'll draw up a loan and make it for several years. That way you'll have a chance to sell some calves and lambs."

I left the bank feeling better. With a few heifers and some sheep, I could generate some income off the ranch. I would also look for odd jobs to have an income. I had day worked during the summer when I was in school. On the ride back to the ranch, I felt better. That was the thing about small towns; people helped one another.

I went to bed early that night after a meal Jose prepared from the supplies I bought. I lay there for awhile thinking of my future. I was twenty-one years old with very little family and maybe the best thing to do would be to put the ranch up for sale. I could take the money and leave, starting over in another place. Maybe somewhere it rained. Then I saw images of my grandparents, Dad, and Mom and knew that I wouldn't leave. I heard a scratch at my door, and getting up, let Hablo in. He immediately jumped upon the bed.

Sometime during the night, I woke up to the sound of machine gun fire. I bolted out of bed and hit the floor, doubling up in a ball, before realizing it was the wind rattling the windows.

Chapter 2

Mattie

I lay in bed listening to my dad scream and cuss at my mother. Although I was two rooms away, every word was plain. It was this way at least once a week. He would come in from work and start drinking. By 8:00, he was drunk and yelling obscenities at Mother, becoming louder the later it became. I assume he continued to drink until he passed out. I couldn't understand why she put up with it.

I was a senior in high school and still had eight months to live in this hell hole. My two older sisters were gone from home, and I saw them only once or twice a year. Now it was just me and my parents. I had been bold enough to ask him why he drank and he said, "It's the only way I can survive living in this dump of a town." I didn't bother to ask him why we didn't move. I didn't ask him why he continued to take his anger out on my mother and occasionally me. I assume that he enjoyed it. I loved this town and the people but living in this house was miserable. I would graduate in May of next year and I was going to be 'out of here'. I was hoping to attend college but that was probably only a dream. I would leave and go somewhere to get away from this. I had friends at school and in town, but my life at home was miserable. I dreaded having to come home every day. I actually enjoyed school since it was a refuge from the constant anger in my home.

I woke up at 5:00 the next morning, which was my usual time to jog three miles. Basketball was starting, and I wanted to be in good shape. I slipped out the door and felt the chill of the morning. We generally had cool nights this time of year and today was no exception. I ran the same route every morning, anticipating which houses I passed that would have barking dogs. It would take between 35 and 40 minutes depending, on how much I pushed myself. This morning I was back in the house at 5:45.

We only had one bathroom, but it was in the hallway close to my room. I took my bath, and drying off I looked in the mirror, experiencing a sinking feeling. I was flat, front and back. So little curves that I could have easily passed for a boy. My best friend, Della, who was shapely, kept telling me that I would be a late developer. That was bull. I was going to be skinny forever. People were always telling me how beautiful I was. I did have a smooth complexion not ever being bothered with acne, with high check bones and a mouth that was too wide. I wore my blonde hair short. Della would cut and style my hair, and at my insistence, attempt to make it look as much as possible like Audrey Hepburn's. I had been an avid fan since seeing her in *Roman Holiday*. I was also self-conscience about a gap between my front teeth. Strangely, I had a number of boys that asked me for dates. I accepted occasionally but wasn't interested in anyone particular.

I loved basketball and had been an All District forward for three years. I had averaged 22 points a game last year as a junior. I was five foot eight inches, but I was athletic and could jump. During the summer, I spent a lot of time in the gym shooting baskets. I seldom made a grade lower than an A and would probably be the class valedictorian, which was not a big deal to me. I did take pride in the fact that I was class president. My class consisted of 32 students with several being Hispanic but no Negroes. They attended a separate school in Abilene.

My pa-pa picked me up at 7:00 just like he always did. My parents were not up which wasn't unusual. He was right on time, to the minute. He had retired from the railroad and was my favorite person in the world. He lived two miles southwest of town on thirty acres. My other love besides basketball was my horse.

I'd loved horses since I could remember. Pa-Pa kept my horse at his place. He was a 12-year-old gelding who I'd had for some time. During the summer, the local riding club had play days each Saturday night. It wasn't that far and I would ride him to and from the arena. It was something that I looked forward to every week. We made a stop on the way to school at a small shack where I bought two burritos. Pa-Pa didn't eat anything since he would meet his friends at the Nook Café and have breakfast there. He stopped in front of the school, and before getting out, I reached over and kissed him on the cheek, saying, "Love you, Pa-Pa."

"Love you, too, Mattie," he responded.

Today, I met Della in the gym a half hour before classes started just as we had been doing for the past four years. We found seats to eat our burritos out of hearing of the other students.

"How're you doing?" she asked.

"Same. Dad drank, screamed at Mother for what seemed like hours and then passed out."

"I'm sorry, Mattie. Just hang on for another seven months."

"That's easy for you to say, Della. You have a wonderful family."

"I know, but you have a lot of things that I don't. You're popular, smart, attractive, and athletic. Some days I would trade if I could be like you."

"I don't feel attractive, Della. In fact, I don't understand how anyone could find me the least bit pretty. You're the one with the boyfriend that'll probably ask you to marry him after graduation."

"Juan is sweet, but I don't know if I want to marry him. I haven't decided yet. Maybe I will. Maybe I won't."

"What does your family think?" I asked.

"That's easy. They want me married and pregnant as soon as possible. That's part of our cultural. Girls are not supposed to have ambition. I would like to attend cosmetology school, become a beautician and own my shop. They'll never support my dream. Of course, my two brothers will be encouraged to be whatever they desire. See, we all have our problems, Mattie."

"I know, Della. I'm sorry for the self-pity. I have a lot going for me and need to decide how to take advantage of it."

"Are you planning on going to college?" she asked.

"Maybe. If I can come up with the money. One thing for sure; I'd like to be a long way from here."

"You're smart enough and I bet your granddad would help you. How long has your grandmother been gone?"

"Almost three years. I miss her and I know Pa-Pa does, too. I don't understand how my dad can be so different from Pa-Pa. It looks like, since he's his son, they would be more alike."

"Doesn't work that way, Mattie. Sons or daughters are not always like their parents. Now, there's the bell, we need to get to class."

I had six classes during the day and seventh period basketball. For the most part, my teachers were good. The one exception was my fifth period English class. We had a first-year teacher that had lost control of our class the first day of school. Being the first period after lunch, probably had something to do with it. She had visited with us and shared personal information from the beginning. When she tried to get down to the business of teaching, students paid no attention to her. We had some boys who were discipline problems and for some reason they had all taken English at this time. The 50-minute class seemed to last forever, and each day I dreaded going. By seventh period, I was always ready for basketball. I actually enjoyed the workouts. With the exercise, I could relieve some of the stress created by my home life. I stayed an extra hour after practice ended today to shoot baskets.

My coach was the high school principal, Mr. Ansley. It seemed strange that a principal would be a coach, but as I understood it, no one else wanted the job. He didn't know much basketball but he was nice and did the best that he could.

While I was shooting free throws, he came over to where I was. "Mattie, I wish our boys had the same dedication that you have. We would win more games."

"Thank you, Mr. Ansley. I enjoy basketball and don't consider it work at all."

"You do plan to attend college, don't you?" he asked.

"Hopefully. If I can afford it."

"You need to go, Mattie. You have so much going for you. I'm sure you would qualify for some loans. Have you ever thought about being a teacher and coach? Women basketball coaches are going to be in demand as the sport grows across the state. There'll come a day when schools are forced to offer girls as many sports opportunities as they do boys."

"To be truthful, I haven't given my career much consideration. I don't know what I want to do except get away from here."

"Well, please give it some thought and look into the possibility of getting a loan. I see very few students with your potential."

He left, and I knew it was time for me to go home. It was a twenty-minute walk, and I took my time, not getting there until after 6:00. My dad, who worked at a local hardware store, was home and already had his drink, watching the news on our one station.

"Mattie, why're you so late?" he commanded.

"Basketball practice."

"That's a waste of time. And spending money on that nag is a waste of money."

"Pa-Pa buys the feed for Spade, and it's my time that's wasted."

"Don't get smart with me, young lady. You still live in my house and I feed you," he said, taking a drink from his glass. He must have been home for a while since his face was red, and he was slurring his words.

I didn't respond, moving toward my room.

"Don't walk away from me when I'm talking to you!" he bellowed.

I stopped and turned back toward him.

"You know, young lady, it wouldn't hurt you to do some cooking around here and help your mother out. She works hard all day in that laundry. You spend all your time playing that stupid basketball and taking care of that nag."

He was still yelling as I went into my room, "You better show me some respect around here, or I'll take a belt to you."

I didn't cry. I had stopped that long ago. I kept repeating the same thing to myself. *I don't have but a few months left.*

I stayed in my room until after 11:00 that night. I knew it would be safe to go back to the kitchen for something to eat since he would be asleep. Thank goodness, he didn't yell at Mother tonight. He was probably telling her what a terrible daughter I am. I found lunch meat in the refrigerator and made a sandwich for my late night meal.

Laying in bed, I kept thinking that children were supposed to love and honor their parents. That was one of the commandments. I loved my mother but felt nothing but anger and resentment toward my daddy. Maybe sometime in the future that would change. I was respected at school and in the community and couldn't understand why he treated me the way he did.

Chapter 3

Gladys

I was at the kitchen table drinking my third cup of coffee, thinking about how angry Leon continued to be at Mattie. Of course, most times when she arrived home he was already drunk. I tried to take up for her, but he interrupted me most of the time and ignored what I said the remainder of our exchange. Mattie was a good girl, and I felt bad not defending her when her daddy went on one of his rampages. He was a bully and I was afraid of him, with good reason.

I didn't have to be at work today until 9:00 since I'd worked late yesterday. I enjoyed the peace and quiet of the morning since Leon had left earlier. We never had, what you would call, a happy marriage; however, it was much worse now than earlier. The drinking was a big part of the problem. He drank because he was unhappy with his life. He had gotten worse the last year and was now a full-fledged alcoholic.

There was a stack of mail on the table that hadn't been opened. Most of them were bills which needed to be paid. The last one, addressed to Leon Quentin, was from the bank. I said aloud, *oh no, it's an overdrawn notice.* I opened it and was correct. That would bring another tirade from Leon. I paid the bills and tried to keep up with our spending. He would blame me even though I did the best I could to see that we met our obligations. We should never have bought the television set. The 21-inch Admiral cost almost $200. I worked for minimum wage at 75 cents an hour, which amounted to a weekly salary of $27 after taxes and social security were deducted. Leon did a little better at the hardware store, bringing home $39 a week. The payments on the house, car, and television, coupled with the electricity, gas, and grocery bill took most of what we made. Leon spent a considerable amount of money on liquor he bought from a bootlegger since the county was dry. Little was left for anything else and some weeks we just couldn't make it until payday. Thus far the bank had failed to return any of the checks but eventually that would probably change.

Looking at the clock on the wall, it was 8:30 and time to get ready to go to work. My friend, Louise would pick me up a few minutes before 9:00. She worked at the drug store, and days when our hours were the same, she would pick me up. Other days I would walk to work. I dressed the same each day, wearing jeans and one of my older blouses. The work was hard and most of the time hot. With a dozen washing machines going at the same time, unbelievable heat was created. The thinking was, the hotter the water the cleaner the clothes would become. I wore tennis shoes because of the amount of walking that I did.

Looking in the mirror to put on some makeup, I appeared to be older than my 53 years. I had more gray hair and wrinkles than most women my age. Of course, I couldn't afford the expensive face creams or a weekly trip to the beauty shop. At least, I wasn't overweight and was blessed with good health. I was interrupted by a horn honk, realizing I had spent too much time getting ready. Louise still had her car running when I opened the door and got in. "Sorry, I spent too long with my coffee this morning."

"No sweat, Gladys. That laundry will still be there. How're you doing?"

"Just got an overdrawn notice from the bank. Maybe we can get some money in the bank tomorrow since it's payday."

"I can loan you some."

"No. No way. We'll get by. I dread Leon finding out."

"Why do you put up with him, Gladys? If he's not a piece of crap, I've never seen one."

"I don't know what I would do by myself. We've been together for over 30 years. Besides, Mattie is still home. I couldn't support the both of us on my salary. I would never leave without Mattie. Maybe after she graduates and gets a job we can get away from him."

"Mattie needs to go to college," she said.

"I know, Louise. She's smart and could make something of herself, but we don't have the money to send her. Mattie's best chance is her pa-pa. He adores her."

"See, there's your answer. He can pay her way to college, and you can get away from Leon and be a much happier woman."

"I wish it was that easy."

The work was hard at the laundry; however, the customers were friendly and the couple that owned it were nice. My job consisted, for the most part, of carrying the bundles of clothes to and from the cars. By mid-afternoon on the busy days, I was usually exhausted.

Most of the customers were women, but sometimes their husbands would come with them. An exception, was Earnest who came alone each Thursday to do his washing. His wife had died the previous year after a lengthy illness. He seemed so sad, and I had tried to make conversation with him but had not been successful. Any question or comment would receive only a one or two word response. I was determined that today would be different.

He was generally one of the first customers and today was no exception. I met him, asking, "How're you today, Earnest?"

"Okay."

"The weather's nice, isn't it?"

"Yeah."

"Looks like you got a big load today. Do you need some soap?"

"I guess," he answered.

Coming back with the soap, I asked, "Are you feeling okay? You look a little under the weather." He didn't answer, but I noticed a single tear role down his cheek.

"Maybe it would help if you talked about it. I'm a good listener." Silence followed.

"You're the only customer, so I have some time," I said.

"We used to come in together. We were married for 32 years."

"I know. You never helped her though," I stated.

"She wouldn't let me. She said it was woman's work. She's been gone over a year, and I miss her so much," he said, with another tear forming. "I'm sorry. I can't help it."

"You have no reason to be sorry. You loved her and miss her. I imagine you had a wonderful marriage for 32 years."

"Yeah," he said, smiling for the first time. "She was my best friend, and we did everything together. Now nothing seems important any more. I get up in the morning, and she's not there. I begin every day depressed and sad."

"Would she want you to be sad?" I asked.

He hesitated before responding, "No. She'd be upset with me."

"Earnest, you need to remember that. Now, I have to get back to work."

"Thank you, Gladys. I'm going to try and do better."

I walked away feeling good that at least Ernest had smiled and seemed to think about what I said about his wife. Some days go by fast and others drag. Today was one of the latter and each time I looked at the clock on the wall it was not as late as expected. By 5:00 that afternoon, with only an hour remaining before getting off, I saw Mr. Wingate come in. He was the owner of the store where Leon worked. He came directly to me and said we needed to talk. Panicking, I led him to a small office in the back.

"Gladys, Leon was gone two hours at lunch and came back drunk. I had to let him go. No way can I tolerate an employee who drinks on the job. I'm sorry."

Stunned, I couldn't speak for several seconds. "I understand, Mr. Wingate."

"Leon was angry and cursed me. I thought it might be necessary to call the law to remove him from the store. He finally left, but I'm worried about what you'll confront at home. Do you have anywhere that you and Mattie can go tonight to avoid being around him?"

"Maybe we could go stay the night at Leon's dad's place; however, Leon will be furious if I don't come home. It might make things worse. I don't know what to do."

"Is there anything I can do?" he asked.

"Louise is picking me up in less than an hour, but I'm afraid Mattie will get home before I do. Could you take me to school, and hopefully we can catch her before she leaves?"

"Sure."

I explained my situation to Mr. Henry, my boss, and he told me to leave immediately.

We arrived at school just as Mattie was leaving. I didn't go into detail but told her we needed to go home together today. She didn't question me, probably knowing it involved her dad.

When we arrived the car was there, so Leon would be also. "Thank you, Mr. Wingate, I appreciate it," I said, getting out of the car.

"I feel bad leaving you and Mattie," he responded.

"We'll be fine."

Before going in, I explained briefly to Mattie what had happened."

"Mother, we can't stay here. Not tonight anyway."

"All right. We'll get some clothes and go to your pa-pa's."

Fortune was with us, as we found Leon asleep on the couch. Wasting no time, we put together a change of clothes and left. He was going to be furious when he discovered we were gone in the car. At least we wouldn't be here.

On the drive to Mr. Quentin's, I gave Mattie more of the details involving her dad losing his job.

"Mother, we have to do something. We can't go on like this. I'm afraid for you."

"I know, Mattie. Maybe your pa-pa can talk to Leon and insist that he get help."

"Pa-Pa has no influence on Dad. We need to get away from him permanently, no matter what it takes."

When we arrived, we found Mr. Quentin at the barn feeding Mattie's horse. I told him about our problem and he immediately responded with, "You're welcome here as long as you want to stay. It's a shame Leon has turned into the kind of man that he is. I'll go over to your house and try to talk some sense into him."

"He was asleep when we left. You may not be able to talk with him until morning."

"You're probably right. He'll need to sleep it off. Let me follow you back to your house and leave his car. You can place a note in his car telling him where you and Mattie are."

After delivering the car, we went by the Dairy Bar to get hamburgers to take home. As I stood at the window and placed our order, the cook was smoking a cigarette with at least half an inch of ash. I kept wondering if it might drop into our burger.

Chapter 4
Sam

The week after I arrived home was spent repairing fences and patching water troughs. I hadn't realized just how dry it was until I had ridden over most of the ranch. It felt good to be back in the saddle again for the first time in three years. Brownie, my ten-year-old gelding, gave every indication of enjoying getting back to work. Our other horse, Jake, was 25 and retired. One of my priorities was going to be finding another horse for Jose.

We did have some grass, but everything was brown from a lack of rain. It was October 23, but it hadn't been below freezing. Ordinarily, we would have had some green grass this time of year. I jumped several deer on my excursions and they were in poor condition. That was not a good sign going into winter.

Of the four stock tanks on the ranch, two were completely dry and the other two could be described as mud holes. The three windmills were still pumping which was encouraging. Jose had done a good job keeping them serviced. Maybe we would have moisture this winter and the tanks would fill up.

I was enjoying being home. After being gone three years and living in constant fear the last two, it was great to feel safe and out of danger. It might take years, and maybe never, to get over the terrible ordeal of killing and seeing men killed. I was young, too young, to go through something like that. They say that young men make the best soldiers and that's probably true. They're the most innocent and naïve, not even thinking of their mortality. Then after being thrust into battle, reality sets in and they see what war is like and they can die like a 90-year-old in a nursing home.

Jose prepared a lunch, usually consisting of meat wrapped in a homemade tortilla with peppers, for me to take when I was gone most of the day. He fixed enough for me to share with Hablo, who was never far from me. I would return in the evening, exhausted. He would have a supper prepared using the supplies that I had bought in town."

We had put in a bathroom my junior year in high school after growing up using an outhouse. It was mighty cold going outside in the winter to use it. The bathroom was a luxury that I'd always appreciate. We had received electricity from the Rural Electric Cooperative the year before that. Those two conveniences were wonderful, and I felt for the people who didn't have them. We still didn't have a telephone or a television but that was no big deal to me. After supper, I would bathe, and listen to music on the radio from a country music station. Hank Williams was my favorite.

I would stay up late as possible, dreading the nightmares that came almost every night. I had gone from a boy worried about what girl to ask to the prom to seeing the horror of war. I tried to put those images out of my mind, but they were entrenched and came back vividly at night.

I went back into town the following Monday to check with the bank to see if I had purchased any livestock. I discovered that a ranch located about eight miles from me had agreed to allow me to purchase 20 heifers and 200 ewes. I signed the note that had been drawn up for me. It would be due in three years, and the amount was $3100. I thanked Mr. Warren and left, feeling like I now had some control of my life, even if I was facing a challenge. Stopping at the feed store, I asked about establishing a credit account, with payment due when I sold livestock. The owner of the store, who I had known for years, told me it wouldn't be a problem.

Leaving, I saw a notice on the window advertising a horse for sale. The price for the gelding was $200, which was reasonable. It stated that he was sound and gentle and would make a good ranch horse. An address was listed where more information could be provided. It required half an hour to find the correct address. The frustrating problem in a small town is no one pays attention to street names. It's actually a waste of time since everyone knows where everybody lives. I finally was able to locate the house.

After knocking for several minutes, I decided they weren't home. I was halfway back to my pickup when someone hollered, "What you want?"

I turned, going back to the house. "My name is Sam Colter, and I'd like some more information about the horse for sale. I saw the notice at the feed store." He didn't introduce himself but began a description of the horse.

"He's a nice one. Gentle enough for anyone. Pretty, too. I hate to sell him, but I need the money. He's twelve years old so he has a lot of good years left. I can't take less than $200 for him."

"I'd like to look at him. Maybe ride him a little if it's all right?"

He hesitated before answering, rubbing his hand over a three-day stubble, "I'll have to get back to you. Let me have your phone number."

"I don't have a phone. Could we just go see the horse now?"

"No. This isn't a good time. Tell you what. Come back tomorrow morning about 9:00. Bring your trailer. You're gonna like this horse. I'll need cash."

"All right. I guess that'll work," I responded.

I left, wondering what this guy was doing with a horse. He didn't appear to be any part of a cowboy. I needed another horse and maybe this one would work. I hadn't deposited my money in the bank yet so I had the cash. Jose and I would have to drive the heifers and sheep I'd bought, the eight miles to our place. It would take the two of us horseback to do it.

After eating lunch, Jose and I went to the ranch where I was buying the stock. We needed to see when we could take possession and also to determine the route to our place that we would take. It was one of the biggest ranches in the area consisting of at least 25 sections. We exited the main road and drove up a lane to a large house. Jose remained in the pickup while I went to the door and knocked. The door was immediately opened by a middle-aged woman.

"Ma'am, I'm Sam Colter. I purchased some heifers and sheep from this ranch. Is Mr. Toller in?"

"Sam, I know who you are. I knew your mother and daddy and even your grandparents. Come in and I'll get Robert for you."

I followed her in, taking a seat in a large cushiony chair. Within seconds both returned. I rose and shook hands with Mr. Toller. "I came to ask you about the heifers and ewes that Mr. Warren purchased for me."

"Sam Colter! You look like a scarecrow! I imagine you have good reason to look the way you do. I've got some good heifers for you and 200 ewes. Hopefully, all of them are bred. You can get them any time you want. I'm sorry we can't help you, but I'm short-handed."

"No problem, Mr. Toller. Jose and I can drive them to our place. It may be a few days until I can get them."

"I'm sure you understand how dry it's been here," Mr. Toller said.

"Yes, sir. It's very evident by the pastures."

"If it doesn't rain soon we're going to be in a world of trouble," he said.

"Sam, do you remember our daughter, Sonia? She graduated last year and is a freshman at Abilene Christian. You probably didn't know that she had a huge crush on you when you were a senior. She saved all your newspaper clippings from football. She kept hoping you'd notice her, but she was only a sophomore."

"I remember Sonia. She was really pretty," I said, embarrassed at the attention and lying with my description.

"Sam, those are good heifers I sold you. Since they're bred you won't need a bull until spring. I can sell you a good one then."

"I appreciate it, Mr. Toller. I need to be going now, Jose is waiting for me."

"Goodness, Jose has been with your family as long as I re-member," stated Mr. Toller.

"Yes. He's been loyal help, and I consider him family," I said.

"Sam, I'd like to have you out for supper Saturday night. You need some home cooking, and it would be a pleasure to have you," invited Mrs. Toller.

I hesitated, not wanting to accept, but realized they had done me a favor, and I couldn't refuse the invitation. "Yes, ma'am, that would be great. What time?"

"Around 6:00 would be fine. We usually eat at 7:00, which would give us some time to visit."

I left, depressed at the thought of having to spend an evening with a family that I hardly knew. They would ask me about the war and that was the last thing I wanted to discuss with anyone.

The next morning, I was in town with my trailer at 9:00. I took $200 in case the horse was what I needed. I only had to knock once before the man appeared.

Without any greeting, he said, "You can follow me, and we'll go look at the horse. I'm busy this morning. I don't have any time to waste."

I followed him to the other side of town, to a place located out of the city limits. He parked and was back at my pickup before I could get out.

"I told you I'm busy this morning. Let's get a move on," he stated, looking around as if he expected someone to appear.

I grabbed the saddle and bridle in the back of my pickup.

"I don't have time for you to ride the horse," he stated, angrily.

That was it for me. I put the saddle back and opened the door to get back in my pickup.

"Where're you goin'?" he asked.

"I'm not about to pay $200 for a horse that I haven't ridden."

"Okay. Okay. Bring your saddle," he said, walking hurriedly toward the barn.

The sorrel horse was nice. If he rode half as good as he looked, he would be well worth the money. I looked him over for blemishes and possible injuries and found nothing to be concerned about. I saddled and rode him for fifteen minutes and was amazed that he was only asking $200 for him. He was nice."

"Okay. That's all. I've got to go. Either give me my $200 or I'll sell him to someone else."

"I'll take him." I left him saddled, and rode him back to my pickup and loaded him in my trailer. I gave the man $200, and he immediately left in his car. That was a strange guy. Maybe I should have asked for a bill of sale; however, I was more than happy with my purchase. He was as nice a horse as I'd ever been on.

Chapter 5

Mattie

It was Tuesday, October 27, and Mother and I were still at Pa-Pa's. I had begun to refer to it as home. He had gone over to try and talk some sense into my dad the day after he lost his job. He came back depressed, saying my dad wouldn't listen to him. He asked for money, and Pa-Pa gave him a few dollars, encouraging him to look for another job. Of course, in a small town word gets around, and it would be difficult for him to find work.

Pa-Pa would take me to school at the usual time and come back for Mother in time for her to be at work, after which he would go to the café to have coffee with his friends. We hadn't seen or heard from my dad and that was fine with me. I could get used to the peace and quiet at Pa-Pa's.

Even though football wasn't over, we had a scrimmage tonight with a neighboring school. It would be the first competition of the season, and I was excited. Many of the girls performed better as freshman and sophomores, and after they began maturing and gaining weight, they wouldn't play as well their last two years. That was not a problem for me. I hadn't developed or gained weight. I was going to be at the top of my game my senior year.

I always ate lunch in the school cafeteria. Some of the students would go to town or walk cross the street to the Badger Den. I had a good appetite even though I was thin. The cafeteria gave us plenty of food, and we had hot rolls every day except Friday, which was hamburgers. There was always honey and peanut butter on the table if you were still hungry after the meal.

Just having sat down at the table with my plate of meat loaf, mashed potatoes, and green beans I saw Pa-Pa come in the door. I knew something must be wrong, and I met him before he got to my table.

"Mattie, you need to go with me. Your mother's fine, but we have a problem at home. I'll explain when we get out of here."

I left my plate on the table and once in his pickup, he began explaining. "Spade was not in his stall when I got back home from the coffee shop. The gate was closed, but there was no sign of him. I drove all over the area, asking neighbors if they'd seen him. I didn't have any success.

A lump came up in my throat and I had difficulty speaking. "Wh-what could have happened?"

"I have no idea. Surely no one would be bold enough to steal him in broad daylight, not knowing when someone would show up at the house."

I started crying. "I can't lose him, Pa-Pa. I love him, and he's the only thing that keeps me going sometimes. Why would anybody take him?"

"We'll find him, Mattie, no matter what it takes. Maybe he'll be back at the barn when we get to the house."

Spade wasn't anywhere around when we retuned to Pa-Pa's place. We drove around the area again, expanding our search from his earlier one. We talked to everyone we could find within the vicinity. All were nice and said they would notify us if they saw him."

"Somebody took him, Pa-Pa. Whoever did, knew you wouldn't be home until later in the morning. There's one person who knows your daily schedule. Go to my house."

"I hadn't even thought of that, Mattie; however, it makes sense."

When we arrived, our car wasn't home. The door wasn't locked, and the house was vacant. I went to their room, noticing that the closet door was open and most of his clothes were gone. *He's left*, I said aloud. I went back to the pickup and told Pa-Pa what I found.

"He must've gotten hold of some money or he couldn't have gone. Mattie, it looks like he may have sold Spade, took the money, and left."

"No one in town would buy my horse from him," I said, beginning to cry again.

"You're right. He probably found a buyer who wasn't from this area. Somebody must've seen something that'll help us," he said. "Let's try the feed store. Horse traders sometime post notices there."

What we found, confirmed our suspicion. The note was still there advertising a horse for sale and our address, to gain additional information. We asked the owner of the store if anyone had inquired about the note.

"No, not that I know of. To tell you the truth I hadn't even seen it. It's not unusual for notices to be posted advertising livestock for sale. I wish I could help you."

We thanked him and left, meeting Carl on the way to the pickup. Carl was actually known as Cobb by everyone in town. He was younger than me by a few years. He'd suffered burns as a child when his nightshirt caught fire, recovering physically but never mentally. He was friendly, always in a good mood, and loved by everyone.

"Hello, Cobb. How're you today?" asked Pa-Pa.

"Good. I got work to do. Sam's back. He's my friend. Bought me a pop yesterday in the feed store. Mattie, you not in school."

Pa-Pa visited with Cobb for a few more minutes before we left. He always had time to talk to him and on occasion would hire him to clean Spade's stall. In the pickup, I asked Pa-Pa who Sam was.

"Sam Colter. We talked about him at the café the other day. He just returned from the service. One of my friends said Sam had been through a tough time in Korea and looked terrible. His parents are dead, and he lives on their ranch south of town in Mulberry Canyon."

"I know Sam. He was a senior when I was a freshman. He was a good football player. Of course, he never had anything to do with me. In fact, he never said a word to me. Probably thought he was too good for me."

"Shouldn't you go back to school?"

"No. I want to keep looking. Is there anything else we can do?"

"We can go to each gas station and see if they have information that might help us?"

Fortunately, after visiting the four stations, the last one in the south part of town told us that a pickup pulling an empty stock trailer had bought gas yesterday. The driver was a young man who he described as thin and sick looking.

We left, with Pa-Pa saying, "I know where the Colter place is. It's about 20 miles south of here, but we'll check it out. Sam's been gone and wouldn't have known the horse belonged to you."

"I just pray that we find Spade."

A half hour later we drove up the lane to the Colter house. A pickup was parked out front with a trailer attached, but no one answered the door. I went around back and knocked on the door of the other small house. No one answered. The stalls back of the house were empty. Returning to the pickup, I told Pa-Pa what I'd found.

"Mattie, he must be working somewhere on the ranch. It's 2:30 and he probably won't come back to the house for several more hours. I don't feel good. It's probably the stress of worrying about Spade. I'd like to go home and rest a few hours. We can come back later tonight or in the morning."

I hesitated, not wanting to leave, but Pa-Pa didn't look good. The only thing we could do was go back to town so he could rest. "That's fine, we can come back later, when you feel better."

Pa-Pa went to his room when we were home. I kept forgetting he was 75 years old. He was still active and able to do much more than most men his age. I picked my mother up at work, and after taking her home, went to the scrimmage that started at 6:00. It was obvious we weren't going to be able to return to the Colter place until morning.

I played terrible, not making but eight points and missing shot after shot. I couldn't get my mind off Spade. Coach asked me what was wrong after the scrimmage. I explained the events of the afternoon, and expressing his concern, said he would help however he could.

When I got home, Pa-Pa still hadn't come out of his room. I asked Mother if she had checked on him.

"I did, a couple of hours ago, and he was asleep. I hated to wake him up. This whole ordeal has been hard on your pa-pa. He's been disappointed in Leon which is understandable. I know he'd have never thought that his son would do something this despicable. Also, he's still grieving over the loss of your grand-mother even after three years. He's a good man and doesn't deserve this."

After eating supper, we watched Dragnet, one of our favorite shows before going to bed. I spent a sleepless night and thought morning would never come. All I could think of was losing Spade. I was up at 4:30 and made coffee, looking over my notes from yesterday's history class since we had a test today. An hour later Mother came in, getting a cup of coffee, and sitting down at the table.

"Have you checked on your pa-pa yet?" she asked.

"No, I was going to give him until 6:00. I know he's always up by then."

"I'm going to see about him, now," she replied.

I heard her knock on his door and a few minutes later she came back, saying, "Something's wrong, Mattie. He can't get up, and his voice is slurred. I've got to call Dr. Sadler."

Going into his room, he said, "Mattie, can't move my legs, what's wrong?" *Oh God please help him, he's had a stroke*, I prayed. I sat down on the side of the bed and held his hand until Dr. Sadler arrived. I left the room during the examination.

Coming out 10 minutes later, Dr. Sadler confirmed what I feared. "He's had a stroke, but I can't tell how bad it is until tests are made. I'll call for an ambulance to take him to the hospital. I'll be waiting when he gets there. It shouldn't take long."

We spent most of the day at the hospital, in the room with Pa-Pa, waiting on more information. He didn't become any worse but no better either. He wasn't in pain but was confused about what was happening. I talked to him constantly, assuring him that everything was going to be all right. He didn't have any visitors, since his friends were not aware of him being in the hospital.

Dr. Sadler came by several times during the day, only staying a few minutes to check Pa-Pa's vitals. On his last visit at 5:00 that afternoon, he asked to speak with us outside the room.

"Every indication is that Hollis had a severe stroke. It's not possible to determine at this time how much he will recover. We'll have to observe him for several days and see how much use of his legs and arms return. The stroke was on the right side of his brain which will allow him to speak. Of course, he will have limited use of his left arm and leg. Just how much, we'll have to wait and see. His age is a disadvantage but you never know. I've seen it go both ways. We're going to do everything we can for him."

"Thank you, Dr. Sadler. We appreciate it," my mother said.

"He'll need help with his meals. I can't spare one of my two nurses to assist him. Will one of you be available?"

"Yes," I replied quickly.

"You're welcome to stay at night, but it's not necessary. I will have someone on duty to check on my patients," he said.

"Mattie, you won't be able to help him with all his meals. You'll be in school and basketball games will start in the next couple of weeks," Mother said, when we were alone again.

"Yes, I'm going to be here for Pa-Pa. I'll talk to Mr. Ansley and work out something."

"I can help some, but there's no way I can miss work. We need the money I make to live on."

"I understand that. Now, if you want to go home for a while, I'll stay until you come back for me. Wait until at least 8:00," I stated.

Mother agreed and left, leaving me alone with Pa-Pa. He was asleep, probably from the medicine that he'd been given. I sat down in the one chair, thinking, *what could happen next? My daddy had lost his job and left town, my horse was gone, the person I loved more than anyone was seriously, maybe deathly ill, and it was going to be my responsibility to care for him. Maybe it was a test of my strength, or it could be that I was being punished for despising my daddy.*

Chapter 6

Sam

After riding my new horse a few times, I was amazed at being able to buy him for $200. He was worth twice or three times that. Jose insisted that I ride him, and he would take my horse. When I asked the man what his name was, he had replied, "Call him what you want," so I had named him Red. He had a lot of sense as well as ability. It remained to be seen if he had any cow in him. He had a good stop and neck reined as good as any horse I'd ever ridden.

I was anxious to get our livestock home. My problem was we'd need both horses and would have to leave my pickup and trailer at the Toller Ranch. After driving the heifers home, I wouldn't have any way of getting back to my pickup. When I went to tell Mr. Toller we were ready to take possession of our livestock, he had a solution. Jose and I would come to the ranch Saturday, drive the heifers back to our place and he would pick me up in time for supper that night. I could return home in my pickup.

I had tried to think of someway to get out of the invitation but couldn't come up with anything that sounded halfway legitimate. I dreaded it with a passion. I kept telling myself that it was a small sacrifice for the kindness they'd shown me. After all, he had sold me the stock at a good price. If I'd had to buy them at the auction, they would have cost more, plus with my small stock trailer it would've required half a dozen trips to haul them home.

Sonia as I recalled was a short, chubby, redheaded girl. I couldn't remember ever talking to her. Well, I was going to eat supper with them and that was that. Worrying about it was a waste of time.

Saturday morning, after a breakfast of eggs, bacon, and toast, washed down with several cups of coffee, we loaded our horses and left for the Toller Ranch. Hablo was riding in the front seat between us. I was surprised that we had a light frost. Usually it was November before that occurred.

"Is good to be going after heifers for our ranch," Jose observed.

"You bet. Now if we can just get some moisture this winter. Regardless, we'll need to feed some."

We were at the ranch at a few minutes after 8:00. I guess Mr. Toller was watching for us because he came out of the house.

"Morning, it's a beautiful day for a cattle drive. Makes me want to be young again. Just pull on down to those corrals where your heifers are penned," Mr. Toller said.

I got out and we shook hands. "I really appreciate it, Mr. Toller. I'm excited about stocking the ranch again."

"No problem, Sam. You shouldn't have any problems until you get to the main highway. There's not much traffic, but be careful. Some folks don't have manners and are too impatient to give you room. You won't have a gate to go through after you leave here until you get home. I'll be over to pick you up about 5:30. How do T-bone steaks sound?"

"It's been a long time since I ate steak," I replied.

"Melba is making an apple cobbler, also. She's determined to put some weight on you. If you and Jose will mount up, I'll open the gate for you. Be careful now. See you this evening."

We started the heifers down the lane toward the three miles of dirt road that would take us to the highway. Hablo wasn't much help, barking at everything and leaving us to chase a rabbit across a field. He came back with his tongue hanging out and trotted alongside me. The road wasn't that wide and was fenced on both sides. It was easy going, and the heifers moved along with little urging. I had brought my rope, anxious to see if Red would be bothered by following one of the heifers and swinging it. Again, I was surprised that he paid no attention. Evidently, he had been roped off of at some time.

Reaching the highway without incident, we decided to cross it immediately and drive them in the ditch on the other side. We had to move west from here for the next five miles. I rode on the side toward the highway and Jose stayed behind them. It became more difficult as we had to pass several side roads on the way. We knew our route, and when one of the side roads was coming up, I would ride ahead and keep them from turning into it. The first problem occurred the third time we had to pass an opening to another road. One heifer was determined not to cooperate, and she got passed us. I moved in behind her, but every time I would get her turned, she would double back. Finally, I fell in behind her, roped her, took a dally and dragged her back to the highway.

Jose was laughing and talking in Spanish. "Vaquero, no olvides lo que Jose te enseno." (Cowboy, you not forget what Jose teach you).

"Get off your horse, and tie him to that tree over there, then see if you can take the rope off this hussy. Maybe she learned her lesson."

"Little Bit, that much horse you ridin'."

"Yeah, I agree. I wouldn't take five times what I paid for him. Now, let's get these cattle moving."

The heifer was exhausted, and Jose was able to remove the rope. All Hablo contributed to this ordeal was to bark at the heifer and nip at her heels while she was tied. We didn't have any more problems the rest of the trip. I'd opened a gate behind the house that was the entrance to a three-acre trap. We'd let the heifers settle down for a few days and then turn them out. I'd bought a few sacks of range cubes in town to feed them until we turned them out into the pasture. Now, if only the 200 sheep that we had to move would be that easy. We'd tackle that job next week.

"Jose, we did okay."

"Sí, Little Bit. We done good."

I started worrying about what to wear two hours before he was to pick me up. I had a pair of dress pants for Sunday. Putting them on, they were even bigger than my old jeans. Trying to cross the room, they fell to my knees. Wouldn't that be something. Shake hands with Mr. Toller and my pants fall down. I didn't have a choice; it had to be the new Levi's. The shirt was another problem. All I had were my old ones that were much too large. I tried on every shirt in my closest, hoping that one would be a better fit. Finally, I chose a dark blue one that didn't swallow me, at least. My good boots did still fit, but all I had was my work hat and it wouldn't do. Giving up and looking in the mirror, I said to myself, *this is the best I can do and it's not much.*

A car pulled up in front at precisely 5:30. I recognized the model, identifying it as a new 1953 Chevrolet. I walked out, opened the door, and was startled to see a girl.

"Hi, Sam. Mom sent me to pick you up. I'm Sonia. You may not remember me."

"Sure. I remember you." Not looking like this, I thought. Wow! In my high school biology class, it was called metamorphosis. What happened to the cubby little redhead? She was really pretty, maybe beautiful. In the army several of the guys had pin up girls glued on their belongings. She could have been one of those girls.

"It's been a long time," she said.

"Yeah. This is a nice car."

"Thanks. Mom and Dad gave it to me for a high school graduation present."

That's great, I thought. My graduation gift was a letter from Uncle Sam.

"Do you like college?"

"It's all right. College is much harder than high school. I haven't decided on a major yet."

"Do you live in the dorm?"

"I do, but I come home on most weekends. There's nothing to do at school, and they have a 10:00 curfew. I have two older brothers who are married and live on the ranch. I enjoy visiting them, also. They insist that I'm my mom and dad's favorite. That may be true since I'm the baby. Do you have any brothers or sisters?"

"One brother and a sister. They live a long way off and never come home."

A deer crossed the road in front of us and she slammed on her brakes, saying, "Damn, that was close."

We both laughed and I thought, this might go better than I thought. She was easy to talk to, and I was already feeling comfortable in her presence. We arrived at her place and suddenly I was conscience of my too-large shirt. Exiting the car, I tried not to stare at her. She was wearing a full skirt and a sweater that was anything but too large.

Her mother met us at the door, saying, "Come in and welcome to our home, Sam. It's so good to have you. It'll be an hour before we eat so I'll let Sonia entertain you."

"Let's go for a walk, Sam, it's too nice a day to be inside. We can come back and watch the sunset from the patio."

"Sounds good," I said, needing a cigarette in the worst way.

"We'll go down to the barn and I can show you my horse."

Her horse turned out to be a paint mare. I didn't have much use for paints or mares.

"She's nice," I said, hoping a complimentary lie would be justified.

"I don't get to ride much, with school and everything," she said turning and brushing up against me. "What about you? Do you ride?"

"I've been riding since I could walk." Maybe that would impress her. I guess it did because she took hold of my arm and pressed up against me.

"I saw you play football and you were wonderful."

"Well, I did the best I could." What a dumb thing to say, I thought.

"Let's get back to the patio and watch the sunset," she said, still holding on to my arm.

We watched the sunset from the patio, in a swing and she never let go. I didn't complain, it was nice. Female attention was something I hadn't experienced for three years. I just kept wishing my shirt fit better.

I was sorry to hear the door open and her mother tell us supper was ready. Oh well, it worked out. I was getting a cramp in my leg from not moving for too long. She held on to my arm until we went into the house.

Mr. Toller said the blessing before we started. The steak covered my plate, with several smaller plates set for the side dishes. I hadn't taken but a couple of bites when Mrs. Toller asked the dreaded question.

"Sam, what was life like in the service?"

"It was okay."

"Tell us about an ordinary day," she said.

Suddenly, the steak tasted like rubber, as I tried to think of a response. I guess my hesitation caused Mr. Toller to come to my rescue.

"Melba, for goodness sakes, let the boy enjoy his meal. We'll have time to visit later."

Feeling relieved, I ate the best meal that I'd had for the past three years. The cobbler topped with whipped cream was delicious.

"Mrs. Toller, that was wonderful," I said.

"Thank you, Sam. Sonia's a good cook, also."

"Let's move to the living room, it's more comfortable," Mr. Toller said.

For the next hour, I dodged questions about my military service, with the help of Mr. Toller. Most of the time was spent discussing the drought and ranching, with a sprinkling of politics. It was a stressful evening, but the meal and Sonia certainly made it worthwhile.

At a few minutes before 9:00, I told Mrs. Toller again how much I enjoyed the meal, and it was time for me to get home.

"Sam, you're going to have to come back often. Our boys are grown and have families, and we miss having a young man around," she said.

"I second that, Sam," Mr. Toller responded.

"Sonia, why don't you see Sam out?"

I really didn't need any help getting to my pickup, but I wasn't going to refuse. She grabbed hold of my arm right out the door.

"It was good to see you again, Sam. Will you come back soon?"

"Well, I have to pick up my sheep. Jose and I will probably do that next week sometime."

"If you wait until the weekend, I'll be home. I could even help you drive them to your place."

"I'll talk to Jose and get back with your dad."

Before I could get in my pickup she reached up and kissed my cheek saying, "Come back to see me soon." The night was cold, but on the drive home I didn't need to turn on the heater.

I was exhausted from the long day, and with a full stomach, I went to sleep when my head hit my pillow.

We could see them coming. We were told we had to defend Hill 112. We didn't understand. It was nothing but a sorry desolate rise of ground. We were outnumbered and my hands were sweating as I gripped the stock of the Browning Machine gun. They started up the hill toward us, and taking aim, I pulled the trigger until I ran out of ammunition. They were still coming and suddenly they were all around, and I knew I was going to die.

I woke up soaked with sweat and gasping for breath.

Chapter 7

Gladys

My alarm clock went off at 6:30, but I'd been awake for some time. It was the fourth day after Mr. Quentin's stroke. We had already worked out a schedule. Mattie would go the hospital and help her pa-pa with his breakfast. She would be back by 7:00, and I would have breakfast for us. She would then take me to work and be at school by 8:00. She would go back to the hospital to assist with the noon meal at 12:00 and then go back to school. She would be through with practice in time to pick me up at work by 6:00. Mr. Ansley and her teachers had been wonderful in allowing her flexibility to follow this routine. In the evening both of us would usually go to the hospital to help him with his supper. If Mattie had school work, I would go by myself to allow her to study.

Thus far, Mr. Quentin had shown no improvement. He could move his right arm but not his legs. He had trouble eating because food would drop from the corner of the left side of his mouth due to a lack of feeling. Mattie was so patient and loving with him. Dr. Sadler was not encouraging, telling us yesterday, that he didn't anticipate much improvement, and we should begin to consider a nursing home. After he left, Mattie told me that she would never allow her pa-pa to go to a nursing home.

I felt sorry for Mattie. She was not only grieving for her pa-pa but also for the loss of her horse. She hadn't been able to get back to the Colter Ranch with her schedule. It was Tuesday, November 3, and she was determined to find out what happened to Spade this coming weekend.

I felt guilty for enjoying the peace and quiet of life without Leon. I'd slept better the last several nights than I had in years. It was too early to make long range plans because I had no idea when he would show up or if he would ever return. I'd like to sell our house and move into Mr. Quentin's. It would relieve me of a house payment, which there was no way I could continue to make on my salary. Of course, if Mr. Quentin died, Leon would inherit this place. That would mean, if we wanted to get away from him, we would have no place to live if I sold our house. The best thing to do would be nothing, until later when we knew more about Mr. Quentin's condition and if Leon was returning. Well, I couldn't lie here wondering about our future. I needed to get a move on and have breakfast when Mattie returned.

"Mother, he was able to move his left leg this morning. It happened while I was helping him with breakfast. I went for the nurse, and she said it was definitely an encouraging sign."

"That's still a long way from walking," I said.

"I know, but it's improvement, and this is only the fourth day. If he would just improve enough to get around, even a little, we could bring him home. He's so sweet and never complains. He cried this morning trying to thank me for helping him."

"Mattie, do you want your daddy to come back?" I asked, changing the subject.

"No. I don't ever want to see him again. He's a mean person, and I hate him."

"Oh, Mattie, you should never say that."

"Why? He treated us terrible! He's a drunk, and he sold my horse to get money to run away."

"He's still your daddy, that should mean something," I said.

"Well, it doesn't. It would be fine with me if I never see him again."

I knew it would do no good to continue this so I changed the subject again. "Do you have a basketball game this week?"

"No. We play Roscoe in football, and you know what a rivalry that is. Everything is focused on the game, Friday night. If you can help Pa-Pa with his supper tonight, I'm going out to the Colter's. I can't wait until the weekend. I have to find out about my horse."

"Sure, Mattie; however, I'm afraid you're going to be disappointed. Even if your horse is there, I don't know what you can do. The man bought the horse and paid for him. He'd have to agree to give him back to you, and I can't see him doing that without having his money refunded."

"It's not right! He's my horse and Daddy had no right to sell him."

"I know, Mattie, and I'm sorry. It's not right, but I don't know what we can do about it."

"I'll buy him back!"

"Mattie, we don't have $200 to buy him back. The man might not even sell him back for that price. You know he's worth more than that." She started crying then, and I felt so sorry for her. She was heartbroken, and I couldn't do anything about it.

"Mother, I have to get him back," she said, sobbing.

I moved over to her, put my arms around her, and said, "I know, honey, and we will get him back, somehow. Now, you have to get ready for school. I need to go by our house and get a few of my things."

Mattie left, and came back within ten minutes. I was always surprised at how quickly she could prepare herself. She used little makeup and wore her hair short. Her complexion was smooth and unblemished, and she was a much prettier girl than she realized. If the school allowed it, she would wear jeans every day.

She drove and I held my breath as we turned the last corner and our house came into view. Breathing a sigh of relief, there was no car. Actually, that was the reason I had wanted to come by.

"He's not here. Do you still want to go in?" Mattie asked.

Embarrassed, I said, "No, not really. I didn't know it was that obvious."

"It doesn't matter. I'm not ever going to live in the same house with him again," Mattie said.

This was the second time she had spoken so angrily about her daddy. It shouldn't surprise me though. It had been building for a long time. "I get off at 5:00. Can you be here that early?" I asked.

"Yes. I won't stay late today."

Chapter 8

Mattie

I was nervous the entire day thinking of going to the Colter Ranch this afternoon. Time seemed to drag but finally basketball was over, and I left to pick up my mother at work. She was waiting for me outside.

"How was your day, Mattie?"

"Okay. I'm anxious to find out if Sam Colter has Spade."

"You need to remember, he didn't have any idea that Spade belonged to you. I'm sure your daddy told him the horse was his. Just be nice, and don't become angry and say things you'll regret."

"I'm going to tell him Spade was my horse, and Daddy had no right to sell him. I don't even know for sure he has Spade."

"You can take me directly to the hospital. It's less than an hour until they bring your pa-pa his supper. You'll be able to get to the ranch before dark."

"I want to go by the house and change clothes. I feel better wearing my jeans." Maybe instead of saying 'feel better' I should have said 'more assertive'.

"How long do you think you'll be gone?" she asked.

"I should be back by 8:00."

When I drove up to the Colter house there was a pickup out front. *Great, he's home,* I said to myself. I went to the door, knocked, and no one answered.

I went around to the back of the house and noticed a horse in the pens, but it wasn't Spade. There was another little house behind the big one, and after knocking, a small Mexican answered the door.

"I'm looking for Sam Colter." My name is Mattie. He came out the door before responding.

"I Jose. Little Bit not here. In pasture riding."

"What horse is he riding?"

Smiling, he said, "New horse. Mucho caballo."

"Did he just buy him last week from a man for $200?"

"Sí."

"He's my horse. My daddy sold him without me knowing it. I want him back."

He frowned and hesitated before answering. "Little Bit, like this horse. His name Red."

"His name's not Red. It's Spade."

"You know Little Bit?" he asked, continuing to frown.

"I remember him from high school. He's older than me."

"He just get back from war. Gone three years."

"Look, he has my horse. I'm sure he'll understand when I explain what happened."

Shaking his head, he replied, "Little Bit not well. Has dreams some nights. Can hear him scream from out here. Little Bit just a boy. See too much death. Loves his new horse."

"He's my horse, and I love him, too," I said, losing patience.

"Please, Little Bit sick inside. Need time to get well."

"What's that have to do with my horse?"

"He no need more problems."

I wasn't getting anywhere with this little man. "When will Sam be back?"

Shrugging his shoulders, he said, "Maybe long time. I tell him you come."

I was about to say I wasn't leaving, when I saw Sam riding through a gate on Spade. Stopping him at his pen, he dismounted, tied Spade and walked toward us. I was shocked at his appearance. I remembered him in school as a big guy with broad shoulders and muscles. What I saw now was nothing like I remembered him. His pants were too large and held up by a belt cinched so tight that it caused pleats in his Levis. His shirt was so large it looked like it was hanging on a rack. His old hat was tattered and filthy. When he was close, and before he spoke, I could see that he had the saddest eyes I'd ever seen."

"I'm Mattie Quentin. You probably don't remember me. I was a freshman when you were a senior," I said, extending my hand.

Shaking my hand, he said, "Sure, I remember. You were a good basketball player. I saw a lot of your games."

"I'm here to tell you that's my horse," I said, pointing to Spade.

"I just bought him from a man in town."

"That was my dad. He's a drunk. He took the money and left town. I had no idea that he was going to sell Spade. He had no right. The horse didn't belong to him. My pa-pa bought him for me, and he was stalled at his place. I want him back! I'll get the $200 for you some way." He didn't answer, just looking at the ground.

"Do you understand me?" I asked.

"Yeah," he replied.

"Do you believe me?"

"Yeah, I guess," he answered.

"Well, are you going to do the right thing and give my horse back to me?"

"I need the horse now. I'm moving 200 sheep this weekend, and it won't be possible without him. It's just me and Jose, and I only have one other horse that we can ride."

"You can keep him until you move your sheep then I want him back."

"Okay. I'll bring him home Sunday," he mumbled, turning and walking toward the house, not giving me a chance to respond.

"Is he always like that?" I asked, turning toward Jose.

"I tell you! Little Bit hurt! You not understand about war. No eres una buena chica," He said, turning and going into his house.

That was rude, I thought. I didn't understand Spanish, but without doubt that was not a compliment. I had my horse back now, but strangely, on the drive back into town, all I felt was sadness.

I was back at the hospital well before 8:00. Pa-Pa was already asleep. "How did he do tonight?"

"Better. He's able to move that leg and he's more alert. It's also easier for him to eat. There're several encouraging signs. Dr. Sadler came by and said he was improving."

"Did he say anything about when he might be able to go home?" I asked.

"No. He didn't mention that. What did you find out?"

I explained what happened, not going into detail.

"You don't seem to be as happy as you should be. You got your horse back. Isn't that what you wanted?"

"Yeah, but it didn't go as I expected. I'll feel better tomorrow and especially when Spade is back in his stall this weekend." For whatever reason, I didn't want to talk about it, now.

I had trouble going to sleep that night. I kept seeing images of those sad eyes and that shell of a person who the little man said was sick inside. I was awake before my alarm went off, got dressed, and left for the hospital. They generally had breakfast at 6:00. Pa-Pa was awake when I went into his room.

"Hi, Mattie. How're you?"

"Good. Did you sleep well?"

"I did. Of course they give me a pill each night. That helps. Look, I can move my leg," he said, lifting it up off the bed.

"That's wonderful, Pa-Pa. You're going to be out of here in no time."

"I hope so. My friends visit me every day, but the days are long. I don't want to be a problem for you and your mother, Mattie."

"Don't be silly, Pa-Pa. We love you. You're not a problem." I changed the subject telling him about getting Spade back this weekend.

"That's wonderful news. I thought Sam would do the right thing. Did he remember you?"

"He did. Tell me about him, Pa-Pa."

"I don't know that much, just what my friends at the coffee shop told me. Of course you knew him in high school. I saw him play football, and he was as tough as they come. He was a ferocious hitter on defense and a fullback on offense. Several of my friends thought he was the best that had come through school in many years. He was drafted right out of high school and ended up in Korea. From what I gather, he was involved in some of the worst fighting of the war. It was a useless war and not worth the lives it cost. The country never supported it like we did World War II. Sam's parents were good, hard working people. Both of them are gone. His mother passed while Sam was in the service. I went to the funeral, and he took it hard. He and his mother were close. It must have been difficult for Sam to come home, bury his mother, and go back to the war."

"What about the man who lives on the ranch?" I asked.

"You mean, Jose. He's been with them as long as I remember. He came from Old Mexico, had no family, and the Colter's took him in. He stayed on the ranch after Sam's mother died. He's a good man and loyal to the family. He was quite a Vaquero, in his younger days. I know that he taught Sam to ride and rope."

"Jose, said that Sam was sick inside. What did he mean?"

"I'm guessing that Sam saw death close up. He may have caused it himself or maybe he witnessed some of his friends dying. Probably both. I doubt if anyone will ever know. Most men who go through that won't talk about it."

"I guess it's going to work out. Did I do the right thing, Pa-Pa?"

"Mattie, Spade is your horse. I know how much he means to you. That's going to have to be your decision and no one else's."

They brought his breakfast before we could talk further about Sam and Spade. It generally took about twenty minutes for him to eat. His appetite was good, and after I cut up his sausage and buttered his toast, he was able to eat without my help for the first time.

After he finished, I gave him a peck on the cheek, told him I loved him, and left. Mother had our breakfast on the table when I got home. I didn't understand why I stayed so skinny. I ate the two eggs, bacon, and toast with jelly almost every morning. Today was Wednesday, which meant chicken fried steak, gravy and rolls in the cafeteria. I would probably clean my plate. I continued to expect my body to begin filling out like most girls my age. I didn't have to look like Marilyn Monroe, but only be normal.

I entered the gym a few minutes before school and noticed my friend, Della, in a serious conversation with Juan. Approaching them, they stopped talking and Juan walked away.

"Morning, Della, is everything okay?"

"No. I'll tell you about it later. How's your pa-pa?"

"Better. He fed himself today. Della, what is, 'No eres una buena chica' in Spanish?"

"Who said that to you?"

"It doesn't matter. What does it mean?"

"It means, 'you are not a nice girl'. That's not true. You're the nicest person I know. Who would say such a thing to my best friend?"

"Doesn't matter. Maybe they're right."

Chapter 9

Sam

It was Friday and I was still sick about having to give up Red. He was the best horse I'd ever ridden. All along, I had a feeling that something wasn't right. He wasn't a $200 horse. I should've known by the seller's actions that he wasn't the owner. The truth of the matter, he was such a nice horse that I ignored the obvious. I had no choice but to give him back to the rightful owner. I remember Mattie better than she realized. She was, and probably still is, an outstanding athlete. She plays more like a boy than a girl. She isn't anything like Sonia and her picture wouldn't be considered for a pin up; however, there's something about her. I can't put my finger on what it is.

I had delayed getting my sheep until the weekend. Sonia had said she would be home and could help us. To be honest, I was looking forward to seeing her again. I hadn't dated anyone since high school. The service wasn't a great place to meet girls.

I was trying to eat more and gain weight. This morning I decided to fry some bacon, scramble some eggs and fix a burrito using Jose's homemade tortillas. After drinking very little coffee when I was in school, I'd become a multiple cup drinker in the service. I'd have five or six cups a day.

I hadn't cut back on my smoking which was discouraging. When I'd wake up from a bad dream, the first thing I would do is reach for a cigarette. Some days I'd go through a pack. I always heard that when you quit smoking you'd gain weight. Maybe that'd encourage me to give it up.

After eating, I went outside to feed the horses, facing a north wind that was much colder than yesterday. I immediately thought of Korea and knew that I would never in my life be that cold again. This time last year, I was living in temperatures below zero, most of the time with snow on the ground.

After feeding and breaking the thin sheet of ice on the water trough, I went to check on Jose. He was dressed and ready to go. Today, I had planned to inform the Toller's that we would get my sheep tomorrow. We'd take my stock trailer and after doing that would pick up some feed shocks from another neighbor. I had made arrangements to buy a hundred bundles from him. I could get that many in my trailer and the back of my pickup.

We hooked on the trailer and were at the Tollers by 8:30. Mr. Toller was down at his pens so we passed the house without stopping. I got out and shook hands with him, saying, "Morning, how're you today?"

"Cold. I don't like winter. You ready to pick up your stock?"

"Would tomorrow be okay?"

Smiling, he said, "Gonna get some extra help? Good, she needs to get off her butt and do some work. We spoil her rotten, but she's a sweet girl. You're all she talked about last Sunday."

"I can sure use all the help that's available."

"What time are you going to be here?" he asked.

"Hopefully, by 8:00. The earlier we start, the less traffic we'll have to deal with."

"Sam, I didn't say anything to you the other day, but the screw worm problem is still terrible. You would think that as dry as it's been it wouldn't be as bad. That's not the case. Maybe it's the mild winters we've had the past several years. Anyway a small cut or scratch has to be doctored right away. Also, it's best to work your calves in the winter when there's not many flies. Remember to doctor the naval cord of your new calves. That's a prime target for the flies. Those heifers you bought will calve in

March. I know that's not what nature intended, but with the cold there'll be less flies."

"Yes sir, I appreciate the reminder."

"Are you going to the game tonight? You know we're playing Roscoe," he said.

"I really hadn't thought about it."

"You should go, Sam. A lot of people would be glad to see you. They remember what a great player you were, after all, it's only been three years."

"I'll think about it."

"My wife told me to invite you over again. When she finds out you're moving the sheep tomorrow, she'll expect you to come back for supper."

"Sure, that sounds good."

Driving off, Jose said, "Little Bit, you watch out. Some girls bad for you."

I decided that afternoon to go in for the game. I was determined to be better dressed tomorrow night for supper at the Tollers. Going in early, I could go to Mellinger's and buy a new shirt that fit me. I'd purposely stayed away from people since coming home, anticipating they'd ask me about the war. Maybe it was time I faced it instead of avoiding the subject. I could say that it wasn't something I wanted to talk about when asked.

It seemed a lifetime ago since I'd been in school and played football. So much had happened since then, which made that time in my life seem trivial. In fact, looking back, it was silly to get that worked up over a game, when winning was supposed to be so important. Comparing football to my last two years made it seem insignificant.

I expected to see a few of my teammates at the game. As for as I know, none of them had been drafted. I was the only one fortunate enough to go through that hell.

Maybe, I felt resentment over that. After all, why me? Maybe some day, I would be a better person because of it. That wasn't the case, now.

I started getting ready early because the stores closed at 5:00. I was going to wear my new Levis and it didn't matter what shirt. It was going to be cold enough to require my heavy coat, which would cover it up. I needed a new hat in the worst way but didn't want to spend the money. I brushed it off but didn't improve the appearance. I had deposited $1000 in the bank and kept out the rest for expenses. That was going to have to do me for a lengthy period of time. It was going to be necessary to find some work to supplement what money I had.

It didn't take me long to buy my shirt and the few groceries I needed. The air in town was thick with smoke from the burning of the cotton burrs at the gin, which was to be expected this time of year. Also, there were more people in town due to the Mexican population that had come in to pick cotton. For some reasons these familiar events made me feel better. They happened each year and this was no exception.

Going by the Queen Theater, I noticed that "Shane" was showing. Maybe I would go see it the next time I came to town if it was still playing. Movies were shown in the service, but they were generally the older ones.

My next stop was the Dairy Bar, the favorite hangout out for students. It was early, and my order was filled quickly. The owner recognized me, saying he was glad I had made it back home. While I was eating in my pickup, a car pulled up and three boys got out. One of them had graduated with me, and I didn't know the other two. I was hoping they wouldn't see me but that wasn't the case. Bennie York, who I had gone all the way through school with, spotted me immediately and came over to my pickup. Bennie was the last person I wanted to see.

"Sam Colter. When did you get back?"

"About three weeks ago."

"Hey. Come over here!" Bennie said, motioning to his friends.

"This is Sam, he just got back from the war. Sam this is Jenner and Ernie. They're friends of mine from Sweetwater."

"How're y'all doing?" I asked.

"Good. We'll be feeling a lot better in a couple of hours," answered Ernie.

Leaning over and speaking almost in a whisper, Bennie said, "We got a big night planned, Sam. Mother and Daddy are out of town. You can go with us if you like. After the game we're going to an all night party in Sweetwater. It's going to be some bash. Pot will be available, too. Mix it with enough beer and you can be out of this world."

"No thanks, Bennie. I've got to move sheep from the Toller Ranch to my place tomorrow. I bought 200 head."

"The Toller Ranch? No wonder you don't want to go with us. That Sonia is a looker."

I hardly knew Sonia, but I didn't like his comment.

"Are you going to the game?" Bennie asked.

"Yeah. Roscoe is special and always a big game. You know how Coach feels about them," I answered.

"We're going, too. We wouldn't go but we have to pick up one of the players who's going with us. We'd already be at the party if it wasn't for that."

Man, I thought. Things must have changed since I graduated. If Coach finds out that guy will never play football again.

"You sure about not going? You're going to miss a lot of fun," Bennie said.

"I'm sure. Got a long day tomorrow. I'll probably see you at the game," I said, hoping they would move on. I guess they took the hint because they went to pick up their order. I couldn't believe someone on the team was going with them.

I was at the game early. I saw several of my teachers who hugged me, saying how glad they were I was home. It made the trip to town worth it. I ran into several students who remembered me, also. I know most of the adults didn't recognize me.

I found a seat in the stands, but after the school songs and the National Anthem I ended up down by the fence. I couldn't get my mind off the fact that a player was breaking all training rules. Going down the list of players in my program, it hit me like a bolt of lightening. Bennie had a little brother that was in junior high when we graduated. Avery York was a 140 sophomore. Bennie was taking his younger brother to the party! What a scumbag!

We won the game 20-6, but my mind was occupied thinking about Avery York. He was about to throw away his high school football career. I went to my pickup and just sat there thinking, it's none of my business. I should just forget it and go home. I started my pickup, but instead of heading home, I drove back to the dressing room and parked in the street so I had a view of the exit. I sat there fifteen minutes before the players started coming out, with Avery being one of the first. From out of nowhere, Bennie and his friends met him. They were parked a good way from me, but I intercepted them before they reached their car.

"Well, looks like you changed your mind. Leave your pickup here, and we can drop you off in the morning," Bennie said.

"I need to talk with you privately," I said, walking away from the group. Bennie followed me out of hearing distance.

"You taking Avery with you?" I asked.

"Yep. It's time that boy found out how to have some fun."

"You know, if Coach finds out, Avery will be kicked off the team," I said.

"What's that to you, Sam? It's none of your business. He's my brother."

"Let Avery go home with me. I can use him tomorrow. I'll bring him home after we finish moving my sheep. You and your friends can go to the party and have all the fun you want."

"I don't know who you think you are to tell me what to do. Does being an ex solder give you the right to order me around?"

"No. Maybe it's none of my business." I moved closer to him until I was only a few inches from his face before continuing. "You know what's right, Bennie. I don't want any trouble with you. I have had enough fighting to last me ten lifetimes. Now, you call Avery over here and tell him he's going with me and don't mess with me tonight." He blinked a couple of times before turning around.

"Avery, get over here!" he hollered.

"What is it, Bennie?" Avery asked.

"Sam needs you tomorrow to help him move some sheep. You're going home with him."

"Awe, Bennie. I told my friends I was going to a wild party. They'll ask me about it and I won't have anything to tell them."

"Just do what I tell you, Avery. Maybe I'll take you next time." Bennie turned and walked away before Avery could plead his case.

I said, in a voice loud enough for him to hear me, "Thanks, Bennie, I appreciate it."

On the drive home, Avery, avoided conversation, giving one word answers to questions and staring out his window.

Chapter 10

Mattie

I went to the football game and nearly froze. Home in my warm bed, I couldn't get my mind off the meeting with Sam Colter. He was using Spade to move sheep tomorrow and then bringing him home. I couldn't decide whether I was worried about Spade or feeling guilty about taking him away from Sam. Either way, I couldn't keep from thinking about it. Maybe it would make me feel better if I went to the Colters tomorrow and helped him move his sheep. That would allow me to make sure nothing happened to Spade and also relieve my guilt. My mother could look after Pa-Pa since she wasn't working tomorrow. I could ask Mother if her friend Louise could take her to the hospital, since I would need to take the pickup. That was my last thought before I went to sleep.

By 6:00 the next morning, I had coffee made. I fixed two pieces of toast and filled a large cup with the strong brew. Before leaving, I woke my mother and told her my plans, asking her to call Louise for a ride to the hospital. I was on the road to the Colters by 6:30, feeling good about my decision. Pa-Pa's pickup was only two years old and had a radio and a good heater. It was cold this morning, below freezing. I'd dressed warm in jeans, flannel shirt, and a heavy sweater. Wearing my warmest coat plus my toboggan, I added two pairs of socks. I was at the ranch a few minutes after 7:00. It was not good daylight yet, but I could see that Sam's trailer was already hooked up to his pickup. No one was outside, so I went to the door and knocked. I waited and was about to knock again when Sam came around the corner of the house.

Looking confused, he said, "I thought you were going to let me use Re--, I mean your horse today?"

"I am. I came to help you move the sheep, if it's okay?"

"Sure. I can't pay you though."

"I'm not asking you to pay me. I'm trying to be nice."

"I appreciate that. You can take your pickup and stay ahead of us. Take my dog with you and keep him in the pickup. That will keep him out of the way. There're several side roads that we pass. You can wait at each and make sure they don't turn up them. That will allow Jose and me from having to worry about keeping them on the route. One other thing, Avery York will be riding with you."

"Am I taking his job?" I asked.

"No. It'll be good to have the both of you. Now, we'll leave in a few minutes and you can follow us. There's coffee on the stove if you'd like some."

"Thanks. I have a cup in my pickup."

Going into the house, I was surprised at how neat and clean it was. It was warm with a space heater in the living room and kitchen. Avery was at the table eating a bowl of cereal.

"Morning, Avery."

"Hi, Mattie. Did Sam hire you, too?"

"No, I'm a volunteer. We're supposed to work together today. You better dress warm. It's cold."

Before Avery could respond, Sam was honking his horn which I assume meant we were ready to go. "Sam said you were to ride with me."

We were at the Toller Ranch before 8:00. The first person I saw was Sonia. Of course, I knew her, but we'd never been friends. She didn't play basketball but had been a cheerleader for three years.

When Sam opened the door to his pickup she was there. Was I seeing things, or did she hug him. How disgusting!

"Wow. She's all over him!" exclaimed Avery.

I just sat there, feeling like a fool. Sam Colter had plenty of help without me. Maybe, I should leave. He unloaded Spade and I changed my mind about leaving. I was going to make sure he was delivered safe and sound.

Mr. Toller came over to the pickup and I rolled my window down. Hablo barked at him like he was defending me.

"Morning, Mattie. I hope you dressed warm for this sheep drive."

"Yes, sir, I did."

"I enjoy watching you play basketball. I make most of the home games."

"Thank you."

"How's your granddad? I heard about his stroke."

"He's doing better. We're hoping he can go home soon."

"He's a fine man. One of the best. Well, stay warm. I'm glad Sam has some extra help. Sheep don't drive nearly as good as cattle."

With the three of them mounted and Sonia on her little paint, Mr. Toller opened the gate and let the sheep out. The drive was under way. We drove ahead a few hundred yards to look for openings that might be tempting for the sheep. When we reached the highway, we took a position that would turn the sheep in the right direction. Hablo tried to escape the pickup, but we managed to keep him in. I wondered why Sam told me to bring him, since all he did was bark at everything.

When they came by us, I couldn't help but notice how well Sam rode my horse. It was obvious that he was a good rider and knew what he was doing. Sonia, on the other hand, was bouncing all over the little paint, which gave me a feeling of satisfaction. Compared to Jose and Sam, she looked terrible.

When we drove around them to look for the next opening that would provide an escape route, Avery commented, "Man, Sonia looks good on that paint, doesn't she?"

I didn't answer, thinking, boys have to be the dumbest animal on earth.

His next comment stunned me. "No wonder, Sam didn't want to go with Bennie and his friends to the party."

"What do you mean by that?" I asked.

"Bennie and his friends went to an all-night party in Sweetwater. Bennie was going to take me. He said it was time for me to learn to drink beer. Then Sam showed up outside the dressing room. He talked to Bennie, but I was too far away to hear what he said. He was right up in Bennie's face. He wouldn't admit it, but he's afraid of Sam. Now here I am, messing with these stinkin' sheep."

"What do you think of Sam?" I asked.

"He should mind his own business. He ruined my plans, and now my friends are going to know I didn't go to the party. I'd told them all about it and said I was probably going to get drunk."

When Sam Colter rode by on Spade, I saw a different person.

On the drive home, I questioned my sanity. I'd told Sam that he could keep Spade to use on his ranch as long as he'd be available for me whenever I needed him. For some reason, I felt good about my decision. Spade would have good care, and I could ride him whenever I wanted. When I told him about my decision, he smiled for the first time and his eyes were not as sad. After saying goodbye to Spade, I believe he was pleased with my decision.

I still couldn't believe Sonia. Why was she interested in Sam? He looked terrible. He was thin, almost a skeleton, and with his big ears and crooked nose, was not the least bit handsome. What did she see in him that I'd missed? Maybe she remembered him the way he was in high school.

Stopping by the hospital to see Pa-Pa, I'd found him in a chair reading the paper. "Look at you. Sitting in a chair."

Smiling, he said, "I've been in that bed too long. The nurse helped me get up. You can't believe how good it feels. I want to show you something. Here, give me your arm."

Putting out my arm, he took hold and pulled himself up to a standing position. Then he let go and even though he was wobbly, stood by himself.

"What do you think, Mattie?'

"Pa-Pa that's wonderful. Does Dr. Sadler know about this?"

"No, I'm going to surprise him when he comes by today."

"I'm so proud of you. When he comes by, ask him when you can go home."

"That's going to be my first question."

I told him about my morning, helping Sam move his sheep. Of course, I left out Avery's story. I did tell him about leaving Spade with Sam.

"That surprises me, Mattie. What changed your mind?"

"I know Sam will take good care of him and he needs Spade. I saw what a good rider he is. Maybe I felt guilty about taking him away from Sam. After all, he paid for him. He's still going to be my horse and I can use him anytime I want. Plus, we won't have to buy feed."

"I know you, Mattie Quentin. You're not telling me everything."

"I feel sorry for Sam, Pa-Pa. He looks horrible. His pants just hang on him and he has the saddest look. He looks like one of those hobos that you see coming through town in a boxcar. I remember what he looked like in high school. I can't imagine what he's been through to change him so much."

"You're a good girl, Mattie. You did the right thing."

"What I don't understand, Pa-Pa is why Sonia Toller is sweet on him. You should've seen her. It was sickening."

"This is coming from on old man so you can take it for what it's worth. Many times what you see on the outside of a person is totally different than what is on the inside. She probably sees the inside of Sam as being attractive."

"From what I know of Sonia, she wouldn't have enough sense to think that deeply. Anyway, that's none of my business."

"Mattie, this is on a different matter, but you need to listen carefully and do what I tell you. My retirement check should be in my mail at home. Deposit it in my account and tell them you need the paperwork that will allow you to check on it. If they give you any trouble, talk to the president of the bank. He'll take care of it for you. You'll need to see that my bills are paid, and also, your mother is going to need some help with her expenses. One other thing. There's a will in my lockbox at the bank. I want you to bring it to me. I need to make some changes. I'd like for you to do this Monday if at all possible."

"No problem, Pa-Pa. I can go by at lunch before I come to the hospital. I'm going to leave now so you can take a nap. Love you."

"Love you too, Mattie."

It was 2:30 but instead of going home, I drove to Della's house. We never did have the opportunity to discuss her problem. She was home but so were her parents. She suggested that we go to my pickup to visit. Once inside, she started crying. I didn't try to say anything, just waited until she was able to speak.

"Juan wants to get married during the Thanksgiving holidays. He says he's going to break up with me if we don't. He's quitting school. His grades are terrible, and he isn't going to graduate. I tried to talk to him, but he won't listen."

"Break up with him, Della. It's not worth it. You have dreams and finishing school is important to you. He's being selfish and only thinking of himself."

"I know, Mattie; however, that's part of our culture. The men believe they're more important, and we should do whatever they wish."

"This is 1953 and times are changing," I said.

"Not in my culture. It'll never change."

"You don't have to follow the culture, Della. Follow your dreams."

"You're right. I know you're right, but I receive no support at home."

"I support you, Della, and will tell that to anyone."

"Here I am feeling sorry for myself, and many are much worse off than me. Did you hear about the terrible tragedy?" she asked.

"No, what happened?"

"You remember Bennie York? He and his brother were in a wreck this morning and both were killed.," she answered.

"What? What're you saying?"

"Their parents were out of town, and they were coming from Sweetwater when Bennie went to sleep and had a head on collision with a truck. The car caught fire and the bodies were burned so badly they couldn't be identified. It was Bennie's car so they knew it was them. Can you imagine how the parents are suffering?"

"I gotta go, Della. Now! Get out quick," I said, starting the pickup.

I left with my tires spinning and Della looking stunned. I had to get back to the Colter's before Sam brought Avery home. I'd never driven that fast before, with the speedometer moving past 70. About ten miles out of town, I met them. Stopping as quickly as possible, I made a U-turn and after several miles caught up and started honking. Sam pulled off the side of the road. I jumped out and went to his door, which he had opened.

"Sam, I've got to talk to you!"

"What's going on, Mattie?"

"Come back here." When we were far enough to prevent Avery from hearing, I told him what happened.

"So everyone thinks Avery was killed, also," he stated.

"Yes, from what Della said. You know how fast this kind of news travels in town," I explained.

"I need to get him home. I'm not going to tell him now. He'll need his mother and daddy when he finds out. Would you come with me?"

I was amazed at how calm Sam was. "Sure. I'll go with you. Let me pull my pickup off the road."

If Avery suspected anything was wrong, he gave no indication. When we arrived at his house, at least a dozen cars were there, including several police vehicles.

"Wonder what's going on? I hope Bennie didn't get into trouble," he said.

We entered the house, and when his mother saw him, she screamed, "Avery! It wasn't them. Avery, where's Bennie? Thank God it wasn't my boys! There was a mistake!" She grabbed Avery, hugging him and crying.

While everyone was carrying on, a policeman came over to us and asked, "What's going on? Where did you find Avery?"

In a quiet, calm voice, Sam explained the events of the previous night to him.

The policeman listened without interrupting and then said, "It was Bennie and one of his friends in the car. I'll explain it to his parents. Thank you."

Sam took my hand and led me out of the house to the pickup. Nothing was said on the drive back to my pickup. When we stopped, he said, "Thank you for going with me. Death seems to follow me around."

"Are you all right?" I asked.

"Yeah. Let me know when you need your horse. Thank you again for allowing me to keep him."

I left, thinking on the way home how rough his hand felt in mine, but also how comforting.

Chapter 11

Gladys

It was Tuesday, November 17. Mattie had a home game tonight with Anson. She'd already left for the gym and I was getting ready to leave in time to go by the hospital. Dr. Sadler still hadn't released Mr. Quentin, saying that he wasn't able to get around good enough to go home. I said that we could look after him, but Dr. Sadler insisted that we didn't need to be in a hurry.

I hadn't heard a word from Leon and was beginning to believe that he might be gone forever. Mattie and I were getting along fine, and it would be all right with me if he didn't return. I didn't know what I would do if he did show up. Our lives were better without him. With Mr. Quentin helping with our bills, we were doing better financially than we had in years. He'd changed his will leaving this house and all his belongings to Mattie. I was going to wait until the first of the year and put our house on the market. There was no use in making a payment on a house we didn't live in.

Since Mr. Quentin had been able to feed himself, Mattie was not having to miss any school. She'd been out to the Colter Ranch several times to ride her horse, although I wasn't sure that was the main reason for her visits. She'd come home talking about Sam. When I questioned her about him, her comment was, "He's just interested in Sonia Toller."

I realized how much more enjoyable life was without Leon. I started fixing up more and had even had my hair done several times. I splurged and bought makeup that made me feel better about myself. When I looked in the mirror some of the lines had disappeared. I'd never been overweight, probably because I worked so hard. Being medium height, I weighted around 120. I didn't consider myself beautiful, but after dressing up a bit and with a little makeup, attractive was a reasonable description. I wore my hair short and had even allowed them to put a rinse on it during my visit to the beauty shop to cover up the gray.

We were going to have our hands full when we brought Mr. Quentin home. He could move around some with the help of a walker but was limited when it came to caring for himself. No way could he get dressed or take a bath without help. I'd not mentioned taking him to the nursing home again. I knew that Mattie would never go for that.

I was at the hospital for supper, but Mr. Quentin needed no help eating. As long as he didn't have to use his left arm and hand, he could do fine. The woman delivering the meal would cut up his meat if it was required. I studied him as he ate, thinking what a wonderful man he was. I'd never heard him curse, but frequently when frustrated, he would say "ah pshaw". He didn't drink but smoked 'roll your own cigarettes'. Most of his shirts had holes burned in them by the ashes that fell from his Prince Albert tobacco. I hadn't seen him smoke a cigarette taken from a pack.

He appeared taller than he was because he was thin. He had a leathery, but kind face, and I'd never, in over 30 years, seen him angry. That was amazing, since his son had provided him plenty of reasons. He'd been retired for ten years, and after coffee at the café with his friends in the morning, usually could be found at the domino hall. He loved baseball and was a devoted Yankee's fan.

Words couldn't describe his feeling for Mattie or hers for him. He'd taken the place of her daddy from the beginning. If it had been required, she would've quit school to care for him. Thank goodness that wasn't the case.

"I'd like to go tonight," he said, between bites.

"Maybe by the time district starts," I responded.

"I haven't missed a home game since she started playing in junior high."

"I know. She'll miss having you there, too. I'm sure you'll get a play-by-play description of the game tomorrow."

"I got my will changed. If Leon gives you any trouble when that time comes, you get a lawyer. I've given him his inheritance many times over through the years. I expect him to show up with his hand out. I want Mattie to use whatever I'm able to leave her to attend college."

After I left the hospital, I went by to pick up Louise who was going to the game with me. She must've been watching for me because she was out of the house as soon as I stopped.

"Hi, Gladys. Thanks for coming by for me. I enjoy the games especially watching Mattie play. You look great. I love your hair."

"Thanks, Louise. I feel better than I have in years."

"You know why, don't you?"

"Yes. It's because Leon's gone. I admit it," I said.

"How's Mattie doing? Probably good, huh?"

"Yes," I said, laughing. "You made your point."

"How's her pa-pa doing?" she asked.

"Better every day. I expect him to be released soon," I answered.

We were at the gym within a few minutes, and before we got out of the pickup, Louise said, "Now I'm going to pay your way in. Don't even think about arguing with me. I get a free ride, so I pay for admission."

The gym wasn't large with seating on one side only. Across the gym floor was a stage. The crowd was small for the girls' game, but would increase when the boys played. We sat in the stands to the left of the entrance, which was considered the home side.

The teams were warming up, and I immediately spotted Mattie going in for a layup. She was smooth, plus being quick and agile.

"Mattie looks good," Louise said.

"She does. Mattie complains about being skinny, but a lot of girls would trade with her."

"Her basketball uniform is a perfect fit. I'd like to look that good," Louise said.

Just before the game started, Louise pointed at the entrance. "Look who just came in."

"Sam Colter. I hope she doesn't see him. It'll make her nervous," I said.

"He looks terrible," Louise said.

"He does. I can't even start to imagine what he's been through. Mattie said he wouldn't talk about it."

"Everybody in town knows he saved that boy's life. It was a terrible tragedy for the Yorks, but it could've been worse if Avery had been in the car," Louise said.

"I know. Mattie said Mr. York tried to do something for Sam. Even tried to give him money, but Sam refused. Sam didn't go to the funeral because he wanted to avoid attention. Mattie went and said it was the saddest service she'd ever attended."

We stopped talking and became involved in the game. If Mattie noticed Sam it made no difference in her performance. She scored 18 points the first half and another 12 the second. The second half they left one of our forwards alone and put two guards on Mattie. We won 46-32.

Sam sat down on the front row in the far corner. Glancing his way several times, he showed no emotion. After the game ended, he left immediately. I waited in the stands for Mattie. She was always one of the last to come out of the dressing room.

"Is Sam still here?" being the first thing out of her mouth when she arrived.

"No Mattie, he left after the game."

"I thought he might wait and talk to me," she said, her voice registering disappointment.

"You played great," Louise said.

"Thank you. We won. That's what's important."

"Are you going to stay for the boys' game?" I asked.

"Yes. Can you believe the number of people who come late to see the boys? Wonder what it would take to get them here to see us play?"

Louise and I ended up staying for the boys' game, since Mattie would need a ride home. It was close, but Anson made a shot at the buzzer to win.

She made a sandwich at home and we visited about the game. "I'm proud of you, Mattie. I'm sorry Sam left without seeing you."

Never looking up, she said, "He's not interested in me."

"That's not true, Mattie. Why else would he come to your game and not stay and watch the boys?"

"I don't know, Mother. I can't figure him out."

"Honey, just be patient. Sam's going through some difficult times."

Chapter 12

Sam

Ishould've stayed after the game to congratulate Mattie on their win and how good she played. People kept coming up to me wanting, to talk about the York family and what I'd done. Becoming uneasy with the attention, I left immediately after the game just wanting to be left alone.

Mattie was something else, being aggressive, yet smart, and was miles ahead of the other players. The Anson girls could do nothing to stop her. She would've been an asset to the boy's varsity team. She probably didn't even know I was there. She'd come out earlier in the week to ride her horse and invited me to the game.

I was having trouble calling her horse Spade. He was still Red to me. I guess he wouldn't mind having two names. She hadn't given me any indication that she was going to take him home, which was a relief. I rode him most days to check on the heifers and the sheep, thus far they were doing okay. I'd made several trips to my neighbors' to buy shocked feed, but still was going to need to find several hundred bales of hay, also.

The last two Saturday nights had been spent at the Tollers. For the most part, I was comfortable there. Mr. Toller must have told them to avoid talking about the war, because they didn't bring it up. On both occasions, Mrs. Toller had made up a plate for me to take home for Jose. I appreciated that and it showed how considerate they were.

Sonia embarrassed me, hanging onto my arm every time an opportunity presented itself. It didn't seem to bother her parents, who paid no attention to her action. She and Mattie were different in so many respects. Mattie, being a year younger, seemed older and more mature. I guess you would have to say that Sonia was better looking, or most boys would. I was confused about why I felt a need to compare them, since Mattie had not shown any interest in me whatsoever.

I wasn't gaining weight and maybe had lost a few pounds. My appetite was not good and some days I ate very little. By the week of Thanksgiving, I knew something was wrong with me. I was getting weaker every day and had thrown up several times. It was harder for me to get out of bed each day and I had little endurance. On Wednesday, the day before Thanksgiving, I gave up and decided to go to the doctor. I asked Jose to go with me and drive. I was so weak it was difficult to climb into the pickup.

When Dr. Sadler finished examining me, with a frown on his face, he gave me his diagnosis. "Son, you're a mighty sick young man. I need to make some blood tests, but I believe you have hepatitis. You may not have noticed, but you have a yellowish tint to your skin and in your eyes. For some reason, your liver is not functioning properly, and that's causing problems. This is not uncommon for men returning from the service. I saw it during the second world war a number of times. It may be a result of the needle they used to give the shots or the unsanitary conditions you experienced. In your case, with the amount of weight you've lost, your immune system is weak and unable to ward off disease. I don't pretend to have the answers. What I do know is you're sick and you need to be in the hospital so we can observe and treat you."

"I can't stay in the hospital. I have too much work at home. Jose needs help looking after the cattle and sheep. I don't even have enough hay for the winter."

"Son, you have no choice," he said, followed by a stern look.

I knew Dr. Sadler well enough, that arguing would do no good. "Well, how long is this going to take?"

"Longer than you want it to. Is Jose with you?"

"Yeah. He's outside in the pickup."

"Send him home to get your bed clothes. We have a room available for you. We'll put you in a gown for X-rays and draw blood to send off for tests. I'm going to have the nurse give you a shot of penicillin and B-12."

That brought a sigh of relief from me. Dr. Sadler was wonderful, but as tough as I was, his shots were something to dread. His sweet, pretty, young nurse, gave shots that you hardly felt.

Dr. Sadler left and in a few minutes the nurse came in, smiling. "I heard about what you did. You're quite a hero around here."

Embarrassed, I didn't know how to respond.

"Goodness, you've lost a lot of weight," she said.

"I have. The food in the army wasn't very good. Lately, my appetite has been poor."

She gave me the two shots, which I hardly felt and then asked me to get on the scales that were in the room.

"Oh me, Sam. You only weight 130. You're just skin and bones. How much have you lost?"

"Probably about 40 pounds since I graduated from high school."

"Come with me. We'll get you in a room and then take some X-rays."

"Let me go talk to Jose first. I'll be back in a few minutes," I said.

My room contained a bed and one chair. I'm glad Jose was bringing my radio when he returned. The nurse left but came by shortly giving me a gown to put on.

"Take off your clothes and put this on. I'll be back in a few minutes to take you for X-rays," she instructed.

"All of them?" I asked.

Yes, Sam, all of them, even your socks," she said, smiling.

I did as she instructed and felt naked when finished. The gown fastened in the back, but I didn't feel completely covered. Maybe no one would be in the hall on my trip to X-ray. I sat down in the chair to wait and my fear was justified. There was nothing between my butt and the cold seat. The nurse returned, telling me she was ready.

I walked behind her down the hall, anxious to get where we were going. We had just passed the entrance, when someone said, "Sam!" I turned around and Mattie was standing there. I couldn't turn and run so I began backing up.

"What're you doing here?" she asked.

The nurse came to my rescue. He's sick, Mattie. Dr. Sadler put him in the hospital. We're going to X-ray.

"I'm here to visit with my pa-pa, Sam. I'm sorry you're sick. I'll check on you later."

I still didn't know what to say. I kept backing up instead of turning.

"Mattie, you better go on to your pa-pa's room. Sam here, is a modest young man and he feels a draft in the back of his gown," the nurse said, laughing.

I couldn't believe this. Of all the people to come in, it would be Mattie. I'd never been this embarrassed. After the X-rays were made, I returned to my room and immediately put my clothes back on. I wasn't wearing that gown another second. I knew it would be an hour or more until Jose returned with my clothes. Laying down on the bed, I felt weak, tired, and depressed. I didn't want to stay here but wasn't going to have a choice.

Jose was back sooner than I expected with my pajamas, razor, and toothbrush.

"Little Bit, no need to worry. I can look after cattle and sheep. Dr. Sadler make you well."

"Winter is here and we don't have any hay."

"I find hay. No problem."

"You go to the Tollers and ask him to help you find some hay," I said.

"I do that. Brought you radio. In the pickup. I get it."

Before he returned, Mattie came in. She was wearing jeans and a long sleeve man's shirt that wasn't tucked in. I was struck by how fresh and clean she looked. She sat down on the side of the bed and gave me a stern look with those big green eyes.

"What's wrong with you, Sam Colter?"

"Hepatitis, maybe. Something about my liver."

"That sounds serious. Did he say how long you would need to stay in the hospital?"

"No. I can't stay long, though. I have too much to do."

"What're you still doing in your street clothes? I see you have your pajamas."

"I haven't had time to change," I said.

"You were cute in that gown," she said, laughing.

"That's not funny. I wasn't decent in that stupid gown. It didn't have a back."

"I know," she said, laughing again. "You have to admit; I've seen more of you than Sonia Toller."

I wasn't that sharp, but I got the pun of that remark. "What's Sonia got to do with this?"

"You've been seeing her, haven't you?"

"I've been out to eat with her family several times," I said.

"Do you like her?" she asked.

"Sure. She's nice," I said. Thinking I probably should say it was none of her business.

"Are y'all going out?" she asked.

"We haven't gone anywhere," I said.

"Why didn't you stay and talk to me after the game, Tuesday?" she asked.

"People were bothering me. I wanted to get away. You played good."

"Thank you."

Jose returned with my radio, interrupting us. He smiled when he saw Mattie. It was obvious he liked her and had told me on more than one occasion that she was a nice girl.

"Hello, Jose. How're you doing?" she asked.

"Pretty good. You look after Sam?" he asked.

"Yes. I'll take good care of him."

"Good. Now I go check on everything at ranch. Take good care of Spade."

"Thank you, Jose. You're a good friend," she said.

After he left, Mattie said, "You're fortunate to have him."

"I know. I couldn't do without him. How's your granddad?"

"He's doing better all the time. I expect Dr. Sadler to let him go home any day. Pa-Pa's really anxious to get out of here."

For some reason, I was worn out by the time she left. Maybe it was the stress of all the questioning. She was different today, being much more aggressive, probably because she caught me in that backless gown. I've never been that embarrassed before. I changed into my night clothes and slept until supper was delivered.

The next day was Thanksgiving, and waking up, I was even sicker than the day before. I threw up before breakfast and again after I ate. Dr. Sadler came by and ordered another shot of penicillin. I didn't even feel like listening to the radio. Ordinarily, I would listen to the Texas /Texas A&M game.

Sonia came to see me before lunch, bringing a heaped-up plate with all the Thanksgiving fare, including turkey and dressing. I was so nauseated it almost made me throw up looking at it.

"Sam, Jose came out late yesterday and told us about you being in the hospital. I'm so sorry. Do you feel better today?"

"No, not at all," I replied.

"Oh, I'm sorry," she repeated. "Maybe you'll feel like eating later. Is there anything I can do for you?"

"No, thank you. Did Jose ask your dad about hay?"

"I don't know. They talked outside and when Daddy came in he told me about you. I wanted to come in last night, but he insisted I wait until today, it was so late."

Sonia stayed another half hour, making small talk. I thought she would never leave. I was doing my best not to be sick in front of her. Finally, I faked going to sleep, prompting her to bend over and kiss me on the forehead before leaving. She hadn't got out the door good, when I grabbed the bed pan and threw up for the third time. After that, I was able to go to sleep.

Mattie came in, waking me up, before supper. Thank goodness I woke up feeling a little better.

"You look terrible. I brought you some of my mother's homemade chicken noodle soup with crackers. If you can get some down, it'll be good for you."

"Thank you. I might try a little. Nothing has stayed down today."

She held the bowl for me while I ate most of the soup. It was good, and I was able to keep it down.

"I see someone brought you Thanksgiving dinner," she said.

"Ugh. I couldn't touch it. It made me sick looking at all that food."

"Do you want me to throw it out?" That way it will look like you cleaned your plate.

"Yeah. Good idea."

"Pa-Pa is going home Monday. He's excited."

"So you won't be coming back to the hospital?"

"Of course, I will. Someone has to look after you. I promised Jose."

"What's the weather like today?" I asked.

"Nice. Going to get cold tomorrow though. Maybe some ice for the next two days," she answered.

"I was afraid of that. Here I am in the hospital and not able to help Jose look after the stock, especially the sheep. I have shelter for them, but they'll need to be driven in. They're not smart enough to come in on their own."

"I could go help him. We don't have school until Monday."

"I couldn't pay you much," I said.

"Would you get off that pay thing? You're ridiculous! I'm not interested in your money. Besides, you're taking care of Spade."

"That would really be good. Jose will have trouble with no help. He generally gets started early."

"It's settled. That'll give me an excuse to ride Spade. Now, I'm leaving and will let you get a good nights sleep."

"Thank your mother for the soup. Thank you for bringing it and for helping Jose."

"Good night, Sam Colter. Hope you have sweet dreams," she said, going out the door.

The nurse came by later and asked me if I wanted a pill to help me sleep. I took her offer and was out in just a matter of minutes.

I was cold and couldn't keep from shaking. I gripped the stock of the Browning, which was sitting on a bi-pod, trying to steady my aim. Hundreds of them were coming up the hill, maybe even a thousand. Orders were to let them get close and make our ammunition count. I could actually see the expressions on their faces when the command came to open fire. The Browning 30 caliber bucked and spit death. I saw them fall, heard them scream as I pulled the trigger.

I woke up to the night nurse shaking me and saying, "It's okay, Sam. You're all right." She put her arms around me and hugged me. "You were only dreaming. You're safe here, in the hospital. You poor boy."

Chapter 13

Mattie

My alarm went off the next morning at 5:00. I lay there in my warm bed and questioned my offer to help pen Sam's sheep. It was the right thing to do, but I was not a cold weather person, probably because I didn't have any fat on me to provide natural insulation. I put on several layers of clothes, including two pairs of jeans. I made coffee but didn't make any breakfast. It was too early to think about eating.

When I left, at a little after 6:00, it was cold but nothing was falling. It was the day after Thanksgiving, and I didn't meet a car until I was ten miles out of town. There was no school today. When I arrived at the ranch I went directly to Jose's house, seeing that his light was on. He opened the door with a surprised look on his face.

"Señorita, what you doing?"

"Jose, I came to help you pen the sheep before the weather turns bad."

"Come in. Mucho frío."

His little house was warm, with the wood stove burning brightly. Everything was neatly arranged, but I hadn't realized how small it was. One room provided the kitchen, bedroom, and den. He did have running water but no bathroom.

"Little Miss, you eat?"

"No it was too early when I left home."

"I fix us something," he said "Coffee?" he asked.

"That would be wonderful." He gave me a steaming cup that would definitely wake you up. In a few minutes he provided me with a tortilla filled with egg, cheese and a pepper. He'd gone light on the chopped-up pepper and it was delicious."

"We get busy now," he said.

It was beginning to get daylight when we saddled our horses, but there would be no sunshine. I know Spade must be wondering what we were doing going out in the cold this early. The wind had increased, and it was getting colder by the minute.

"Jose, do you have any idea where the sheep might be?"

"Sí. Think maybe so."

We left the barn and headed north, right into the wind. There were some mountains, which in other states would be called hills, at the back of the ranch, and within half an hour we had reached them. By that time, sleet was falling, stinging my face. We found one group of about 50 at the bottom of one of the hills.

"We move these," he said.

That was easier said than done. They didn't want to move. After twenty minutes of moving easy and coaxing, we were able to get them moving south toward the shelter. We were successful driving them to a set of low covered pens about three hundred yards behind the house. The pens faced south and provided shelter from the wet and protection from the north wind. Once we had the sheep under the sheds it was evident they wouldn't venture out. They weren't the sharpest animals, but they had enough sense to know they were in a good place.

Three more trips to and from the hills enabled us to have most of the sheep in a shelter, according to Jose. By the time we rode back to the horse pens, it was mid-afternoon. I was numb. My teeth were chattering, and I was shaking all over. I don't believe another trip would've been possible. Jose insisted that I let him unsaddle and put the horses up. I put up a feeble argument and then went to his house, moving as close to the stove as possible. It still had some heat but was going to need more wood. After getting feeling back in my hands and feet, I put more wood in the stove from his supply behind his house.

By the time Jose was back, a nice fire was going. He took a pot out of his ice box and put it on the stove. In a few minutes, a wonderful aroma was filling the room.

"Need to eat. Help get warm."

The dish proved to be chili and it was wonderful. It was spicy, but not too much, and after two bowls, I began to feel like I would survive. "That was awesome. Thank you, Jose."

"Couldn't pen sheep without help. Gracious. You tell Little Bit sheep safe?"

"Sure. I'll stop by the hospital on the way home."

On the drive back into town something was still falling, and my windshield began to ice over. My vision became limited, with only a small space available to see the road. I had to drive slow because I could feel the road becoming slick. On the curve outside of town I lost control, hit my brake, started spinning, and ended up in the ditch. I should never had applied the brake, I thought. Not enough moisture had fallen for the ditch to be muddy and I was able to get out and back on the road. I slowed down to a crawl and made it to the hospital before supper was served.

I met Dr. Sadler in the hall. "Bad day to be out, Mattie."

"How's Sam today?" I asked.

"Not good. He's a sick young man. I've arranged for him to go to the veteran's hospital in McKinney. They can provide better treatment than I can here."

"Have you told him?" I asked.

"Yes. He didn't even argue with me. That's how sick he is."

"When will he be leaving?" I asked.

"I scheduled an ambulance to take him tomorrow morning. After you see him, I'm going to have the nurse put a 'Do Not Disturb' sign on his door. He doesn't need company."

Entering the room and seeing him, I gasped, before being able to prevent it. He was lying motionless, staring at the ceiling.

It seemed an effort for him to turn his head toward me. His skin had become more yellow and his eyes had a hollow, vacant look.

When he spoke it was more of a whisper. "Mattie, how're you?"

"Almost thawed out. We penned the sheep. Jose thought we got most of them," I said.

"Great. Is it cold?"

"Freezing cold. The roads are icing up."

"I'm going to McKinney tomorrow," he said.

"I know. I talked to the doctor."

"Got to get well."

"Don't worry about anything here. I can help Jose."

"Thank you," he mumbled, closing his eyes.

I knew it was time for me to leave and let them put up their sign on the door. The night nurse stopped me in the hall, asking how well I knew Sam.

"Not very well. We had an issue involving my horse shortly after he returned. I've spent some time with him since then. I know he's very sick."

"That's not all. He has terrible dreams at night. I'm not able to stay with him very long at a time. Other patients require my attention at night. Would it be possible for you to stay in the room with him until morning? I'll bring a cot for you to sleep on. I spoke with Dr. Sadler and he told me it would be all right."

"I guess so. Do you think it would help?"

"Yes. Somebody needs to be with him. Usually people who have nightmares wake easily but that's not the case with him. Sometimes it takes several minutes to wake him up and assure him everything is okay."

"I'll call my mother and tell her not to expect me home." Thank goodness Pa-Pa had a phone.

"Good. Thank you. It'll make my night go much easier."

I spoke to Mother and explained everything to her. She was understanding and didn't object. When I returned to the room the nurse had already set up a cot for me.

"Sam hasn't been able to eat today. I doubt if he wakes up. Feel free to eat his meal when it's delivered. I'll bring you some magazines to look at to pass the time. Also, I don't believe the radio will bother him in the least. In fact, it might be helpful. Thank you again. It's sweet of you to stay."

Sam didn't wake up when they brought his supper. I'd eaten late and wasn't hungry. I nibbled a little on the sandwich but didn't touch the soup. Time dragged by and finally at 9:00, I lay down on the cot, determined to sleep. It must have taken me at least an hour to doze off. Later, I woke to the sound of moaning, becoming louder and louder. I moved over to the bed, gently shaking him. Then he started mumbling.

"No, no, no, don't die. Hang on. Medics are coming." I continued to shake him harder but it did no good. Suddenly he bolted upright in bed, trembling.

"It's okay, Sam," I said, putting both my arms around him. He continued trembling and gasping for breath. I was about to call the nurse when his breathing became more even; however, he continued to shake. "Sam, you're okay, wake up. Everything's all right."

He let out a soft moan and lay back down. He would stop trembling for a few seconds and then start again. The firmer I held him, the less he shook. Finally, I lay down beside him and held him as close as I could. His breathing became regular, and he stopped trembling all together. I lay there for what seemed hours and then someone had their hand on my shoulder. Looking up, it was the nurse.

"Honey, you've done your job. It's morning. Breakfast will be here shortly. Thank you again for staying with him."

Getting up, I went to the bathroom, and coming back in, he was awake. "Morning, Sam."

"Mattie. You stayed with me?" he whispered.

"Yes." He sounded even weaker this morning.

"Thank you. Can't stop the nightmares. Almost every night. Glad for morning to come."

Dr. Sadler came in before I could respond. "The ambulance will be here at 10:00. Maybe the roads will be better by then. I'm going to give you a sedative for the four-hour trip. How did you sleep?"

"All right. Mattie stayed with me," he answered.

"Nice to have a friend, isn't it?" he questioned, smiling.

"Yeah. I appreciate her."

"Honey, now you go home and get some sleep. Be careful. The roads are slick," Dr. Sadler instructed.

"Sam, don't worry about anything. Jose is taking good care of the stock. If he needs help, I can provide."

"Thanks," he said, closing his eyes.

There was no traffic on the way home. The roads were terrible, and it took me twenty minutes to go about three miles. It was hard to believe Sam had become so sick in only a few days. Maybe the doctors at McKinney would be able to provide him with the care he needed. I know another issue was the money to pay for his care. That would've never been an issue for Dr. Sadler, but if he'd sent him to a regular hospital rather than a veteran facility it would've been.

Suddenly, it dawned on me. We had a basketball game last night at Hamlin. Surely it was canceled. I'd totally forgot about it. Surprised at how my priorities had changed in such a short time, it made me wonder what was happening.

Chapter 14

Gladys

Mattie's conduct the last several days had been confusing. When she called last night to tell me she was staying at the hospital with Sam it was a surprise. She hadn't even mentioned the ball game that was scheduled. Of course, it was canceled, but she probably didn't know that. The only explanation would be that she forgot about it, which was not like Mattie.

At home this morning she had talked nonstop about Sam and how worried she was about him. Mattie had never shown more than a casual interest in a boy. In fact, she seldom dated, even though she had multiple opportunities. Finally, my curiosity got the best of me, and I asked, "Did you forget about the game last night?"

"Yes. I'm sure it was canceled, so it's no big deal."

"You do remember that your pa-pa is going home Monday?" I asked.

"Sure. It'll probably be lunch so it's no problem. I'll go to the hospital then and take him home. I can get him settled before going back to school."

"Mattie, I expect your daddy to show up any day. I won't know what to do."

"That should be easy, Mother. Tell him he's not welcome. Pa-Pa will back you up. After all, it's his house. If he wants to stay in town, he has a place to live. He can make the payments and leave us alone. I don't want anything to do with him, now or in the future."

"That's harsh, Mattie, but I can't change the way you feel."

The next week our routine changed with Mr. Quentin being home. We'd get up early enough to have breakfast and get him settled. He could get around with his walker and was able to come to the table for meals. He needed help getting dressed and, of course, couldn't bathe himself. His attitude was positive, and he never complained. He didn't want to stay in bed, so we would get him to his favorite chair in front of the television before we left.

I'd take Mattie to school before going to work. The laundry was slow this time of year. People still washed their clothes, but not nearly as much as in the summer. I would go home for lunch with Mr. Quentin and was off work in plenty of time to pick up Mattie after practice.

After the ice storm, the weather had turned off beautiful, with cold nights but sunshine and warm days. I would go by my old house each day, expecting to see Leon's car, feeling relief when it wasn't there.

This Thursday, regular as clockwork, Earnest came in to do his washing. Since our conversation last month he'd been more talkative. I asked him if he needed any help.

"No thank you, Gladys. I have a light load this week. Haven't done much to get my clothes dirty. How're you doing?"

"Good. We have Mr. Quentin home and he's doing well," I answered.

"Haven't heard from Leon?" he asked.

"No. Not yet. He's been gone over a month. Not a word."

"Hard to understand why anyone would leave you, Gladys."

I didn't respond, not knowing what to say. Actually, it was not hard for me to understand. Leon was unhappy with his life, including his family. He got hold of some money and left, looking for something better. I hope he found it and didn't come back.

"You seem to be doing better, Earnest."

"You know, I'm feeling better. Ever since our visit things don't seem as bad. The point you made about my wife being upset if I didn't get on with my life really struck a cord. I stopped feeling sorry for myself and looked at what I have to be thankful for. It's working."

"Good for you." I said, turning to another customer.

I was getting off work every day at 5:00. Friday was the usual day to buy groceries, but since Mr. Quentin was home, we were out of everything. I went by the grocery store before picking up Mattie. I had a charge account that I paid every Friday. I bought milk, coffee, bread, hamburger, and lunch meat. I'd come back tomorrow and buy more. Hamburger meat had gone up since my last purchase, being 26 cents a pound. My total came to $2.43, with the coffee being my most expensive purchase. I would use the pound of hamburger to make a meatloaf, one of Mr. Quentin's favorites. The owner of the store, Mr. Wilson, stopped me going out the door.

"Gladys, have you got a minute?"

"Sure. Let me put my groceries in the pickup." Confused, I went back into the store to his office.

"Gladys, this is a busy time of year for us. One of my checkers has quit. Would you be interested in going to work here?"

Stunned, I didn't know what to say. "I don't know. You caught me off guard."

"I know you're a hard worker and dependable. That's the kind of employee we need. The pay is $1.15 an hour and you would be working six days a week. There would be pay increases after you're here for a length of time."

I put the numbers together and realized my salary would be around $50 a week. Much more than I was currently earning. "Do you think I could do the work?"

"We'll train you. It's not that difficult."

"When would I start?" I asked.

"Soon as possible. With the cotton picking season underway and many more people in town, we're busy."

"I would have to give the laundry notice and time to find a replacement."

"Yes. I understand that."

"Can I let you know tomorrow?" I asked.

"Sure," he said.

My heart was pounding when I left the store. I'd never been offered a job before. Especially, a good job making that kind of money. It would mean six days a week, but I'd have Sunday off. I couldn't think of one reason not to accept the offer; however, I wanted to talk with Mattie before making a decision.

Mattie was waiting on me when I arrived at school. On the drive home, I told her about the offer.

"Mother, that's wonderful. I'm proud of you. Someone else recognized what a hard worker you are. You're going to accept, aren't you?"

"Do you think I can do it?"

"Of course you can. Just think, working in the winter with heating and the summer with air conditioning. You deserve a good job."

"We could sure use the extra money. Of course, I'll need to buy some new clothes to wear to work and that will cost. I didn't ask what my hours would be and that might be a conflict having only the one pickup."

"Mother! We'll make it work. It's wonderful that you're getting a good job. Now, stop worrying. When you get your first check, we'll go shopping, maybe even to Minters in Abilene. It'll be fun."

"You're right, Mattie. I'm having trouble accepting the fact that we have something going our way. I should be thankful."

"I haven't heard anything from Sam. He's been gone four days now, and I thought he might call," she said.

"The way you described him, he's probably too sick. I expect you'll hear from him when he's feeling better. I'm glad Dr. Sadler sent him to McKinney. I'm sure they'll take good care of him, since it's a veteran's hospital. I hope and pray the poor boy is able to recover physically and mentally."

When I turned the corner and Mr. Quentin's house came into view, I gasped at the sight of the car parked in front.

Chapter 15

Sam

I remember being loaded in the ambulance but slept the entire trip. I was taken to an office when we arrived and a lady behind a typewriter commenced to ask me questions. They ranged from my birthday to when I was released from the service and everything in between. She must have asked me a hundred questions. I finally told her I was sick and about to throw up and that ended it.

I was taken to a room that I would share with another patient. There was a sign on the door which read Quarantine. That was the first indication my sickness was contagious.

For the next several weeks, I slept as much as possible. When awake, I was sick and miserable. Doctors were in and out, night and day. I was awakened several times during the night to take pills after being given a pill to allow me to sleep. Food had no appeal to me and most of the time I threw up after eating. Then gradually, the third week of my stay, I began to feel better and could keep down food. I was still weak but could feel myself gaining some of my strength back. A doctor visited with me that week.

"Sam, you're improving. You have been a sick young man. The concern of several of us that have been treating you is your mental state. You have dreams regularly that obviously are a result of your experiences in the war. We believe that you should be treated for your mental as well as your physical condition. It's not unusual for us to see this, because after all, it is a veteran's hospital, but your case is worse than most."

"I'm sorry, Doctor Olsten. I can't help it."

"There's nothing to be sorry for; however, we need to help you if possible. Have you talked about your experiences with anyone?"

"No. I avoid talking about the war. In fact, it frightens me to even think about having to relive that time in my life."

"But, Sam, you're doing that almost every night in your dreams. I believe it might help if you would speak with someone."

"I don't think that would be possible," I said.

"The thing about it, Sam, is that your mental health is going to slow your physical recovery if it's not addressed."

"Who would I talk to?"

"We have a chaplain here who served in both World Wars. He's seen it all, and I believe would be a good person for you to visit with about your experiences in Korea. Of course, we cannot and would not force you to engage in this session with him."

"I'll try."

"Good. I'll talk with him today and he can come by your room."

"Could we talk somewhere in private?" I asked.

"Certainly. You don't need to be under quarantine anymore, and you can go to his office."

After the doctor left, a feeling of dread came over. I never expected to talk of the war with anyone... ever again.

The next day a nurse came and escorted me to the chaplain's office.

He introduced himself as Phil, saying, "Welcome, Sam. I'm glad to meet you. Believe it or not, I was young at one time. Of course, that was some time ago."

He was older than I expected with white hair, wrinkles, and a nice smile. I should've expected him to be older, since he'd served in the first world war.

"Thank you for seeing me, Mr. Phil."

Laughing, he replied, "Just Phil, please. Now, tell me, Sam, what's your favorite thing to do?"

Surprised at the question, I thought a minute before answering. "I enjoy animals. I am happiest when riding my horse early in the morning with my dog, Hablo, along."

"Are you a cowboy?" he asked.

"I never thought about that. I can ride and Jose taught me to rope. I guess you could call me a cowboy. I do have sheep and some heifers."

"Who's Jose?"

"He's a Mexican, who's been with us as long as I can remember. He came from Mexico and stayed. He's a good and loyal friend. I consider him family."

"What about your mom and dad?"

"They're both gone. Dad when I was ten and Mom two years ago."

"Are you lonely?" he asked.

"I don't know. I live in a small town and the people there are nice. Maybe I am. To tell you the truth, I don't know."

"Do you have a lady friend?" he asked, with a smile. I didn't know how to answer. Was Sonia a lady friend? Or Mattie? Maybe neither.

"No, probably not," I said.

"You don't sound so sure, Sam. Let me ask you this. If you were in trouble and needed help immediately, do you have a girl you would call?"

I didn't need to think long about this. "Yes."

"Good, I have my answer. You do have a lady friend," he said. "That's all for today, Sam. I look forward to our next visit."

Stunned, I went back to my room, thinking, we didn't talk about the war. I thought that was what this was all about.

The next day our session started out much the same way as the first, with Phil asking me about the ranch.

"It's been in the family for several generations. It's small and we're in a drought so it's going to be tough to come out on the livestock. I may have to find additional work," I explained.

"Do you worry about being able to make a living?" he asked.

"No, not really. I can always find work if the ranch doesn't provide enough income."

"Do you attend church regularly?"

"No. I haven't been to church since coming home," I answered.

"Did you attend the worship service that was offered in the army?"

"Sometimes… at first."

"But you stopped after a while. Is that correct?"

"Yes."

"What caused you to stop?" he questioned.

I was beginning to get uncomfortable. When I failed to answer he continued.

"Did you attend church before you went into the service?"

"Yes. We seldom missed a Sunday. I also went to Sunday school from the time I was five or six years old. My parents insisted I go; however, I did enjoy it. There was a small church in the community where we lived that we attended."

"Will you ever attend your church again?" he asked.

"I don't know."

"You are a believer, aren't you?"

"I don't know," I answered.

"You know, Sam, it's strange the way war effects us differently. Many times, I witnessed men's faith become stronger in combat. Other times, the opposite was true. I assume the latter would fit you."

"Honestly, I haven't thought about it."

"Did you make a lot of friends in Korea? Usually that happens when you're in combat."

"Yeah. I did."

"Any one friend better than the rest?" he asked.

I hesitated, dreading going further. Finally, I answered, "Yeah."

"Would you like to tell me about him. What was his name?"

"Flint."

"He was from Texas?"

"Yeah, from a farm in the Panhandle," I explained.

"Did you know him before the service?"

"No. We met in boot camp at El Paso. He missed his home even more than me. We became friends right off. Maybe because I was a country boy also. I think that helped him with his homesickness. I don't know. He was a good guy."

"You said, 'He was a good guy'. What did you mean by 'was'?"

I couldn't go any further. I just sat there and stared at the floor.

"Tell me about being a cowboy," he said, changing the subject.

"I've never competed in a rodeo. I learned to rope on the ranch with the help of Jose. He's quite a vaquero and can do a lot of rope tricks even when he's riding."

"Would you like to compete?"

"I never thought about it. My hometown did have a rodeo a year or so back. Three brothers put it on. I attended several before I was drafted. I do remember thinking it would be exciting."

"Everyone needs something to do that's fun. Maybe you should consider it when you get back home," he said. "That's all for today. You did good, Sam. See you tomorrow."

Back in my room, I thought about the session with Phil. I didn't 'do good' as he said. Phil was kind not to put pressure on me. I didn't believe he'd ever do that. He was an intelligent man and probably had talked with hundreds of soldiers like me. I'd try harder tomorrow.

The next morning Phil sent word that we were going to skip a couple of days before we met again. Something had come up which required him to be out of town.

It worked out, because Sonia and her parents came to visit that afternoon, staying several hours. I asked them about my livestock and Mr. Toller told me not to worry. He'd found hay for Jose and everything was good at the ranch. I thought of asking about Mattie but decided that was not a good idea. Mrs. Toller and Sonia did most of the talking, concerning news in the community and Sonia's school. Mrs. Toller did have an offer for me.

"Sam, you're going to need someone to look after you when you go home. I suggest that you stay with us until you're fully recovered. It won't be any trouble for us and we'd be glad to have you."

I didn't know what to say. The last thing I wanted do was stay with the Tollers. It would create an awkward and uncomfortable situation for me. Mr. Toller noticed my hesitation and came to my rescue again.

"You need not make a decision now, Sam. You're probably going to be in here several more weeks and you can decide later what you want to do."

I appreciated them coming but was glad when they left. Since I wasn't under quarantine, I was afraid they would ask me to go eat supper with them at a restaurant. Thank goodness, that didn't happen. My appetite was much better, and I was eating most of what was brought to me. This evening the meal was a hamburger patty with mashed potatoes, green beans, and cake for dessert.

My roommate had been dismissed and I had the room to myself. After eating, I listened to the radio until bedtime. I seldom missed The Louisiana Hayride, with Slim Whitman and Kitty Wells being two of my favorites.

I had the worst night since coming to McKinney. One dream followed another and it seemed daylight would never come. I woke up tired and drained, unable to eat my breakfast. I realized recovery would not be possible if this continued. I spent the next day thinking of a way to describe my experiences to Phil at our next session.

After lunch two days, later, I had the opportunity to talk with the chaplain again. He sensed a change in my behavior immediately.

"You look tired, Sam. Nightmares again?"

"Yeah. Worst since coming," I replied.

"Do you want to talk about it?"

"I'll try. Can we stop at any time?" I asked.

"Certainly."

I couldn't look directly at him so I focused on a picture hanging on his wall of snow covered mountains. "I was drafted a few months out of high school. I've often wondered, why me? No one else in my class was. My mother was devastated and wanted to appeal to the local draft board. I begged her not to do that."

I hesitated before going on, trying to organize my thoughts. "I was sent to Fort Bliss in El Paso for basic training. I was in good physical shape and had no problem, but many of the guys complained constantly. I met Flint during that time. He was having a hard time being away from home. He had just graduated also and had never been away from his family and friends. After basic training we remained at Fort Bliss for the next year, which was 1951. Our commanding officer was good to see that we had furloughs at the same time. Flint was overweight, and unlike most, he didn't lose any pounds during basic training. He loved soft ice cream, saying it was a great invention. He constantly complained because I could eat everything in sight and not gain. He had a girl friend in his hometown and received at least one letter a week from her. The only letters I received were from my mom, who was still living at the time."

I stopped, took a deep breath, and continued. "We received our orders on January 10, 1952 sending us to Korea. I'll never forget that day. We were in the 7th Infantry Division and arrived in Seoul on January 25, which was a Friday. We were transported by truck to the front lines."

Hesitating for several seconds, Phil asked me if I wanted to stop. "No, not yet. It was cold... brutally cold. The roads were covered with snow and ice. Our first stop was a warm-up bunker that was located a safe distance from the front lines. We saw worn out soldiers that were getting warmth and much needed rest. An officer explained our mission to us. We would be on the front lines to guard against a surprise attack which he said was unlikely during the winter. They didn't waste any time getting us placed. Our home for the winter turned out to be a log and dug out bunker in the side of a mountain. It was five or six feet wide and eight to ten feet long. We had a stove that burned coal, a straw covered floor, and bunk beds made of poles and mesh."

"What about weapons?" Phil asked.

"We had a BAR 30 caliber machine gun that was sitting in an above ground opening. That was the weapon assigned to me beginning in basic training. In our own minds we never had enough ammunition. Our thinking was that the more ammunition we had the more security we had. Flint had trained with an M-1 rifle. The other man in the bunker with us had an M-1. We had a supply of grenades, also.

We saw very little action during the winter. The cold was unbelievable. We alternated watching for the enemy who seldom made an appearance. We were allowed to return to the warm-up bunker a few hours each week. We could bathe and shave there since they had running water. The best thing was being able to get warm for a few hours."

"How did you spend your days in the bunker?"

"Talking mostly. I learned about farming, with Flint describing the tractors and other equipment he used. I could probably be a cotton farmer with the information I gained from those long days. I told him about ranching and livestock. We both enjoyed fishing and we traded stories about days spent at stock tanks and lakes. Not a day went by that Flint didn't say he was going to eat all the ice cream he wanted when he got home. We never mentioned the possibility of not making it.

In March, with the spring thaw and warmer weather, all hell broke loose. The enemy launched an all out offensive against our position. We were able to hold out until reinforcements arrived. Wave after wave of North Korean and Chinese troops came at us. As I said previously, our greatest fear was running out of ammunition. On one particular charge, they came so close I could see their faces, but we held our ground and they fell back. I-I- was s-shooting and k-killing. Their faces a-are in some o-of m-my dreams. I was reacting; i-if I h-had t-thought a-about it, m-maybe,

I c-couldn't h-have done it. When it w-was done, o-over c-come with emotion, Flint and I cried. That's all I can d-do."

"That's fine, Sam. Maybe it will help after telling someone. Do you want to have another session?"

"Yeah. I've got to do something to stop the nightmares."

"We'll meet again tomorrow," he said.

"Okay," I said, getting up and leaving.

I hadn't been back in my room but a few minutes when a nurse appeared, telling me I had a phone call and to follow her to the office. I thought it was probably Sonia or her mother.

"Hello," I said.

"Sam. Is that you?"

"Yeah."

"This is Mattie. How're you doing?"

Surprised, I said, "Better. It's good to hear from you."

"Probably expected it be Sonia, I bet?"

Should I lie or just not answer the question? "How're you doing, Mattie? How's your basketball going?"

"I'm averaging 28 points a game. We've only lost twice so far."

"Have you been to the ranch since I left?"

"Of course, silly. I've been out to ride my horse several times. Jose and I are getting to be good friends. He's a sweet man."

"Has it rained or snowed since I left?"

"No. All I hear from the farmers is 'we need some moisture'."

I couldn't think of anything else to say or any other question to ask. Silence followed until I confessed to her about the session with Phil, where he asked me if I had a lady friend. I told her about his question "Do you have someone you would call if you had trouble?" My answer prompted me to say that I did.

"You must have been thinking of Sonia," was her response.

"Is that what you think? If it is then you're not as smart as I thought you were."

"Oh, Sam, I want to think it might be me. But when I compare myself to her, it's depressing."

"That's easy, stop comparing yourself to her. Now, when I get home, we'll go to the picture show or something and have a real date."

Silence followed my comment. Finally, I asked, "Would you like that?" This time the response was quick.

"Yes, I would like that."

Chapter 16

Mattie

When we went into the house, my dad was sitting at the table with Pa-Pa. Smiling, he said, "Well, it's good to be home with my family." I didn't respond, just staring at him.

"Where've you been?" asked Mother.

"All over. I've been looking for work. Didn't find any, so I'm back. Maybe something will come up here."

"Why did you leave without telling us anything?" Mother asked.

"I just wanted to get away from here as quick as possible. I hate this town and the people."

I'd stayed quiet as long as possible. "Why did you come back if you hate this place?"

"I missed my family. We can go home now and be together," he said.

"Bull! I'm not going anywhere with you."

"You'll do what I say, Mattie!"

"No, Leon. Mattie can stay here as long as she wants. I think it best if you leave now and we can talk later," said Pa-Pa.

"All right. Let's go, Gladys. I'll deal with Mattie later."

My mother stood there, not saying anything, looking frightened.

"Well, woman, get a move on! We're going home." Still, she didn't move.

He grabbed her by the arm and pulled her toward the door, saying, "You're going with me."

"Take your hands off my mother!" I screamed.

"It's okay, Honey, I need to go with him. Please don't worry about me," she said.

Mother left with him, and I broke into tears.

The next two weeks I only saw my mother at basketball games and twice when buying groceries. I didn't see Leon at all. I'd stopped thinking of him as my daddy and referred to him by his name. I hated him. Mother and I had little chance to talk, but she did attempt an apology after one of my games.

"Mattie, I didn't know what to do. Leon was going to cause trouble if I didn't go with him. I was frightened for you and Mr. Quentin. I'm sorry you're disappointed in me, but I do my best."

"Mother, I don't understand. Why can't you tell him that you're leaving and that's final?"

"I'm terrified of him, Mattie. I believe he might kill me if I left him. He's angry with his life and everything around it. I need to do everything possible to keep him away from you and his dad."

"Go to the police and tell them you're afraid he'll hurt you. Maybe they can talk to him."

"I don't know, Mattie. I'm doing okay now. He's usually asleep by the time I get home, after drinking most of the day. The best I can hope for is that he'll leave again."

I left, feeling sorry for her, but at the same time discouraged that she wouldn't stand up to him. Maybe in the future that would change, but I wasn't optimistic. One thing for sure; I wasn't afraid of him.

My days were busy, with the responsibility of taking care of Pa-Pa and school. He was getting stronger and was able to do more for himself, which helped. He could actually dress himself now, and was able to perform more tasks without my help. One of his friends would come by every morning and take him to the coffee shop, proving again that Leon was wrong about this town. The people here were wonderful and looked after one another. I was having my best season in basketball, and we had a good chance at winning district which started next week. Boys seemed to notice me more during basketball and several had asked me out, but I wasn't interested.

On Wednesday, December 16, before our first district game on Friday, I received a note from my favorite, teacher Mrs. Fields saying she needed to talk with me. I did have an idea what it was about, and sitting down in her vacant classroom, was proven right.

"Mattie, I need to let you know, your grades have come down in several of your classes. If you don't bring them up, Keri is going to be the valedictorian. She knows how close it will be and is working hard. I know you have a lot on your plate with your granddad, but you need to focus on your studies more."

"I'm not worried about it. I can live without being valedictorian. It's not nearly as big a deal for me as it is for Keri."

"I know it's hard on you, Mattie. I also know that you'd like to attend college. The valedictorian does receive a scholarship to the state school of their choice. It's not a great amount, but it would help."

"Right now, college doesn't seem to be realistic," I said.

"That's your choice, but I'd like to see you further your education. You have a great deal going for you, and a college degree would open up many opportunities for you."

"I'll think about it and try to concentrate more on my studies."

"One more thing, Mattie. I heard through the grapevine that you've been helping Sam Colter. Sam was one of my all time favorites. I understand he needs a friend now, and I appreciate everything you've done. I wasn't at all surprised about his action that saved Avery. Every time I see him in the hall, I think; he wouldn't be here if not for Sam. Sam had this way of looking after people that needed help. I don't believe he realized it, but to the ones who knew him well, it was obvious. You know we still have hazing here for the freshman students. Sam never took part in that tradition when he was a senior. In fact, I witnessed him take up for underclassmen a number of times."

"Sam's in the hospital at McKinney. He has hepatitis," I said.

"That's what I heard. How's he doing?"

"I don't know. He hasn't called and it's been three weeks."

"Why don't you call him?" she asked.

"Do you think it would be okay?" I asked.

"Of course, Mattie. Why wouldn't it?"

"He might not want to talk with me."

"Believe me, Mattie, he would love to hear from you. I get around, you know. I hear things most don't."

"Thank you, Mrs. Fields. I need to get to my next class," I said.

After basketball practice, I went by the hospital and the nurse gave me the number for the veteran's hospital in McKinney. I was nervous about calling Sam. He would probably be expecting a call from Sonia. She probably called him several times a week or maybe every day.

I was wrong again. He was actually pleased to hear from me. I was delighted at the conversation. No, thrilled is a better description. I kept comparing myself to Sonia and thought Sam did, also. Maybe I was wrong about that, too. When we said goodbye and hung up, I thought; why did I wait so long?

I felt good and was humming while cooking supper for Pa-Pa. He was easy to please, but I tried to cook his favorites at least a couple of times a week. Tonight was grilled cheese sandwiches and tomato soup. I wouldn't call myself a good cook, but we got by. He came in, sitting down at the table.

"You're in a good mood, Mattie. What's the occasion?"

"I talked to Sam. He's doing better and was glad I called."

"Kinda like Sam, don't you?"

"He's all right."

Laughing out loud, he replied, "Don't try to fool your pa-pa, Sugar. I know you too well. He's more than all right."

Changing the subject, I asked, "Have you talked to Leon this week?"

"No. After our last conversation a couple of weeks ago, I haven't made another attempt to talk some sense into him. He's angry and won't listen to anyone. How's your mother doing?"

"She likes her new job. She's afraid of him and believes he might hurt her if she left."

"It's hard for me to believe that he would be dangerous; however, I guess it's possible, he's so full of hate. I haven't told him that I changed my will, leaving everything to you. When he finds out, that could really set him off."

That night, I spent more time studying. My grades had gone down in English more than any other subject. I detested the teacher and the feeling was probably mutual. She hadn't regained control of the class, in fact, several of the boys had virtually taken over. I was disgusted, and unable, or maybe unwilling, to hide it. I could expect a paper she returned of mine to be at least ten points lower than it should be when compared to my friend, Della's paper. I'd asked her on more than one occasion to explain her grading to me but she refused, becoming angry. Maybe the fact that she was young had something to do with her unfairness. I'd about given up and accepted the fact that I was going to make a low grade in English. It probably didn't make any difference if I was valedictorian. I couldn't leave Pa-Pa. There was no one else to take care of him, and the nursing home was not an option. I could probably find a job here in town after I graduated.

Attempting to read Julius Caesar, which was required for English, my mind began to wonder. *It would soon be Christmas and we didn't have a tree. I hadn't even thought about presents for anyone. I wanted to buy something for Mother, Pa-Pa, and Della. Should I think about buying a gift for Sam? Probably not. There was a good chance he wouldn't be home by then. What about Jose? I'd been out to the ranch several times to ride since Sam left. Jose had become a good friend. Yes, I would get him something. We were getting out for Christmas holidays next Tuesday and would be off two weeks. I was going to get a tree and buy some presents, hopefully getting into the Christmas spirit.*

I was on fire at Friday night's game with Clyde. Everything I put up went in, scoring 42 points, and by the final buzzer we had won 58-26. It was my best game ever and several of my friends were waiting for me when I came out of the dressing room to congratulate me. After hugs and praises, I went into the stands to see Pa-Pa. I'd brought him to the game, finding him a seat on the bottom row. He was all smiles.

"Mattie, you were awesome. I'm so proud of you. People have been coming by and congratulating me, like I had something to do with it."

"Thank you. It was just one of those nights when everything seemed to click." I felt rather than saw someone standing behind me. I turned around and Avery York was there.

"You were great, Mattie. My parents are here and would like to talk with you," he said.

"Sure," I said, following him up several rows in the bleachers.

"Mattie, you were wonderful," Mr. York said.

"How in the world do you make those shots look so easy?" asked Mrs. York.

"They don't always go in like they did tonight," I said, with a smile.

"Mattie, we wanted to let you know we're going to McKinney Sunday to see Sam. Would you be interested in going with us? I know you're looking after Hollis, but we should be home by 4:00 in the afternoon. We're worried about him and are going to see if there's any way we can help."

The offer caught me by surprise. I could ask one of Pa-Pa's friends to look in on him and he would be fine. I took so long to answer that Mr. York felt a need to comment further.

"I believe Sam would be pleased if you came to visit him."

"Yes. I'd like to go with you," I said.

"Great, we'll pick you up around 6:00 Sunday morning," he said.

"I'll be ready."

When I returned, Pa-Pa asked me what that was about. I explained the offer and my acceptance.

"Good for you, Mattie. Can we stay and watch the boys play? Maybe they'll win a game."

Chapter 17

Gladys

It was Friday and Mattie had a home game tonight. When I arrived from work, Leon announced that he was going with me. Usually he was asleep on the couch, but that was not the case tonight.

"I'm tired tonight and have a splitting headache. All I want to do is take some aspirin, fix supper for you, and go to bed," I said.

"Did you get paid today?"

"No. We get our checks tomorrow."

"I need a few dollars," he said.

I looked in my purse, took out my billfold, and gave him a five-dollar bill. I knew that was how much a bottle of liquor cost at the bootleggers. It was worth it to keep him from going to the ballgame.

"I'll be back in a little while," he said.

I didn't have a headache and sure wasn't that tired; however, I wanted to keep him away from Mattie, if at all possible. I was surprised that he wasn't already drunk when I got home but now the reason was obvious. He didn't have money for liquor. He'd spent at least a third of what I made ever since coming home. No way could we pay the bills on my salary, especially with his drinking. It was still an hour until the game started. Maybe he would be home and drunk by then and I could still make the game. I had to do something but what? I was still afraid of him and going to the police would make him furious. He'd threatened me if I tried to leave, but that is as far as it had gone. Every time I thought of standing up to him, fear won out.

He was home within fifteen minutes, poured a drink, and went to his favorite chair to watch television.

"Would you like supper?" I asked.

"Not now. Gonna watch the news. Maybe later. I'll let you know."

"I took two aspirin, and my headache is better. I'll make supper for you and leave it on the stove. You can eat whenever you're ready. I'll still have time to make the game."

"Leave me a cold supper, huh?"

He came into the kitchen and poured another drink saying, "You can stay home tonight and spend a relaxing evening with me."

"I want to see Mattie play. This is her last year."

"Mattie turned out to be hateful and has no respect for me."

"Leon, please be reasonable. I'll make supper and you can heat it up when you're ready to eat." By now, he was feeling the effects of the liquor, and I knew arguing was useless.

He came over to me and put his arms around me. "Awe honey, don't you want to stay with me tonight?"

Something came over me and I pushed him away. "No! I want to go see Mattie's game! Please!" Then he shoved me against the stove so hard I fell.

"Not good enough for you, huh? Uppity bitch! Got a good job so you can treat me like this."

I was trying to get up, and he took his foot and pushed me down again. "Leave me alone. You hurt me. Let me get up."

"I warned you! You didn't listen!" he yelled, pushing me down to the floor again.

"Please, Leon. You're hurting me. I'll stay with you, tonight."

"That's better. Maybe you learned your lesson," he said, draining his glass.

I guess something like this had to happen to force me to make a decision. After he passed out on the couch, I put some clothes together and went to Mr. Quentin's, vowing to never return. No one was home, which I expected, since they were at the game. Mr. Quentin's house had three bedrooms, and I put my clothes in the one that was vacant. My side was hurting where I'd hit the stove, preventing me from taking a deep breath. I wasn't going to be able to attend the game. I locked all the doors, thinking that he might find a way over here. I knew this day was coming, it was only a matter of time. Leon had to take his anger out on someone. I tried to remember a time when we were happy and realized it had been years. He'd treated the older girls better than Mattie, but he hadn't been drinking as much then.

I was 22 when I met Leon and about given up on marriage. I was still living with my parents, working as a waitress in a neighboring town. He began coming in each evening to eat and would linger until my shift ended. He started taking me home, and one thing led to another, until we were married six months later. I knew very little about him except he worked at odd jobs and hadn't graduated from high school. I'd always been shy, and he was outgoing and full of confidence; maybe that was what attracted me to him. Actually, in the back of mind, I think it was the fear of being an old maid. After all, in 1923, most girls were married before they reached my age.

Three years later we had two girls and then Mattie wasn't born until ten years later in 1935. By the time Mattie was in the third grade, both her sisters were gone from home. The depression years were hard, and we lived from week to week on the few dollars Leon made at odd jobs and what I earned cleaning houses. We had enough to eat and that was about all. He'd always drank, and by the time Mattie started high school, he was an alcoholic, becoming meaner and more unreasonable each year.

It was after 10:00 when Mattie and Mr. Quentin knocked on the front door. Opening the door, Mattie hugged me, knowing something was wrong.

"What happened, Mother?"

"I had to get way from him."

"Did he hurt you?" she asked.

"A little. Not much. You were right. I can't stay with him any longer."

"You're welcome to stay here as long as you like," Mr. Quentin said.

"I brought clothes, but I need to get the car back to the house. Mattie, can you follow me?"

"Sure."

Thank goodness we were able to leave the car without waking him up. I held my breath until we were out of sight.

The next morning was Saturday, and it was difficult for me to get out of bed. My side was hurting, and any kind of quick movement brought terrible pain. Mattie noticed something was wrong immediately.

"Mother, you're hurt. You can't go to work today. We need to take you to the doctor and see how serious it is. You may have a broken bone."

"We're busy on Saturdays. The groups of Mexicans that are here picking cotton always come to town on Saturday to buy groceries. It's nonstop from the time we open. I'll take some aspirin and try to make it through the day. Tomorrow is my day off and will give me time to improve."

By the time Mattie took me to work, I was feeling better and in less pain. That didn't last but a couple of hours, after bending over and unloading the baskets onto the counter. The pain came back worse than it ever had been. My checkout line became longer as I fell further behind. Mr. Wilson came over and asked me if I was all right.

"I'm sorry. The pain in my side is terrible."

"You need to go home. We can get by without you today. Call Mattie to come get you," he said.

I didn't argue. The pain had become unbearable. I called Mattie and she was there to pick me up within minutes.

"Mother, we're going to the doctor. Dr. Sadler is open until at least noon."

"No, I want to go home. I'll take some more aspirin."

"I'm going to turn him in to the law and file charges against him," Mattie said.

"I don't want to cause trouble. It's better that no one else knows. I'm not going back to Leon."

"He should be held accountable," she said.

"It's over, Mattie. I just need to move on."

Leon's car was parked in front of Mr. Quentin's when we arrived. I asked Mattie what we should do.

"Now's as good a time as any to settle this," she said.

Expecting the worst, we entered the house, and Leon was sitting in the living room with Mr. Quentin.

"Where've you been? I stopped by the grocery store a few minutes ago and you weren't there. I thought you might have left town. I'm sorry about last night. I over-reacted. It won't happen again," he stated.

"You're right about that," Mattie said.

"You shut your mouth! This is between me and your mother."

"No, Leon. Mother's not going back with you. Never! Now, you can leave, or I'm going to call Mr. Fulton. If I have to involve the law, then so be it."

"What about it, Gladys? Are you going to listen to her?" he asked.

"Yes, Leon. I agree with everything she said. Please leave us alone. I'm never coming back to you," I said.

"You're going to be sorry; the both of you. Just mark my word. You're going to be sorry."

"Leon, you need to leave," Mr. Quentin said, speaking for the first time.

He walked over to me and shaking his finger in my face said, "You'll pay for this, Gladys!"

He stormed out, slamming the door. I sat down on the couch, too weak to stand and shaking with fear. Mattie went to the door and locked it. Coming back, she sat down and put her arms around me.

"Don't worry, Mother. We're going to be fine. Now to something that's more important. You have to help me decide what to wear tomorrow on my trip to McKinney."

Chapter 18

Sam

It was Friday, December 18, and Sonia had called saying she was coming to see me tomorrow. They were already out for the Christmas holidays, and her parents had agreed to let her come alone. I was looking forward to seeing her, especially since I was feeling better. My yellow complexion remained, but it didn't seem to bother her since this would be her third visit. I had to admit she was an attractive girl and easy to talk with, mainly because she did most of the talking. The nurses had been teasing me about my girlfriend coming to see me. They commented on how pretty she was and what nice clothes she wore.

Today would be the fourth visit with Phil. I had to stop during our last session for fear of becoming too emotional. I knew it was important that all of my experiences causing the dreams be expressed out loud to him; however, that was going to be hard. I had given a lot of thought as to how that could be accomplished. Maybe if I could tell him a little bit at a time it would be possible. Anyway, that was my plan.

We had been meeting after lunch, but the nurse came for me at mid-morning. Entering his office, he greeted me with a handshake, asking how I was doing.

"I guess you could say fair," was my response.

"Still having the dreams?"

"Most nights," I answered.

"Do you ever dream about anything else, like that cute girl that visits you?"

"No. Unfortunately, the dreams are about the war," I replied.

"Sam, we'll start wherever you wish today. You can end the meeting at any time. Please try to be as comfortable as possible."

I sat in silence for several minutes, thinking of where to start. "Last spring, sometime in March…I'll start there. Rumors were going around that negotiations were in progress that could end the war. We had high hopes of going home soon. I guess because of these talks both sides became more aggressive. We assumed the thinking was that whoever was winning would have the upper hand in the peace agreement. We didn't know but were only guessing.

It was constant fighting almost every day. For some reason, the hills in the area were the focus. We would take a hill and then defend it, only to be forced to retreat when the enemy brought in reinforcements. It was stupid and useless. Everybody knew it, but we followed orders. Causalities were high. I witnessed death close-up, almost daily. There was one instance where the fighting became so fearless that it was hand-to-hand because we had run out of ammunition and were trying to retreat." I stopped and took several deep breaths.

"Do you want to stop?" Phil asked.

"You wouldn't have a cigarette, would you?" I asked.

He opened his desk and took out a pack of Lucky Strikes, giving me the package and a lighter. I lit one, took a drag and put it in the ashtray he had put on the arm of my chair.

"Could I ask you a question?" I said.

"Sure. Anything you wish."

"Have you heard these kind of stories before, and were the men as messed up as me?" I asked.

"Oh, me, Sam. War does terrible things to people. I won't say that I've heard it all, but your case is certainly not the worst. I've provided counsel to men who took their own life, unable to go on. You're going to make it. Just trust me and continue to move forward with your life. I know it must seem like more than you can handle, with your illness and terrible memories, but we're going to get you through both."

"Do you have a personal memory of combat that is your worst?" I asked.

"That's easy, Sam. When a friend died in my arms. Nothing comes close to that," he said.

I sat in silence, thinking about whether or not to continue. Finally, I stared at the painting on the wall and said, "It was late April, not long before the end of the war. There was this hill that was barren, just made up of rock and dirt, but orders came to take it at all costs. We went in the dark but floodlights exposed us. Flint and I always stayed together. We were about halfway up the hill and under heavy fire, when-when…I can't go on!" I said, sobbing, unable to stop.

"You're a brave young man, Sam. I consider it a privilege and honor to be your friend. Let's stop there."

"I just don't understand why it had to happen. The men I fought with were so brave. The war was almost over, and we were trying to take a worthless hill that meant nothing. I was angry, maybe furious is a better description, when Flint died, and it became even worse when the war ended later. I blamed our leaders even more than the enemy. My commanding officer recommended another medal for me. I have my medals, but I never look at them. I lived through it and that was enough. I thought returning home and back to a normal life would stop the dreams. Of course, that wasn't the case."

"Did you ever consider visiting Flint's parents and his girl-friend?" he asked.

"Briefly, but it would've been too emotional for me to handle. Maybe it would have helped," I answered.

"You might consider it in the future," he said.

"Maybe. Flint was special. You know, he didn't even play football in high school but was in the band. He didn't have a mean bone in his body. Of all people, he should never have been in a war. A boy who wanted to marry his high school sweetheart, farm, and eat soft ice cream gave his life for a worthless cause."

"It's going to take time, Sam; after all, these events that you're describing happened only six months ago. Of course, your illness has slowed the mental recovery of the war. I'm praying that being able to talk about it will help."

"I'm feeling stronger physically."

"Sam, I'd recommend that you find something you enjoy to supplement your work on the ranch. I believe that staying busy will be good therapy. Also, please resume attending the church in your community. You have friends there who miss you and will be glad to help any way they can. You were too young to go through what you did, but I see a strength in you that will prevail."

"I appreciate your effort to help me. Will we have more sessions?"

"Yes; however, the next time I'd like to talk about the happier times in your life. I understand you have a visitor coming tomorrow. Maybe you could introduce her to me."

I didn't go back to my room but went to an outside patio. Phil had given me the package of cigarettes and the lighter. I sat down in one of the chairs and lit another cigarette. It had a terrible taste, but I smoked it anyway. After going this long without smoking, it would have been a good opportunity to quit.

I was glad to be able to tell someone of that horrible experience during the last few days of the war, even though I couldn't talk about it in detail without breaking down. In some ways, I did feel lighter and more free after the session. Maybe it was going to help. I should have gone to Spearman to visit with Flint's parents. I owed that much and more to him and his parents. Deep down, I was afraid of reliving his death with them.

Phil said our next session would involve some of my happier memories. It had been so long since dwelling on them, but thinking back, there had been many. Football came to mind first and foremost. I loved the game and excitement it created in me and the community. The pep rallies were good memories and several games stood out. My junior year we beat Anson on the last play of the game. I ran the ball in from the five-yard line with no time on the clock. There was a huge celebration. The next week, I broke my nose for the first time in a game against Ballinger. At the recent game I attended, a few of the players were wearing helmets with face protectors. If I'd had one of those, my nose wouldn't be so crooked. It would only be a matter of time until all the players would probably be equipped with those.

The best recollection I have of my dad was him taking me fishing. We always went to a neighbor's stock tank a few miles from our place. If I remember right, his name was Curb. It was a large tank, and we nearly always caught enough fish to eat for one meal. It was something that I looked forward to and missed after my dad died, when I was ten. My mother would take me after that, but it was never the same. Later, a friend would go with me, or I would go by myself. Fishing was a good memory that I hadn't thought about for a long time.

I had spent many days with Jose and even more after my dad passed. I would watch him do rope tricks for hours and then attempt them myself. I never gained his expertise but did learn to rope, first on the ground and then horseback.

We would attend church every Sunday and that continued after my dad passed. Sunday school was fun, but during church, I would watch the large clock on the wall behind the pastor, planning my afternoon activities. Phil had suggested that I resume attending church; however, I was reluctant to do so, at least for now. His question, as to whether or not I was a believer, bothered me. I couldn't answer him. Before the war, even prior to combat, there was no doubt. Now, I wasn't sure either way.

As I had begun feeling better, the ranch and livestock came into my thoughts more often. Without rain, we would need to buy more feed. The more feed we bought the more it would eat into our profits. I began to doubt if it was wise to go into debt to restock the ranch. It might have been better to find a job and have a steady source of income. Too late now. I had an obligation to repay the loan. Mr. Warren, the banker had called me the first week I was here in McKinney, asking me if I needed anything and telling me not to worry. That was kind of him, but it made me even more determined to repay the loan and interest.

Sonia would be here tomorrow and was coming by herself, which concerned me. Her parents being here helped with the conversation. I could talk with her dad about ranching, the price of livestock, and the weather. Without them, it would be more difficult to think of subjects to talk about. She usually did most of the talking, but I knew that more would be expected from me tomorrow. Sonia had confidence and why shouldn't she? Expensive clothes, a new car, college, and being nice looking would have something to do with that. I still didn't understand what she saw in me. She may be thinking of the muscular high school senior in 1950 that was popular, athletic and full of confidence in himself. I was a far cry from that now.

Chapter 19

Mattie

I was awake when my alarm went off at 4:30, having found sleep difficult. The Yorks were picking me up at six. Surely an hour and half would be enough time to get ready. I'd laid out my best Sunday outfit to wear… a simple chocolate brown wool dress with matching wide buckled belt, handed down from a distant cousin. My ma ma had given me a matching earrings and necklace set…pink cameos…a gift to her from my pa-pa for their first anniversary. Of course, I would wear them.

My shoes would not be a difficult choice since I only had two pair, except for my boots. I would wear my brown penny loafers, which were my school shoes. My other pair were the white tennis shoes I wore when playing basketball. I would wear bobby socks since I owned no hose or shoes that required them.

Since it was cold, I would need a coat. That was not a problem, in fact, it was my best piece of clothing. Mother had given it to me last Christmas, a wool camel colored one. Somehow, she had managed to save enough money to buy it in a spring sale and save it until Christmas. It was tailored but had an inverted pleat in the back which allowed for extra movement, a large cowl collar, and large blackish-brown buttons. It felt elegant because it had a satin lining. With that, I was good to go. I was watching for them through the window when they drove up at five minutes till six.

It was a four or five-hour drive and the conversation, at first, was awkward with questions about my mom and Leon. They had no way of knowing about the separation and seemed embarrassed when I told them. By the time we'd driven for an hour, Avery was asleep and Mr. and Mrs. York were involved in a discussion about family matters. The death of Bennie was not mentioned, even though it had occurred only two months ago and was surely on their minds.

A couple of hours later we stopped for a bathroom break and gas in Weatherford. It was daylight by now and Mrs. York commented on how nice I looked.

"Thank you," I responded.

"I just love that coat," she said.

"It was a gift from my mother," I explained.

"Are you and Sam a couple?" she asked.

Startled and not knowing what to say, I didn't answer. She felt a need to explain further.

"I mean, is he your boyfriend?"

"We're just friends. He keeps my horse at his place and I've helped him on the ranch several times," I responded, hoping that would satisfy her curiosity.

"Sam's tough. I want to be like him one of these days," volunteered Avery.

When we resumed our journey, Avery went back to sleep and the conversation continued in the front seat with me being ignored... thank goodness. I didn't know what my relationship with Sam was; however, he did say we would go on a date, maybe to the picture show. I felt in my purse for the small package that contained a pocket knife. After talking with Sam last week, I'd bought the knife at Bullock Hardware. It was going to be a Christmas present. Pa-Pa had given me the eight dollars for the purchase, which seemed high. I felt sorry for him having to spend Christmas in a hospital with no gifts. I'd wrapped it and would insist that he wait until Christmas to open it.

We didn't stop again until we reached the veteran's hospital in McKinney. It was a few minutes after 10:00 when we were escorted to a receiving room to wait for Sam. I was nervous, not knowing how he would react to seeing me.

When he came into the room he seemed surprised, smiling and shaking hands with Mr. York and Avery, before hugging Mrs. York. He came over to me, extended his hand and said, "Mattie, it's good to see you." I guess a hug would've been too much for him.

The nurse had remained in the room. "If you'll come with me, we have a more comfortable room with better chairs where you can visit," she said.

We followed her to a larger room where Mr. York and Sam started talking about the drought and the effect it was having on the local economy. Mrs. York and I were left out of the discussion. Sam then asked Avery about his school and basketball. Mrs. York finally got in a word by asking Sam how he was doing.

Before Sam could respond, Avery said, "Sam have you seen the new car Chevrolet has come out with? It's called a Corvette and is awesome."

"No, Avery, but it sounds exciting. Mrs. York, to answer your question, as you can see, I'm yellow because of the jaundice. I'm stronger and feeling better each day. I've gained a few pounds, but the doctors tell me that it's going to take time."

After another half hour of small talk which didn't involve me, Mr. York said, "Sam, if it's all right, we're going to get some hamburgers and drinks. We'll bring them back here, and we can have lunch together. I assume that's not against the rules."

"No, sir. That sounds great. I get tired of the food here," he answered.

"Mattie, that will give you and Sam a chance to visit while we're gone," Mr. York said.

After they left Sam asked, "How're you doing, Mattie? I'm glad you came."

Given a chance to talk, I over did it, telling him about Mother and Leon. The last thing he probably needed was depressing news. After blabbering for a good five minutes, I stopped. "I'm sorry, Sam. You're not interested in my family problems."

"Sure I am, Mattie. Will your mom ever go back to him?"

"I hope not. He's terrible."

"Have you been to the ranch lately?" he asked.

"It's been over a week. With basketball and final exams, I've been busy. Now that we're out for the holidays, I'll go for sure. I miss riding Spade and visiting with Jose. I'll be sure to give him a report on you. I know he's anxious to hear how you're doing."

"You're looking good," he said, out of the blue.

"Thank you, Sam." That upped my confidence, and I was opening my purse to give him his gift, when looking up, I saw her walk through the door carrying a large gift-wrapped box. Of course, she looked great. She was wearing a forest green suit, with a linen blouse. She had on black pumps and hose. The skirt was straight with a panel front closed by large leather buttons. I couldn't even imagine what the outfit cost. She looked like she stepped right out of the pages of Vogue. Her shape resembled Marlon Monroe's, but at least she wasn't wearing her white sweater that was a size too small and seemed to be her trademark.

She came straight to him and as he stood, she put down the box, hugged him, and kissed him on the cheek at the same time.

"Sam, it's good to see you. You look better each time I'm here," Sonia said.

Sam turned red even through the yellow. "Sonia, how're you doing?"

"Great. Oh, hi, Mattie, I didn't mean to ignore you."

"Hello, Sonia," I replied.

"Sam, I brought you a little something for Christmas. You can go ahead and open it," she said.

Sam began to unwrap the box, being careful not to tear the paper. When he was finished he lifted the lid off and took out a new Silverbelly hat. "It's great, Sonia. I needed a new hat."

"Go ahead, try it on Sam," she said.

He followed her orders, saying, "It's a perfect fit! How did you know?'

"I cheated a little. My dad went by your place, and Jose let him borrow your old hat. We took it to Roberts Hat Shop in Abilene, and they made this one for you. I bet you never had a custom-made hat."

"Not hardly. Thank you. It's a wonderful gift, and I appreciate it."

I'd always been told that three was a crowd. Realizing how true that was, I said, "I'm going to wait in the lobby for the Yorks."

Sam opened his mouth, I assume to object, but Sonia intervened, "Sam, I've got some good news for you. Daddy went by the bank and co-signed your note. Wasn't that nice?"

I was out of hearing distance before Sam's answer. That was just great. Now he was going to be obligated to her because of her dad. Things had gone from good to bad with her arrival. My pa-pa who never cursed, had a saying for such occasions. "The ice cream turns to poop." I waited in the lobby until the Yorks came in carrying our lunch. Mrs. York asked me why I wasn't with Sam.

"He has another visitor who showed up after y'all left. Sonia Toller is with him now," I said.

Mr. York must have sensed the disappointment in my voice. "She'll just have to find her lunch elsewhere. Come on, Mattie, let's break up this meeting. After all, we got here first."

Of course, the Yorks knew Sonia, and the greetings were friendly. Mr. York took the initiative in explaining our plans. "Sonia, we have lunch for Sam and us. Unfortunately, we didn't expect him to have company."

"No problem, Mr. York. I can eat in the cafeteria while y'all have lunch together."

Avery, who hadn't taken his eyes off Sonia since coming into the room, had the solution. "I'm not hungry, Sonia. You can have my hamburger. I had a large breakfast before leaving home this morning."

I would've liked to reach over and pinched him hard. He ate in the cafeteria at school and always went back for seconds and sometimes thirds. The little twerp was lying just to impress her.

"Why, Avery, are you feeling okay? I've never known you to miss a meal," his mother said.

"I might be a little car sick from that long ride. Sonia can have my dinner," he repeated.

That ended the problem and we ate our lunch together with Sonia. I didn't taste my hamburger, only wishing we could leave. Sonia talked throughout the meal about everything from her school to her family. Avery didn't take his eyes off her, captivated by everything she said. Mr. and Mrs. York got in a few words but not many.

After we'd finished eating, Mr. York put me out of my misery. "Sam, we need to be going. We have a long drive, and it's already nearly 2:00. I've told you this before, but if you need anything please let us know. I'm glad you're doing better, and I'm sorry that you won't be home for Christmas."

"Thank all of you for coming. It's good to see friends from my hometown. Also, thank you for dinner."

A repeat of the greeting that morning occurred, with Mr. York, Avery, and me shaking hands with Sam while Mrs. York received a hug. We left Sam then with Sonia, who was smiling as we walked away. I left the knife with the receptionist, asking her to give it to Sam when he was alone.

We didn't get out of town before we had to stop at a drive-in diner where Avery ordered two burgers with fries and a shake.

We were home before dark, and Mother had to hear all about the trip. I tried to be positive, but she saw through it immediately.

"You didn't know Sonia was going to be there?" she asked.

"No idea. I wouldn't have gone if I'd known."

"I'm sorry, Honey. I'm sure Sam was glad to see you," she said.

"Maybe. At least before she showed up with that $100 custom-made hat."

"Mattie, gifts are not going to win Sam. He's a good boy and will make decisions based on his feelings. I don't believe you're giving him enough credit."

"You're probably right. I just feel that she has so much more to offer, it's hopeless."

"Sam will make that decision, Mattie, not you. Changing the subject, but I thought you were going to get a Christmas tree," she said.

"I'm going out to ride Spade Monday. I'll ask Jose to help me find a cedar tree in their pasture. It's only a few days until Christmas so it should stay fresh if we put it in water."

"Now, that's better. We need some Christmas spirit around here. Did you get Jose something for Christmas?" she asked.

"Not yet. Do you have any suggestions?"

"Braggs has a sell on their flannel shirts. That might be nice. I can give you enough money to buy one," she said.

"Sounds great. Are you sure we can afford it?" I asked.

"It's amazing how much further our money goes not having to give Leon money for liquor. We're doing fine."

I took Mother to work Monday morning and went directly to the ranch. It was colder today and seemed more like Christmas. Maybe I was getting into the spirit. Jose hadn't left the house yet, and he seemed pleased when I asked him to help find me a Christmas tree. I gave him a report on Sam, and his face lit up when I described how much better he was doing.

We decided to drive my pickup into the pasture to look for a tree rather than riding our horses. After looking for the better part of an hour, we found a nice tree about the same height as me. It had a good shape and the best part was the cedar smell. Jose cut it down with an ax and trimmed around the bottom so it would fit in a stand.

On the drive back, Jose asked, "Little Bit like his hat?"

"Yeah. It was beautiful. Did they bring his old hat back?"

"No. Little Bit not like it if he not get it back."

When we got back to the house, I saddled Spade and rode through the pasture toward the hills at the back of the ranch. Spade felt good and spooked when we jumped a deer. At the mouth of a canyon that led into the hills, a powerful smell met me. I knew it must be something dead that was rotting, and unfortunately, I was correct. I rode upon a ewe that was dead and partially eaten. It had been warm up until today, and she probably hadn't been dead over a couple of days. That would account for the rapid decay and the fact that Jose hadn't found her. She may have become sick and died, but that thought was proven wrong when I found two more. It was obvious they'd been killed by some kind of varmint.

When I returned to the house and told Jose about finding the dead ewes, he responded with one word, "Coyotes."

"Why would they kill three?" I asked.

A deep frown with a look of anger came over Jose before he responded. "Do not kill just for food. Kill for fun. Bad. Now, big problems. Will not stop killing sheep."

"What can we do?" I asked.

"Need to move them up here into trap by house. Watch closely. Maybe coyotes leave country after a bit. Can you help?"

"Sure. I have to be back in town by 5:00 to pick up Mother from work. We can get at least some of them moved. I can return in the morning to help pen the rest of them."

We spent the next four hours moving sheep into the three-acre trap behind the house. By the time I had to leave to pick up Mother at work, we had about half of them penned. We hadn't even taken time out for dinner. They were more scattered this time than they were before when we penned them. I promised Jose to return early the next morning to finish moving the rest of them.

We put up our tree after supper that night and after decorating it, was surprised at how pretty it turned out. It was only three days until Christmas and should stay fresh.

The next day we penned the remainder of the ewes but found two more that had been killed by the coyotes. I dreaded Sam finding out about the loss of five of his sheep.

I invited Jose to come for Christmas dinner. It was a hard sell, but I stayed after him until he finally agreed. I promised him he wouldn't have to stay long and could leave whenever he chose.

My shopping was finished that afternoon, with only two days left before Christmas. I was pleased with the Sunday dress that I bought for Mother. It was expensive, but Pa-Pa insisted on getting something nice for her and said it could be from him and me. I found Jose a nice flannel shirt for $4.00 and Pa-Pa house shoes and a robe. It didn't seem right using Pa-Pa's money to buy his gift, but I had no other choice. One of these days, I'd make it up to him. I found a pair of earrings for Della at Wilson's that completed my list. The town was full of people doing their last-minute shopping, and just as I was getting into the pickup someone hollered, "Mattie." I looked up and Carl (Cobb) was waving and coming my way.

"Carl, what're you up to, today?"

"Get Mother a Christmas present. I got lots of money."

"What're you going to get her?"

"Don't know. Something good."

"Do you want me to help you pick something out for her?"

"Yeah. You my friend."

We went back to the jewelry store and found a nice matching necklace and earring set that was beautiful. We waited while they gift wrapped it for him. Cobb thanked me and took off in that long stride of his that covered a lot of ground, speaking to everyone he met. I smiled and said to myself, *I wish there were more Cobbs' in the world. It would be a better place.*

Mother was up early Christmas morning to put the turkey in the oven. She would make cornbread dressing, which was wonderful. She would make Pa-Pa a small pan of oyster dressing which he liked. Sides would be candid yams, green beans, homemade rolls, and a fruit salad. Dessert would be my favorite... pecan pie.

Since dinner would be late, we always had breakfast on Christmas before we exchanged gifts. We had just sat down to eat when the phone rang. I thought it would be Della wishing me a Merry Christmas, so I answered it.

"Mattie, is that you? This is Sam."

It took me a few seconds to speak, I was that surprised.

"Mattie." He repeated.

"Yes, Sam. It's me."

"Merry Christmas."

"Merry Christmas to you, Sam. I'm glad to hear from you. Are you still doing better?"

"Everday. I'm ready to come home. I pinned them down yesterday and they said maybe in two weeks. How're you doing?"

"Good. We have a lot of good things to eat today. I wish you were here," I said.

"Me too. Mattie, about last Saturday. I'm sorry."

"What do you mean?" I asked.

"Sonia, interrupting our visit. She didn't mean any harm. That's just the way she is. I appreciate you coming with the Yorks and thank you for the knife."

"Well, it wasn't much compared to the custom-made hat."

Laughing, he replied, "You know, I was going to buy a black hat when I had the money. I'll actually use the knife more than I wear the hat."

"Oh, Sam. That's not true. You're just trying to make me feel better."

"Is it working?"

"I think so. It's nice of you, anyway."

"I better go now. I'm running up a phone bill for the hospital. I look forward to coming home and seeing you. Remember we're going to have a real date," he said.

"Thank you, Sam, for calling. It was my best Christmas present," I said.

Going back to the breakfast table, Pa-Pa was smiling. "You see, Honey, there is a Santa Clause."

Chapter 20

Gladys

It was Friday, January 15, and over a month since Leon had shoved me against the stove. I'd gone back to work the Monday after it happened, but even now if I moved a certain way or took a deep breath the pain would return. He had come back to Mr. Quentin's twice wanting me to come home. I refused and told him if he continued I'd get a restraining order. He left angry, making threats, but he hadn't been back since then.

Mattie had a district game tonight at Roscoe and Louise had asked me to go with her. I knew the only reason she was going was so she could take me. Mattie had been in good spirits all week, mentioning several times that Sam was coming home tomorrow. Dr. Sadler had made arrangements for him to be transported by ambulance to the hospital here, where he would examine him. Sam had called her last weekend and told her about his release.

She was having a good year in basketball and thus far they were undefeated in district play. Opposing teams had tried everything to stop her and had not been successful. She was now averaging 30 points a game.

A problem had come up at school with one of her teachers. Mattie was not one to complain about or criticize anyone, but she'd made an exception for her English teacher. She'd received a C in English after making A's on her papers. When she approached the teacher it only made matters worse. Finally, I told her to schedule a conference between her and the teacher with the principal. I was surprised when I received a call from the principal asking me to be present for the meeting, which was scheduled for Monday morning. I'd already made arrangements to take off work for an hour.

On the drive to Roscoe for the game, I told Louise about the problem Mattie was having with the teacher.

"Have you seen this teacher?" she asked.

"No. Mattie's always been such a good student, I never visit the school."

"Well I'll tell you, Gladys; she looks like one of the students. She can't be over 21 years old, and I've heard things about her. She has no discipline in her class, and some of the parents have been to school and complained to the principal."

"If Mattie keeps receiving bad grades in English she'll not be the valedictorian. When I try to talk to her, she brushes it off, saying, 'It's no big deal, anyway.'"

"Maybe she has the right attitude about being valedictorian, Gladys. If it's not that important to her, I wouldn't worry about it."

"You're probably right."

"What're you going to do about Leon? Are you going to file for a divorce?"

"Yes, definitely. He'll be furious, but that's my only option."

"When?"

"I don't know. I keep putting it off," I said.

"In my opinion, the sooner the better."

Mattie scored 32 points, which turned out to be more than the Roscoe team scored, and the game was a rout, with us winning 50-26. By the time the game ended, the weather had turned bad. When we walked out of the gym it was snowing and much colder. The change in the weather was unexpected. I went back in and waited on Mattie, asking her if she would ride home with us. Of course, it was not a problem for her coach.

We left Roscoe at about 10:00, and the roads were already snow covered and slick. Louise finally pulled over and asked Mattie to drive.

"Mattie, I'm a nervous wreck. You can handle this better than me."

With Mattie driving at a reduced speed, we didn't get home until after 1:00 Saturday morning. Whether it was the stress of the trip home or worrying about what to do about Leon, I couldn't sleep. After tossing and turning for four hours, I gave up and went to the kitchen to make coffee. Looking outside, I noticed the ground was snow-covered and had drifted up over the porch. I didn't have to be at work until 8:00 and was as quiet as possible, not wanting to wake Mattie and Mr. Quentin. We shouldn't be busy today because of the weather and the fact that most of the cotton was out. With the drought, the cotton crop had been sparse, with not as many families coming into town for the harvest. Still, most of the Saturdays up until a few weeks ago had been busy. I liked my job and had already received a ten cent an hour raise. I couldn't ask for a better, more kind boss than Mr. Wilson.

I was proud of Mattie, not only because of her basketball, but also for the young lady she had become. She was mature beyond her years, and the fact that Louise had asked her to drive us home last night was testimony to that. The one thing that bothered me was her anger toward Leon. He had not been a good father or husband, but I didn't want her to hate him.

I was on my third cup of coffee when Mattie came into the kitchen. "Morning. You're up early," I said.

"Did it snow much?" she asked.

"Several inches. There're drifts up to the porch. It's stopped now."

"If the roads are bad, Sam won't get to come home today," she said.

"Maybe they'll clear by noon."

"It's still an hour before I have to be at work. Would you like for me to cook breakfast?"

"No. I'll eat with Pa-Pa when he gets up."

Mattie couldn't hide her disappointment about the possibility of Sam not being able to come home. "Do you think Dr. Sadler will let Sam go home after he examines him?" I asked.

"I don't know. Sam looked better when I saw him, but his complexion was still yellow and he'd not gained much weight. He did seem stronger. He's going to be disappointed if Dr. Sadler keeps him in the hospital, but that might be best for him."

I tried changing the subject to her basketball, but nothing was successful in cheering her up. Finally, I gave up, telling her it was time for me to go to work. When she dropped me off, she said she was going by the hospital and see if there was any word on Sam.

When she picked me up at 6:00 that evening, things had gone from bad to worse. Mattie didn't say a word on the drive home. In the house, I asked her what was going on.

"I didn't get to the hospital until after Sam arrived. You know who was already there. I hardly got a word in. She started in telling me she was going to take care of Sam after he went home. Then she went into detail about how she was going to care for him, including cooking, washing his clothes, and even cleaning his house. Can you believe that? She probably can't boil water and she's never cleaned house. I guarantee you that! She makes me sick."

"Just calm down, Honey. What did Sam say during all this?"

"Nothing! He just lay there like an invalid."

"Had Dr. Sadler examined him?" I asked.

"I don't know. I left."

"It'll be all right, Mattie. Sam has a mind of his own. I can't see Sonia telling him what to do."

"She was doing a pretty good job of it, Mother."

"Why don't you go back to the hospital after Sonia leaves and talk to Sam. You can ask him what the doctor said."

"It probably won't do any good. She has her claws in him. What I don't understand is what she sees in him. She's beautiful, rich, and going to college. Surely she could do better than Sam. He's not that handsome. I guess he's a little cute."

I tried not to laugh but couldn't help it. "Listen to you, Honey. Trying to convince yourself that Sonia's too good for Sam. Here you are, thinking Sam is the best thing to come along since sliced bread. That's quite a contradiction. Maybe she sees Sam the way that you do."

"Mother, I'll admit it. I like Sam. There's something about him that's different. He's real. He's kind and wholesome. Most of all, he needs me. More than HER."

"Be patient, Honey. It'll work out for the best."

"I'll take your suggestion and go back to the hospital, but not until 9:00. Surely she'll be gone by then."

"Good. I'm going to predict this visit will be much better."

I didn't wake up when Mattie came home from the hospital, but she was in a much better mood at breakfast the next morning.

"Mother, you were right. She was gone and we had a long visit. Sam was sweet and apologized for Sonia. Of course, I could still smell her perfume everywhere. He insisted that he could take care of himself when he got home."

"Is he going to remain in the hospital?" I asked.

"For at least a few days."

"See, it's all going to work out, Honey," I said.

"The thing about it, Mother, Sonia is not a bad or evil person. She's just who she is and so different from me. Not only in looks but in personality. I don't believe I hate her. It's just that I hate what she is; a spoiled child who has gotten everything she ever wanted and now she wants Sam."

I was at school Monday morning for the conference. In fact, I stayed and waited after Mattie went to class. The meeting was at 8:30; hence the wait was short.

Mr. Ansley was nice, and when the teacher arrived, he introduced me as Mattie's mother. The teacher's name was Miss Vaughn, and I was struck by how pretty she was. She was carrying her grade book across her chest like she was afraid someone might take it away from her. Mattie arrived a few minutes later and the meeting began.

"Miss Vaughn, Mattie and her mother have some concerns about her grades. Can you help us out and explain your grading system?"

"Well, first of all, Mattie doesn't show me any respect. I have a college education and should be treated as such. She thinks she knows more than I do. I can see that by the expression on her face when I'm talking to the class."

"Miss Vaughn, now would you explain how you arrive at a grade for your students, including Mattie?"

At this point, she opened her grade book and said, "I give a grade each day for student participation. It's based on the student's attitude and how they respond to my instruction. This last six weeks, Mattie's daily grade was no higher than 60 and some days much lower."

"How much does this daily grade count toward their six-weeks average?" Mr. Ansley asked.

"I count it as half the grade," she answered, clutching her grade book.

"So, if Mattie made A's on all her papers she would still receive a C."

"That's correct."

"On the other hand, if someone failed all their tests and received a good daily grade for participation, they could receive a C also?" Mr. Ansley asked.

"That's correct."

I spoke for the first time. "You don't like Mattie, do you?"

"Mattie doesn't give me the respect I deserve. I don't like that," she said.

"Have you earned the respect of your students?" I asked.

"I shouldn't have too earn their respect. I'm a college graduate. They should respect me when I walk into the classroom."

I looked at the principal, and he was looking at the floor frowning and shaking his head. "I believe that's all we need to know. Thank you, Mrs. Quentin, for coming. You and Mattie may leave. Miss Vaughn you need to remain."

Out in the hallway, Mattie said, "Thank you for coming, Mother. I doubt it did any good."

"Believe me, Mattie, it did."

Tuesday night the regular season ended, with a game against Albany that would decide the district championship. Mr. Quentin went with me when I took Mattie to the gym at 5:30. We'd have to wait an hour for the game but we didn't mind.

Leon had found me during my lunch break at the drug store today and demanded that I come home. I told him that I was filing for divorce. He stormed out, saying, "You'll be sorry, I promise you."

My stomach was all in knots when the game started. I knew it'd be close, but throughout the first half the lead changed every minute or so. The half time score was 18-17 their favor.

The second half was the same, with neither team being able to get a substantial lead. With thirty seconds remaining, the score was 35-34 in our favor. Albany had the ball, and with ten seconds remaining, their best forward was fouled. She went to the line and made both shots. Now it was 36-35, Albany.

We had the ball and with two seconds remaining, Mattie shot from the top of the key, making it and the crowd went wild. Final score, 37-36.

Louise and I were jumping up and down, hugging one another. I couldn't stop the tears. People were going out on the court to offer congratulations. I didn't see him until he touched my arm. Turning, I saw Mr. McWilliams, the fire chief.

"Gladys, Hollis's house is on fire. You need to get him and come home."

Chapter 21

Sam

The sound of sirens going off were heard even though the radio was on. I suspected it was a fire alarm since it was not tornado season. The men who were members of the volunteer fire department would respond. I continued listening to music and thinking it was time for me to get out of here and go home. A few minutes later the nurse that was on night duty came into my room and confirmed it was a house that was on fire. For some reason, it gave me an uneasy feeling, and half an hour later I found out the reason. The nurse came back and told me it was the Quentin house that was burning.

I dressed quickly, and finding the nurse, I said, "I've got to get to their house. Would you let me borrow your car?"

"I guess so, but the doctor won't like you leaving."

"I'll take full responsibility," I said.

"Okay, but I get off at 7:00 in the morning. Be back before then," she said.

When I arrived at the Quentins, a large crowd was gathered, and it was evident that the house was going to be destroyed. The fire department was spraying water on the fire, but it was out of control, and the walls were already collapsing.

I moved through the people looking for Mattie and found her toward the front, closest to the fire. I reached and touched her on the shoulder and she was immediately in my arms, sobbing. I held her, not saying anything. Her mother and granddad were standing quietly as if they couldn't comprehend what was happening. Another woman had her arm around Mrs. Quentin.

"We've lost everything. All we have is the clothes we're wearing," Mattie sobbed.

I did know how to respond to that statement, holding her tightly, I said. "No, Mattie. You haven't lost everything. You, your mother, and Pa-Pa are alive. I've seen men who have lost everything. You still have each other and a future."

She relaxed in my arms. "You're right, Sam. We could've been in the house and burned with it."

We stood for the next half hour and watched the remainder of the house burn. Finally, the crowd began to disperse, until only a few people remained. Several had come by before leaving, offering condolences and help with anything that was needed. A familiar face appeared, talking with Mattie's mom. They had moved out of hearing distance and I realized that it was her dad, who I had bought the horse from. After some time, her mom came over and said, "Mattie, he wants us all to go home with him. I don't know what else to do. Louise has offered her house, but it's so small we would be crowded. We could stay with Leon until something else becomes available."

"No way, Mother. Forget it! I'm not about to stay in the same house with him!"

"Listen to me, Mattie. We have no choice until we can find a place to live. Please be reasonable."

"No! The answer is no! You and Pa-Pa can stay with him if that's what you want to do. Not me!"

"Mattie, I'm worried about your pa-pa. He hasn't said anything since we got here."

Mattie turned and asked her pa-pa, "Do you want to stay with Leon?"

He didn't respond but only had a blank look. She asked him the same question again, reaching out and touching his arm.

"It don't matter, Honey. I had no insurance on the house. We don't have anywhere to live and not enough money to rebuild. I'm sorry."

Mattie's dad had moved over and spoke to her mother. "You might as well come with me. You have no other choice," he said.

It was obvious that she was caught in an impossible situation. Mattie wouldn't go with them, and they had no other option.

"Mattie, please go with us. I promise it will only be temporary until we can find a place to live."

Mattie didn't respond, only shaking her head.

"You spoiled little brat. You do what your mother told you, or I'll take off my belt and whip you right here and now!" her dad bellowed.

I stepped in between them, not knowing what I'd do if he tried to carry out his threat.

"What do you think you're doing? I guess you're the big, brave solider that's going to protect her. I might just have to take care of you, too," he said.

I could smell the liquor even from several feet. "No sir. I'm not big or brave. I've been a solider for the past three years but not now. I've been sick and certainly couldn't be much of a protector. Mattie's my friend and I don't want to see her hurt."

"Then you best stay out of my way," he said, taking off his belt.

I immediately turned to Mrs. Quentin. "Ma'am, you're welcome to stay with me until you can find somewhere to live. I have plenty of room and it wouldn't be a problem. In fact, I could use some help around the house when I go home. Of course, Mattie and her granddad will be welcome, also."

That caught everyone by surprise, including Mattie's dad. Nothing was said, and I thought that maybe they didn't hear me.

Finally, Mattie's Pa-Pa, said, "Sam, that's very kind of you. If it's all right with Mattie and her mother, we'll take you up on your offer."

Mattie moved to my side. "Thank you, Sam. That'll be fine with me."

Her mom remained silent, looking confused. She looked at Mattie and then her husband, opening her mouth but not being able to speak.

"You're going with me, woman. Let's go!" he demanded.

That must've brought her back to reality. She moved over to stand beside Mattie and said, "No, Leon. I'm going with my daughter. Now, please leave us alone."

He took a step forward, shaking his finger at Mattie and her mom. "You're going to be sorry. I promise you that!" He left, cursing and making more threats.

"If you'll follow me, we'll go to the ranch and get you settled. I'll need to return to the hospital, but that's no problem."

"Could I ride with you, Sam?" Mattie asked.

"Sure."

Very little was said on the 20-mile drive, but Mattie did move over next to me and put her head on my shoulder.

I was back at the hospital by midnight. The nurse was relieved to have me and her car under her care again. I went to bed but was not able to sleep, thinking of what lay ahead. I'd gotten my guest settled, with Mattie and her mother having one of the bedrooms and her pa-pa the other. I was thankful that the house did have three bedrooms even though they were small. Mrs. Quentin had said that they were paying me board, and I knew it would be useless to argue. She insisted that she was going to work the next day. I'd told Jose to come get me tomorrow. I'd stayed in a hospital long enough, and I was hoping Dr. Sadler would not disagree. I felt good about being able to help Mattie and her family. Her dad was a piece of work and was probably going to be a problem in the future. Phil had asked me if I was lonely. Maybe having company was what I needed.

I finally slept a couple of hours before my breakfast arrived at 6:00. I hadn't dreamed and was hungry… two good signs.

Dr. Sadler came in a little after 7:00, asking me how I was feeling. I explained my situation and decision to go home. He asked me several questions about Mattie's family. He didn't insist on me staying but emphasized that I would need help at home. He wrote prescriptions and told me to come back to see him in three days.

I was dressed and ready when Jose showed up. As we were leaving, Dr. Sadler's nurse stopped me in the hall and gave me an envelope.

"Sam, this is to help the family replace their clothes. They'll receive second-hand clothes from generous people in the community, but this is for new outfits."

"Thank you," I said. Opening the envelope at my pickup, there was a check for $100 from W.T. Sadler.

On the drive to the ranch, I asked Jose how he felt about the Quentins staying with us.

"Good to have more people on the ranch, Little Bit. They nice. Mattie my friend and she likes you. I think maybe you like her, too."

Laughing, I replied, "I think you may be right."

When we arrived home, there were several cars parked in front of the house. Going inside, I found three of my neighbors that lived in the Canyon and they had brought clothes for Mattie, her mother, and Pa-Pa. That was only the beginning. Throughout the day, people kept bringing items by for them until I thought we might run out of a place to put them. Mattie was emotional and cried several times during the day. By the time her mother arrived from work, they each had several wardrobes.

The next month, I realized that Dr. Sadler was correct when he told me it was going to take a long time for me to recover. Being stubborn, I had not accepted his prediction. I slept a great deal during the day, and the least bit of effort left me exhausted, looking for a place to sit or lie down. I could never have made it living by myself, even with Jose close by. I was waited on hand and foot by my guests and was too weak even to object.

You would think, with the drastic change in our lives brought on by the fire that a great amount of confusion would've been present; however, that was not the case. Mrs. Quentin went back to work immediately, with Mattie riding with her to school. Of course, I wasn't able to do physical work and stayed in the house most of the day with Hollis. He'd insisted that I drop the Mister. Jose took care of the ranch work and cooked lunch each day for the three of us.

Mrs. Quentin went by school and picked up Mattie before coming home. Basketball ended the first week I was home when we lost to Ranger. After that, Mattie rode the bus to the ranch after school.

Mattie's mom insisted on paying me $30 a month for board even though she and Hollis paid for most of the groceries. Financially, I was better off, plus getting good meals. Hollis bought a television, saying that was the least he could do. Jose, with Hollis' supervision, installed the antenna, and the picture was clear most of the time on the channel we received.

I still dreamed of the war, but much less frequently, and usually was able to go back to sleep after waking up. When I was about to give up on getting better, my strength began to return. By the middle of February, I was able to be up and around for at least part of the day. I began spending more time with Mattie, and one spring-like day the last of the month, let her drive me through the pasture to look at the livestock. What I saw, was shocking. Without moisture, most of the grass was already gone. The heifers were not in good shape and were due to calve within two months. The ewes were not much better and would start lambing any time. Both stock tanks were dry. We were going to be forced to add to our feed bill, which was already high. I'd made a mistake stocking the ranch during a drought. All the moisture we had received this winter was in the form of two inches of dry snow. Mattie realized something was wrong.

"What is it, Sam? You got so quiet. I thought you were feeling better."

"We need rain or some form of moisture. The stock are running out of anything to eat. I have a loan to repay."

"It's not due for months," she said.

"With an increasing feed bill I won't have any profits when I sell the calves and lambs."

"Sonia's dad co-signed your note. If you can't pay it, he will," she said.

"No. I don't want any charity. I'll pay my own bills."

"I know she comes to see you while I'm at school. Pa-Pa told me."

I thought it best not to respond to her observation. Sonia had been over several times since I'd come home. She made it clear that she wasn't any too happy with my guests. She was spoiled, which became evident the more time I was around her.

"Have you made a decision about going to college?" I asked, moving to another topic.

"No. I don't know what to do. Probably just get a job and forget college. I have no idea what I would major in if I did go."

"You mentioned teaching and coaching to me one time," I reminded her.

"I know. That's probably not realistic though," she said. "We need to find a place to live. If I had a job, more money would be available."

"You've been a big help to me. I couldn't have come home and lived by myself, even with Jose."

"I guess it did work out for the both of us," she said.

"Tomorrow's Saturday. Would you like to go to the show? I said we would go on a date when I came home."

"Yes. That would be nice."

"We can go to the Pioneer Drive-In or the Queen in town. You choose which one," I said.

"If you were taking Sonia, where would you go?" she asked.

"What's that got to do with anything?" I asked.

"People make out at the drive-in. I figured you'd want to take Sonia there."

"You're impossible, Mattie! We'll go to the Queen in town. If you mention Sonia one time on our date, I'm going to put you out and let you walk home," I said, laughing.

Chapter 22

Mattie

I was tired of school and ready to graduate. I looked forward to getting back to the ranch each day. My grade in English had improved since the meeting with the principal, but without basketball school held little interest for me.

My best friend, Della, and I still visited each day. She had broken up with Juan when he dropped out of school. Almost every day she had questions about my temporary home. On Monday, the first day of March, she was even more persistent.

"So, tell me all about the date," she demanded.

"There's not that much to tell. We saw *Sabrina* and it was wonderful. Audrey Hepburn, of course, is my favorite actress. She gives us skinny girls hope."

"Did he hold your hand during the movie?"

"Most of the time."

"What do you mean, most of the time?" she asked.

"The last part of the movie he put his arm around me," I explained.

"Oh. This gets better all the time. Did he…you know…did he get fresh with you?"

"No. He was a perfect gentleman."

"Oh. Well, did he kiss you?"

"Did it ever occur to you that's none of your business?" I asked.

"We're friends, Mattie. Friends tell each other everything."

"No Della. Not everything." The first bell rang, which thankfully, ended our discussion.

I went to my first period class but spent most of the time thinking of Saturday night. I had a great time and hopefully Sam did also. The movie was great and afterwards we went to the Dairy Bar for burgers and drinks. We were home by 11:00, sitting outside in his pickup and talking for another hour. Della would be disappointed to know that he didn't kiss me, but that was fine. It would eventually happen.

We hadn't found a place to live that was suitable. Mother didn't seem to be in a hurry, after looking at several rent houses in town. With Sam improving and not requiring as much help, that would probably change. Pa-Pa had talked about putting the thirty acres up for sale that he owned.

I'd taken Pa-Pa to his place several times after it burned. Looking through the rubble, we found nothing that could be used. He did notice a five gallon can beside the house that he swore was not his. It had been burned but was still intact. He didn't say anymore about it, but both of us were wondering the same thing. Could the fire have been set intentionally, and would Leon have been capable of performing such a terrible act?

I was riding the school bus to the ranch each day, and Friday when I got off I noticed a familiar car parked in front. Walking the quarter mile to the house, I kept telling myself, *she has every right to be here. I don't own Sam Colter. After all, I get to see him every day.* When I reached the house, I went around to the back porch, and sat down in one of the chairs placed there for that purpose. It was a cloudy and cold afternoon, but I had my coat. I was determined to stay outside until she left. When I saw Jose ride in from the pasture, I met him at the barn. He greeted me, asking me how I was doing.

"Okay, I guess. Sam has company so I'm staying out of the house."

"Little Bit like you more. No worry about her," he said, smiling.

"How do you know, Jose?"

"Know Little Bit all his life. Better than anyone."

"Well, I hope you're right. How're the heifers and ewes?"

"Coyotes back," he said, frowning. "Killed two lambs last night. Got to do something. Most lambs not come till next month. Few ewes bred early."

"How do you know it was coyotes?" I asked.

"Saw them. They no afraid of me."

"Maybe you and Sam could shoot them," I suggested.

"Eyes bad. Can't shoot."

"What about Sam, since he's improved?"

Shaking his head, he said, "Little Bit no touch guns. Too much war and death."

"Do we need to move them back to the trap behind the house?" I asked.

"Maybe. Ask Little Bit what to do."

"I see she's leaving, Jose. I'm going back to the house and get warm. I'm cooking tacos for supper. Come eat with us. It'll be ready about 7:00."

When I walked into the house, Pa-Pa was sitting at the kitchen table. I spoke to him and then went on into the living room, but it was vacant. I thought, Sam must have gone to his bedroom. I knocked on his door, but nothing. Maybe he had gone to the bathroom, I thought. I went back into the living room and sat down to wait on him. After ten minutes, I went back into the kitchen, asking Pa-Pa where Sam was.

"Honey, he left with Sonia. She had invited him over to eat with them tonight. She's going to bring him home."

"Oh. I didn't realize…I just saw her car leave." I couldn't sit around and mope. It was already 5:30 and I needed to cook supper. I'd invited Jose over and the tacos weren't going to make themselves. I should've known this would happen. Sonia wasn't going to give up. They would probably not be home until late and it wouldn't do any good to worry. There was nothing I could do.

That was easier said than done. I burned the hamburger meat for the tacos and cut my finger slicing vegetables. By the time I had supper ready, Mother was home and Jose was there. Mother asked me where Sam was when we sat down to eat and Pa-Pa answered before I had a chance.

"Sonia picked Sam up to eat supper with them tonight."

"They won't have a meal this good, I bet," she said.

"Oh, Mother. They'll probably have steak or shrimp. They're rich," I said.

"Jose, I heard the coyotes, last night. They sounded close," Pa-Pa said, moving the subject away from Sam.

"Killed two lambs. Need to tell Sam."

"Can you get close enough to shoot them?" Pa-Pa asked.

Jose told Pa-Pa what he had told me about his eyesight and Sam's reluctance to shoot anything.

"I wouldn't be any help either, however, Mattie's a good shot. I taught her how to shoot, and she was always more accurate than me or her daddy. Of course, we only shot at cans. What about it Mattie, would you shoot a coyote?"

"I'd try. They're killing those helpless lambs, and Jose said they not only kill for food but do it for fun."

"Early morning best time. Before sun come up. We go in the morning?" he asked.

"All right. Just tell me what time?" I said.

After we finished eating, Jose went to Sam's room and came back with a gun. "This bolt action 30-30. It kicks some but not bad. We use it."

I reached for the gun, and it was much heavier than the .22 I'd learned to shoot with. I told Jose I would be ready at 5:30 and have coffee made for us.

Jose left, Pa-Pa moved to the living room to watch television, and Mother helped me with the dishes. Being the loving Mother she was, it was impossible for her not to try and console me.

"Mattie, I know Sam feels obligated to the Tollers. They've been nice to him since he returned home. He couldn't afford to turn down their invitation. It would've been rude."

"Mother, I'm fine. Don't worry about me. When're we going to find a place to live of our own?"

"The places I've looked at to rent are dumps. I keep thinking something nice will come up," she explained.

"Sam doesn't need us now. The sooner we find a place the better," I said.

"Mattie, have you noticed how much better your pa-pa has been doing these last few weeks? It's been good for him to be here with Sam. He's felt useful."

"We can't stay here forever, Mother."

"I know, I know, Mattie. Please be patient. I'm doing the best I can."

I was being unreasonable and knew it, because of Sam leaving with Sonia. I was trying to not let it bother me but wasn't successful. As the night wore on, it didn't get any better. I went to bed early since we would be leaving the house before daylight. I tossed and turned, looking at the clock on the table by the bed every few minutes. At 12:05, I heard the car drive up. I lay there, wondering how long they'd sit and talk or whatever before he came in. At 12:30, I went to the window, looking out. That was stupid. What was I looking for? At 1:00, I was mad! What were they doing out there?"

The minutes dragged and at 1:15, I got up and turned my light on. I was beyond reasonable thought, and going to the front door was about to open it when Sam beat me to it. I've never felt so humiliated, standing there in my pajamas with my mouth open but no words coming out.

"Mattie, what're you doing up so late?"

"I turned, went back to my room, got back into bed and covered up my head. I stayed that way until my alarm went off at 5:00, which wasn't necessary since I was awake. I eased into the kitchen, hoping not to awaken Sam, and put the coffee on.

Thank goodness, when Jose arrived at 5:30 Sam was still in his room. I poured coffee for us, and taking our cups, we left.

Jose drove and we found a large flock of ewes at the bottom of the hills.

"This right spot. They here yesterday," Jose said.

It was still dark when we parked the pickup and waited. Jose had loaded the gun and given it to me. I was nervous, wondering if I could shoot at an animal with the intention of killing it. Gradually it began to get light enough to see. We waited, and waited some more, as the sun began to come up.

"Maybe not come today. Full bellies from yesterday," Jose said.

The words were barely out of his mouth when I saw movement come out of a canyon. I gasped as three coyotes appeared, moving toward the ewes. Before I could do anything, one of them had grabbed a lamb by the neck and was shaking it, with his mother running off. I judged the distance to be about 100 yards. I opened the pickup door and stepping outside, steadied the gun against it, took aim and fired. The coyote jumped, dropping the dead lamb and falling, not moving.

"Shoot others!" Jose exclaimed.

They'd turned and were moving back toward the canyon, where they had come from. I aimed and shot again, this time kicking up dirt behind them. I aimed and shot again, this time not seeing where my bullet hit. Then they were gone.

"You do good, Mattie."

I was shaking…maybe from excitement or just amazement that I could kill an animal so easily without even hesitating. I checked the gun to make sure there were no shells left in it. I fired three and that's all it held, but I wanted to be sure. The first shot, I didn't notice the recoil, but the second and third hurt my arm.

"How many would they have killed, Jose?"

"More. Until they got tired. Not hungry, killing 'cause they like it. Maybe now, they be afraid of pickup. You do good," he repeated.

We drove over and put the dead coyote and lamb in the back of the pickup before going to the house. Now I had to face Sam, which I dreaded with a passion. He must think I was out of my mind last night.

Mother had already left for work, but Sam and Pa-Pa were eating breakfast. Jose, excitedly told them what happened, exaggerating the distance of the shot that killed the coyote. He used a lot of hand motions with his descriptions.

"I told you she was a good shot," Pa-Pa boasted.

"Thank you, Mattie. I appreciate it. We can't afford to lose lambs," Sam said.

"If you're hungry, there're sausage and eggs left on the stove," Pa-Pa said.

"No. I'm going to try and catch up on my sleep," I said. No way was I going to stay and face Sam. He might start asking me questions about last night.

In my room, I lay down on the bed but couldn't relax, thinking, I killed an animal this morning and made a complete fool of myself last night. Maybe I should just stay in bed all day. I wish it wasn't Saturday and I could go to school. Suddenly, I decided that riding might be the best therapy for my depression. After Sam went about his business, I would saddle Spade and ride... maybe the entire day. I felt better immediately.

Chapter 23

Gladys

The 20-mile drive to work gave me time to think. Mr. Quentin told me about finding the five gallon can and that the fire might have been set intentionally. I questioned him about why anyone would do such a thing, never considering it could have been Leon. Later, after thinking more about it, I realized that it was definitely a possibility, given his threats made before and after the fire. He was angry and vindictive enough to do it.

I knew we should move as soon as possible; however, I felt more secure for me and Mattie, living at the ranch. Up until recently it could be justified, because we did provide necessary help for Sam. Since he was improving and could care for himself, it was going to put more pressure on my conscience to find a place of our own. We were paying board so that helped justify our stay somewhat.

Poor Mattie. She was wanting to move immediately when Sam had supper with the Tollers. She adored Sam and couldn't believe he might feel the same way about her. Her answer to deal with the situation was to run from it.

Everything was going fine until the fire. Now there was so much uncertainty in our lives. I loved my job and the extra money was helping. We actually had a little left each month after paying bills. Of course Mr. Quentin helped out, also. My thoughts went back to the conversation we had last week when we were alone.

"Are you anxious to find a place to live?" I asked.

"You know, Gladys, I haven't given it much thought. I've been fine here. In fact, there were so many memories of Ava in my house that I believe it helped to get away. I miss her terribly, as you know. I still haven't gotten over her. Being here, I wasn't reminded of Ava everywhere I looked. Also, I've enjoyed Sam immensely. He's a special young man. To answer your question more directly after thinking about it; no, I'm not looking forward to leaving. I know it'll be necessary to eventually find a place of our own."

"You've done better since we moved," I said.

"Yes. I never expected to recover to the extent that I have. I miss going to coffee with my friends, but Sam fills that void. We have coffee together almost every morning after you and Mattie leave. He never mentions the war, but it's obvious he has scars that will never heal. I believe we're good for Sam, also. He's lonely and us being here, helps. I don't think Sam is in a hurry to see us leave either."

"Sam still smokes," I said.

"Yes. That's a habit we share. He tries to get me to smoke his Camels, but I have my Prince Albert with papers to roll my own. We enjoy our cigarettes with our coffee after you and Mattie leave."

"Does Sam ever talk about Mattie?" I asked.

"Not much, but I tell you something, Gladys; whenever her name comes up he smiles. It never fails, and Sam doesn't smile very often. There's something there between them. They may not know it but it's there."

"I hope you're right."

"Gladys, I keep wanting to apologize for Leon. I don't know where it went wrong. Maybe being the youngest of my children had something to do with it. I wish he was different, but it's not going to happen. I hesitate to give you advice, but it would be in yours and Mattie's best interest to get a divorce. I'll do my best to see to it that he leaves you alone."

"It's not your fault Leon turned out the way he did. I should never have stayed with him this long. I didn't have the confidence to leave him, and to be truthful, have always been afraid of him. I do plan on getting a divorce."

"Another suggestion is that we work together to encourage Mattie to attend college. We can come up with the money somehow. She has the potential to make something of herself, and I want to see she has the opportunity to do so," he said.

"I agree with you. School will be out soon, and we need to start pushing her toward college now."

Thinking back on the conversation with Mr. Quentin, I realized he was right on all counts. I made it to work on time, and the day went fast. This was Saturday and payday, which was always nice. At 6:00 promptly, Mr. Wilson brought my check by the register.

"Gladys, I appreciate your work. You've been an asset to our store, and I made a wise choice in hiring you," he said.

The check was important, but the compliment meant more than anything to me. I was gaining confidence and this job was a big part of that change.

I didn't get home until after 7:00, since I'd spent time buying groceries. Mattie had supper ready, waiting for me before putting it on the table. She was becoming a better cook with each meal. Tonight we were having beef stew with cornbread and a bread pudding for dessert.

When we sat down at the table, I suggested that we have a blessing. I asked for a volunteer but didn't have any takers. I asked them to bow their heads and assumed the task myself. I began, *thank you for the blessings we have. Thank you for this makeshift family and the love within it. Thank you for this food. Amen.*

"Now, I have a suggestion. I would like to attend church in the morning. Preferably at the church right down the road. Will anyone go with me?" I asked.

Silence followed. Then Sam spoke, "I haven't been to the new church. I'll go with you."

"Me too," said Mattie.

Mr. Quentin didn't speak so it was settled. Me, Sam, and Mattie would attend church at the Pioneer Methodist Church on Sunday, March 7th. Maybe the compliment by Mr. Wilson gave me the confidence to suggest something that I felt this family needed. I had a good feeling about my action.

When we were cleaning up the kitchen, Mattie said, "We can wear our new outfits we bought with the money Dr. Sadler gave us after the fire."

"Yes, we can."

"What made you suggest that we go to church?" she asked.

"I believe it will be good for all of us. We haven't been since the fire and it's time we started back. Going to Sam's church will make it easier on him. I'm glad he consented to go."

"I was gone most of the day, riding Spade, and haven't had a chance to talk with Sam. I waited up for him last night. He was late getting home and I made a fool out of myself. I don't know what got into me, Mother."

"I doubt if Sam has given it any thought. Besides, you can't change what has already happened," I said.

The next morning when Mattie came out of her room dressed in her new outfit I stared in amazement at how lovely she looked. With her part of the money she had bought a two-piece deep wine colored suit. The skirt was solid and topped with a matching wine and black plaid fitted jacket. The jacket had a Peter Pan collar and cuffed long sleeves. A thin belt at her waist closed over the jacket which fell just below her hips. After looking in the mirror, she had to know how pretty she was.

She smiled and said, "I look pretty good, don't I?"

"You're beautiful, Mattie."

"This suit makes me look curvier than I am. That's why I picked it," she said.

"You look beautiful," I repeated.

"You look mighty good yourself," she said.

I'd bought a simple gray tweed fitted dress and a pill box hat. I felt good about myself...better than I had in years. We were actually ready to go before Sam was.

When Sam appeared, he was wearing dress slacks and a sport coat, both of which were too large for him. He stopped and stared at Mattie, saying, "You look good, Mattie. I'm sorry my clothes are too large. You may be embarrassed to be seen with me. My jeans I bought fit much better, but Mother never allowed me to wear jeans to church."

I felt so sorry for him. No wonder Mattie adored him. I went over and hugged him, saying, "You look great, Sam, and we're proud to go to church with you."

Coming in from outside, where he had been smoking, Mr. Quentin commented, "My, my, two beautiful ladies. Sam, you're a fortunate man."

We went in Sam's pickup, with Mattie sitting in the middle. It was only a few miles to church and we were early. We decided to remain in the pickup for a few minutes before going in.

"I was surprised that Hollis didn't come with us," Sam commented.

"He has never attended church, yet he's the best man, I've ever known. If he has faults, I've not discovered them," I said.

We were some of the first inside the church, taking seats toward the back. When people started entering, almost all of them stopped and spoke to Sam, either hugging him or shaking his hand. Every one of them said how glad they were to see him in church. It was obvious their affection for him was sincere.

It was a beautiful church and almost filled when the service started. Sam sat next to the aisles, with Mattie in the middle and me on the inside. The singing was amazing, with Mattie adding her musical talents but Sam remaining silent. The pastor's message was positive and uplifting, much like what I was used to hearing in the Presbyterian Church. At the end of the service, as we exited the building, the pastor spoke directly to Sam.

"I haven't met you, Sam, but I've heard many good things about you. I'm so glad you came today and brought your friends. Please come back."

It took us at least fifteen minutes to get back to the pickup. People kept stopping us and talking to Sam. It was like everyone wanted to say something to him. I could see that Sam was embarrassed. On the drive back to the ranch, I asked Sam if he expected the reception he received.

"No, not really. This was the first time I'd been to church since returning. I'd forgot how much of a family the church is. I've missed it."

"They love you, Sam. That's obvious," I said.

I had put a roast in the oven before leaving for church. It was done when we arrived home. Mattie, helped me set the table and as we sat down for Sunday dinner, I asked if anyone would like to say the blessing and once again…silence. I said a short prayer before the meal.

After we finished, and before we left the table, Sam asked Mattie if she would like to take a short trip with him. I could see the surprise on Mattie's face but she answered, "Sure."

I told them to go ahead that I would do the dishes.

Chapter 24

Sam

We were in my pickup heading east from the ranch. "Where're we going?" Mattie asked.

"To the cemetery where most people that lived and died in this area are buried."

"Oh," she said.

"Were you waiting up for me Friday night?" I asked.

"Yeah, I guess so. I was worried about you."

"Why were you worried?"

"It was so late. I thought you might have had trouble with your pickup," she answered.

"You wouldn't be telling a lie would you? We just left church a couple of hours ago."

She didn't answer, turning her head and looking out the window. Suddenly, I was ashamed of myself for embarrassing her. "That's all right, Mattie. I'm glad someone is looking after me, especially someone who can shoot. Now, move over here next to me. She still didn't say anything, but moved over beside me. I reached down and squeezed her leg. Nothing else was said until we reached the cemetery.

"This is the White Church Cemetery, named after the church that was here for so long. It's the church I grew up in. I want to show you where my mother and daddy are buried. I'd have brought some wild flowers, but it's too early for them."

"For some reason, I thought they were buried in town," she said.

"No. They both left instructions to be buried here. When I came home for my mother's funeral, I told Jose, this is where I wanted to be buried, in case I didn't make it home alive."

I took her to the Colter family plot where my parents and grandparents were buried. "This is the first time I've visited the cemetery since coming home. It makes me sad. I'm going to try and come more often. I've seen too much death."

She reached down and took my hand. "I'm sorry, Sam. You need to forget the past."

"I-I know, but it's not easy," I said, trying to control my emotions.

"You have many friends here, Sam. I could see that at church."

"I know, Mattie, I love this area. It's my home. I thought about leaving but that's not possible. This is where I belong. Let's go home. It looks like we have a norther coming in. Maybe, we'll get some rain."

On the drive back to the ranch, the cloud in the north became darker, the wind began to blow, and the sun disappeared. Before we were home, I had to turn on my headlights to see the road. I'd never seen anything like it.

"Mattie, what's going on?"

"It's a dust storm. We had several last spring."

We made it home and into the house, to find Mrs. Quentin and Hollis sitting at the kitchen table. The lights were turned on in the house.

"How long will it last?" I asked.

"Maybe a few hours or all night," answered Hollis.

"I've never seen anything like it," I repeated.

"It was like this in the dust bowl, during the '30s," Hollis said.

"Why?" I asked.

"No crops on the plains. Nothing to stop the soil from blowing away. This is a bad drought, Sam. I'm afraid it's going to get worse before it gets better," explained Hollis.

"What can we do?" I asked.

"Pray for rain. That's all that will help," he answered.

It was time to shear the sheep. They'd start lambing in a month or so and have time to get over the stress created by the shearing. I'd been in touch with Mr. Toller, and he was shearing next week. After they finished, the crew he was using, would come to my place. Of course, he had several thousand and it would take all week to do that many; mine could be done in two days, easily.

We'd had about two inches of rain since I bought the heifers and ewes. The stock tanks were dry, and one of the windmills had quit pumping. It being only a matter of time until there wouldn't be sufficient water for my stock.

Mr. Toller had offered me day work to help gather his sheep. I was appreciative of the possibility of extra income. The pay was ten dollars a day, which would be from early morning until late evening. It would soon be six months since I took out the loan, which was for three years, but I wanted to pay the interest and some toward the principle each year. What made that difficult was my feed bill, which continued to grow. The ewes and heifers both needed protein since they would be delivering soon. The high protein feed was expensive. If we didn't get moisture, a large part of the sale of my lambs and calves in the fall would have to go toward my feed bill.

Another expense was approaching. I would need to buy a bull to put with the heifers and several rams to put with the ewes. Even buying them from Mr. Toller, the cost would be several hundred dollars. There was only about $800 left from the money I brought home. Cattle and sheep buyers had dwindled with the drought, and the market was weaker than when I purchased stock for the ranch in October. At this point, I didn't have anything going my way. I shouldn't think like that, and it wasn't true. I was stronger and feeling better, which was more important than anything. I weighed 150, according to the scales at the feed store, which was 20 pounds more than two months ago. My new pants were getting tight and my old ones were still too large.

Also, I had enjoyed having the Quentin's living with me. They had become like family, and I dreaded the day they would leave. Hollis had become a good friend and someone I was comfortable talking to. Mrs. Quentin was nice and reminded me of my mother. I was confused about my feelings toward Mattie. I respected and admired her maturity and intelligence. Actually, she was amazing. She had shot and killed another coyote this week, no doubt saving several lambs. She was awesome in basketball. She was just as attractive as Sonia in her on way. We had spent little time alone since they had moved in with me. I did enjoy being with her, but had to admit Sonia was fun also.

I worked three days at the Toller Ranch, with five of us gathering up the sheep, including Mr. Toller, his two sons and one-full time hand. At first, I thought it might be my imagination that his two sons were not at all friendly. By the second day, they were making every effort to show me that I wasn't welcome. If I needed help in moving a group of sheep, they ignored me, only working with their dad and hired hand. At the end of the third day when Mr. Toller paid me, he explained the problem.

"Sam, sometimes your kids never grow up. I apologize for their behavior. It was brought on by jealously, plain and simple. My wife and I have bragged on you often and in their presence. Of course, Sonia has done the same and this is the result. My two sons' conduct was childish and immature. I'll talk to them in a few days, after they've had a chance to think about how they acted."

"No problem, Mr. Toller. I appreciate the work." My statement was true. It was no big deal to me if the brothers didn't like me.

I thanked him again and left, feeling good with the thirty dollars in my pocket. By the time I was home, supper was over, and Mattie and her mother were doing the dishes.

"Have you eaten, Sam?" asked Mrs. Quentin.

"No ma'am."

"I'll heat you up a plate," Mattie said.

"Thanks. I'm hungry. It seems I have my appetite back. It's been a long time since that sandwich I had for lunch. How was school today, Mattie?"

"Boring. Just a little over six-weeks left. I can't wait," she answered.

"What's next, after school?" I asked.

"Get a job and help pay the bills. Don't you start in on me about going to college. We don't have the money for that. I don't want anyone doing without so I can continue school."

"You're kind of touchy tonight," I said.

"Sam, we've been encouraging her to go to college. Her pa-pa and I have both tried to convince her that was the thing to do so she would have a future," Mrs. Quentin explained.

"Sounds like to me she's getting two big for her britches," I said, smiling.

She turned around from the stove where she was heating my supper and glared at me with those green eyes blazing. "Sam Colter, I would like to get too big for my britches like someone else you know. Maybe you would be nicer to me then."

"Oh, Mattie. I'm nice to you most of the time. By the way, I agree with your mother and Pa-Pa. You should go to college. If I was as smart as you, I'd probably go myself."

She sat my plate down in front of me and stalked out of the room. "I guess she's going to be mad," I said.

"Don't worry about it. We've been on her pretty hard about going to school. She's determined not to let us do without because of her. Also, every time you go to the Toller Ranch she gets out of sorts. Maybe she'll be in a better mood since you finished today."

I went outside to smoke and found Hollis sitting on the back porch. "It's a nice evening," I said.

"Sure is. Sit down and talk to me, Sam. We've been after Mattie to attend college but haven't been successful. It's all about money and she's determined that we not pay for her school. Do you have any suggestions?"

"No. She's already mad at me for telling her she needs to go to college."

"All we can do is try. That girl has a mind of her own," he said.

"Hollis, it's been a week since we had the dust storm. How soon can we expect another one?"

"No way of knowing. Could be tomorrow or next week or a month from now. Most of the time they're a result of a cold front that blows in, picking up dirt off the plains."

"Were they this bad during the dust bowl in the '30s?" I asked.

"Worse. Some of the ones back then actually killed people who were caught out in them. They would suffocate. It was our fault, because at the beginning of the century farmers began turning the prairie into farm land. When the drought hit there was no vegetation to hold the dirt. The soil just blew away. Sometimes we are our own worst enemy."

"How long can this drought last?" I asked.

"It's started right after you left for the service so we're in our fourth year. Surely it won't last much longer. If it does, many of the small ranchers and farmers will go out of business."

"What would you do if you were me? Would you give up and sell the heifers and ewes or try to wait it out?" I asked.

"I could tell you my opinion; however, if I was your age, my decision would probably be different than it is now. You have to decide, Sam. You're young and can overcome a bad decision."

"So, if you were me, you would sell out?" I said.

Laughing, he said, "I didn't say that. A wise man once told me never send good money after bad. That was sound advice then and still is."

He continued, "I will tell you something everyone should know, based on experience. I thought many things were important until I had my stroke. After that, everything seemed insignificant compared to my health. Now, the fact that I can get around without a walker and take care of my personal needs is so far ahead of any worries I have. You're young and alive, Sam. Be thankful, and don't spend time worrying about the future."

We continued to talk for another hour before going inside. Mattie was in her room, and Mrs. Quentin was watching television. I asked her if Mattie had been out of her room since supper.

"Just briefly. She informed me that she would ride the bus to school in the morning. It looks like we're all in the dog house.

She's a stubborn young lady. I guess we might as well give up on the college idea. I'm not feeling well. Maybe the stress of arguing with her is making me sick. I'm going to bed."

I went to my room, turned on the radio and lay down across the bed. Hollis was right even though he wouldn't come out and say it directly. He would sell out, pay off the loan and not depend on it raining. Maybe that would be the best thing to do. He was also right about what was important. I was fortunate to be here at the ranch instead of in the family plot at the cemetery. I came as close to being killed as you could, not just one time but several times.

I slept really good, not waking up until after 7:00 which was unheard of for me. When I went to the kitchen Hollis was drinking his coffee.

"Gladys is sick today. She went back to bed. She asked Mattie to call Mr. Wilson from school and tell him. She left a few minutes ago to catch the bus, still in a bad mood."

I poured myself a cup of coffee and sat down. Since it was just me and Hollis, I lit up a Camel. I'd just taken one sip of coffee when I heard the front screen door slam. Mattie stalked in the kitchen.

"The bus left me! I was running up the road and he just left me! I can't believe it! I'm turning him in to the school board!"

"Honey, just calm down. Everything's going to be all right," Hollis said.

"I'll take the pickup to school today," she said.

"No. You can't do that. Your mother said she was going in at lunch if she felt better," he said.

"Then, I won't go to school today. I'm tired of school anyway. Maybe I'll just quit altogether."

"I'll take you," I said.

"I thought you'd be going back over there today," she responded.

"No. We finished yesterday. I need to go into town anyway. If you'll let me finish my coffee, I can take you to school."

"That sounds like a good offer," her pa-pa said.

"I'll wait on you in the pickup," she said, leaving.

I gulped down my coffee and was in my pickup within a few minutes. "Your day's not starting out very good, is it?"

"No."

On the drive into town, I tried to make conversation. "You look nice today. Is that a new dress?"

"Not quite. I've worn it about a hundred times."

"Mattie, your mother and pa-pa only want what's best for you."

"I want to be left alone to make my own decisions. Is that asking too much? I'm eighteen and old enough to know what I want. They need to stop nagging me. I'm going to get a job and make some money so I can help out with the bills."

"I believe you should go to college, Mattie. That's what your mother and pa-pa want."

"What's it to you?"

"I want what's best for you, too. I believe college will be best for you."

"I guess you prefer college girls," she said.

"No. I prefer girls who smile and are happy."

That ended the conversation until I stopped in front of the school. A large group of students were gathered outside the building.

"Well, here we are, Sunshine. How about a goodbye kiss for your taxi driver?" I leaned over for a peck on the cheek.

She got out and slammed the door, without saying a word.

Chapter 25

Mattie

I didn't look back when walking away from Sam's pickup. He hadn't left when I reached the building and went in. He thought he was being smart, telling me to kiss him goodbye, then presenting his cheek, like I was a child. I don't see how my day could get any worse.

My first period teacher, who was standing at the door greeting her students, stopped me, saying, "Mattie, Mr. Ansley would like to see you in his office. He came by earlier and told me."

It was probably about this valedictorian thing, which everyone except me seemed concerned about. When I arrived, his secretary told me to go right on into his office.

"Morning, Mattie. How're you today?" he asked.

"Well, I tell you, Mr. Ansley, I could be better. I hope my day doesn't get any worse.

Laughing he replied. "We're not going to talk grades, if that's what you mean. I'll get right to the point. I have a long-time friend at Wayland Baptist College in Plainview. He is currently a professor there and we stay in touch. I've been telling him about you for the past several years and asking him to relay it to the coaches. To make a long story short, they evidently listened to him. The girls' coach was at the Roscoe game this year. I visited briefly with him, and he told me he would be in touch. I never heard from him and thought that was the end of it. He called me after school yesterday and informed me that he would like for you to come for a tryout in May. What do you think about that?"

Suddenly, I was having difficulty breathing and my heart was racing. "You mean the 'Flying Queens,' I mumbled."

"Yes, that's what they're called now."

"I'm not that good," was all I could think to say.

"Well, would you like to find out? They need to fill three slots and they've invited twenty-five girls to try out."

"I don't have the money to attend college," I said.

"If you make the team, that's no problem. They're the first college to give girls' basketball scholarships. Your room and board plus your tuition would be paid. It would amount to about $800 a year. You would receive a free college education if you made the team."

"I wouldn't have a chance," I stated.

"Listen to me, Mattie. They're looking for two rovers, who as you know play the entire court. That requires speed, stamina, and the ability to shoot. I only know of one player who has all those qualities and she's sitting right across from me. You're special, not only because of your ability and determination, but because you play smart."

"I haven't picked up a basketball since the season ended."

"We can take care of that," he said, opening his desk drawer and taking out a key. "This is to the gym. I'll let you keep it and you can practice whenever you like…day or night. You have six weeks before the tryouts."

I didn't know what to say. My hand seemed to act for me as it reached out for the key. I thanked him and left, going back to my class in a trance. When I entered the room, the teacher asked me if everything was all right.

"Yes ma'am, I guess so."

I might as well have been in another world the remainder of the day. I kept repeating to myself, *this can't be real. The Flying Queens, me trying out for a spot on their team.* I made it through the day somehow and using the phone in Mr. Ansley's office called the grocery store and asked if my mother was there. A minute later she picked up.

"Mother, you came to work at noon?" I said in the form of a question.

"Yes. I got to feeling better."

"I'm not going to ride the bus today. Could you pick me up after work? I'll be in the gym."

"Sure. Basketball's over. What're you going to do in the gym?" she asked.

"Just shoot some baskets. I'll explain later."

I went directly to the gym after talking to my mother and was surprised to find someone already there. He saw me, saying, "Hi, Mattie, come on in and join me. I wanted to shoot a few baskets before going to feed my steer."

"How did you get in?" I asked.

"Easy. We always leave a window cracked so we can open it and come in whenever we feel like it."

I must be doing something right. I walk into the gym to start practicing and find the nicest boy in school already there. Jimmy was president of the FFA and a good athlete. He was one of the most popular boys in school, especially with the girls. He was so cute it kinda took your breath away. We had gone all the way through school together and he was a senior also. He dated the most beautiful girl in school.

"Let me go put on my gym clothes," I said. The dressing room wasn't locked, and my workout clothes were still hanging in the locker. I didn't have my shoes, but I could go barefoot. When I returned, Jimmy was still there.

"You miss basketball?" he asked.

I decided he was going to be the first to hear the news. I told him about my invitation for a tryout and that I was going to start working out immediately.

He stopped and stared at me. "You mean the real Flying Queens? They're becoming famous. You're good, Mattie. I hope you make it. You could have played on the boys' team this year. We didn't have anyone that could shoot like you."

"Thanks. I'm going to give it my best shot. Do you want to play some one on one?"

"Sure, if you'll go easy on me," he replied.

For the next hour, with only a few breaks, we competed one on one. Jimmy was good, and the workout was just what I needed to get started. We finally sat down on the floor, exhausted.

"Thank you," I said.

"No problem. Just let me know what days you're going to practice and I'll help you. That was fun today. I need to go now and work with my steer."

After he left, I thought, what's going on? What did I do to deserve this? Jimmy was big in FFA and showing steers. I would never have thought he would pay any attention to me. Of course, he had always been nice, but he was that way with everyone. His girlfriend would be upset when she found out he was spending time with me.

I had trouble containing myself on the way home, but I was determined to make the announcement at the supper table with everyone present. Time dragged and I thought it would never be time to sit down at the table. My opportunity finally came after Mother said the blessing.

"I have an announcement," I said. It was quiet while I gave them the news and then Mother burst into tears. Pa-Pa clapped and even Sam got up and hugged me. Supper was forgotten as the questions poured in. Of course, I didn't have any answers yet. I went over, again, the meager information that Mr. Ansley gave me.

"I expect to hear more from the college in the next few weeks. Right now, it's important that I go to work on conditioning and gym work. I may not have the most ability of the other girls in the tryout, but I can work harder than they do."

"Is there anything we can do to help?" asked Mother.

"Just give me time in the gym. Oh, I didn't tell you. Jimmy worked out with me today and said he would be willing to help me anytime."

"Jimmy?" questioned, Mother.

"Jimmy Russell," I replied.

"Oh, my goodness, Mattie. He's handsome and so nice."

"I remember him. His daddy runs the locker plant. He's big into show cattle and the FFA. His daddy ropes every year at the Fourth of July Rodeo that's held in the Canyon," Sam said.

"Why would he help you?" Sam continued.

"He's nice. I think he's always been a little interested in me," I answered, hoping I wasn't stretching the truth enough for my response to be called a lie.

He didn't respond but went to eating his supper. "I like to run in the morning before school. Until I get a three-mile route, I'll just run to the gate and back. If I do that six times that should be about three miles. What do you think, Sam?"

He didn't look up, continuing to eat. "Yeah, that should be at least three miles. Will you be staying in town every day?"

"Probably so. I can ride home with Mother."

"Mattie, we're so proud of you. It doesn't matter whether or not you make the team. It's a great honor to even obtain a tryout," Pa-Pa said.

"I'm going to check on the heifers. They should start calving anytime. I'm glad we moved them into the trap behind the house so I can watch them." He got up and left after making the announcement. I smiled, aware of him changing the subject.

"Mattie, I didn't know Jimmy had ever been interested in you," Mother said.

"Well, we've gone to school together for twelve years and had many classes together. He's the one who nominated me for class president."

"Poor Sam. I think it upset him that Jimmy was helping you," Mother said.

"That's tough. Maybe Sonia can console him," I said.

"Mattie, be careful with Sam. I can't imagine what he's been through the last two years. He's fragile and we all need to consider that fact," Pa-Pa said.

If anyone could make me feel guilty, it was my pa-pa. I had so much respect for him and the way he lived his life. I can't remember ever doubting anything he told me. He was right this time also. I was jealous of Sonia and couldn't help it. On the other hand, I was feeling great about Jimmy paying attention to me, of all people. Flaunting it was an opportunity I couldn't pass up.

I finished my supper, then went outside and sat on the back porch. I could see Sam walking among the heifers. It was a nice evening and the sun was just beginning to go down. My pa-pa kept looking for an evening when the sun would set behind a bank, saying that could mean rain.

This had to be one of the most exciting days of my life. I still couldn't grasp the idea of trying out for a college basketball team, especially the Flying Queens. Pa-Pa was right. It was an honor to get a tryout; however, that wasn't going to be enough for me.

I continued to wait on the porch until Sam returned. "How are they?" I asked.

"Several are about to pop. All of them won't be able to have their calf without help. I need to get up at least once tonight to check on them."

"What about Jose? Can't he do that?" I asked.

"We're going to trade out. He'll take tomorrow night. That way it won't be as hard on us," he explained.

"I'm going to get up at 5:00 to run. I could check on them then if you want," I offered.

"That would be great. Mattie, I'm proud of you. That's really neat. I hope you make it. Maybe I could come watch you play. Of course, I'll miss you. It's strange, but since y'all have been out here, the demons have left me alone. That's what I call the dreams that used to come almost every night. I'll never forget you lying down beside me in the hospital and holding me. You were all that got me through that terrible night."

Now I felt horrible after trying to make him jealous. I understand what Pa-Pa had said about him being fragile. I had to change the subject before the tears came.

"Will all the heifers have calves?" I asked.

"Hopefully, at least fifteen will. The problem is, it's going to take most of the money the calves bring to pay the feed bill. The same is true with the lambs. If it doesn't rain, there's no way I can pay off the loan. Some days, I want to sell everything and give up. I should never have borrowed money to buy stock during a drought. I don't have anyone to blame but myself."

I moved my chair over next to him and took his hand. "Why did you take me with you to the cemetery yesterday?"

"I've been trying to get up the nerve and I couldn't do it by myself. With you going with me, I was able to go. I miss them, Mattie, especially my mother. When I walk into the kitchen in the morning, I expect her to be at the stove cooking my breakfast. I wasn't even here for her when she passed. I know she suffered toward the end."

"Is that chair big enough for the both us?" I asked.

"Maybe. We could try if you like."

Moving over to his chair, I sat down on his lap, putting my arms around him. We spent the next hour gaining strength and resolve to face the future in that embrace.

Chapter 26

Gladys

The next month passed quickly, with Mattie working tirelessly to get ready for the tryouts in Plainview. She was pushing herself to the point where she'd lost weight. I tried to persuade her to slow down but to no avail. She'd be up at 5:00 in the morning to run and had increased her route to five miles. She stayed in the gym to practice after school and on weekends.

I worried about the effect it'd have on Mattie if she failed to make the team. She talked constantly about what it would be like to play for the Flying Queens. The local newspaper ran an article about the tryouts with a picture in her basketball uniform. She would not discuss a backup plan, saying, "I've got to make it." After the article came out in the paper, it seemed that every other person that came through checkout at my counter congratulated me for Mattie's honor. Everyone already had her playing for the Flying Queens. She'd received additional information about the tryout. They would be held on the 17th, 18th, and 19th of May.

Poor Sam. It had been a terrible month for him. Thus far only six calves had lived and one of the heifers had died giving birth. Only eight heifers remained to calve and the best he could hope for would be to have 14 to sell this fall. Added to his disappointment, after his sheep were sheared, we had a cold, wet norther and he lost a dozen ewes. The wet didn't amount to much moisture, only enough to chill the sheep. Watching him sit at the table doing calculations on a scratch pad, attempting to figure out a way he was going to pay his feed bill and repay a portion of the loan, my heart reached out to him. No one as young as he should have had to go through what he had in Korea and come home to the problems he was facing. I wished we had the means to help him.

I'd hired a lawyer and filed for a divorce, charging Leon with assault. Leon said it was not going to happen, but I was determined. My confidence had grown, being away from him so long, and I realized how miserable my life had been with him. I felt better and looked better than I had in years. No way was I going back to that life. My lawyer didn't believe it would be a problem, since Mattie would testify in court if that became necessary.

My job was great, but I hadn't found a place for us to live yet. Sam insisted there was no hurry, but I felt like we were imposing. I wanted my own place before Mattie left for tryouts. If she made the team, she would have little time at home before moving to Plainview. Since Leon was living in our house in town, I'd stopped making payments on it. I was surprised the bank hadn't taken possession and put it up for sale. To my knowledge, Leon didn't have a job and wasn't making the payments.

On Friday, April 30, when I picked Mattie up at the gym, she announced that she was going to be the valedictorian. "It's official. Mr. Ansley called me and Keri to his office today and told us. Keri cried, and I told Mr. Ansley to give it to her, that it wasn't a big deal to me. He said that wasn't possible. She finally settled down but never did congratulate me. To me, everyone is making a big issue out of nothing. Now I have to make a speech at graduation, which is the pits. Graduation is the 14th and tryouts start on the 17th. I don't want to be thinking of a speech when my mind will be in Plainview."

"Mattie, I'm proud of you and it's a big deal for me. I bet your pa-pa can help you with the speech."

"I thought Jimmy might help me. It's strange. We went all the way through school together and waited until now to become friends. Of course, we've been together in the gym almost every day. I promised to let him know about the tryouts. He's leaving for Arizona right after graduation to work on a ranch.

She continued, "Sam's been acting strange lately, like he's in another world."

"I know, Mattie. He's worried about repaying the loan, and it's been a terrible month for him. You've been occupied with your training and have spent little time with him. Maybe it would be a good idea to offer him some encouragement."

"Are you going to be able to take off work to go with me to Plainview?" she asked, changing the subject.

"I don't see how, Mattie. It would mean missing four days' work and we can't afford to lose the money. You'll have expenses with the trip also. I'm sorry, but it's not going to be possible. I'll need Mr. Quentin's pickup to get to work. The only thing I know to do is get you a two-way bus ticket. You'll need to leave Sunday and return on Wednesday."

"I'll probably be the only one at the tryouts that arrives on a bus."

We had been going to church each Sunday and I was getting to know some of the congregation. They were a friendly group and it continued to surprise me about how they took on over Sam. The men would shake his hand, pat him on the back, and tell him how glad they were to see him. Many of the women would hug him and comment on how nice he looked.

Our seating arrangement was always the same. Sam would sit next to the aisle on the second row from the back, with Mattie sitting next to him, and me on the other side of her. He would never sing loud enough to be heard, but Mattie had a beautiful voice and could be heard by everyone present. She had been asked to sing in the choir but didn't accept, saying, "Maybe later."

Sam and Mattie's relationship seemed to be at a standstill; not moving forward or backward. Sam was preoccupied with the ranch and Mattie with the tryouts. Sam went to eat at the Tollers every Saturday night, but it didn't seem to bother Mattie. I think she was focused on basketball to the point she didn't see much of anything else. I felt badly about not being able to take her to Plainview, but it would mean giving up too much of my weekly pay. Also, the bus ticket would be cheaper transportation.

When I told Mr. Quentin our plans he insisted on buying the bus ticket. He surprised me with a suggestion about our housing problem.

"Gladys, it seems a shame to not do something with the thirty acres I own. When I went to town last week with Sam to buy feed, we drove around and looked at vacant houses. There're several that aren't bad and could be made into nice homes. Why don't we see about buying one and having it moved to my property? I already have a water well plus a septic tank. I believe the bank would loan me the money, with my property for collateral. We can buy one of the houses for $2500 and have it moved for another $300. I have some friends who have offered to help with repairs. I believe we could come up with a nice home that Mattie would inherit after I'm gone. What do you think?"

"Are you sure about going into debt?" I asked.

"I need a place to live and someone to help me. Hopefully, I can stay out of the nursing home for a few more years. It would be sort of an investment for you and even Mattie, if she decides to live here."

"It's a great idea and I appreciate it, Mr. Quentin."

"I believe it would be good for the both of us," he said.

His suggestion made a lot of sense and took pressure off me to find a place to live. Of course, it would take time, but at least we could be looking forward to a place of our own. When I told Mattie, she agreed with me, saying, "He's right, Mother. He needs us, and we need a place of our own."

Graduation day arrived, and Mattie had her speech prepared. She practiced before she left for the commencement ceremony, wearing a favorite Sunday dress and her first pair of high heels. She was tall and beautiful, causing Sam to stop and stare when he came into the room.

Pa-Pa joined the audience, expressing my thoughts, "Mattie, you're beautiful, elegant, and all grown up. It just seems like yesterday when you would crawl up in my lap and I would tell you stories. Now, look at you."

"Mother, would you time my speech?"

Her speech was eight minutes long and wonderful. She spoke of the advantage of living in a small town where everyone looked after one another; where friendship lasted a lifetime; where people's first and middle names were used. She praised her teachers and said how fortunate she was to have me and her pa-pa in her life. She talked about dreams of the future for her class and how they could be attained with hard work and perseverance. Mattie was modest yet confident, and listening to her, it amazed me that I could bring something like her into the world.

When she finished, we all applauded, with Sam saying, "Mattie, that was great. You didn't even look at your notes."

"I'll be more nervous tonight with so many people. I'll be glad when it's over," she said.

"You can't imagine how proud of you we are, Mattie. One of these days when you have children and grandchildren it will be easier to understand," her pa-pa said.

I drove Mr. Quentin to town and Sam took Mattie in his pickup. If anything, Mattie's speech was better than her practice one. Of course, I cried and her pa-pa's eyes were moist also.

Chapter 27

Sam

I waited on Mattie while she talked with friends after graduation. She was surrounded by a number of people who I assume were praising her for the speech and her other honors. I stood off a good distance and couldn't hear what they were saying. Watching her, for the first time I realized how beautiful she was. After half an hour, she joined me, and we made our way to my pickup.

"You did really good tonight, Mattie. Your message was better than Keri's salutatorian speech. I noticed you didn't throw your cap up in the air at the end like everyone else did."

"I guess it dawned on me that it was over. I'll miss my classmates and most of my teachers. It's sad knowing that we'll go our separate ways and some of us might not see one another again. Mrs. Mac congratulated me and said I was one of her all-time favorites. She's so sweet and her class was one of my best experiences. She could fill the blackboard up with that left hand."

"Would you like to get something to eat? I know you were too nervous to eat before graduation. It seems like we should do something to celebrate. By the way, you're beautiful tonight."

Silence followed my comment, and I thought maybe she didn't hear me. I glanced over at her and she was crying. Maybe I said something wrong. "Are you all right?" I asked. She nodded but kept crying. She kept wiping her eyes as if trying to stop, but the tears continued.

Finally, she said, "I'm sorry. It's been an emotional night, and your comment was more than I could handle. I've never felt beautiful."

"Well, you are and you might as well get used to people saying it," I said.

"Could we see what's showing at the drive-in?" she asked. "We could get hot dogs and drinks there."

"Sure, that's a great idea."

The choice was a success. Watching *On the Waterfront* and eating our hot dogs, we couldn't have asked for a better conclusion to a special day. She hadn't wanted onions on her hot dog and I hadn't smoked a cigarette since leaving the ranch. I guess both of us knew what was going to happen, especially since we were at the drive-in. The first time we kissed, the film had broken and the screen went blank. I guess both of us figured it was now or never. It wasn't a long kiss just short and sweet. As the night wore on, they became longer and took our breath away. To tell the truth, we missed a great deal of an academy award winning movie. On the way home, she moved over and put her head on my shoulder. Sonia Toller was the furtherest thing from my mind.

The dust storm came in sometime Saturday night or early Sunday morning. When we got up it was dark and still that way when Mattie's mom and Hollis left to take her to the bus station at 11:00. I didn't go, knowing it was going to be emotional and hating goodbyes, anyway. I hugged her and attempted encouraging words, which later I thought, seemed trivial.

Alone, I started thinking again of my situation. The dust storm and darkness added to my depression. To date, I had eight healthy calves with only five of the heifers left to calve. At the last count, I had 64 lambs. Being optimistic, I should be able to count on that many more when the lambing ended. Still, in the fall, when I took the calves and lambs to the sale, there would be little money left after the feed bill was paid. I needed a bull now and also several rams. I had to decide whether to continue sending good money after bad or cut my losses and sell out. Added to my problems was a shortage of water. All my tanks were dry and one of my windmills was producing little more than a trickle. Everything depended on a rain, and today seemed to be sending a message that was clear...forget it.

I'd started paying Jose a monthly salary. It wasn't much, and he tried to refuse, but I insisted. He wasn't working for anyone else now and needed some income. Mr. Toller had been allowing me to work at least one day a week for him which helped a little. The other ranchers in the area were suffering with the drought, also, and couldn't afford to hire extra help. I kept trying to think of somewhere to work, at least part time. My skill was limited to working here on the ranch with horses, sheep, and cattle. I wasn't a bad student in school, but couldn't see myself sitting behind a desk, selling anything, or even working inside a building.

I needed to think of positive events in my life. I'd gained weight, tipping the scales in the feed store at 161 last week. I'd been going to church and now was able to mix with people without fear of them asking about the war. I was regaining my faith and had even been praying for rain. Then there was Mattie. The longer I knew her the more amazing she became. When she was up on the stage Friday night delivering her speech, I saw her in an altogether different manner. It's hard to describe, and it doesn't matter anyway. The fact was, I had never felt this way about anyone.

I'd been seeing Sonia every Saturday when I had supper with them. We'd spend several hours together, and her mom and dad made a point to see that we had time alone. She was aggressive and wanted a more serious relationship than I did. I dreaded her school being out because she would expect to see me more often. Now I was back to thinking of my problems.

My thoughts were interrupted when Hollis and Mrs. Quentin came in from taking Mattie to the bus station. "Did she get off all right?" I asked.

"I feel bad sending her on the bus, especially in this terrible dust storm. It'll be even worse where they're going," Mrs. Quentin said.

"This is the worst one we've had. I keep thinking the wind will stop and it'll clear up. We still used our headlights coming home and it's after 1:00 in the afternoon. This used to be the time of year we received a good rain," Hollis added.

"There weren't but five other people on the bus. I worry about the kind of characters she might run into," Mrs. Quentin continued.

"Gladys, Mattie can take care of herself. No use worrying," replied Hollis.

"The Yankees and Orioles are playing on television," I said, trying to lighten things up.

"Sounds good to me," said Hollis.

We spent the remainder of the afternoon watching baseball. The dust storm ended late in the evening, in time to have a blood red sunset.

The next day was bright and sunny, with no hint of the previous day's storm, except dust covering the furniture and inside of my pickup. I don't see how dust gets in, with everything shut up, but it does.

After breakfast, I drove to each of the windmills, and discovered the one that had been producing a small stream was not pumping any water. This was despite the fact that the windmill was turning and the sucker rod was moving up and down. I mumbled to myself, *well, it's gone dry*. The other two were still pumping a good stream but how long that would last was anybody's guess.

When I was growing up we always had plenty of water. In fact, two of the stock tanks had never been dry. Now the only water was coming from two windmills. It was evident; I couldn't keep the stock. No way could I afford to haul water. I would ask Mr. Toller about who could haul my sheep to San Angelo. I could take my heifers to the auction in Abilene to sell. It would take several trips with my stock trailer, but it would still be cheaper than hiring someone. I felt better since the decision was made.

When I returned to the house, Hollis was sitting on the back porch smoking one of his 'roll your owns'. I joined him, saying, "I'm selling out. One of my windmills isn't pumping any water this morning. I keep thinking what you said about sending good money after bad."

"Sam, I believe it's a wise decision. It'll rain sometimes, but when, is anybody's guess. If you sell out and cut your losses, it's always possible to start over when this drought is broken. It might happen tomorrow, but it could be several more years. If it were to be that long you'd be in debt so bad it'd take years to recover."

"Hollis, I dread y'all leaving. I've thought about it a great deal since Mrs. Quentin told me your plans."

"I'm not in any hurry either, but Gladys has made up her mind. It'll be a while before we're able to move. Repairs are going to be needed to the house and that will take time."

The next morning, Jose and I drove the heifers and the calves into the pens. I'd told him last night about my decision and he remained quiet. I know he hated to sell, but it was the best decision. I could haul six of the heifers at one time in my stock trailer. The sale was on Tuesday and Thursday each week. I decided to go ahead and take them today for tomorrow's sale. If I waited I might change my mind.

It was almost noon when I drove through the unloading dock at the sale, after waiting in line for an hour. The man tagged and unloaded them, while another drove them to a pen. I asked the man if they had many cattle coming in.

"Yeah. We're going to have a big run tomorrow. I'm guessing, 2000 head. The drought is causing many of the guys to give up and sell."

He stopped talking when an older man carrying a walking stick approached us. He was tall with a large mustache.

"Daryl, how're things going?" he asked.

"Good, Mr. McDaniel. They're coming in at a steady rate. Looks like a big run tomorrow."

Looking at me, he said, "Bob McDaniel, I own this place. You selling all your stock?"

"Yes, sir. Running out of anything for them to eat or drink. Now I have to find a job," I said.

"I might could help you. I'm short of alley help. One of my men was run over last week by a bull and can't work for several weeks. The pay is 75 cents an hour and lately the hours have been long."

"What time would I come to work?" I asked.

"Since you'll be in the alley, not until the sale starts. That would be 10:00."

"When would I start?"

"Tomorrow. Just report to Andy. He's in charge of the alley. Come by the office first and we'll get you signed up."

"I'll be here," I said.

Driving away, I couldn't believe it. I had a job with income. It wouldn't be much but any little bit would help. If I worked ten hours that would be $7.50.

I would bring another load of heifers today and bring the rest tomorrow when I came to work.

Chapter 28

Mattie

I took a seat on the bus about halfway to the back, trying to sit as far from anyone as possible. It was 11:00 in the morning and my arrival time in Plainview wasn't until 5:00 this afternoon. That meant several stops and some wait times.

The seats were comfortable compared to those on a school bus, and I thought a nap might be possible but that didn't work. My thoughts kept racing from tryouts, to Sam, and back again to tryouts. My nervousness kept interfering with my excitement. I was probably being dumb to think I had a chance of making a college basketball team, let alone the Flying Queens. They'd probably send me home the first day telling me to "get real." My next thought was of getting off at the first stop and catching a bus back home. What was wrong with me? That would disappoint everyone, especially Pa-Pa. Then I would always wonder, "*what if?*"

I switched over to Sam and smiled. Graduation night had been wonderful; not the ceremony, or my speech, nor the congratulations from everyone, but the drive-in. Sam had been special since the first time we met. I realized that, now. I kept trying to put my finger on what it was that made him that way. It certainly wasn't his looks, even though he was cute. Maybe it was the hurt he was suffering because of the war and the mystery surrounding it.

Didn't matter. I'd never felt this way about anyone. I just hoped he felt the same way.

Our first stop was at the Snyder Station, and the dust storm was even worse here. The driver informed us that we'd have a fifteen-minute break and to be back promptly. Exiting the bus, it was difficult to walk into the wind, and I could barely make out the bus station. It was noon and had been a long time since breakfast. I found a snack bar and bought a coke and candy bar before returning to my seat. When the other passengers started loading, I noticed a young Negro lady who had a child about two years old. She took the seat across from me. I smiled and told her the little boy was cute.

"Thank you. He's a handful. We're on our way to Amarillo to meet my husband. He's in the Air Force and is stationed there. Where are you going?"

"Plainview. I have a basketball tryout at the college," I explained.

"How exciting. I hope you make it," she encouraged.

The little boy was climbing all over the place. Fortunately, the seat behind them was vacant, and she was able to catch him when he tumbled over the top of theirs. She brought him back to their seats and was holding him in her lap when the bus driver returned. Looking in the mirror, he spoke in a gruff, stern voice.

"You need to move to the back."

Confused, I looked around, trying to see who he was talking to. Nobody moved and he spoke again, in a louder voice.

"You need to move to the back of the bus! You know, I'm talking to you, colored woman. Our rules say that coloreds sit at the back of the bus."

"I have a weak stomach, and the fumes or worse at the back. It makes me sick to my stomach to sit there. I'm sorry," she said.

"That's not my problem. We have rules, and I expect everyone on my bus to obey them. Now move, or I'll have you put off the bus."

I couldn't believe what I was hearing. In my sheltered world, I was aware that Negroes had separate water fountains and restrooms in department stores; however, I had no idea they were treated this way when traveling. Her husband was in the service and here she was being told to sit at the back of the bus. She rose, and carrying her little boy, moved to the back. I immediately followed her.

"I'm sorry. That man is terrible," I apologized.

"It's okay. I'm used to it," she replied.

"I'm Mattie."

"My name is Cabrina and this little monster is Jesse."

He was struggling to get out of his mother's lap and was finally successful. From there he started back up the aisle before she caught him. He wasn't ever still, not even for seconds. She reached in a bag, bringing out several toys, including a small truck and a train caboose. She put them down on the floor, and he commenced to play with them, making all kinds of noises.

We hadn't gone far until it was obvious about the fumes in the back. I could see how they could make anyone nauseated. We visited back and forth for half an hour, then she became quiet. I could tell by her expression that she was ill, and by this time, Jesse was tired of his toys and was trying to escape and explore the rest of the bus. This time, I caught him going up the aisle.

"Thank you. I'm sorry," she said, bending over and gagging.

I felt badly for her, asking, "Can I do anything to help?"

"Maybe," she said, reaching in a bag and bringing out a bottle of milk. "He should be weaned, but I keep this for emergencies."

When he saw the bottle, he began reaching for it, making a grunting noise resembling someone trying to pick up a weight that was heavy. I took the bottle, and it was no problem getting him in my lap. He lay back in my arms and latched onto that nipple and at that moment I made myself a promise. *I will never breast feed my baby.* He sucked that bottle dry in two minutes, with milk running out of the corners of his mouth. Looking at him lying in my arms, my heart melted. He was beautiful, with those big eyes, long lashes, smooth skin, and smell that all babies have.

"Do you know how to burp him?" Cabrina asked.

"I think so," I said, putting him up on my shoulder and patting his back. Immediately, a large burp erupted. I put him back down and his eyes were already shut.

"That's what he always does. I swear he just passes out from exhaustion after eating. He'll sleep now for at least an hour," Cabrina said.

I took a cloth she handed me and wiped the corners of his mouth. He was a beautiful little boy, and rather than put him down, I continued to hold him while he slept. We stopped at Post for fifteen minutes and were on our way again. His mother was leaning against the side of the bus with her eyes closed. I know she wasn't asleep but only trying to keep from throwing up. Thank goodness Jesse didn't wake up until we stopped in Lubbock at 3:00. My arm was numb and tingling from not moving it for so long, but I was determined to let him sleep as long as possible.

His big, brown eyes popped open when we stopped and he said, "Go."

"We're potty training him and that means he needs to go. Can you take him, please?" she asked.

Oh me. I was getting all kinds of experience. "Sure. I'll take him with me. I need to go, too," I replied.

The bus station was large, and as we made our way through the crowd, Jesse, kept wanting to get down. Finally, I gave him his wish and was amazed at how well he walked. We found the restrooms, and entering, it was crowded. While waiting for a stall, a woman asked me, "Is that little nigger yours?" I didn't respond, refusing to meet her gaze.

A stall came open and we went in, closed the door, and started our business. I didn't know where to begin. I pulled down his pants and lifted him up to sit on the pot, but he objected saying, "No." I gathered that he wanted to stand up so that's what we did. I tried to lift him up to hit the potty but that was futile. When he started, it went everywhere, except in the commode. On the floor, on the walls. He soaked it all. It was like he had been saving for just an occasion. All the time he was giggling, like this was so much fun. He finished, finally, and I pulled up his pants and we went to another stall. I felt guilty, not cleaning this one up, but hey, I can only do so much. I had to go. All was fine until I finished and turned around to flush the commode. I heard a scream in the adjoining stall.

"What's this little darkie doing in here?" she screamed.

Jesse had crawled under the petition into another stall that was occupied.

"Jesse, you get out here, now!" I said.

He crawled out under the door, looking innocent.

The lady came out of the stall saying, "You need to keep that little Nigger out of the women's bathroom. Is he yours?"

"Yes, he is," I answered.

"That's disgusting. What's this world coming to?"

I didn't respond, picking up Jesse and hurriedly moving out the door. On the way to the bus, I noticed a man with a badge, gun, and big western hat. He was not talking to anyone, only sipping a cup of coffee. I approached him thinking, *it's worth a try.*

"Excuse me, sir. Could I talk to you?"

"Sure, young lady. What's on your mind?" he asked, smiling.

I started from the beginning, when Cabrina and her baby got on the bus, and told him the entire story. He listened intently, never interrupting me. My final statement was a request that maybe he could help with the situation.

"Which bus are you speaking of?" he asked.

"The one over there, going to Amarillo," I said, pointing out the bus.

"You're very kind, young lady. Thank you for the information," he said, turning and walking off in the opposite direction from the bus.

Well, anyway, I tried. I guess the bus rules have to be enforced. When I was back on the bus, Cabrina was still in her seat.

"Would you like to go to the bathroom?" I asked.

"No. I'm afraid to get up. My stomach is turning flips. How was Jesse in the bathroom?"

"We made it. He missed the potty. I'm surprised he hadn't gone in his pants he did so much."

"I'm sorry. I should've warned you. He won't sit down. He's seen his daddy go and he wants to stand up. His aim is not good. I suspect he doesn't even try."

I couldn't suppress the laugh as I replied, "It was like a hose with high pressure that was dropped on the ground and water going everywhere."

Passengers were filing back on the bus, which was about half full by now. The bus driver entered and sat down, closing the door, saying, "Everyone better be accounted for, we're leaving. I have a schedule to keep."

The bus had been left running, but before he could shift into gear there was a knock on the door. He swung the door open and the sheriff I'd talked with, climbed into the bus. He looked over the passengers until his eyes rested on us. He moved down the aisle to where we were sitting.

He addressed Cabrina. "Ma'am, I'm Sheriff Webster. I understand you have a weak stomach and can't tolerate the fumes given off by the engine."

"Yes, sir. I'm sorry," she answered.

"Let's move you more toward the front of the bus. Maybe that'll help. This young lady told me about your plight. She must be a good friend."

He motioned for her to get up and follow him. There were two vacant seats three rows back of the driver and that's where he led us. There was a vacant seat across from where he sat them, and I settled there. We thanked him as he left. The driver stood up, stopping him in the aisle with a book in his hand and a page opened.

"Our bus rules say clearly that coloreds are to sit at the back of the bus. It's right here," he said holding up the book inches from the sheriff's face.

The sheriff spoke softly, but it was so quiet he could be heard throughout the bus. "Sir, I don't give a tinker's damn what your rule book says. Your bus is sitting in Lubbock County which is my territory. Now, this soldier's wife can sit anywhere she pleases on this bus. If you have any ideas about changing her seating arrangement, I have a good friend who's sheriff in Hale County which you will enter next. He'll greet you in Plainview and see to it that this seating arrangement is in tact. Also, the sheriff of Potter County will meet you in Amarillo and do the same. Is that clear?"

The bus driver turned, without speaking, and sat back down in his seat, to the loud applause of the passengers, including myself.

The remainder of the trip I played with Jesse. First paddy cake and then peek-a-boo. I let him ride the horse on my leg until exhausted. When we arrived at the bus station in Plainview, I gave him back to his mother. She thanked me over and over, asking for my address so we could stay in touch. I asked Jesse for a hug before leaving. Bending down to allow him to reach me, he kissed me squarely on the mouth. Exiting the bus, my eyes were wet.

It was not a problem getting to the college. I'd met a lady from Plainview on the bus whose husband was picking her up. She offered to give me a ride which I gladly accepted.

The campus was smaller than I expected. I asked a student for directions to the athletic office, and she pointed to a building not far from where we were standing. I found a custodian who directed me to an office. Standing in the open doorway, I introduced myself and told the man sitting behind the desk my purpose for being here.

"Welcome, Mattie, to Wayland Baptist College. How was your trip?"

"It was fine. I came on the bus."

"Let's get you settled. I'll show you to the dorm where you'll be staying for the next several days. I also have a meal ticket for you. The cafeteria isn't open since it's Sunday, but breakfast will be served in the morning beginning at 6:30. Workouts will start at 8:00. We'll break for lunch at 12:00, come back at 1:00, and finish about 6:00 tomorrow evening."

At the dorm, I was directed to a room by an elderly lady, who I assume was the dorm supervisor. It was small, with two beds, and no bathroom. She told me the bathroom was down the hall and used by all the girls on the floor. I thanked her, and after she left, I sat down on the edge of one of the beds thinking of my day. *I'd gotten my first taste of the 'real world' today. I had witnessed evil and hate along with goodness and love. I was astonished at how Negroes were treated. What would Sam have thought about a soldier's wife being told to go to the back of the bus? And then the sheriff who I thought had ignored me, doing everything to assure that Cabrina and Jesse were treated decently. There were good people and bad in the world. I had witnessed it first hand today.*

I was at the gym fifteen minutes early the next morning and would have been there sooner if it had not been for an incident on the way. I was stopped by a man whom I assume was a teacher and told that shorts were not acceptable on campus. I had to go back to the dorm and put a skirt on over the shorts.

Several girls were already sitting in the bleachers, and all of them had on some sort of clothing to cover their workout attire. The coach came in shortly after and asked the girls to all come down to the gym floor.

"Ladies, welcome to our campus. Please make yourselves at home. As you were told, we have three scholarships available. During the next two days you'll be given ample opportunity to demonstrate how you can add quality to this team. I would request that you not view it as competition but rather a determination to do your best. I assure you that being here on this campus, trying out for the Flying Queens, is an honor within itself. Now, your dressing room is through that door," he said, pointing to a corner of the gym. "You will find lockers where you can leave your clothes. Showers are available for those of you who wish to use them. I'll see you on the court in ten minutes."

Most of us were back in five minutes. I counted 18 as we gathered around the coach and he announced that we would have a prayer before we began. He commenced to pray, and I have no doubt that it lasted at least ten minutes.

"Ladies, we're going to go through some fundamentals that will allow you to demonstrate your abilities."

We formed two lines and began going in for layups. I missed my first one. How could that happen? I never missed layups. *Calm down*, I said to myself. I didn't heed my own advice and matters became worse. We formed a circle and attempted ten foot shots. I hit two out of ten and was almost in tears.

The girls were all shapes and sizes, but they had one thing in common…they were outstanding athletes. After the first two drills, I wanted to go hide out somewhere until it was over and go home. The third drill consisted of passing the ball back and forth. I didn't see how it would be possible to mess up on this; however, I dropped several passes. We took a break after this drill and Coach led us in prayer before starting again. I don't know what kind of coach he was but that man could pray. I found out later he was a Baptist minister.

By noon, when we broke for lunch, I was ready to quit. I'd been terrible at everything. Looking in the stands, most of the girls had parents or relatives present who were offering them congratulations as they left for lunch. I went to the dressing room, put on my skirt, and headed to the cafeteria. It was a beautiful day after the dust storm. I wasn't hungry but knew that I needed to eat.

Sitting down at a table by myself, I thought of my morning and what could be wrong that caused me to perform so poorly. Was it nerves and trying too hard? Probably, I thought. Looking at a big clock on the wall, I took my pulse, which was 90. Unbelievable! It was usually between 50 and 60 because I was in such good physical condition. *Relax*, I said to myself. *Why are you nervous? You're not going to make the team anyway. You've already blown it! What've you got to lose? Be yourself and stop trying so hard!*

I took several deep breaths and ate my salad. I'd noticed they had chocolate cake for dessert, and returning to the line, scooped up the largest piece available.

Chapter 29

Gladys

I slept little Monday night, worrying about Mattie. I kept thinking we should have been there to support her. Finally, at 4:30, I went to the kitchen and made coffee. Sitting at the table, drinking a cup, Mr. Quentin came in, asking why I was up so early.

"Couldn't sleep. I kept thinking we should have gone with Mattie."

"We do what we can. It wasn't possible for us to be in Plainview. Mattie will do fine. She's a fighter. Now, stop worrying, and let's talk about something more pleasant."

"Leon, has agreed to a divorce after threatening to take him to court and telling him that you and Mattie would testify. I guess that's positive. It should be final in the near future. I just hope and pray that he leaves me and Mattie alone."

"That is positive, Gladys. You need to put that part of your life behind you and move on. I'm ashamed of Leon for what he's become. I'd like to change him but know that's not likely to happen. You're still a young, attractive woman and you need to get on with your life."

"You're doing well, aren't you?" I asked.

"Better than that. My recovery has been something of a miracle. After the stroke, I would've never thought it possible to be where I am today. I can walk, dress, and care for myself.

If placed in a nursing home, I'd have probably withered up and died. You and Mattie cared for me, and I'll always be grateful."

"I guess that's enough positive for now. It's 7:00 and time to get ready for work."

"One more thing, Gladys. What do you think about getting a phone put in? I know we plan on moving to our own place, but it would be here for Sam. We need to do something for him."

"That's a great idea. I'll start on it today."

Standing in front of the mirror, putting on my makeup, I noticed the bags under my eyes were gone. My skin looked healthier, and the rinse on my hair gave me a look more like my age. I walked taller, having more self-assurance, and felt good about myself for the first time in thirty years. Mr. Quentin was right. I did need to move on and not dwell on the past. I heard voices and realized that Sam was up. I finished getting ready and returned to the kitchen. He had already started breakfast with the bacon sizzling.

"Morning, Mrs. Quentin. How about something to eat? I thought a good breakfast would help me through my first day at the auction. We'll have a big run today and that means working a lot of hours."

"Don't have time. I'm running late, after getting up early. Thank you anyway and I hope you like your new job."

On the drive in to work, I ate the bacon sandwich that Sam had made for me. I was going to need to watch my weight. My appetite had improved, with everything else, and it was obvious by the way my clothes fit that I'd gained.

When I drove into the parking lot behind the store, an unwelcomed sight greeted me. Leon was sitting in his car, occupying my space. I parked and took a deep breath, telling myself to *be strong*. He exited his car and put himself between me and the entrance.

"I need to talk with you, Gladys. Please."

"We have nothing to discuss," I replied, attempting to walk around him. He moved over to block me.

"Please… Gladys. Just listen to me. I'm sorry. I'll do better. Give me another chance."

"Leon, you've had enough chances. I don't want anything to do with you and neither does Mattie. Now, move. You're going to cause me to be late for work."

"Please, Gladys. I've lost everything. I promise to change. I'm begging you to give me one more chance."

"No. You've had too many chances, and I'm not letting you come back. We're through, once and for all. The divorce will be final in a few weeks. Please, get out of my way." He moved over, and I went into the store.

I halfway expected him to follow but he didn't. Looking out the window in the door, he was getting back into his car. I breathed a sigh of relief and thought, maybe that's the end of it.

The day drug by, as I had expected. Earnest, my friend from the laundry did come in. He stopped by often and was in better spirits than when I would see him at the laundry. He generally made an effort to come through my counter and visit for a few minutes. Today was no exception.

"Gladys, you're looking good this morning. You've changed since the laundry. You look younger and even prettier," he said.

"Why thank you, Earnest. That's a nice thing to say."

"It's easy for me to tell the truth. Are you and Leon still apart?"

"Yes. The divorce will be final in a few weeks."

"Do you think we might spend some time together, after the divorce?" he asked.

Blushing like a teenager, I replied, "I don't see why not."

"Good. I look forward to it."

As Earnest left, a voice inside my head spoke. *You're not wasting any time getting on with your life.*

During my lunch break, I went to the telephone company and made arrangements to have a phone put in at Sam's. The person I spoke with was familiar with the location, telling me it would take at least a week to complete the job.

I still had time to go by the drug store and eat a sandwich. Mr. Quentin insisted on buying his medicine here, commenting that Dave, the pharmacist and owner, was the next thing to a doctor. On more than one occasion, when he had run out of medicine and Dr. Sadler was out of town, Dave had given him enough to hold him over until a new prescription could be written. Small town folks took care of one another. That's what I loved about living here.

When I returned to work, we had few customers, and being a slow day, I began stocking some shelves. We had two checkers and that left one available. It gave me time to think about Leon and what he'd said. Surely he didn't expect me to believe him after the way he'd treated me. I wasn't about to go back to that life. Mattie would agree with me, and Mr. Quentin would understand. I felt good about standing my ground which I know surprised Leon.

That evening after supper and the dishes were done, I settled down in front of the television to watch two of my favorite shows, "I Married Joan" and "My Little Margie" Mr. Quentin didn't share my enthusiasm for the selection and went outside to sit on the porch and smoke.

I had trouble concentrating on the show, with my mind wondering to Mattie. I hoped she did well in the tryouts and was pleased with her performance. After all, that's the most she could do since the final decision would be in someone else's hands. It was important to her. Maybe the most important event of her life. She should be home by the time I got off work tomorrow.

I stayed up as late as possible but still didn't sleep well. I gave up at 6:00, getting dressed and going to the kitchen to make coffee. Sam still wasn't home, and I was worried about what happened to him.

Sitting at the table drinking a cup of coffee, Mr. Quentin came in and joined me.

"I'm worried about Sam. He should've been home hours ago," I said.

"No need to be concerned, Gladys. With the drought, they probably had a large run of cattle. I've spent a good many hours at the sale and generally they can run between 75 and 100 through the ring an hour. It wouldn't surprise me to learn they had 1500-2000 head. This drought is causing everyone to reduce their herd or sell out."

"Sam's not back to full strength, though. I can't imagine him having to work all night."

I couldn't see our driveway from the kitchen, but lights suddenly reflected inside the house, meaning a car had driven up. That would be Sam. Then I stiffened, thinking it might be Leon. Within a minute someone knocked at the door. After the second round of knocks, I went to the door and opened it, seeing the sheriff and a deputy.

"Mrs. Quentin, we need to talk with you," said the sheriff.

"Come in, please. What's wrong?" I asked. *Please, God, don't let it be Mattie,* I prayed.

"Please sit down," I said, motioning toward the couch. Mr. Quentin had joined us.

"I'm afraid we have some bad news for you. Your husband, Leon, was found dead at his house about an hour ago," he said.

"W-what h-app-ened?" I mumbled.

The sheriff looked at the deputy before he spoke, like he was seeking help. "It appears that he took his own life."

"Oh, my God, no!" I cried.

This time the deputy spoke. "Leon committed suicide tonight. He put a garden hose in the muffler of his car and run it through a window. A neighbor called authorities when she discovered what had happened."

A half hour hour later, the sheriff and deputy were gone, and we were sitting at the kitchen table. Sam had gotten home from working all night at the auction sale. Mr. Quentin had taken the news better than I expected.

"Do we need to try and contact Mattie?" I asked.

"What do you think, Sam?" asked Mr. Quentin.

"Nothing would be accomplished. It'd be better for her to hear the news directly from us and not by phone. After all, she'll be home today."

"I agree," said Mr. Quentin. "Could you meet her at the bus station? I hate to ask you, but she'll take the news better from you."

"Sure. I can do that."

"Why would he do this? I'd never have guessed that he'd take his own life. Something must've happened to cause him to do such a thing," said Mr. Quentin.

I remained silent, my heart pounding, thinking, "*How can I ever live with this?*"

Chapter 30

Mattie

The beginning of the Monday afternoon workout consisted of shooting free shots. I assume the coach thought we needed something less strenuous after lunch. We shot until we made one and then we shot until we missed. While in line waiting my turn, the smallest girl on the floor started up a conversation.

"Are you staying in the dorm?" she asked.

"Yes. I came in yesterday."

"My parents brought me this morning. We live in Spearman which is not that far. I'm going to stay tonight. My name's Charley. I know it's a boy's name, but my daddy wasn't expecting a girl and already had a name picked out."

"I'm Mattie."

"Mattie, I understand we're going to play some two-on-two this afternoon. Would you be my partner?"

"Sure. The way I've been playing though, you could find someone better," I answered.

"I haven't been doing so great myself," she said.

When it came my time to shoot, I took a deep breath, and commenced to make 15 free throws in succession. Me and one other girl finished tied with most in a row. I felt better. At least I could do something.

We did half a dozen more drills, involving ball handling, dribbling, passing, and shooting. I wasn't great but was much better than this morning. Then, like Charley had predicted, the coach called us together and told us to choose a partner. We were going to play half court two on two. It so happened that two more had showed up this afternoon and we had an even number of 20. He explained that the team that reached ten first would win and advance to the next round. I was feeling good about this drill; however, it was obvious from the start that this was going to be an out-for-blood event. Watching the first group, there was pushing, shoving, bumping, and elbowing, with the coach ignoring most of the fouls.

When it came time for us, our opponents were two girls about the same height as me, only heavier. They took the ball first and missed a shot from the corner. I blocked out, ready for the rebound, when I found myself on the floor. One of the girls had moved into me and knocked me down. She got the rebound and put it back in. We took the ball at mid-court and moved it down toward the goal. I faked a pass and went in for a layup which was good. They missed their shot and this time I was ready when I blocked out. The girl moved into me again, but this time I moved toward her also, causing contact which jolted us both. I snatched the rebound and moved back to mid-court. They anticipated that I would drive for the basket and left Charley open in the corner. I passed to her and she shot, moving the ball from her hip, giving her the force necessary to reach the basket. The shot was perfect, hitting nothing but net.

We followed the same pattern in the next two games after winning the first. I would drive to the basket or shoot a short jump shot. One girl couldn't guard me. The one-on-one practice sessions with Jimmy had prepared me. After they became frustrated and the other came to help, I would pass off to Charley who was a deadly shot. I hadn't understood how someone so small could be invited to the tryout. Now, it was obvious.

The final game involved a tall girl who was at least six feet and a chunk who was about my height but weighed at least 200. They had been watching us and had a plan. The first time we had the ball, my guard, the tall one, gave me an opening for a layup. I went in and the chunk hit me in mid-air, knocking me clear up against the wall. I saw stars for a few seconds and then the gym was spinning. There were three Charleys as she bent down over me.

"Mattie, are you all right?"

"I don't think so," I mumbled.

I heard the coach announce we would have a ten-minute break. I saw Chunk standing over me. Only one of her was visible…three wouldn't fit.

"That's what's going to happen on a layup. You're too pretty to play basketball. You need to go home and get married," she gloated.

She addressed Charley next. "Squirt, you better watch out or you'll get mashed into the floor."

"Could I ask you a question?" Charley whispered in a soft, polite voice.

"Suit yourself, Squirt."

"Was your mother really a cow?"

Oh, no. Charley was going to get smashed," I figured.

Instead, Chunk turned and stomped away, cursing loud enough for us to hear but not coach.

Can you get up, Mattie?" Charley asked, offering a hand up.

"Maybe." When I was standing, the room was still spinning. Coach came over and asked me if I wanted to continue.

"I can't, now. Could we wait a while?" I asked.

"Tell you what. We'll finish in the morning. It's nearly time to quit anyway."

"Thank you," I replied.

Charley and I went directly to the cafeteria. Of course, we had put a skirt on over our shorts, and she had her overnight bag with a change of clothes. I had invited her to be my roommate.

"Are you hungry?" I asked.

"Always."

We went through the line, filled our trays, and found a table that wasn't occupied. The fare was meatloaf, I thought, until it required a knife to cut it up. The cream potatoes were okay, and the green beans were just green beans.

"Mattie, have you noticed how stuffy everyone around here looks? I haven't seen anyone smile yet. Everyone has this serious look like they expect something bad to happen."

"Now that you mention it... yes," I replied.

"How're you feeling? Are you still dizzy?"

"Better. I'm not seeing double, and my head's clear. I do have a slight headache, though. Do you think we have a chance in the morning?"

"David slew Goliath, didn't he?"

"Charley, why do you think the coach let it become that rough?"

"My guess is he wanted to see how tough we are. I've heard stories about these college games and they let the girls get by with a lot of rough-housing."

We finished eating and went to the dorm, where for the next two hours we talked about boys, basketball, and our families, in that order. Before turning out the lights, we planned our strategy for the two-on-two the next day.

After warmups the next morning, the first event was the finals of the two on two. We got the ball first, and when I dribbled down the court, the tall one moved out of the way when I came within eight feet of the basket. She was expecting me to drive for the layup, where the 'cow' as we had renamed her, would demolish me; however, I stopped and made a jump shot, unguarded. The next time I drove for the layup making it easily. They became frustrated, double teaming me which freed up Charley, who was amazing from outside. To sum it up, we won 10-2 and received applause from the remainder of the group.

We went through the same drills as the day before and I did better, especially with my shooting. At the end of the day, Coach informed us that we were going to do a couple of the most important drills. The first was a speed drill. We would put one foot on the wall, run to the other end of the gym, touch the wall and return. We divided up into 4 teams of 5 each. The winner of each team would compete in the finals. Thank goodness, Charley and I were on different teams and both of us won our races. I didn't win the finals, but Charley did, and I finished third, which pleased me.

The next drill was to determine our vertical leap. We would run to the basket, jump and see how high we could reach. I felt sorry for Charley, knowing this was going to be difficult for her; however, this was one of my strengths. Most of the girls could touch the net. Several were even able to touch the back board. I was one of the last to go, and running full speed toward the basket, I jumped with all my strength and reached the rim, hanging from it. There was a gasp from the other girls as I swung for a few seconds and let go, dropping to the floor.

Charley came over to me when I returned to the line, saying, "Mattie, that was awesome. How can you jump that high?"

Laughing, I replied, "I don't have anything to hold me down. I'm skinny and this is what you can do when you're made like a boy."

"Oh, Mattie. You're so pretty that doesn't matter."

Charley's parents were there for her when the tryouts ended. We exchanged addresses and promised to stay in touch, whether we made the team or not.

I ate supper in the cafeteria, returned to the dorm, and packed my meager belongings for my return trip home in the morning. I went to bed early, wondering if I had a chance.

Chapter 31

Sam

I was exhausted after working all night, but no way could I sleep after hearing the news of Mattie's dad. As we talked of the event, I was amazed at the calmness of Hollis and somewhat confused at Mrs. Quentin's reaction. Rather than grief, it reflected something closer to panic and desperation. Now, I had to meet Mattie this afternoon at the bus station and give her the news of her dad. The fact that he took his own life added to the difficulty of telling her of the tragedy. I had no idea how she would react, due to the harsh feelings she had toward him.

I was going to accompany Hollis and Mrs. Quentin to Starbucks where they would make funeral arrangements. They were trying to decide whether to have the funeral at the church or just graveside rites. I remained silent, not wanting to give any advice.

Another problem was what to do about going to work tomorrow. I hated to miss my second day, but the right thing to do would be to stay with Mattie. My first day at work had been a marathon. I took a few minutes and reflected on the previous day.

I had found Andy Tuesday morning in plenty of time for him to show me my job. The alley was about ten feet wide and probably seventy-five yards long, with pens on each side. Each pen had a gate with a number on it. I was responsible for six pens, three on each side. After a cow sold, a number would be called over a speaker, and the alley worker responsible for that pen would open the gate which covered the alley. They had nowhere to go except in the pen. My six pens were located about mid-way down the alley. It was the responsibility of the men stationed along the alley to keep the stock moving until they reached the correct pen. I was given a round stick about six feet long to encourage the stock to move by me.

The sale started at promptly 10:00. It wasn't an exciting job, but occasionally the man calling out numbers on the speaker would announce to be aware that a bad one, usually a bull, was coming. I learned to take that warning seriously. I wasn't relieved until 4:00 that afternoon, and the only thing I wanted more than something to eat was to find a bathroom. The floors inside were wooden, with spittoons placed at strategic locations. The air was thick with smoke from cigarettes and cigars. After the bathroom, I found the café. I was starved and looking at the menu, ordered a hot steak sandwich which cost 50 cents. That was forty minutes' work. Thursday, I would bring my lunch and a water jug to take to my work spot. The meal consisted of fried steak and gravy on toast with fried potatoes.

Thirty minutes later, I was back at my work place. I wasn't relieved again until 10:00 that night. I visited the bathroom again and only ordered coffee in the café, hoping to rest and regain some energy. I wasn't back to full strength from being sick, not realizing it because I'd not pushed myself.

It was after 4:00 in the morning before the last head came down the alley. I'd worked for eighteen hours and was exhausted. I made it to my pickup, lay down in the seat, and slept for two hours. Waking up, I decided to see if the office was open and get my check for the cattle I sold. Fifteen minutes later I walked back to my pickup with a check for $1,637. I had hoped for more, but at least I could pay my bill at the feed store and have some left over to pay on the note.

Now the adrenaline had taken over and my energy was returning. It was going to be a tough day. For the past three years it seemed that death had been a constant companion.

I took my own pickup into town instead of riding with Mrs. Quentin and Hollis. We were at the funeral home at about 11:00. Since Mattie was due in at 2:00, I would stay and wait for her. I waited in the office while they picked out a casket. Returning, we sat down, and I listened as they told Mr. Starbuck they had decided on a graveside service that would be held on Friday morning at 10:00.

"Could you tell us what the cost will be for everything?" asked Hollis.

After several minutes of calculations on a sheet of paper, Fred handed the bill to him. I could tell by the look on his face that it was bad. "I can't pay all of this. Right now, $865 is a lot of money. Could we pay it out over a year?" he asked.

Before he received an answer, I said, "I'll take care of it, and you can repay me later." I had the money from my stock and still had time left to pay off my note.

A look of relief came over Hollis. "Thank you, Sam. It seems we're always thanking you."

"We'll pay you back," said Mrs. Quentin.

After writing a check for the funeral expenses, I left, still having two hours to kill before Mattie was to arrive. Mrs. Quentin and Hollis were attempting to get in touch with a preacher to do the service, using the phone at the funeral home. They were also discussing who would sit up at night with Leon. It was a tradition, in small towns to have two people sit with the deceased during the night. Usually the shifts were three hours or four hours, with friends volunteering. I decided to walk around to Woozy's and eat lunch. The café was nearly full, but I found a vacant table toward the back and ordered a hamburger, fries, and tea. The waitress had just left and a commotion toward the front door caught my attention. A man with his western hat on crooked staggered through the door, weaving from side to side, knocking over several chairs. Even with the tragic day, I had to smile. Hollis had told me about his friend, CK Russell, who would pull this antic ever so often, especially with strangers in town. The entire crowd stopped eating and it was evident who didn't know what was going on. Whenever he reached the counter and sat down, straightening his hat, laughter erupted. He'd obtained the reaction he wanted, and it was obvious that he was a hometown favorite. CK was short, maybe 5'2", and had on low-top boots with his breeches tucked in.

The hamburger and fries were good. While I was eating, several people came by, saying they were sorry to hear about Leon. Of course, in a small town, word travels fast, and by nightfall everyone would have heard the news. I paid my ticket and walked back to my pickup. I still had over an hour to wait, which gave me time to stop at the feed store and have them figure my bill. I wasn't surprised to find that my bill was over $400. Again, I realized selling out was the best move. I had enough money in my bank account to settle up. The owner assured me it wasn't necessary but I insisted. Leaving, I felt like a big load had been lifted from me.

I parked on the right-of-way across from the bus station. The traffic was heavy on Highway 80 going through town. At 2:00 the bus hadn't shown up, and after another thirty minutes, it still hadn't arrived. I'd been going over what I would say to Mattie and was ready to get it over with. Finally, at 3:05, the bus came to a stop in front of the station. I got out of my pickup, knowing she would see me. She crossed the highway carrying her one bag, and I had the door open for her.

"Sam Colter, aren't you even going to hug me?"

"I responded, holding her longer than she expected."

"What's wrong?" she asked.

"Get in and we'll talk about it," I instructed.

"There's bad news, Mattie, concerning your daddy."

"He hurt my mother, didn't he?" she interrupted.

"No, just let me talk. Your daddy is dead. He took his own life last night. We found out this morning and decided to wait and tell you in person today. I'm sorry."

"W-wh-y w-ould he do that?" she asked, beginning to cry.

"We don't know. They didn't find a note."

"Where are M-other and Pa-Pa?"

"I left them at the funeral home making arrangements, but they're probably at home by now. Your pa-pa is taking it better than I would have expected. I can't tell about your mother. I'm sure they both need you."

"Let's go h-ome."

She was silent on the drive to the ranch but continued to cry softly. I didn't know what else to say. Arriving at the ranch, she went inside, but I walked down to the barn, where Jose was working.

"Bad day, Little Bit."

"Yeah. I'd like to be able to do more. I don't know what to say."

"You here, Little Bit. Need your strength. That enough for now."

"I can't decide whether to go to work tomorrow or stay around here."

"Ask them. Do what they want, Little Bit."

"Thank you, Jose. That's good advice."

When I entered the house half an hour later, everyone was sitting at the kitchen table. That always seemed to be the gathering point for serious discussion. They asked me to join them and then told me about the plans for the service. I remained silent until they finished and then asked if there was anything I could do.

"Could we go for a ride?" Mattie asked.

"Sure. I'll saddle the horses." It was already 4:00 but that would still give us several hours of daylight.

I had the horses saddled and was waiting when she walked up in her jeans and boots. The sun was warm and she was wearing a cap and had on sunglasses. She looked good...better than good.

"I'm ready," she said.

"Is there anywhere in particular you would like to ride?"

"No. Just a long way," she replied.

It was two miles later before she started talking. "Why did he do it, Sam?" I would've never thought of him taking his own life."

"Don't know. I guess we'll never find out. I can't imagine anyone doing it. I spent two years doing everything to stay alive."

"I told Mom I hated him. That was wrong. I didn't hate him but hated how he treated us. Now I regret being that angry, and it's too late to correct it. When I was little, maybe four or five, he was nice to me. It was in the later years that he became mean. I know the drinking played a part in it."

"Try to remember the good times, Mattie, even though they occurred a long time ago. Forget the recent memories if you can."

"Something's wrong with my mother. She's not acting right. I can't put my finger on it. Do you know what I mean?"

"Yeah. Maybe she'll eventually tell you what it is."

"Let's stop awhile," she suggested.

We were at the bottom of a hill. We tied our horses and walked about halfway up to a large flat rock to sit down. From there we had a good view to the east, west and south.

"Look, you can see Castle Peak from here," I said.

"Have you ever climbed it?" she asked.

"Many times but not for years. Have you?"

"No. Could we do it together sometimes?" she asked.

"Sure. No problem. Now, do you feel like telling me about the tryouts?" I quizzed.

The mood became lighter as she told me about the first half day and how terrible she was. For the next half hour, she went into detail about the drills and two-on-two. She ended with the speed and vertical jump drill.

"When will you find out something?"

"They said it would be at least a week and maybe two. I left feeling pretty confident, but the closer to home I became that evaporated into doubt. Now the doubt has developed into the certainty that I don't have a chance."

"It sounds to me like you did good. I predict that you're going to make it."

"I have trouble imagining anything that exciting happening to me," she replied.

"Changing the subject, Mattie, but I can't decide about working tomorrow. Do you want me to stay with you?"

"We talked about it, Sam. Pa-Pa and Mother both thought you should go to work. I agree with them. This job is important. You'll be here Friday for the service."

She continued, "I thought all the way home about what you'd do when you saw me. It seemed like I'd been gone longer than three days. I imagined that you might grab me and kiss me. When you didn't I was disappointed. Of course, I understood why when you told me about my dad."

I immediately reached out, pushed her down on the rock, and tried to make up for her earlier disappointment.

Chapter 32

Gladys

I was miserable. That was not a strong enough description. There wasn't a word to describe my feelings with guilt occupying my thoughts 90 percent of the time. I couldn't concentrate on anything without being interrupted by a voice saying, *you caused it.* I couldn't eat. I couldn't sleep. Two weeks after Leon was buried, I admitted that recovery and acceptance of what'd happened was going to require help. I considered Louise but knew that she'd just try to make me feel good and insist that it wasn't my fault. After much consideration, I decided on the pastor of the Methodist Church we'd been attending. I called the pastor with our newly installed telephone before I left for work on Monday, June 7, and he agreed to see me that day.

Arriving at the church, Pastor Frank greeted me at the door. It was a warm day, but the sanctuary was cool. It was late afternoon, and the building was darker than usual, which added to my comfort. We sat down in one of the front pews.

"Pastor, I have a problem that I need to discuss with someone. I appreciate you seeing me on such short notice."

"No problem, Gladys. Maybe I can help. Many times it helps to talk about it."

I started from the time Mattie and I left to live with Mr. Quentin and told him what occurred up until Leon's death. I told him about my conversation with Leon on the day he took his life. I described it word for word. He listened without interrupting, not speaking until I finished.

"My words seem so little to address the guilt you must feel. The Scripture that comes to mind right off is, John 1:9; '**If we confess our sins, he is faithful and just to forgive us our sins and to cleanse us from all unrighteousness.**'

"I'm not going to try and help you justify what you did. I don't believe that will ever be possible. It's obvious that you're blaming yourself for Leon's death and regretting the things you said to him. I expect that's something you will live with the rest of your life; however, if He forgives you and He is the ultimate judge, what right do you have to continue to punish yourself? I'm not going to preach you a sermon either. I would expect you to have more patience and compassion for others after this experience. I expect your faith to become stronger as you work through this and trust Him for forgiveness."

"B-but...but, I can't stop thinking about it. Mattie keeps asking me what's wrong and I keep saying, 'nothing.' If I'd just let him come back, he'd be alive today. I can't get it out of my mind."

"Have you considered telling Mattie?" he asked.

"No. I'm afraid of what she would think."

"I would suggest that you tell her, Gladys. She knows something is wrong and probably worries about you. I believe it would help both of you to talk about it. I wish it were possible for me to give you peace of mind. I would suggest that you memorize and recite the Scripture that I shared with you every time you start feeling guilty. Also, please remember we all make mistakes that result in sin. Jesus is the only One who has walked the earth that has been perfect. Many of the great men and women of the Bible had terrible sins and were forgiven, going on to become people we admire. You're a good person, Gladys, and God loves you. Please remember that."

We visited a while longer before I thanked him and left. I didn't feel much different, but I was going to think about what he said. Also, I was going to talk with Mattie about what had happened the day her daddy died.

When I returned home, Mattie was in one of her moods, which had become all to frequent lately. She had been going to the mailbox daily, looking for a letter from Wayland. It had been over two weeks. No letter had come today either and she met me at the door and started in, "I don't know why I expected to hear anything from them! They probably knew from the first day; I wasn't good enough. I'm not going to the mailbox tomorrow!" She continued for several more minutes, before announcing, "I'm going to town with you tomorrow and find me a job and quit this stupid dreaming."

After the blowup, she went to her room, slamming the door. I knew this wasn't the time to tell her about Leon and what I had said to him, leading to his death. Maybe later on tonight she would get over her disappointment at not hearing from Wayland.

My thoughts turned to Sam. He was working Tuesdays and Thursdays at the auction and was happier after making the decision to sell out. Of course, he couldn't pay off his note, since he had loaned us the money for the funeral expenses. I hated to accept his offer, but we had no choice. He insisted it wasn't a problem because the note didn't come due for two more years. He'd gone to the Tollers again Saturday night for supper. That had set Mattie off. "If he really cared about me, he wouldn't go over there. I might as well forget Sam Colter and playing basketball in college! I never did understand what he saw in me anyway! She has it all...money, looks, and the assurance that she's going to get what she wants!"

I felt sorry for her but didn't know what to do. I believe that Sam felt an obligation to the Tollers for being good to him. I don't think he was that interested in Sonia but didn't want to refuse their invitations.

Sam and Mr. Quentin got home, but Mattie didn't come out of her room until I called her for supper. I saw immediately that she had been crying. After the blessing, silence dominated until we were halfway through the meal.

"Mattie, there's a new singer performing Wednesday night at Anson. It's a fundraiser for the local fire department. Would you like to go?" Sam asked.

"Who is it?"

"I can't remember his name. Some of the guys at the auction were talking about it last week. They said he was supposed to be really good," Sam said.

"I'm not in the mood for a concert, especially from a nobody," she replied.

"Mattie, why don't you go? It would be good for you and who knows, it might be someone who'll be famous some day," I said.

"Are you sure you want to take me?" Mattie asked.

"Well, I could take Hablo, but he's not much for music. He just likes to talk."

"Go, Mattie. It'll be fun," said Pa-Pa.

"I'll think about it. Maybe I will. Maybe I won't."

"Please go, Mattie. I'm afraid Hablo will pee on someone's leg," Sam said, bringing laughter from me and Mr. Quentin.

"I'll let you know tomorrow," she replied.

"I'm working at the sale tomorrow, and it'll be late when I get in."

"Then I'll let you know Wednesday morning," she replied, getting up and leaving the table.

"That girl can be stubborn. She's into self-pity and misery now," said Pa-Pa.

"Thank you for trying, Sam. Maybe she'll go," I said.

The next morning Mattie was up early and dressed ready to go with me into town. She hadn't backed down on the statement that she was going to get a job. It might be the best thing for her. Having to work eight or nine hours every day might cause her to think twice about not going to college. On the drive in, I asked her why she was being difficult with Sam about attending the concert.

"I'm not being difficult. I just can't decide if I want to go. The guy is probably terrible and can't even get a job singing in a bar. After all, how many singers do concerts for the fire department?"

I thought about telling her about Leon but decided against it. She was still in a foul mood. Maybe tonight after Mr. Quentin had gone to bed. Sam wouldn't be home, either.

"Where are you going to apply for a job?" I asked.

"I'm going to start at the Rural Electric Co-op. I heard they might be hiring. After that, I'm going to each business in town. I'm not particular."

"You look nice today. There won't be anyone prettier that applies," I said, hoping flattery might improve her mood.

"Mother, right now, I feel like a nobody. I was someone in school, even at the tryouts, but now I'm lost. You care and Pa-Pa cares but who else believes I'm good for anything. Maybe Sam does sometimes, but who knows. He's still going over to 'her' house every week. Sunday morning when we go to church, I can still smell her scent on him. I know I have a lot to be thankful for, but now going from a somebody to a nobody, is making me miserable."

"I'm sorry, Mattie. I wish something could be done to make you feel better. Would you meet me at the drug store for lunch at 12:00?" I asked.

"Sure. How long do you have off for lunch?" she asked.

"An hour. Maybe we can see if Mellinger's or Bragg's have any sales after we finish eating," I suggested.

Mattie was in a better mood at lunch. Her interview at Rural Electric had gone well. We sat down in a booth and had to wait several minutes because the waitress was talking at the other end of the counter. I don't know whether she didn't see us or was in no hurry to get our order. We both ordered pimento cheese sandwiches and cokes.

"The man at Rural Electric was so nice. He'd seen me play basketball and was impressed. They do have an opening, and he'll let me know in a few days if I get the job. I feel better. I didn't apply anywhere else. After my interview, I went to the cemetery. I don't understand why they call it *Rose Hill*. There's not one rose in the entire cemetery. I went to Daddy's grave and apologized to him. I guess it's too late, but I had to do it."

"That was a good thing to do, Mattie. It's not too late." Should I go ahead and tell her now or wait until tonight? I decided on the latter.

Chapter 33

Mattie

I stayed up after Mother and Pa-Pa went to bed thinking that Sam might get home from the sale earlier tonight. I was going to try and be more positive. I kept telling myself there was nothing to do but accept the facts. It wasn't easy because everything that had happened since I returned home from Plainview had been depressing, beginning with the death of my dad. I was plagued with guilt over the way I had talked to him at our last meeting. Going to his grave and apologizing had done little to end my feelings of remorse.

We were told that within two weeks a letter would be sent to us from the college. It had been over that and I had not heard anything, which meant no college scholarship for me. I hadn't realized what it would be like to suddenly go from being recognized in high school for my athletic and academic accomplishment to being nothing upon graduation. I guess many students go through a similar experience.

Sam wasn't going to be able to let Sonia go. She had her claws in him and was going to hang on. I know he had feelings for me, but they weren't strong enough to stop seeing her. I was going to the concert with him, if you could call it that. I knew all along my answer would be yes, that I was just being difficult because of my frustration with everything.

Finally, a positive event happened. My interview with Rural Electric was encouraging, and from every indication, I had a good chance of getting the job. It was, in my opinion, the best job I could get without going out of town. I needed to accept the fact that college was not in my future.

At 1:00 I went to bed, giving up on Sam coming home. I dreamed that Sam and Sonia were getting married. I stood outside the church, crying, and watched them drive off in his pickup…Just Married written on the back windshield.

I woke up to the sound of people talking. It was several seconds before I realized it was coming from the kitchen and must be Mother and Pa-Pa. I thought about my dream and realized my head was hurting. I lay there a few minutes, thinking, how pitiful my life was at this moment. Angry, I jumped out of bed, put on my robe, selected jeans and a t-shirt, went to the bathroom, and got dressed. I didn't even bother with makeup or my hair, which was sticking out everywhere. I did brush my teeth.

When I joined them, Pa-Pa said, "Sam's not home yet. They must have had some kind of cattle run. I feel sorry for that boy. I'm afraid he hasn't recovered enough to work these long hours."

I didn't respond, and Mother asked, "Are you going to the concert tonight?"

"I don't know why they're calling it a concert. Some guy is going to sing in Anson who I don't even know. It would be a concert if we were going to Abilene to see Hank Williams or Kitty Wells. Yeah, I'm going. There's nothing better to do."

"Mattie, please be nice to Sam. He's done so much for us."

"He's a good boy who's been through a terrible ordeal in Korea," added Pa-Pa.

Again, I didn't respond, thinking, *I've heard this a dozen times, and he still goes to Sonia's every Saturday night. Worse, he carries her scent around for several days which means more happens than sharing a family meal.* I heard someone drive up, and assuming it was Sam, rose and went to my room to put on some makeup and brush my hair. I stayed away from the kitchen as long as possible but finally gave in and returned.

"Mattie, how are you this morning?" Sam asked.

"Fine. You had a long day."

"We ran 2500 through the sale. I'm beat. I had a new job today. Mr. McDaniel took me out of the alley and put me in the ring. My job is to move the cattle around so the buyers can see them and when they sell move them onto the scales. It's easier, because I get a break every several hours. I rotate with another guy. His name's James, and he's really nice."

"Would you like some eggs and bacon?" I asked.

"That would be awesome, if you don't mind," he replied.

I immediately began cooking his breakfast and suddenly my anger had vanished. He was dirty, and his old hat was filthy. He hadn't worn the custom made hat 'she' gave him in my presence. He wasn't skinny anymore but had regained his muscles. He was more than cute. He was handsome in a rugged sort of way. I know he must be dead tired after working for almost 24 hours. Sitting his plate down in front of him, I said, "I would like to go with you tonight if the invitation is still open."

"That's great. I'm going to rest for a few hours, and maybe we could go for a ride this morning. The horses need some exercise. Since the stock is gone they're getting fat and lazy."

"I'd like to sit and visit, but it's time for me to leave for work," Mother said.

"I'm going outside to smoke," announced Pa-Pa.

That left Sam and me alone. I moved over behind him while he was eating and began messaging his shoulders and neck.

"Oh, oh, oh. That's wonderful, Mattie. I may go to sleep right here. Why're you being so nice?"

"I'm trying to accept my new role as a 'has been nothing.'"

"What do you mean?"

"I'm not getting a scholarship. You're going to see Sonia every Saturday night. I'm just trying to accept what I am…nothing."

"You're impossible, Mattie. Thank you for the breakfast and the massage. I'm going to sleep for a couple of hours," he said, getting up and leaving.

Now you really messed up, I thought. I went back to my room to select some clothes to ride in. What would be appropriate? Smiling, it hit me. I was going to wear shorts…my smallest ones and a t-shirt…my smallest one. It took me several minutes to squeeze into the shorts which I hadn't worn in over a year. The t-shirt was easier but was at least a size too small. Looking in the full length mirror, I spoke to myself; *I don't look half bad.* I may have gained a little weight since not working out for two weeks. Of course, I'd need a lot more padding to look like Sonia. I did have nice legs even though they were too big for the rest of me, but they were smooth. I'd been wearing shorts since school was out as evidenced by my tan. My complexion was my best quality. My skin was smooth and with the wide mouth, and high cheek bones, I might could have been a model if not for the muscular legs.

My tennis shoes completed my attire for the morning ride. I couldn't wear boots, with the outfit I'd selected. I decided to go ahead and saddle the horses ahead of time. They'd be frisky after the time off and being tied would take some of the edge off them. Sam had said he only wanted to sleep for two hours.

It was a nice morning, but by noon it would be hot. It still hadn't rained and most days the temperature would approach 100 with a strong south wind. I saddled Sam's horse first without a problem. When I went to halter Spade, he made a circle around the lot, kicking at me. This was not going to be easy. I finally penned him in the corner and haltered him. Leading him out, he was dancing around and kicking up. I opened the gate, and he jumped sideways toward me landing on my right foot. I screamed, trying to get him off, but he seemed to bear down with all his weight. Finally, I let him go and he ran off. Unable to stand, I slumped to the ground, suddenly feeling nauseated. I thought for a minute, I might pass out, the pain was so bad. I lay on the ground for at least ten minutes before trying to stand. No way could I tolerate the pain brought about by my first attempt. I sank back down and thought, it could be another hour before Sam comes to the barn. I crawled out in the open so anyone coming out of the house would see me.

Spade had stopped about twenty yards from the barn and was looking at me as if to say, "I didn't mean it." My foot was hurting so badly it was hard to think straight. Should I try and crawl to the house? Probably not. The pain when I moved was unbearable. Why would I wear tennis shoes to ride? Stupid! The same reason you wore shorts and a t-shirt. To impress Sam. Angrily, I said aloud, *it's your fault Sam Colter, I hate you.* Then I cried.

Pa-Pa found me within half an hour after it happened. He'd come outside to smoke and saw me. Coming as fast as possible, he asked me what happened.

"Spade, stepped on my foot. I think it's broken."

"Honey, just stay there and I'll get Sam," he said. Just like I could do anything else but stay here.

Sam drove up in his pickup a few minutes later, getting out and asking, "Are you all right, Mattie?"

"No, Sam! I'm not! Now, help me get in the pickup." He reached down and put his hands under my arms and lifted, causing me to scream, "Not like that! You're killing me!" He abruptly, dropped me, causing more pain.

"Hollis, if you'll open the pickup door, I'll put her in," Sam said, reaching down and gathering me up in his arms.

The pain was fierce with my foot dangling with no support, but he got me inside before saying, "I need to get your shoe off. The swelling is so bad I'll need to cut it off with my knife." I looked at my foot and could see he was right. He tried to be easy, but the pain was still horrific.

"We need to take you in to see Dr. Sadler. We'll stop at the house and get you some aspirin."

"I need to change clothes," I said.

"Why? That's just going to mean more pain."

"These clothes are not appropriate," I said.

"For crying out loud, Mattie, you're going to the emergency room! It doesn't matter what you're wearing. Besides, you look fine."

I didn't argue. By the time we arrived at the hospital, the aspirin had done little to relieve my pain. Pa-Pa had called Mother and she was waiting on us. We parked in the back, and Sam went in and came back with a wheelchair. Dr. Sadler met us as we went through the door.

"What happened to you, Honey?" he asked.

"My horse stepped on me."

"Let's get some X-rays and see what we're up against. We'll get you a shot to relieve the pain."

An hour later Dr. Sadler came into the waiting room, saying, "Honey, you definitely have a broken bone. There's too much swelling to do anything today. You can stay here and we'll put ice on it or go home and do it there. If you choose to go home, I'll get you some pain medicine. If the swelling is gone down tomorrow, we'll put a cast on it."

"I want to go home."

"That's fine, but I want to see you tomorrow," he said.

It was only 2:00, so my mother went back to work and Sam took me home, but not before going by the ice house. He wrapped the block of ice in newspaper to keep it from melting. The first thing he did after getting me in the house was to take an ice pick and chip up enough off the block to place in a bucket with water. I would place my foot in the water for as long as I could stand it then remove it and wait ten minutes or so before repeating the process.

After two hours the swelling had decreased. The pain medicine had taken effect and I was able to move to the living room and elevate my foot. Sam had been sweet, looking after me and never asking what I was doing wearing tennis shoes to ride. I was using crutches obtained at the hospital to get around and had changed into my warmups, which were more comfortable than the shorts which I think must have cut off circulation to my lower body.

Sam went to his room to catch up on his sleep and I was reading a book when Mother arrived home at 5:30. She came directly to the living room, presenting me a letter from Wayland College. My heart began to race as I opened it.

Dear Mattie,

Congratulations. You have been selected to be a part of our women's athletic program at Wayland Baptist College. A full scholarship will be provided and more information will be forthcoming from your coach. We are proud of the Flying Queens and know that you will add quality to the team. The fact that you were the valedictorian of your school and the class president weighed heavily on our decision.

Sincerely,
Dr. Marshall

I started crying. My broken foot would prevent me from playing basketball for months. It was already June, and practice would probably start in August. Mother, of course, thought it was a rejection letter since I was crying. I handed her the letter to read.

"Oh, my, Mattie. That's wonderful! Why're you crying?"

"I can't accept the scholarship. No way can I be ready by August with a broken foot. I'll have to notify them to give the scholarship to someone else."

"Don't make any decision until we talk to Dr. Sadler. He can tell you how long it will be," Mother said.

I read the letter again. I'd made it. A full scholarship to play college basketball. I blew it! I re-read the letter a dozen times before Sam came in and discovered the news. He tried to be optimistic.

"Just calm down, Mattie. We don't know anything about how long it will take your foot to heal."

"It's not fair to take a scholarship that someone else who is healthy, could use," I said. "Why is this happening? It seems everything's against me. I want you to go to the concert. Just leave

- 220 -

me alone. I'll be fine. Go have fun. Take someone else if you want to."

"Don't be that way, Mattie. I'm not going to leave you feeling this way. Like you said, it's not really a concert. It's a nobody performing who can't find work. I did remember that his name is Elvis something or another."

Chapter 34

Sam

Jose had gone back to Mexico for a visit after the stock was sold. I'd taken him to Del Rio where he would catch a bus for another four hour ride to his destination. When I asked him when he was returning he shrugged his shoulders, saying, "Don't know, Little Bit, maybe a month, maybe more." When we parted, he hugged me, which was strange, since he hadn't done that since I was a little boy. He would have probably saddled the horses had he been here and Mattie wouldn't be in the fix she was.

It had been six weeks since she broke her foot and was due to get her cast off in another two weeks, which would be around the last of July. With a great amount of persuasion from all of us, she'd agreed to see how she did before turning down the scholarship. The Rural Electric Co-op saved us from having to put up with her all day. They called two days after she broke her foot offering her a job. After telling them she had a broken foot, they assured her that wouldn't be a problem since she would be at a desk all day. It worked out, since she and her mother had similar hours and could ride together.

She was walking on the cast while at home, despite our repeated warnings that she needed to stay on the crutches. I think she did it to just aggravate us. Several times a week we would sit on the porch after supper and discuss our day. She was enjoying her job and after getting her first check bought a new pair of tennis shoes to replace the one I had to cut off her foot.

Mattie told me about her mom's guilt over her dad's suicide. She admitted her guilt also and had been dealing with that. She thought that together she and her mother would get through it. I tried to be a good listener and not offer any advice. I'd always believed he was the one who burned down their house, but it would have done no good telling her.

I liked working at the auction, even though the hours had been long. I'd taken my trailer the last several times. The guy who worked the ring with me had told me about bargains that came through. Sometimes they might be sick, other times just needing something to eat. The market was poor anyway, and it was amazing how cheap some of them sold. James, my friend, would signal to me when he saw one come through the ring that had a good chance of being profitable and I'd buy it. He also bought some, and I learned to identify the type of stock he favored. One day, I bought four and the following sale three more. Within a few weeks, I had twenty head in my pen at home, in all kinds of conditions. James had warned me that I would lose some but the ones that made it would more than compensate. It was hard to believe, but I had only paid an average of $10 a head for the twenty. It kept me busy on my off days doctoring and looking after them. The first thing I would do was give them a shot of penicillin for several consecutive days. When they were going better, I would turn them out to graze and by supplementing them with a small amount of oats, they did fine.

We still hadn't received rain to amount to anything. I was glad to have sold my sheep and cattle when I did. We were in the fifth year of a drought, which old-timers, including Hollis, were saying was the worst they'd ever seen. It was not unusual to see tumbleweeds rolling down main street in town. Some of the ranchers were burning prickly pears for their cattle to eat. Many were giving up and selling everything, as evidenced by the large runs at the auction.

Mattie's cast was removed on July 29 and her progress after that was something to behold. Whether it was stubbornness or determination, she started her training immediately and never looked back. She ran five miles each morning before leaving with her mother for work and spent as much time in the gym as her job would allow.

She had received information from Wayland that she was to report on Monday, August 23. Workouts would begin the next day and school would start on September 7. She had given notice that August 20 would be her last day to work at Rural Electric. Her boss had assured her that she would have a job next summer when she returned from school. After receiving her last check, she had saved $280 to be used for spending money, and it seemed that everything was going to work out.

Friday night before I was going to take her to Plainview on Sunday Hollis fell, attempting to get to the bathroom. He was sore the next day but insisted that nothing was broken even though he couldn't get out of bed by himself. Her mother and I attempted to reason with Mattie the next day, which proved to be impossible.

"I'm not leaving him and that's final!" she exclaimed.

"Mattie, honey, be reasonable. You can't just abandon your plans and stay here. We'll take care of your pa-pa. I know Sam will help me and his friends will, also."

If he doesn't improve you'll send him to the nursing home. There won't be anyone to care for him. You and Sam work. We don't have the money to hire a full time nurse. If I'm here, he'll not have to go to the nursing home."

"Mattie, I'm sorry, but you're not thinking clear. You would work, too, and couldn't be with him during the day. Listen to your mother," I said.

Through the tears, she replied, "He'll die in a nursing home."

"We can't predict how he'll recover. We never thought he would be able to walk and care for himself after the stoke but he did," I pleaded.

Hollis evidently heard us arguing. "Mattie," he called from his bedroom. "Come here please."

She returned five minutes later, walking past us and through the door without saying a word. I found out later that her pa-pa had told her if she didn't go to Plainview the next day, which was Sunday, that he was moving to the nursing home on Monday. Her pa-pa didn't speak untruths, and I've no doubt that he would've carried through with his threat if she hadn't done as he wished. Hollis was a special man; unlike anyone I'd ever known. My respect for him grew even more after his talk with Mattie.

I was with Mattie when she told her pa-pa bye, Sunday morning. "Mattie, honey, I'm so proud of you. I never dreamed that you'd be playing for the Flying Queens."

"I'm going to miss you, Pa-Pa. I owe you so much, and I love you."

"Now, don't get all emotional on me. I plan on seeing you play and looking forward to holidays when you come home. I couldn't be happier with the way everything turned out. Of course, I'm sorry for causing all this trouble by falling."

"I'll write and call once a week," she promised.

I guided her out of the room before she started crying; however, Mattie and her mother both were crying when we drove away. She'd stopped sniffling by the time we were on Highway 80 headed west. Mattie had few words until we were between Snyder and Post. Then she surprised me with several personal questions.

"Sam, do you ever have those terrible dreams?"

"I still dream about the war, but not as often, and they are less real. I wake up more easily and usually can go back to sleep."

"Do you think that a time will come when the dreams go away completely?" she asked.

"No."

"Will you miss me?"

"Sure."

"You don't sound very enthused."

"I dread you leaving, and also, your pa-pa and mother. I've been happier since your family came to live with me. I was lonely. All I had was Jose."

"Maybe I shouldn't go to college. I have a good job and a future with the REA."

"Don't even think about it, Mattie. This is a great opportunity, and you'd always regret not taking advantage of it."

"I know you're right; however, it's going to be hard leaving. I'll get homesick for sure. I don't know why I'm worrying about it. My foot may not heal to where I can play basketball, especially at that level. I may be home within a few weeks. I guess you'll be going over to Sonia's more?"

"It's really warming up," I said, rolling down my window. "It'd be nice to have an air conditioner."

"You changed the subject, Sam."

"I don't want to talk about her, Mattie. Tell me about your roommate."

"Charley is from Spearman. She's small but can shoot like no one I've ever seen. I'm pleased she made the team and that we're going to be roommates."

"It's a small world. I had a friend that was from Spearman," I said.

"You never told me that. What's his name?"

"Doesn't matter now. Just forget it. I shouldn't have mentioned it," I said.

"Just tell me his name and I won't ask any more questions."

"Flint."

After stopping in Lubbock to eat, we were in Plainview at Mattie's dorm by 2:00 that afternoon. I helped carry her luggage inside but not to her room. We went back outside to a bench that was shaded by one of the few trees on campus. Sitting down, she became talkative, probably because she was nervous.

"I've never been away from home for any length of time. I'm scared, Sam. Right now, I wish I hadn't made it. We'd just be getting home from church and eating lunch. All this is strange to me. The people here are not friendly."

She kept talking and for some reason I noticed how green her eyes were and how her lip began to quiver. I wanted to do something or say something to make her feel better. I moved over next to her and put my arm around her.

"Mattie, you're going to be fine. If you become too homesick, I'll come visit you. It's only a four-hour drive."

"Will you, Sam? Promise?"

"I promise, Mattie."

By now, she was crying. She grabbed and hugged me and then was up and running to the dorm. Watching her go, a feeling of loneliness came over me that I hadn't experienced since the day I left on a bus for El Paso to begin basic training. I sat there a few minutes staring at the dorm before returning to my pickup for the long drive home.

Chapter 35

Gladys

Mattie was gone, and I missed her already. After they left, I continued to cry for some time before telling myself, *she's going to make something of herself. You should be rejoicing and not mourning. This is what she wanted more than anything, and you have to move on with your life.*

I went outside and sat down on the porch. I had no choice but to move back into my house in town. Driving 20 miles back and forth to work, would not allow me time to take care of Hollis. Maybe it was for the best. It would be hard, being constantly reminded of Leon, but it was the only thing to do.

Now that the decision was made, I didn't waste any time getting some of my things together. I didn't leave until mid-afternoon since Hollis convinced me that he would be all right staying at Sam's by himself. Sam should be home in a few hours and he could tell him our plans. Sam could bring him into town tomorrow or the next day. Hollis was reluctant to leave with Sam being gone, and I understood and appreciated that.

On the drive into town my thoughts returned to Mattie. We'd never been apart for any length of time, and it was going to be hard. I'd finally gotten up the courage to tell her about Leon and our conversation the day he died. She'd reacted much like I'd expected, insisting that it wasn't my fault. She confessed feeling badly about the way she'd spoken to him. I feel relieved after telling her, but still had not come to grips with my feelings. Ernest had been insistent, asking me out numerous times, beginning two weeks after Leon's death. I refused and was sorry for not being able to tell him my reason.

My house, I guess that's what it should be called now, was filthy and smelled awful. At least I'd have something to keep me occupied the remainder of the afternoon and well into the night.

The first objective was the kitchen and cleaning the fridge, which accounted for the smell. Next, I swept and mopped the floor with Pine-Sol and cleaned the counters and table using water mixed with bleach. Satisfied with the kitchen, I moved to the living room. I assumed it was much the way Leon had left it the day he died, except for a layer of dirt on everything. I froze when seeing the half-filled glass of dark liquid sitting on the small table by Leon's chair. It would've been his last drink that he hadn't finished. I turned and left the room, going out the front door and getting in Mr. Quentin's pickup, muttering, *I can't do it, not today, anyway.*

I drove to my friend, Louise's, needing to get away from that place. She came to the door, hugging me, knowing from my look that I was hurting. I told her my plans about moving back into my house and what'd happened.

"Gladys, you should've called me, and I would've cleaned the house. That must've been horrible to go back in and see it the way it was the day he died. You're going to stay with me tonight, and we'll decided later about what to do."

"I'll be all right tomorrow. It was just too much today, with Mattie leaving. I wanted to stay busy and cleaning the house was going to be a way to do that."

"I know it must be a terrible day with Mattie leaving. I'm going to miss her, too. Just think, though, she's going to get a college education. I'm so proud of her," said Louise.

"That's what I keep telling myself, but it falls on deaf ears. I'm sure you noticed that my two other children didn't even attend Leon's service. Both called and said it was just impossible for them to get away. Isn't that something? Too busy to bury their dad. Mattie's really my only child and we've always had each other, even when Leon was so mean to us."

"You need to move on with your life, Gladys. I know Ernest has been asking you out. I don't understand why you don't accept. He's a nice guy and y'all would be good company for each other."

"I have my reasons, and they're personal."

"Gladys, we've been friends a long time and have kept few secrets from one another. Please tell me what's keeping you from accepting Ernest's advances."

Louise was right. We'd been as close as friends could be for a long time. We had depended on one another in the tough times. I was there for her when her husband died six years ago. I spent many a night sitting up and talking with her. I started from the beginning when Leon approached me about getting back together and told her the entire story. By the finish, I was crying. She didn't say a word until I had stopped crying.

"We need to take a short trip, Gladys. We shouldn't be gone long."

We drove downtown to the small building that served as the constable's office. Louise hadn't told me anything about where we were going or why.

Mr. Fulton invited us in and asked us what we needed. Two chairs were opposite his and we sat down without an invitation.

"Mr. Fulton, you need to explain to Gladys about Leon and what was going on with him when he committed suicide."

I could tell by his expression that he didn't like what he was being told to do. "Why? It'll serve no purpose whatsoever. That's all in the past," he said.

" Please, do as I ask. It's important that Gladys knows. Trust me. She's my best friend."

He hesitated so long, I thought he was going to refuse. Finally, he began, "We had a strong suspicion that when Hollis's house burned it was arson. We conducted an investigation, interviewing neighbors, and putting pieces together, until we had a good case. All the evidence pointed to Leon, including an eye witness. We were going to pick him up the next day, and you know how a small town is. One of the guys that work for the city knew about the investigation and told him that afternoon. I understand they were drinking buddies. He was fired, but it was too late to prevent Leon from taking his life. Leon knew he was going to jail, and he chose the alternative. This was a black mark against law enforcement. Also, we could see no reason for you to know that Leon had burned down Hollis's house. I still don't understand why you needed to know."

I sat there, silent and stunned, letting it soak in. He didn't take his life because of me. It wasn't my fault. I was speechless.

"We appreciate it A.D. I know you don't understand, but believe me, you did a good thing by telling Gladys what happened," Louise said.

In the car, I found my voice. "I suffered all this time, thinking it was me. I should've told you earlier. How did you find out about the investigation?" I asked.

"Like he said, it's a small town. Working in the drug store, I hear just about everything. I actually overheard the law talking about it after Leon's death. I didn't tell you because, like A.D., I didn't see any reason for you to know. We were both protecting you, without having any idea what you were going through."

"Should I tell Mattie?" I asked.

"Doesn't she feel guilty" she asked.

"Yes. We both were sorry we said the things we did. Looking back, we were taking the blame for standing up against the terrible treatment we received from Leon. I'll definitely tell Mattie."

"Now, do you feel better?" Louise asked.

"I think so. It hasn't soaked in yet. It's been on my mind constantly. I'm so thankful to find out the truth."

The next day was Monday, and before going to work I called Mr. Quentin to see if Sam had gotten home. He told me that Sam was home by nightfall. I didn't mention the information received the day before. There was no reason to give him anything else that would make him think less of his son.

Leon's car hadn't been moved from the driveway. I hadn't opened the door or even looked inside. I'd been driving Mr. Quentin's pickup. On the way to work, I stopped in at the Ford dealership and talked to a salesman. I asked him to pick up the car at my place and see what kind of deal he could make me on another used car. He agreed, and I told him the keys should still be in the car. Of course, he knew the story of what had happened.

I felt like a load had been lifted from me when I got to work. Ernest came in early and bought a few groceries, checking out at my register. He was friendly, but for the first time didn't mention us getting together. No one was in line behind him, and when he was walking away, I asked, "Ernest, would you like to ride out to Sam's with me when I get off work this afternoon and visit with Hollis?"

His face lighting up, he said, "I'd love to spend some time with Hollis."

Chapter 36

Sam

I was home by dark from Plainview, and Hollis told me that Mrs. Quentin would be staying in town. Walking to the barn I checked on my calves that weren't in good enough shape to be turned out. When I left this morning, one was down. I'd doctored him before leaving, hoping he'd be up by the time I returned. He had died sometime during the day. I sat down on the ground in the shade and lit a Camel, fighting the sinking feeling in my stomach. My friend, James, had told me this would happen. Somehow, I'd thought with enough care and medicine it could be prevented. This was the first one I'd lost, with over half of them being healthy enough to turn out in the pasture. My thoughts came out in a mumble. *What makes you think you're so special that you can cure illness? You couldn't even save your friend. Remember, he died begging you to keep him alive.* I pushed my cigarette butt into the dirt, got up, and pulled the dead calf out of the pen.

There was a pit in an open space about a hundred yards from the barn. I had used it to burn the remains of the ewes and lambs killed by the coyotes. The dead calf was small and no problem to drag. I piled dead limbs on him and started the fire with gasoline. At least the varmints wouldn't get to him. I continued to feed the fire until dark, before walking back to the house. I wasn't hungry but made a sandwich from a left over roast, forcing myself to eat. I visited with Hollis briefly, hoping to overcome my loneliness and despair. I tried watching television but gave up and let Hablo in the house. I decided to go to bed early, intending to sleep through my misery. I turned on the radio to a county station and lay their listening to music for two hours before going to sleep.

His voice was clear. Sam, please don't let me die! Please don't let me die! I was going as fast as possible, slipping and sliding down the hill, screaming, Medic! Medic! Medic! I stood and watched as the medic stood up from his examination, shaking his head. I knelt down and watched as they placed him in a body bag.

I woke up trembling and gasping for breath to the sound of Hank Snow singing, "I Don't Hurt Anymore."

As the days passed and turned into weeks, I started seeing Sonia more often. The fact that she decided to stay home this semester and drive back and forth to school each day made it possible. At first it was twice a week and then it increased to three times and then most evenings I wasn't working. I was lonely and depressed and being with her gave me something to look forward to each day. She interpreted my action to mean I was becoming more interested in her. Nothing could have been further from the truth.

Mattie had written every week at first, but after her school started, it became less often. By October 15, a month had passed since hearing from her. She admitted enjoying college and basketball. She hadn't seemed the least bit homesick, which disappointed me. I talked with Mrs. Quentin each week and her experience with Mattie had been the same as mine. Hollis had recovered from his injury and was living with her. I tried to see him once a week for a brief visit.

The demons were coming regularly again. There was no predicting when or why my dreams would occur, only that they continued. Most times, they included the horrors of war, but occasionally I would get a reprieve and Mattie would appear. I had thought often of going to see her, but she'd never mentioned it in her letters. The impression I got was that she was busy and didn't need interference from me or anyone else.

The dry weather continued with no end in sight to the drought. I now had 25 calves that I'd nursed back to health. My friend James had been right. Even though I'd lost one and would probably lose more, I was going to make good money. My expenses had been small, and even being conservative, they could triple what they cost, when sold.

I kept expecting Jose to return. He now had been gone over four months. His presence would help with the loneliness and relieve some of my dependence on Sonia, who was becoming more demanding. It didn't bother her to be aggressive, showing up unannounced at my house some days when I hadn't planned to see her. Sometimes she'd come on the pretense of bringing food she'd cooked.

The third week in October was especially bad. The demons were fierce and came every night. After one of the worst nights since coming home, on Saturday morning, the 16th of October, I decided to go after Jose. I had packed some of my belongings and was loading them when Sonia drove up. She immediately asked me where I was going.

"After Jose. He's been gone longer than I expected. I need him here."

"Why? You don't have but a few calves to look after," she said.

"Doesn't matter. I need him," I said, running out of patience.

"I'll go with you. If we need to be gone longer than two days, I can miss school. It's not that important anyway."

"No. I'm going by myself. I don't know how long it will take. I know the name of the town where he was going, but not the location of his home. It may be several days before I find him."

"I still don't understand why you need him. You have me to help with anything."

I remained silent, going back into the house with her following me. Inside, I tried again, "Look, Sonia, I want him back here. This is his home and has been since I can remember. He may be sick or not have the bus fare to get back to Del Rio."

"Fine. I guess you don't need me. You're probably going to take that stupid dog with you," she said. "All he does is bark at everything."

How'd I ever get into this mess, I thought? "Yeah, you're right. Hablo's going with me. There's no one here to take care of him."

"You're not being very nice, after all me and my family have done for you. I guess you've forgotten about that."

"No, I appreciate it. I'm leaving now," I said, walking out the door. I called Hablo to load and he accepted the invitation. I drove off with her crying and shouting something that I couldn't and didn't want to understand.

It was approximately 220 miles to the border. I stopped in Sonora at 2:00 for gas and something to eat. I drove the last 90 miles to Del Rio and the border, arriving at 4:30. The crossing wasn't busy, and I was in Mexico on Highway 29 an hour later. Jose had told me that he was from Sabinas, a small village 20 miles outside of Monclova. I hadn't been able to find it on a map but did locate Monclova which was a large city.

After changing to Road 57 and driving three hours, I came to the village, which consisted of a scattering of small houses, a gas station with a cantina behind it, and little else. It was dark by now, and I was hungry. This would be as good a place as any to start inquiring. "Hablo, you be good. I'll bring you something to eat when I come back." He responded with a series of barks. Entering the building, it was difficult to see at first. The only light was coming from lamps on the walls and at each table. I found a place to sit down, and a large, older lady appeared.

"Drink? Eat?" she asked with a smile, probably speaking the only English she knew.

"¿Qué es bueno?" (What is good?)

"Her smile widened as she replied, "Todo nuestra comida es buena." (All our food is good.)

"¿Qué recomendarias para un hombre hambriento?" (What would you recommend for a hungry man?")

She put her fingers to her lips and blew a kiss into the air, saying, "¡ Mi gueso es el major de México!" (My gueso is the best in Mexico!)

"Bueno eso es lo que quiero. ¿Tu cerveza esta fria?" (Good, that's what I want. Is your beer cold?)

"Más frio en México." (Coldest in Mexico.)

"Bueno." (Good.) No way was I going to drink the water.

She left and came back with my beer and a glass. It was cold. A few minutes later she returned with my meal, which included tortillas and a bowl of peppers. Setting it down proudly, she stood with her arms crossed, waiting for me to begin.

I took a bite, exclaiming, "Delicioso, el major que he tenido nunca." (Delicious, the best I have ever had.)

Satisified, she left. I wasn't lying. The gueso was wonderful, tasting even better since I was starved. The peppers were hot, and I had to have another beer. I finished, and after paying my bill at the counter, asked her if she might have any scraps for my dog. She came back a few minutes later with a bag full of various meats that, I assume, had been left over from the day's business.

"Gracias, eres muy amable." (Thanks, you're very kind.)

"Hablas bien nuesro idioma." (You speak our language, good.)

I thanked her, asking if she knew Jose Samaniego. Her smile faded with the question, and she hesitated before answering.

"Sí, lo sé." (Yes, I know of him.)

¿Puendes decirme dónde encontario?" (Can you tell me where to find him?)

She hesitated longer this time before answering. "Te dibujaré un camino." (I will draw you a way.)

The drawing she gave me seemed easy enough to follow. She added that it was only about two miles. I thanked her again, going back to my pickup. Hablo was glad to see me, especially when I presented him his feast. It had been dark for two hours, and I decided to wait until morning to find Jose. It would be easier in the daylight, and he always went to bed early. I drove across the road to a vacant lot and settled down for the night.

Hablo woke me up the next morning barking. At what, I have no idea. I actually slept pretty good, being tired from the long drive. The two beers probably helped. I looked at the directions given to me and drove immediately toward my destination, finding the house within a few minutes. It was sitting at the end of a dirt road in a pasture surrounded by small trees. The house was in better shape than most I had seen. There was no car parked in sight. Letting Hablo out with me, I approached the door and knocked. No one answered, and hearing Hablo barking, I went around to the back of the house. I spotted him and it took me a few seconds to grasp what I saw. There were five crosses, which obviously were grave markers, and Hablo was laying across the last one that was covered with fresh dirt. Grief swept over me as my heart sank. I had found Jose.

Chapter 37

Mattie

The first few weeks had been hard, but as time went by and I became familiar with college, it became easier. By the end of August, I was enjoying my new life. The other girls on the team were not only fabulous athletes but nice as well. Rather than being fearful we would take their place, they encouraged us at every opportunity. I'd never seen such focus on teamwork, as evidenced by their play. They were all stars but never made it about themselves. One of the seniors became my big sister. Sarah would answer my questions about not only basketball but academics as well. She explained the rules and traditions of the team and helped me with my registration. Sarah was one of two girls that had once played for an amateur team before coming to Wayland. She was in her mid-twenties and was one of the best athletes on the team. She was high point in our first game. Being 6'1" didn't hurt her.

It took me a while to get used to my schedule. I took 16 hours, which was probably too many. It was more difficult than high school; however, not nearly as much time was spent in class, giving me more time to study. We were required to attend chapel once a week. I discovered that many of the students were going to become Baptist ministers.

I was fortunate to have Charley as my roommate. We had many things in common, including being from a small town and seldom traveling anywhere outside the county. She was a Methodist, and I had been attending the Methodist Church in Mulberry Canyon. She came from a family who could not afford to pay for her college, as I did. Both of us were frightened out of our minds on our first plane ride with the Hutcherson Flying Service. Three planes took nine of us to the races at Ruidoso during the Labor Day weekend. They made sure to include the freshman, since none of us had flown before or even been close to an airplane. I came close to throwing up. We closed our eyes during takeoff, but within a short time were marveling at the tiny figures on the ground. We had whispered before takeoff that if we were going to die it would be with the handsomest man we had ever seen. We were referring to the pilot, who was the boys' basketball coach.

We didn't crash, spending two exciting days at the races and staying in one of the nicest motels in Ruidoso. All of our expenses were paid, and Mr. Hutcherson gave each of us twenty dollars to bet on the races. I had never had so much fun in my life. Both Charley and I had money left after the second day. We tried to return it to Mr. Hutcherson, but he refused, telling us the money was ours. Flying home after the races on Sunday, high in the clouds, I thought it must be a dream.

I tried to call home once a week and talk with my mother and pa-pa. I would occasionally talk with Sam. As time passed and my days became busier, it was more difficult to remember to call. With the approach of basketball season, the workouts became longer and harder. By the end of the day, I was exhausted, and usually had studying to do after supper.

Of course, neither me or Charley were on the first team. I was one of the rovers and Charley was a forward. We had talked constantly about whether or not we would make the traveling team as the first game approached, which was in Iowa.

We had just returned from a fiery sermon on Sunday, October, 15, when Charley asked the question again, "Do you think our names will be on the traveling list when it's posted this afternoon?"

"I don't know. One minute I'm optimistic, the next, I don't see how."

"It won't be the end of the world if we don't make it. We have 12 road games," Charley said.

"Can you believe the traveling suits they gave us?" I asked. "I've never had anything that beautiful."

"I know, and they fit perfect. Finding the right size is always a problem for me because I'm so small."

The traveling roster was to be posted in the gym at 3:00 that afternoon, and we were waiting anxiously at the site. I held my breath going down the list and my name was not included; however, Charley's was the last one. I was disappointed, but happy for her. We returned to the dorm, with me attempting to cheer her up and not feel badly for me. She was about to start on a grand adventure.

The team left Tuesday morning and several of us that didn't make the trip went to the airport to see them off. They looked stunning and professional in their travel suits and somehow Charley managed to get on the plane with the handsome pilot. Looking through the window and smiling, she waved at me as the plane sped down the runway. I returned to the dorm, sad and feeling a little sorry for myself. At the moment there were two rovers and I was number three. It was going to be up to me to beat one of them out.

Tuesday was a busy day for me, with three classes. I didn't finish until 4:00 in the afternoon, and since there would be no workout, was free the rest of the evening. After eating supper in the cafeteria, using the pay phone in the hallway of the dorm I called home. Mother answered, and I commenced to tell her about not making the traveling team.

"Don't worry about it, Mattie. You'll make it the next time," she said.

"How's Pa-Pa doing?" I asked.

"Good. You know him. He never complains, but I'm worried about Sam. He left Saturday to go after Jose and hasn't returned. He was supposed to work today, and it's not like him to miss. I called him last night and early this morning, and then just a few minutes ago I talked to a lady at the auction. I don't know what to do."

I didn't respond, and she continued, "Mattie, are you still there?"

"Yes. Something must be wrong, Mother. Sam would never miss work."

"I know. What should I do?" she asked.

"Keep trying to get in touch with him."

"I'll do that."

"Please call me if you find out anything," I said.

After we hung up, the more minutes that passed, the more panic I felt. Sam would never go off and stay, missing work and not telling anyone. Thinking back, I realized it'd been a month since talking to him. Had it been that long? Yes, it was almost like I had forgotten him. I had been absorbed in myself and thought of little else. I hadn't even thought about him spending time with Sonia. What if something bad had happened and I would never see him again? I left the dorm, going for a walk around the campus. It was almost dark and the north wind was cold. I was wishing for my coat rather than the sweater that wasn't doing much to break the wind. I had been told that the winters would be much colder here than at home and could believe it now. I gave up and headed back to the dorm and warmth. When I entered the hallway, the pay phone was ringing, and answering, it was my mother.

"Mattie, he's home. I just talked to him on the phone a few minutes ago."

"Thank God, I was worried sick," I said.

"That's not all, Mattie. There's bad news. Jose died."

"Oh, no!" I cried, breaking into tears. "What happened?"

"Sam wouldn't talk about it. Really, I don't think he could. I felt so sorry for him. He's hurting in a bad way. Jose was like a father and grandfather to him, all rolled into one. I tried to get him to come stay a few days with us, but he refused."

"I'll call him." I said.

"Mattie, I'd wait a day or two. It's too early."

"Maybe I should come home for a few days," I suggested.

"Mattie, you can't do that. Sam will be all right. We'll check on him every day. Give him two days and call him."

"I loved that old man," I said.

"I know, Mattie, and Sam did, too."

After saying goodbye, I put my big coat on and went back outside, sitting on the bench where I'd last seen Sam. I had become more religious in the last few months. I'm sure, due in part, to attending chapel. I bowed my head and mumbled a prayer. *Please, God, be with Sam in his time of grief and help him to be strong. Thank you for the life of Jose and what he meant to all of us. Amen.*

I stayed up as late as possible, knowing sleep was going to be difficult. I was correct and remained awake most of the night. Every time I closed my eyes, a vision of Jose appeared.

The team arrived back in the early afternoon. Charley couldn't contain her excitement as she gave me the details. We had won the game easily and increased our winning streak to 30 games. She had gotten to play a good part of the fourth quarter and scored six points.

"Mattie, it was wonderful! It was evident that the other team was afraid of us and intimidated. They were never in the game. Our team is so classy. We could have scored more but we slowed down our offense to keep from embarrassing them. So, what did you do?"

I told her about Jose, trying not to become emotional. I'd not spoken of him or Sam that often since the first few weeks on campus. There was always, other day-to-day happenings, that occupied what time we had to visit.

"I'm sorry, Mattie. He must've been a special person."

"He was, and Sam will be devastated," I said.

"Doesn't Sam have other family or friends he can depend upon?" she asked.

"No family nearby and he has only mentioned one friend, and he wouldn't talk about him. It was strange. I told him about you and Spearman being your hometown. He said it was a small world; he had a friend from Spearman. He wouldn't tell me anything about him, and after pressuring him, he finally told me his name was Flint."

When Charley didn't respond immediately, I noticed she had an odd look on her face. "What's the matter?" I asked.

"Flint. What was his last name?"

"Sam didn't say. He wouldn't talk about him after that."

"Flint McGowan was his name. He was several years older than me, and his family farmed like mine did. We were neighbors, and our families were close friends. Flint was nice to everyone, young and old. People in the community talked of what an injustice it was for him to be drafted. He was killed in Korea, and his funeral was the saddest that I'd ever attended. You told me Sam was in Korea. Flint must have been the friend he was talking about. It's a small world."

"That explains why Sam wouldn't speak about his friend," I said.

"At the funeral there were pictures of Flint in his uniform. In one of them he was shown with another soldier. That must have been Sam. Do you think Sam would be willing to visit Flint's family? I know it would mean a lot to them."

"I don't know, Charley. He's suffered and grieved over his experience in Korea. I understand better now why it's been that way."

"Mattie, Sam's special to you, isn't he? You haven't talked about him often but I can tell."

"Yes. I've been involved with basketball and my classes and had forgotten just how much he means to me. There's this other girl that he sees. I hadn't thought of her either, but now I realize she'll be there for him during this difficult time. That worries me more than a little."

Chapter 38

Sam

I stood, staring at the grave, thinking, I should have known. Maybe I did and didn't want to consider it. He would have never been gone that long unless something was wrong. I'd refused to consider my life without him.

"Señor?"

I turned, finding a man standing behind me. I had been so absorbed in my thoughts, his presence surprised me.

"You are...are Sam?" he asked.

"Yeah. That's me."

"Jose tell me you come. I expect you sooner."

"How long has he been gone?" I asked.

He hesitated, before saying, "Two months, three days."

I noticed the man favored Jose, and was probably in his sixties, maybe older. It dawned on me he was speaking English. I asked him if he was related to Jose.

"Sí. He was my uncle. He say when he get here, 'I come home to die and be with family.'" As he told me this, he pointed to the other graves.

"Who are the others?" I asked.

"His wife, and three sons. They died many years ago."

"What happened to them?" I asked.

"Hung for treason by the rurales. Jose never tell you?"

"No. He never spoke of his life or his family in Mexico," I said.

"We go inside, and I tell you about Jose before he cross border."

I had to call Hablo several times to get him to go with me toward the house. He followed me into the house which was dark and cool. The man pulled the shades on several windows, providing enough light to see. He motioned for me to sit down at a table. I noticed how neat and clean the room was. He set about lighting a gas stove and putting on a pot of coffee. After completing his task, he sat down and introduced himself as Miguel.

"Jose speak well of you. Consider you family. Sad to leave you by yourself."

"Why didn't he tell me he was ill? Maybe we could've gotten him medicine."

"Jose know it would not help. Jose very old. Knew it was his time."

"Why was his family killed?" I asked.

"Jose a revolutionary. A solider. Support Francisco Madera uprising against the government of President Diaz in 1909. Bad time in Mexico. Much killing. One revolution and then another. Jose always support Madera. Madera overthrown in 1912. Jose fight for Mexican independence from dictators."

"Why did he leave Mexico?" I asked.

"His leader assassinated in 1923. Jose know he next. Have to leave or die. Crossed the border and find your family."

"He returned to Mexico several times," I stated.

"Sí. Visit graves of family and stay a few days. Much sadness here for Jose. Beautiful wife, three sons killed. Boys, 16, 14, and 13."

"I can't imagine Jose being a solider."

"I give you something. Jose said it was to be yours when you come."

He went to the cupboard and took out a box. He opened it and laid a watch with a gold chain on the table. "Jose want you to have this. His friend tell his wife it was to go to Jose if he was killed. After friend assassinated, she give Jose watch."

Opening the watch, the inscription read...¡Viva México! *Pancho Villa.*

I sat and stared, trying to envision this quiet little man that I loved, riding into battle with the famous revolutionary. It had been over forty years ago. How he must have suffered when his family was killed. He came to the ranch in 1923, ten years before I was born. Maybe I was a substitute for the sons he had lost.

"Jose teach you to ride and rope?" asked Miguel.

"Yeah. He was a great horseman and could do rope tricks," I said.

"Not teach you to shoot?" asked Miguel.

"No. I never saw him touch a gun." Now, it was obvious why he was so understanding of my feelings when I came home from Korea.

Miguel explained further that he still worked as foreman for a large ranch near here. The ranch, owned by an Anglo, was the reason he learned English. Jose had taught him to ride and rope when he was a boy, also.

Miguel told me I was welcome to stay as long as I liked. Miguel lived at the ranch where he worked most of the time, only returning occasionally to check on the house. I had more questions but didn't feel like talking now. I asked him if he would return tomorrow.

"Sí, if you like."

"Yes, thank you. I'll stay a few days. I would like to talk some more with you later," I said.

After assuring me he would be back late tomorrow afternoon, he left in a late model pickup, which I assumed belonged to the ranch. I went back to Jose's grave, speaking to him. *I'm sorry for not realizing you were sick. I would've done anything to help you get well. I don't know what I will do without you. You were my only family. You kept your secret well and hid your sorrow from us. It amazes me that you could have gone through what you did and endured. I always respected and admired you and now, knowing what I do, that feeling has increased. I'll never forget you, Jose. Thank you, with all my heart, for everything.*

Returning to the dark house, I realized it would do no good to remain and ask my questions. It would only add to my sadness. I decided to stay tonight and start home tomorrow. It was past noon and I hadn't eaten breakfast. I drove back to the cantina and ate lunch, with Mia making a big fuss over me. She had introduced herself as Mia because that's what her ten grandchildren called her. The food was really good and she kept bringing me more each time my plate was empty.

She told me how she loved Jose and how good a man he was. One of her grandchildren was named after him. He had been a hero to this community, respected by everyone. Stories about his bravery and fight for freedom had been handed down from generation to generation.

When I left, she hugged me with tears in her eyes, saying, "Vaya con Dios, mi pequeño amigo." (Go with God, my little friend.)

Before leaving the next morning, I left a note for Miguel, which included my address, thanking him and saying I was going home. I went to Jose's grave, told him goodbye, and started my trip back to Texas.

I was at the border checkpoint by noon and expected a quick entry back into Texas. To my surprise, a guard instructed me to exit my pickup. He padded me down, looking for a weapon. He directed me to an office and put me in a room by myself, where I waited for two hours. I was concerned about Hablo, who was left in the pickup. Finally, two men entered who appeared to be officers, and started asking me questions. One of them spoke good English, and I remained silent about my Spanish-speaking ability. He started the questioning.

"Why are you in Mexico?" he asked.

"I came looking for my friend. He'd gone back to his home in Sabinas. I discovered he'd died and I was going home," I answered.

"A wetback, huh?"

"No! He was family and I was worried about him!" I replied angrily.

"We have a report of a young gringo who is smuggling drugs," he said.

"Well, that's not me. All I have is my dog," I replied, running out of patience.

"This man, you were looking for, what was his name?"

"Jose Samaniego," I answered. "He worked with my family ever since I can remember."

"Is there anyone we can contact to prove you are telling the truth?" he asked.

"Miguel Samaniego works on a ranch outside of Sabinas. He's a nephew of Jose," I replied.

"We will see if your story is true."

They left, and I couldn't believe this. What was going on? They must have me confused with someone else," I thought.

Three hours later, the original guard who had brought me to this room, appeared saying, "Puedes ir." (You can go.)

"¿Dónde esteá mi perro?" (Where's my dog?)

He smiled and shrugged his shoulders. "Tal vez se fue." (Maybe gone.)

"Quiero a mi perro." (I want my dog.)

"¿Tienes aigo de valor?" (You have something of value?)

So that was it. A shakedown. I couldn't go home without Hablo. I replied, "Tengo un reioj valioso." (I have a valuable watch.)

"Déjame ver." (Let me see.)

I took the watch out of my pocket that Miguel gave to me. He looked at the watch and inscription and started laughing. "Usted crees que soy estúpido. Gringo? Es falso." (You think I'm stupid, Gringo? It is fake.)

I took out my billfold and gladly gave him $10, which proved to be enough to get Hablo back.

With a sigh of relief, I crossed the bridge and was on Texas soil. It was already getting dark, and I decided to stay the night in Del Rio. I bought baloney and a loaf of bread at a grocery store for our supper, found a vacant lot, and slept in my pickup.

I woke up early, and after getting coffee at a small café, was on the road. I had been occupied yesterday with the problems at the border, but now the sadness set in. I couldn't get my mind off Jose and the fact he would never be a part of my life again. The farther I drove, the more depressed I became. Hablo moved over, lay down and put his head on my leg, knowing something was not right.

Today was Tuesday and I was going to miss work. I would call the auction when I arrived at home and explain my absence. It was important to keep the job, even though little money was involved. At least some income was available for bills. I hadn't given any thought to my calves while away; maybe, I hadn't lost any. It would soon be time to sell several of them.

I tried to think of other things, but my thoughts kept returning to Jose. Right after I crossed the Devil's River, a deer ran in front of me, causing me to swerve, barely missing him. Something broke inside me and I pulled off the road with tears streaming down my face. I got out of my pickup and walked around, allowing Hablo to mark foreign territory, thinking of my situation. *I had to get control of my emotions. I'd seen and caused death in Korea, had come home to bury my mother, had lost my best friend in the war, and now I had to accept the fact that Jose was gone. How much more could I take? Why was death following me everywhere? Surely, if there was a God he would see I couldn't take any more sorrow.*

A shadow on the ground interrupted my thoughts, and looking up, an eagle was circling overhead. My first thought was how much ranchers hated to see them because they killed lambs; however, as I watched he continued to circle around me, becoming closer on each rotation. Now, I could make out the different colors of his feathers and even his claws and beak, he was so close. It was as if he was trying to tell me something. I watched in amazement as he came so near I could almost touch him and then he was gone. For some reason, Hablo, who barked at everything, anything, and nothing, was silent through the whole spectacle.

I left the Devil's River with a strange feeling that there was something more important than my sorrow. I felt somewhat better until I was a few miles from the ranch, then the sadness hit me again, realizing the house would be empty.

Arriving at the ranch, before going into the house, I went to the little shack out back. I sat down in one of the two chairs and thought of my friend until I heard someone calling my name. The person calling my name turned out to be the mailman. He had a registered letter for me which required my signature. I couldn't imagine who would be sending me registered mail. I signed for it, thanked him, and went inside my house. Before reading the letter, I called the auction sale and explained my absence.

Directing my attention back to the letter, I noticed the only return address was the US Army. I opened it and began reading.

Dear Sam,

I hope this letter finds you well and recovering from your experience in Korea. I have thought of you often and consider it an honor to have had you in my unit. I was recently contacted by a representative from the motion picture industry about a film being considered about the Korean War. They were interested in locating a young soldier who was in the midst of the war and could describe his experience. I immediately thought of you, since no other solider was involved in more combat. I took the liberty of giving them your address and you may or may not hear from them. Compensation would be involved. How much, I do not know.

Thank you for your service to this country. God Bless.

Sincerely,
Sargent Maurice Rutherford

I laid the letter on the table and thought, why would I want to relive my experiences again? That would only increase the demons. No amount of money would make me go through that hell again. Sargent Rutherford was a nice guy and never asked me to do anything he wouldn't do. I have the greatest amount of respect for him. The guys above him who were actually handing down orders are the ones I hate. I reached for the letter, wadded it up and threw it in the trash.

Chapter 39

Gladys

It was Wednesday and I was getting ready to go to work, thinking whenever something positive happened it would be followed with tragedy. I became aware that my guilt about Leon was unfounded and then Jose dies. Now I was worried sick about Sam. I had never known him to be as depressed as he was yesterday when we visited on the phone. He was going to be lonely, and we weren't going to be there for him. He had been there when we needed him, and I was determined to do the same for him.

Going out the door, Mr. Quentin, who was sitting on the porch, said, "Gladys, we need to do all we can for Sam."

"I know. That's just what I was thinking. Do you have any suggestions?"

"I'm not good for much, but maybe if I stayed with him a few weeks it would help. Let's drive out to his place after you get off work today."

"Sure. At least you can offer to stay with him," I said.

"How do you like your new car?" he asked.

"So far, I like it. It's two years old. but it's new to me, and I think it was a good deal. I really like the automatic transmission."

"Ford made a good one in 1952. I'm glad you like it. You deserve a good car," he said.

I arrived at work ten minutes early and sat in my car enjoying the time alone with my thoughts. Mr. Quentin had recovered from his fall and was doing well. He was no trouble whatsoever and I didn't mind looking after him. Also, with his pension and my salary, we got along well financially, with me even having a little left over each month. Bragg's was having their fall sale this week and I was going to buy some clothes for both me and Mattie.

I'd been seeing Ernest on a regular basis since finding out about Leon. We didn't go anywhere much, but he would come over for supper several times a week. Occasionally, we would have a big night and go to Abilene, eat out, and attend a movie at the Paramount Theater. He was a sweet man, and we enjoyed one another's company.

Mattie's calls had become less frequent as time went by. When she first left, I would get a call once a week. After a month, it would be every two weeks, and this last month she had gone three weeks without calling. Expressing my disappointment to Hollis, he reminded me that she must be doing well or we would hear from her. I realized he was correct but couldn't help but be concerned that she was forgetting about me all together. Also disappointing was the fact she wasn't coming home for Thanksgiving because they had a tournament during the holidays. Yesterday, when I told her about Jose, was the first time she had shown any interest in what was happening here. I know that Sam was getting the same treatment since we had visited about it on more than one occasion.

I continued to enjoy my job, and we were busy with the cotton chopping crews that came to this area. Most would stay and pick cotton later this fall. The crops were poor because of the drought, but many of the farmers were hanging on, looking for next year to be better. I'd actually checked out a group whose bill was $50 last Saturday. That was a record for me. I assumed they pooled their money, and the purchase would feed 15 or 20 for a week. Of course, we had our regular customers, many who I had known before coming to work. Most were nice, but on occasion one would scold a sack boy for not putting their bread on top or dropping their bananas and bruising them.

I met Louise for lunch at the drug store, which was not a problem since she worked there. She worked the register at the pharmacy. We took a seat in a booth and ordered our sandwiches.

"Gladys, why do we always eat here? Let's start going somewhere else. I'm here all day and a change would be nice."

"Where would you like to go?"

"Anywhere, to get away for an hour."

"Tell you what, Louise. As soon as we finish eating, let's go check out the sale at Bragg's."

"Sounds good to me."

"What's the news around town?" I asked.

"Mostly football and the drought. Coach comes in most mornings for coffee and meets with a group of men. Boring stuff to me. Of course, everyone is wishing for rain. Oh yeah. It looks like the Baptist Church will be looking for another minister. That's the talk, anyway."

"What about Ernest?" she asked.

"He's coming for supper tonight," I said.

"You're going to marry him, Gladys."

"It's too soon. We've only been seeing one another for a couple of months."

"Gladys… Gladys. How old are you?"

"Fifty-four last month," I stated.

"Nothing's too soon, girl. Go for it! Y'all make a beautiful couple."

"He's got to ask me first, Louise."

"Gladys… Gladys…Gladys… don't be such an old foggy. There're ways around that. Drop a few hints here and there. Ernest is smart. He'll get the message."

We finished eating, thank goodness. I was not comfortable with the conversation. We went to Bragg's and I spent three days' salary on outfits for Mattie and me. It was a good sale, and Louise bought several items, also.

Leaving, I told Louise, "I've gained weight. I had to go up a size. Maybe a diet is in order?"

"No Gladys. You look great."

That afternoon, when I got off work we went to the ranch. Sam's pickup was home, but he wasn't around. Spade was gone, so we assumed he was riding. We waited for him an hour before he returned. He didn't stop at the barn but continued on to the house. I could see immediately that he was in a bad way.

"Sam, we wanted to check on you and see if there was anything we could do," Mr. Quentin said.

"No, I guess not. I've been riding in the pasture. I only have a few calves, but Spade hadn't been ridden lately."

"We were sorry to hear about Jose," I said.

"Does Mattie know?" he asked.

"Yes. I called her yesterday after talking to you. She was upset," I replied.

"Will she be home Thanksgiving?" he asked.

"No. They have a tournament. Sam, why don't you take off a few days and go see her."

"I have several sick calves that need to be doctored. Besides, she hasn't asked me to come. I don't think she has time for me."

I didn't know how to respond. She hadn't given me any reason to believe that she could spare a few minutes to call me. Thank goodness, Mr. Quentin changed the subject.

"Sam, would you like for me to stay a few days with you? I'm not good for much except company."

"I appreciate it, Hollis, but I'll be fine. I just have to get used to Jose not being around. It's going to take some time. I'm glad to see that you have recovered from your fall."

"Sam, will you let us know, if we can help?" I asked.

"Sure. I appreciate it. I need to put Spade up and feed. Would y'all like to stay for supper? My cupboard is almost bare, but I can rustle up something."

"Oh, no, but thank you anyway. We need to be getting back home," I said.

I left with an uneasy feeling that we had accomplished nothing by our visit. I expressed this to Mr. Quentin who agreed with me.

"We did what we could, Gladys. The boy has gone through too much suffering and loss for anyone to endure without consequences. I just hope and pray that he can recover. He's a special young man and no one, regardless of their age, should have to go through what he has. I just wish we could do more for him."

"I know. The next time Mattie calls, I'll encourage her to invite him for a visit. Right now, he needs someone in his life to fill the void left by Jose."

I didn't sleep well that night, with my thoughts going from Sam to my relationship with Earnest. Was there anything we could do to help Sam? Did I really want to marry again? Was Mattie going to put me out of her life?

Chapter 40

Sam

Thursday morning, getting ready to go to work, I realized a year had passed since coming home. A lot had happened during that time…most of it bad. I was in debt, we were still in a drought, the two people that I was closest to were gone. One had left for college, the other had died. I still had not completely recovered from a sickness, and the dreams continued. I was lonely and that was a fact. I didn't expect this when I returned.

On the drive to the auction, I considered the positive things in my life. I had a job, even though it was only two days a week. I was going to make money on the calves that I had bought, thanks to my friend James. The decision to sell my stock was a good one, or my debt would be greater now. The people in the community had been more than good to me, especially the Tollers, which brought me to Sonia. I'd not seen her since returning from Mexico. I'd like to spend some time with her if she'd only back off a little. A couple of times a week would be good and her company would be appreciated. My feelings for her were not anything like she imagined and never would be. My actions or lack of them should've gotten the message across but evidently it hadn't. Her brothers' attitudes toward me hadn't improved, based on their conduct whenever I day worked for Mr. Toller. I think her mother already had me as part of the family, which was scary.

When I arrived there was time for a cup of coffee. I had made friends with Eddie, the cook and operator of the café. He joined me, asking how I was doing. Word had already gotten around about Jose.

"It's been hard," I answered. "It's difficult to accept that he's gone. I depended on him and he was always there for me."

"Sam, you have friends. Not like Jose, but still, that's important. People around here like you. I know you've taken up with James and he's one of the best. Just give it time and things will get better. Now, I have to get back to work. Early lunch crowd will be coming in soon."

I paid my bill and left for the ring, going through the lobby. I liked the smell of the building, which was unique and always present, being a combination of cigar smoke and scents from the café. I could always depend on it being there; maybe that was the reason it gave me a good feeling. Also, the sound my boots made on the hardwood floor was pleasant. I could use a whip in the ring to move the cattle or a walking stick. My choice was the latter most of the time. It was ten minutes until sale time when I climbed down into the ring. I saw, my friend, James in the box next to the auctioneer. He motioned for me to come over.

"Sam, I'm sorry to hear about your friend. Is there anything I can do?"

"No, but thanks. I should have expected it, due to his age. I guess we never want to think about losing people that have always been a part of our lives," I said.

"Sam, I've got a new job. I'll be writing tickets starting today. It'll mean more money, which I can sure use. Hopefully, I won't make too many mistakes. You'll have a new partner to work the ring with you."

"That's good news. I appreciate you helping me buy calves. They're doing good and some will be ready to sell in a month or two."

"Some people make fun of me for the type of stock I buy, but they make money. That's what counts," he replied.

"Right." It was time for the sale to begin so I took my spot in the ring. I continued to be amazed at the auctioneer as he spoke in his rhythm, never seeming to run out of breath. It was something to watch him pick up bids in the audience and never let up. The bulls sold first and when one entered the ring, the person who was sitting by the auctioneer, would call out a price. If it was by the pound, then it would be something like 35 cents. The auctioneer would pick up from there and the bidding would start. After the animal sold, it was my job to run them through a gate onto a scale where the weight would show up on a screen and the purchaser could determine its cost. Sometimes they would sell by the head and not by weight. A cow and calf might be started at $100.

My friend James had the job of writing down the tag number on the animal and the buyer's name. The ticket would be sent to the office where the transaction was completed before the animal could be picked up. I had no doubt but what James would do a good job. He was smart and knew cattle better than anyone I'd ever known. I heard people call him Jaime, which was Spanish for James. When I asked him about it, he laughed and said, "I'm dark and it's not unusual to be mistaken for a Mexican." I discovered that he was the uncle of Mattie's friend Jimmy who had helped her prepare for the basketball tryouts.

The third bull that came into the ring was a bad one. I climbed up on the fence to get out of his reach, but that didn't stop him from trying. His kind didn't come in that often but when they did, it paid to be careful. The worst were the Angus cows. They would kick you before you knew it. I learned quickly to stay out of range. It was an interesting job, with a lot going on, and time passed more quickly than working in the alley.

We only had a few head over a 1000 and by 7:00 that evening the sale was close to ending. The last to be sold were the cancer-eyed cows. The open wounds were full of screwworms and you could smell them from a distance. Surely in the future something could be done to eliminate the worms caused by fly eggs. The word around was that test were underway that would accomplish this. Hopefully, it wouldn't be too many years before it happened.

It was dark before the drive home. It was good to be around other people and stay busy. It kept me from dwelling on Jose and my grief; however, by the time I was approaching the ranch, depression had set in. I was going to be greeted by an empty house filled with sad memories. Driving through my gate, I noticed a light on in the house. The car parked in front belonged to Sonia. As much as I hate to admit it, she would be a welcome sight. Hablo welcomed me with a series of barks from the time he saw me drive in. Of course, he wasn't in the house. He and Sonia didn't get along ever since he hiked on her foot one day while we were sitting on the porch.

She met me at the door, saying, "Oh, Sam, I'm sorry about Jose," than hugging me. "I called the sale and found out when it would be over. I fixed supper for you and brought it over. I'm sorry for my temper tantrum the day you left for Mexico. I don't know what got into me."

"That's all right," I said, finally getting a word in.

"You just relax and I'll heat up your supper."

I admit the fried pork chops and gravy, with red beans was good. It made me nervous the way she kept looking at me, wanting a compliment. Finally, I gave in, saying, "Sonia that was very good. I appreciate it."

"I'm glad you like it. I'll wash the dishes while you watch TV. It won't take me long."

I didn't follow her direction and went outside to smoke. Hablo joined me, lying down at my feet. "Well, boy, you shouldn't have peed on her foot, and you might have gotten a pork chop." He responded with a series of barks, which I assumed meant it was worth it. She interrupted my conversation with Hablo, saying she was finished and we could watch TV. I wasn't in the mood but decided she was owed that much for the fine meal. We settled down to watch Dragnet. Halfway through the show, it wasn't surprising that with my loneliness and her aggressiveness, we were wrapped up on the couch. The ringing phone interrupted the action which was probably good.

Picking up the phone, a voice I didn't recognize said, "Sam?"

"Yes. This is Sam."

"Sam, this is Brad York. I'm sorry to call this late, but Sandy and I didn't know what else to do. We're having problems with Avery. He's not the same boy he was when his brother was killed. He's rebelled against everything, especially me and his mother. You can't imagine how he's changed. He quit football today and is threatening to quit school and leave home. We were hoping that you might be able to help. Avery respects you, at least he used to. Could we talk to you about help you might provide?"

"Sure, Mr. York. Anytime."

"Please, just Brad. We owe you so much already, Sam, and I hate to ask, but we are desperate. I know it's late, but could we come out tonight?"

"That'll be fine," I said.

After the call ended, I explained to Sonia, which didn't go over well. "Couldn't they wait until tomorrow?" she asked.

"Evidently not. I appreciate the supper and thank you for coming over."

She took a deep breath before asking, "Could we continue where we left off, tomorrow night?" she asked.

"I guess so if that's what you want," I said, a little concerned about what she meant.

She kissed me, longer than usual, and left with Hablo barking and probably saying "good riddance." Something must be wrong with me. I didn't want our relationship to go any further. Here I was, a lonely guy with a beautiful girl falling all over him, and all I wanted was some company. I wonder what Phil, my counselor at McKinney would say about this. Probably just scratch his head.

It was after 10:00 before the Yorks arrived. After listening to them for 20 minutes, the situation was much worse than I thought. Avery was associating with the wrong group, which was probably the reason he had quit football. Both parents were confused about why this was happening. It had been going on for some time and became worse by the day. They had tried punishing him but that proved to be useless. He would come in all hours of the night and refuse to get up in the morning, being late for school almost every day.

"Do you think that losing his brother has something to do with the change?" I asked.

"Maybe, but that's been over a year ago. I know we spoiled him after we lost Bennie. We tried to give him everything he wanted and bent the rules to allow him more freedom. We've talked to our minister and he suggested the same thing. We've tried to talk with Avery, but he becomes angry and tells us to leave him alone. The final straw was quitting football. That broke my heart. He'll be a senior next year, and they have a fabulous group of athletes in his class. I have always predicted that the season of 1955-1956 would be one to remember. His friends, up until he changed, have always been athletes. This group he's fallen into does nothing but party and cause trouble."

While he was explaining Avery's behavior, Mrs. York began crying. I felt sorry for them, but didn't know what to say or do. Brad answered that question for me.

"Sam, I know it's a lot to ask, and we owe you so much already. We would like for Avery to live with you for awhile at least. You're our last resort, and if something isn't done we're going to lose another son. Would you consider it? I'd be glad to pay you for his room and board."

No way could I refuse the request. I didn't know the first thing about being a parent, and it would be a challenge to put it mildly; however, they were desperate and had run out of options. "I'll try to help you. I work two days a week, and most of the time it's late when I get home. We'll need to make some kind of arrangements on those days. Of course, he can ride the bus, but he'll be here by himself for several hours."

"We bought him a car, thinking that might help. Looking back, it was probably the wrong thing to do," Mrs. York said.

"Could you contact the school tomorrow and tell them that I'll be coming by to see Avery? Also, you might want to inform them he'll be staying with me and I will be the contact person in case he gets into trouble. If it's okay, I'd like to be the one to inform him that he's going to live with me."

"Yes, we'll be glad to do that. Thank you, Sam. We can never repay you," said Mrs. York.

"Honestly, I don't know if it'll work. He may not respond to me either," I replied.

We visited another 15 minutes, with them giving me more information about Avery, including the fact that he was failing several of his classes. At least when they left it was with more hope than when they arrived. I followed them to the car and lit a Camel after they left, thinking, *what a day; from depression to reluctant lover to parent, all in a few hours.* Hablo barked a number of times, as if to say, at least she's gone and I can come in the house.

Chapter 41

Mattie

I felt guilty about profiting from someone else's misfortune, but Thursday's practice after talking to Mother the opportunity presented itself. The rules allowed for two rovers from each team to play the entire court. One of the starting rovers sprained her ankle and would be out for at least a week, maybe two.

Friday, when the traveling team was posted for an out-of-town game, Saturday with the Tulsa Twisters, my name along with Charley's was on the list. I had assumed that our games would be with other colleges; however, all but a couple were with amateur athletic teams that were sponsored by businesses. I don't see how they called them amateur, since some of them played for ten years or more. A business, such as an automobile dealership would hire them, and they, in turn, would play basketball. It was a form of advertising for the business and gave the girls an opportunity to continue to play basketball. Few colleges had a girls' program at this time. From what I understood, the pay was not good, but it was the only chance the girls had to continue to play.

I tried to call Sam Friday night, but he didn't answer. I was hoping to cheer him up with my good news. I was disappointed about not being able to go home over Thanksgiving, but it wouldn't be that long until Christmas.

Charley and I stayed up late Friday night talking about the next day. "Will we need to take other clothes besides our traveling suits?" I asked.

"Only to lounge around in at the hotel. We'll wear our traveling outfits to and from the game. It's exciting, Mattie. Even more than I'd expected. You feel special with the nice clothes, good food, great lodging, and flying. We're fortunate. I would've never dreamed of being a part of something like this."

We were at the airport at noon the next day in plenty of time to load our belongings. A small carry-on bag with our uniform, shoes, and leisure wear was all that was required. I felt elegant in my travel suit, not ever wearing anything that fit so good and was made with such expensive material. A hairdresser from Amarillo had come over early this morning, working on the nine of us who were going on the trip. For the first time in my life, I felt beautiful. I'd never known anyone as generous as Mr. and Mrs. Hutcherson who paid for everything plus furnishing the four airplanes for our trip. Mr. Hutcherson was an immaculate dresser, wearing a suit and a bow tie. Mrs. Hutcherson was dressed to the hilt, wearing heels, and looking fabulous.

The upperclassmen loaded in the plane piloted by Mr. Hutcherson, since they received first choice. The next group loaded with Coach Redin, the boys' basketball coach, and my group was riding with one of the pilots that worked for Mr. Hutcherson's Flying Service. Charley and Sarah (my big sister) were in my group. Since she was a senior, she had her choice, and she chose to ride with me. That made me feel even more special. I was tense during takeoff, afraid of getting sick, but closed my eyes and made it.

"Are you sick?" asked Charley.

"A little. Not bad. I can't turn around three times without getting queasy. Motion sickness, I guess."

Within two hours we were checking into a hotel in Oklahoma City. I had never stayed anywhere close to as nice. They had carpet throughout, with the bathrooms having a shower and a tub. Each room even had a television and a telephone. My roommates were Charley and Sarah.

We rested that afternoon, before having a pre-game meal at 4:00 consisting of roast beef, baked potato, green beans, and dry toast. No dessert was allowed. Charley leaned over and whispered, "We'll have a great supper after the game."

Several taxis were out front of the hotel at 6:00 to provide a ride to the gym which was a high school facility. It was the largest city, with the tallest buildings I'd ever seen. I gawked at everything on the ride, just like a country girl who had gone to town for the first time.

"What are you looking for?" Charley asked.

Embarrassed I said, "The buildings are tall. I've never seen anything like it, and they're so many cars and people."

"You've never been to a city?" she asked.

"Just Abilene. It's nothing like this," I said.

"You better get used to it, girl. We're going to be traveling to some big cities," she replied.

I'd been so caught up in sightseeing that it seemed like no time until we arrived at the gym. We were shown to our dressing room, and on the way saw two rough looking women sitting in the stands smoking.

After we passed them, Sarah asked, "Did you see two of our opponents taking a break before the game?"

"That's who we're playing? They look, uh, they look…."

"Tough. Believe me, they are."

We took the floor at 7:00 for warmups. The gym began to fill, and by 7:30, which was game time, it was almost to capacity. I guessed the gym would seat somewhere around a 1000. The air was thick with smoke, since no restrictions existed. Neither Charley or I started the game. The rules were different than high school. There were two forwards and two guards for each team on their respective ends. Two rovers were in the middle of the gym who could play the entire court. Whatever end of the court the ball was on would have four players from each team. I was recruited as a rover because of my speed and stamina.

The first quarter was close with the Twisters matching us point for point. By the middle of the second quarter, our conditioning and discipline began to show, with us pulling away. Sarah was awesome and scored 14 points. By halftime the score was 28-16. Coach told me and Charley that we would start the second half. Sarah caught me by the arm before I went on the court. "Mattie, remember who you're playing for. Play hard, but smart, and remember the strategy that we practiced. Everything else will take care of itself."

Of course, I was nervous. We got the ball and were on offense. Going down the court, I could feel my heart pounding. Sarah set up at the post, and of course, they swarmed her. She passed to me, and I shot a 12-foot jump shot that hit nothing but net. I could've screamed with joy, but instead picked up my girl to guard on defense. The rest of the quarter was a dream, as Sarah kept feeding me the ball, and I made four jump shots in a row. Finally, they backed off Sarah and began to guard me. When that happened, she began scoring again. We scored 20 points in the third quarter and were leading 48-22 when it ended. Going to the bench, everyone was congratulating me. I scored six more points in the fourth quarter with the final score being 65-29. It took all my effort to control my excitement after the game ended. Charley had played well, too, scoring six points.

I expected other team members to be excited, but by their reactions, you couldn't even have told if we'd won. Then it occurred to me, the only thought in their minds was that we would win. It was only a matter of how much. It was almost as if it was a waste of their energy to celebrate an outcome that was never in doubt. I was going to have to get used to this kind of confidence. Of course, my excitement was due to the fact I'd proved my ability to play on this great team that had now won 32 straight games.

We had come to the gym dressed in our game uniforms under our warmups. We went directly back to the hotel where coach had us meet in the lobby. Mr. and Mrs. Hutcherson hugged me, saying they were proud of me. Coach led us in a lengthy prayer, told us we played well, and sent us to our rooms to dress for supper.

The compliment that meant the most came from Sarah, my big sister. "Mattie, welcome to the Flying Queens, we're going to make basketball history together."

I tried to stop the tears, but a few slipped as I responded, "Thank you for helping me. I'm so excited."

The taxis were waiting for us when we had finished showering and getting dressed in our traveling uniforms. We drove to a nice restaurant, and by the reception I knew they were expecting us. We were seated four to a table and within a few minutes were served. A waiter set a plate containing a T-bone steak and a pile of French fries in front of me. A dinner salad in another bowl, along with a basket of hot rolls, was sat down next to my plate. I looked at Charlie, and she smiled, mouthing silently, *I told you so.*

I'd not eaten real steak but a few times in my life. It was too expensive. Certainly, I had never eaten this kind of steak. When I had cleaned my plate, it was removed and replaced with another one containing a piece of pecan pie with a dollop of ice cream. I thought, surely this will mean a weight gain; however, looking around me at the other players who had been eating like this in the past, they were as thin as me.

"What do you think?" Charley asked.

"That was the best meal I've ever eaten," I replied.

"You need to become accustomed to it. This is a normal-after game meal," Sarah said.

Everyone finished at about the same time and we were taken back to our hotel. We went to our rooms, and since it was after 11:00, prepared for bed immediately. There were two double beds, and we knew without asking what the sleeping arrangements would be. Sarah, with her height, would get one bed, with Charley and I sharing the other.

We arrived back in Plainview the next morning in time for church. Church service was not an option; everyone was expected to attend. The team generally sat together. Charley nor I were used to the type of sermons we heard which included a lot of scary stuff. Going to hell was mentioned frequently for a number of shortcomings that we admitted having. At first, guilt accompanied us back to the dorm. After talking it over, we decided that the doctrine we'd been taught included a loving God who was quick to forgive if we were sincere. After that, we left the church on Sunday or a chapel meeting during the week feeling less guilty.

When I arrived back at the dorm after church, I tried to call Sam again but received no answer. I spent the next two hours trying to write him a letter but finally gave up with a dozen wadded up papers on the floor. I couldn't come up with the right words. I was torn between consoling him about Jose and telling him about my wonderful weekend. I couldn't, with any amount of effort, make them compatible. I went to the pay phone in the hall and tried his number again…no answer. He was probably with Sonia, being comforted by her. Then, I remembered how long it had been since calling or writing him. I'd been too busy to do either. He should understand that. *Come on Mattie*, I said to myself, *don't lie to yourself. You were occupied with basketball and school, not thinking of Sam.*

I tried calling one more time before going to bed and hung up after ten rings.

Maybe he had forgotten me all together.

Chapter 42

Sam

I went to school the next morning and found Coach in the gym with a PE class. When he saw me, he came over to a corner, out of hearing of his students. "How's it going, Coach?" I asked.

"Sam Colter! Bless my soul. It would be a lot better if you were suiting up tonight. It's good to see you," he said.

"Thanks, Coach, I miss football."

"Football misses you, too, Sam. I wish we would've had the face guards when you played. Your nose wouldn't be as crooked," he said, chuckling.

"Coach, I'm here about Avery. I know he quit yesterday. His parents have asked me to keep him for the time being. I don't know what's happened to him, but evidently he's not the same boy he was last year."

"That's an understatement. I've never seen anyone change the way Avery has. He got in with the wrong crowd and became a different person. I was sorry to see him quit. He wasn't getting a lot of playing time, but I was counting on him for next year. We have an outstanding group coming up."

"Would you allow him to come back?" I asked.

"Sure. He only quit yesterday after practice. In fact, he can suit up for tonight's game, if he comes back."

"I haven't spoken to him yet, but hopefully he'll be around to talk with you sometimes today. Maybe we can get him back in the program. I appreciate it, Coach."

"No problem. Thank you, Sam, for what you're doing. If Avery will listen to anyone it should be you, after what you did for him. I know you've been through some tough times, but you'll make it. I've coached few, if any, players that were as special as you."

I left the gym with a good feeling. Coach didn't pass out compliments unless he meant them. My next stop was the principal's office where I asked to see Avery. I assumed his dad had already called school because the secretary was nice and cooperative. She directed me to an adjourning room and said that Avery would be here shortly. I didn't have to wait long before he arrived. It had been several months since I'd seen him, and his appearance had changed. He'd always dressed neat, but now his hair was longer and his shirttail was out.

"Avery, how're you doing?" I asked, as he slumped down in a chair.

"All right. I guess you're here to tell me how bad my attitude is," he stated.

"No. You're going to be staying with me for awhile. I needed to let you know."

"Why?"

"Your parents asked me. They're worried about you," I said.

"Don't I have anything to say about it?" he asked.

"No. You'll be my responsibility beginning today. From here, I'm going by your house and get your clothes. I understand you have a car. Also, at some time today, you need to talk to Coach and ask to get back into football. Don't try to argue with me about this. There's only three weeks left, and you're not going to quit this year. If you don't want to play your senior year, that'll be your choice. Now, you can go back to class and I'll see you this afternoon. You come directly to my house after school, and I'll take you back with me to the game tonight." Before he could respond, I got up and walked out of the room.

It was a toss-up whether or not he would follow my instructions. I needed to decide what to do in case he refused. He was already 17 and had been pretty much telling his parents what he was going to do, with or without their permission. Force was out of the question. Maybe he still respected me enough to follow my directions. Hopefully, that would be the case.

We were having another good football season and the game with Winters tonight was a big one. I had been to several games and the underclassmen were going to be something else. It wouldn't surprise me if a state championship wasn't in Coach's future.

I was home by noon and went to check on my calves. I only had five in the sick pen, with the others doing well enough to be turned out. The five were holding there own…standing, eating, and drinking. That was all I could ask for. I was thankful to have found my friend, James. With his help, I was still in the cattle business but on a much smaller and more profitable level. James was a huge football fan and made all the games. One of his nephews graduated last year and another was currently a sophomore.

As long as I stayed busy, it wasn't so hard, but with nothing to occupy me, my thoughts would return to Jose. I hadn't been back inside his house since the day I returned. After lunch, I made myself go back. I needed to examine his belongings and if he did have anything of value, send it to Miguel. He had so little but never complained. I sat down in a chair at the table, and my thoughts returned to when I was a small boy while my dad was still living. I must have been five or six years old. I could hear his voice as if he was here.

"Little Bit, we teach you to rope. You be mucho vaquero one day. Got to do it over and over.

We would practice every day for at least half an hour. He had me rope an old milk can that had belonged to my grandparents. Within a year he had me swinging a rope on my old horse. When no one was around, I would rope the chickens, roaming around the barn. The next year I was roping calves in a large pen from my horse.

From the time I could remember, he never called me anything other than Little Bit. No one else used that name for me, it belonged to him. He began teaching me Spanish words when I was three, maybe four and never stopped until we could communicate in the language. By the time I was in junior high, my Spanish was as good as any of the Mexicans in the area.

"Little Bit, my language beautiful. Is a gift to you from me. No one takes it from you."

After my dad died, when I wasn't in school I was with Jose. We didn't have the money to hire extra help during the busy times of the year… it was just me and him. By the time I was 12, I was doing man's work. I would practice the rope tricks for hours that he made look easy but was never able to come close to him.

Without doubt, I filled a loss in his life that must have been devastating. Looking back, it made me feel better that I was able to do something for him.

I expected Avery by 4:00, since school was out at 3:30. At 5:00 he still hadn't shown. At 6:00, I called his parents and his mother answered.

"Have you seen Avery?" I asked.

"No, I thought he was with you."

"I told him to come directly to the ranch after school. He should've been here by now. I'll come by your house when I get to town. If he has a close friend, you might contact the parents and see if he's missing, also."

I met Sonia on the way out, not stopping to talk with her. I didn't have time to visit and she'd be upset about me leaving. I was at the Averys by 6:30 and no one was home. I waited for an hour before they arrived. Judging by their expressions, they didn't have any good news. Brad explained what they had found out.

"Sam, we know where he is, or we think we do. It took a while, but after talking to parents of several new friends Avery has made, we're pretty sure he's in Sweetwater at the Gunter Hotel. There's a party in one of the rooms every Friday night for those who aren't interested in a football game. Some older guys furnish the liquor and drugs. They charge a fee to the younger boys to get in. We believe it is the same party that Bennie had attended the night before his accident coming home. We don't know what to do. Should we call the police in Sweetwater or go after him ourselves?"

"It would be hard to believe that the police didn't know about the party, since it's been going on for this long. I told Avery this morning he was going to be my responsibility. I'll go see if he's at the party and bring him home. I'll let you know the outcome."

"Sam, we're sorry for putting you through this," said Mrs. York.

"I thought he might do what he was asked." I said.

When I walked into the Gunter Hotel the lobby was empty. I asked a man at the desk if he knew of a party being held. He smiled and asked, "You interested?"

"Maybe. I need a room number."

"Actually, they rent two adjoining rooms. Quite a crowd usually. I tell them to keep the noise down. Try room 221."

I left, going up the stairs. The hall on the second floor was quiet. When I knocked on the door, it surprised me to be looking at a man who must've been 30.

"You ready to party? You been here before?" he asked.

"No."

"Ten bucks to get in. Most think it's worth it. Lot's of booze, maybe a little something else to make you feel good," he said.

I took out my billfold and gave him two fives. "Is Avery here?"

"How the hell should I know? We don't exchange names."

I went into the room and was surprised to see half a dozen boys sitting around smoking and drinking. Some had beer, others had a glass of something, probably vodka, or gin. Avery wasn't among them, so I went through a door to an adjoining room. This room was full, having at least a dozen boys sitting in chairs and on the floor drinking. Some were older than the ones in the first room... maybe in their twenties. I spotted Avery in a corner chair, holding a can of beer, talking to another boy. He didn't see me until I was standing in front of him.

"What're you doing here?" he slurred.

"Come to get you."

"I'm not going with you. I have friends here. Just go away and leave me alone."

"No. You're coming with me. Now get up and let's get outta here."

By this time the room had become quieter, with Avery's loud voice getting attention. I reached down and took his arm, but he jerked it away, screaming, "Leave me alone I said!"

"Avery, your parents are worried about you. Please go with me. This isn't a place for you." I didn't see him but felt a presence behind me. I turned and the older guy who let me in, was standing there. Another man, who was in his twenties was standing beside him.

"You bothering this young man?" he asked. "Are you a relative?"

"No. Just a friend," I answered.

"It seems that he doesn't want to go. You better leave. We don't want any trouble here. The boy paid his ten dollars and is entitled to a good time."

"I'm not leaving without him," I said.

The men looked at each other and smiled, like they had a secret. The one doing the talking said, "Yes, Sonny, you're going to leave," as he pulled a gun out of his pocket and pointed it at me.

Seeing the gun, was the last thing I remember well. I reacted as if it were a life or death situation, like the ones experienced in Korea. When my mind could once again comprehend what was happening, three policemen were holding me down on the floor and putting handcuffs on me. One of the police was calling for an ambulance, saying men had been injured at the Gunter Hotel. As I was led out of the room, I saw the two men lying in blood on the floor.

At the jail, I was fingerprinted, photographed, and placed in a cell by myself. I still didn't know exactly what happened.

I remembered the man pointing the gun at me and there was something about a knife, but that was all. Maybe later what happened would be clearer. I lay down on the bed and closed my eyes hoping to remember everything that happened. After about an hour, a man came and unlocked the cell, indicating that I go with him. When we reached the outer office, Brad and his wife were present.

"Sam, are you hurt?" Avery's dad asked.

"No. I don't think so. I just can't remember what happened."

"Let me refresh your memory," a man who I assume was a detective said. "I talked with a number of boys at the party and they all told the same story. You kicked the victim between the legs, took his gun away from him, pointed it at his head and pulled the trigger several times. The gun was not loaded are you would be facing a murder charge. You then clubbed him with the gun. You still may be looking at a murder charge because the other guy you attacked, had a knife and you took it away from him and cut him several times. He's in ICU now, and his condition is critical. After you did all that damage, you sat down on the floor like nothing had happened until the police arrived."

"Officer, our boy was at the party, and he's a minor. Sam went to the party to bring him home. From what I understand, these men threatened Sam with a gun. How can any of this be Sam's fault?"

"Witnesses said this man was a maniac, intent on killing these men. He went beyond protecting himself. They had never seen anything like it, was the comment I heard over and over."

"What about bail?" Brad asked.

"A hearing will be scheduled for Monday and the judge will determine bail. Until then, he will be held. A lawyer will be provided if he can't afford one."

"He'll have a lawyer for the hearing," Brad said.

I was escorted back to my cell, and exhausted, laid down and went to sleep.

They were coming, and I only had part off a magazine of ammunition left, that was feeding the Browning. I squeezed the trigger and several fell and then click, click, was the only sound. Two were coming with bayonets pointed at me, screaming. I moved aside the first, pushing my knife between his ribs, jerked his weapon away from him and thrust his bayonet into the second one, seeing the look of surprise as he slumped to the ground.

I woke up trembling, remembering now, what had happened last night. I couldn't go back to sleep and lay there until the jailor brought my breakfast. I wasn't hungry but tried to eat the scrambled eggs and toast. I got most of it down, with the coffee that wasn't bad. Later when the jailor came back to get my tray, I told him that I didn't want to see any visitors.

The remainder of the day, I spent a lot of time thinking since there wasn't anything else to do. I needed to treat Sonia better. She cared for me and was doing everything she could to help me. Mattie, on the other hand, had her own life now, and it didn't include me. It would be Christmas before I saw her, which was two months away. We hadn't stayed in touch like I thought we would. It might be best if I didn't even see her Christmas.

That afternoon a lawyer came to talk with me. I told him my version of the incident which had occurred. After finishing, I asked him, "What will be the charges against me?"

"I'm not sure. Maybe assault. The way I understand it, they may have a difficult time coming up with a charge. After all, you had no weapon. I talked with two of the boys who saw the incident, and they told me it wasn't unusual for Reeves to pull his gun on someone. According to them, he was always flashing it around. He used the gun to bully people. You had no way of knowing that it wasn't loaded. He just picked the wrong person to bluff this time. The one thing that we have to overcome is the fact that after you took the gun from him he was no longer a threat, but you pointed it at him and pulled the trigger several times. Of course, after that you clubbed him with it. The knife incident shouldn't be a problem. It wasn't your knife. Also, I checked at the hospital and Sloan will recover. He's out of ICU and in a room. Most important, they were serving alcohol to minors which is against the law."

"What about bail?" I asked.

"Shouldn't be a problem since Sloan is out of danger; however, Judge McCloud is something else. He stays in a foul mood most of the time. He's been on the bench over thirty years and needs to retire, but no one has the courage to suggest that to him. There's no telling what he might do on any given day. I'm going to have a talk with the prosecutor in the morning and feel him out. He's young, ambitious, and full of himself. He'll probably try anything to draw attention to himself. Can I get you anything before I leave?"

"Are we allowed to have a radio?"

"Let me check," he said. He left and came back with a radio a few minutes later.

Giving me a piece of paper, he said, "My phone number is on this. Call me if you need anything. The jailor will let you use the phone. I'll see you tomorrow."

The radio helped with the boredom, and I slept through the night without the demons visiting me.

Pierce, my lawyer, was at the jail by mid-morning the next day, which was Sunday. He had talked to the prosecutor but got nowhere, saying, "Looks like we go before the judge in the morning at 10:00. It'll be interesting to see what charges they bring against you. I was young once, but never as impressed with myself as this prosecutor.

"What will happen in the morning?" I asked.

"They'll say what the charges are and ask how you plead. Then I expect them to ask that bail not be allowed. I'll be permitted to speak at that time."

"Is there any chance that the judge will dismiss the case?" I asked.

"Slim and none. As I told you yesterday, this judge is a piece of work from the old school. Our best chance will be to get you out on bail and when we go before the Grand Jury get a no-bill."

"Which will mean?"

"It's over. You'll not go to trial."

"Can we smoke in here? I asked.

"Yeah. Do you have cigarettes?

"A few. Can you bring me another pack?"

"Sure."

"One more question. How much do you charge?"

Smiling he replied, "You don't have to worry. That's been taken care of. I have to go now, but you'll have cigarettes shortly.

After another long night, I thought 10:00 would never come. Two officers came in, handcuffed me, and led me to a car. It was a short drive to the court house and Pierce met me out front. It was cold this morning, and without a coat, I was shivering by the time we were inside. There were several people in the court room including, Brad and Mrs. York, Mr. and Mrs. Toller, Hollis and Mrs. Quentin, and I was surprised to see my boss from the auction, Bob McDaniel.

The judge came in shortly and everyone rose. He was medium height and thin. What set him off was his hair or lack of it. He was bald in front but had allowed what little hair he had in back to grow down over his ears. He looked angry when the announcement was made that the court was in session. The prosecutor commenced to lay out the charges against me.

"Judge, we have a dangerous man here. He's a killer, and two men are fortunate to be alive after Friday night. The charges are assault with a deadly weapon, in fact, two weapons, resisting arrest, and possible manslaughter if one of his victims dies."

"How does the defendant plead?" the judge asked.

"Not guilty, Your Honor," I said.

"Pierce, do you have anything to say?" Judge McCloud asked.

My attorney rose, thanked the judge, and commenced to tell my side of the story. He was remarkable, with his accuracy, professionalism, and speaking ability. I marveled at how smooth he was and how his voice varied when he wanted to make a point. When he reached the issue about my resisting arrest his voice became angry. "I'm appalled that an outright lie of this kind would be told in your courtroom." His final statements addressed my military service.

"Your Honor, Sam Colter served two years in Korea. I did research and found out about his service. None of this information came directly from him but from his superiors. Sam was in the midst of the fighting during his tour and was sited for bravery many times. He was awarded the Distinguished Service Cross which, as you know, is the second highest military decoration. It is for extraordinary heroism. Sam was reacting Friday night to a threat on his life, exactly the way he did in Korea. I looked at his records, which included a note from his commanding officer. 'Sam Colter was a warrior and killed as many or more of the enemy than any other American in the Korean conflict.' Your Honor, we locked up a hero over the weekend, and I am ashamed of it." Pierce sat down.

The judge, hesitated, took a deep breath, and looked at the prosecuting attorney.

"I believe this is a waste of time and money. I want you and Pierce to go in that room over there and work out some kind of agreement to end this. Don't come out unless you have something that is reasonable for this young man. Do you understand? Son, you need to go with them."

Evidently, the prosecutor got the message, because, once in the room, an agreement was reached in a matter of minutes. Pierce recommended, I take it. I was to receive a six-month jail sentence that would be probated and a fine of $500. When we returned to the courtroom the judge was smiling for the first time.

"So, let's hear it," he said.

"Judge, my client has agreed to a six-month jail sentence, that will be probated and a fine of $500."

"Sounds fair, except let's reduce the fine to $250 if that's agreeable?"

The prosecutor opened his mouth intending to disagree but a stern look from the judge changed his mind and he nodded in agreement.

Jenkins, this is a small town and I'm not supposed to be aware of anything when I come to court. That is ridiculous. I received calls from half a dozen parents over the weekend that were happy to see someone do something to bring attention to this party that has been going on for years. Also, I heard the description of what happened several times. Now, this boy didn't resist arrest. You lied in my court. You're young and not blessed with much intelligence so I'm going to overlook it this time. If you do it again I will see to it that you never practice law again. Understood?"

Jenkins, nodded, saying, "Yes, Your Honor."

"Another thing, Jenkins. I notice you have on white socks with a dark suit. Get you some colored socks before you come back into my courtroom."

Slamming the gavel down hard enough to make everyone jump, he said "This court is adjourned."

Chapter 43

Gladys

It was Tuesday, November 23, and Thanksgiving would be the day after tomorrow. Of course, Mattie wasn't coming home, but something very exciting had happened. Mattie had called last week and explained the event. It was a tradition that the freshmen Flying Queens have a chance to play before their home fans. This weekend was going to be her opportunity to do just that. Sunday, on the way back home from their tournament, the team was going to play an exhibition game at Dyess Air Force Base Gym. It would just be an intrasquad game but would give Mattie's hometown fans a chance to see her play. Mattie said that the Hutchersons were responsible for this act of kindness and consideration. Of course, they owned the flying service that furnished planes for travel to out-of-town games. Mattie could not say enough nice things about Claude and Wilda Hutcherson.

The local newspaper had a nice spread about the game in the paper. I think everyone in town knew about the game, at least it seemed that way, by the number of people coming in the store mentioning it to me. The one problem that concerned me was Sam. He hadn't asked me about Mattie in over a month. Sonia had been with him on most of his visits to buy groceries. He was always polite and spoke, asking about Mr. Quentin and myself, but never Mattie. I didn't know what was going on and was afraid to find out. Evidently, she was spending a lot of time at his ranch. Sonia was a pretty girl, and I could see how boys would be attracted to her, but somehow she didn't strike me as being Sam's type. Maybe that was because I wanted Mattie to be his type.

Mr. Quentin and I were relieved that Sam didn't receive jail time for the episode in Sweetwater. We were at the bail hearing and everyone was surprised at the judge's decision. I didn't tell Mattie about Sam's trouble, on the advice of Mr. Quentin. Avery had only stayed a short time with Sam after that. He was back living at home, and from what I heard, doing well.

It wasn't going to be much of a Thanksgiving without Mattie. Earnest was coming over, but it would only be the three of us. Mr. Quentin had called Sam yesterday and invited him to join us, but he had already made arrangements. I assume that meant he would be at the Tollers. I hadn't mentioned Sonia spending so much time with Sam, but maybe I should. When I asked Mattie about Sam, she was evasive, changing to another subject. She was totally involved in school and basketball. She was now starting as a freshman and couldn't contain her excitement when describing the games and her experiences as a Flying Queen. They now had a 37-game winning streak and were receiving state as well as national attention.

We had a busy day and it would be even more so tomorrow with everyone stocking up for Thanksgiving Dinner. At noon, I met Louise for lunch at the drug store. She suggested that we walk around to Woozys' and eat. They had a lunch special each day and it was usually good. After we ordered, I told her my concern about Sam.

"I tell you, Gladys, it doesn't sound good. You know, I hear everything in the drug store with the beauty shop being there. The gossip, and there's plenty of it about Sonia, is that she has all but moved in with Sam. Everyone is saying that her parents should be ashamed for allowing her to be so bold. I don't know what to believe but that's the talk. They've been in the drug store together several times, and the way she acts you would think they were already married."

"It doesn't surprise me that her parents allow it. They like Sam, and who wouldn't. He's a nice boy and has been through so much, with the war and all. He must be terribly lonely after Jose died, and I imagine that's part of his willingness to allow this to be going on," I said.

"You're so positive and yet naive, Gladys. It could be because she's a pretty young lady that's willing to do anything to catch a man and Sam's taking advantage of a situation."

"I hope that's not the case. I believe that Mattie cares about Sam but is caught up in this excitement of playing for the Flying Queens and is ignoring him. When she calls, all we talk about is the last game they played and how much she is enjoying herself. She's looking forward to playing at Dyess on Sunday."

"Will Sam go?" asked Louise.

"I honestly don't know. What do you think would be worse? Sam not going or being there with Sonia?" I asked.

"If he was there with Sonia, maybe that would be a 'wakeup call' for her; however, Mattie may be over Sam, with all the attention she's receiving," she said.

"I know Mattie, Louise. I don't think that's the case. I just believe that right now there's not room for anything in her thoughts except basketball and college."

Our food came and I changed the subject to something less stressful.

Thanksgiving turned out better than I expected, with Louise eating with us. The four of us enjoyed our dinner, with the talk centering around Sunday's game, the drought, and politics. With the depression being a vivid memory for Mr. Quentin and Earnest, they were die-hard Democrats. For the most part, Louise and I stayed out of that discussion.

Earnest had asked me to marry him and I had agreed but asked that we wait until after the first of the year. That would allow me to tell Mattie in person when she was home for the holidays. I was satisfied with my decision and could see no reason not to get on with my life. Mr. Quentin had insisted that he would make other arrangements after we were married. I knew this meant going to the nursing home. I didn't argue with him but wouldn't allow him to do that since he was doing so well. We would cross that bridge when we got to it. He and Earnest got alone great and something could be arranged.

Late that evening, we had a cold front move through, bringing wind and sand. The temperature dropped drastically over the next several hours, and it looked as if winter had arrived.

The game Sunday was to start at 3:00, giving people plenty of time to attend church. We took my car, and Mr. Quentin, Earnest, and Louise were passengers. We left early, hoping to be there when the planes landed. When we arrived, I parked close to the runway. We didn't have a long wait as the first plane landed, followed by the second, third, and fourth. It was an incredible sight to watch and when the girls stepped off the planes in their traveling suits it took my breath away. When I saw Mattie exit the second plane, I started crying, unable to help myself. She was beautiful, and when she started toward us, the closer she came, the more I could see the change. She was a young lady now, and not a little girl.

She hugged her pa-pa and then me, asking, "Mother, why're you crying?"

"I'm sorry, Mattie. I can't help it. You... you look so grown up and professional. I expected to see my little girl."

"I'm still your little girl, Mother."

Before I could answer, a man and woman approached, introducing themselves as Claude and Wilda Hutcherson. Mattie introduced us and she spoke first.

"Mrs. Quentin, we just love Mattie. She's a joy to be around and we know much of the credit for that goes to you. We are not supposed to have favorites, but it's hard to hide our affection for Mattie."

"Mrs. Quentin, Mattie is a remarkable addition to the Flying Queens. We're looking forward to her being with us for three more years. She has the most beautiful jump shot I've ever seen," said Claude.

"Mother, we have to get dressed now, but I'll see you after the game," Mattie said.

A crowd was already gathering in the gym, even though it was an hour before the game. Many were there to see Mattie, but a good number were strangers. The fame of the Flying Queens was growing, and the Abilene Reporter News had also run the story about the game.

It was exciting to watch the warmups on both ends of the court. The girls were tremendous athletes, and it was easy to see how they had a 37 game winning streak. By 3:00, the gym was full, with standing room only. We had been early enough to get seats. When the game started, I was surprised to see they were playing full court with boys' rules. Mattie was on the first team and the second team was no match for them. They would get the ball into the tall post and she would either drive to the basket, put up a beautiful hook shot, or feed the ball back outside, many times to Mattie. I couldn't help but keep count of the points Mattie made. Every time she scored a roar went up from the hometown fans. They only played six minute quarters, but by the end of the game Mattie had scored 15 points. The only player scoring more was the tall post. Throughout the game, during time-outs, I noticed Mattie looking into the stands. When she came back out for the second half, she spent several minutes surveying the crowd. I know she was looking for Sam, but he wasn't there, and maybe that was for the best.

When the game ended, Mattie was swarmed by friends. Some of the children were even asking for her autograph. I stayed back until they thinned out and then we had a few minutes to ourselves. Her first observation didn't surprise me.

"Sam wasn't here. I thought he would come."

"When's the last time you talked to him?" I asked.

"I've tried to call several times but couldn't get him. I don't have time to write."

"Sam had a hard time when Jose died. We tried to do something, but I'm afraid we weren't much help. It's only a month until Christmas. You can see him then," I said.

Her pa-pa had been standing back, giving me a few minutes alone with her. Mattie left me, going over and hugging him. "What did you think, Pa-Pa?"

"You were awesome, Mattie. Who's the big girl that plays post?"

"That's Sarah, by big sister. Isn't she amazing?"

"The best I've ever seen," he said.

"I need to get dressed now for the trip home."

"We'll wait and watch you take off," I said.

After she left, Mr. Quentin said, "Gladys, can you believe how she's changed. She doesn't even look the same. Tell me what's so different about her."

"Confidence, self-assurance...she believes in herself," I said. "As far as her looks, she's gained weight, and isn't as thin."

"Did she ask about Sam?"

"Yes, but she didn't seem that disappointed he wasn't here."

We watched the girls enter each plane, waving at Mattie just before she went out of sight. The take-off was even more impressive than the landing, with each plane going down the runaway and lifting off. Mattie was in the second one and we stood and watched until they were all out of sight.

I knew it would be something special, but it was even more than that," Louise said. "It must be like a fairy tale for Mattie."

"Who would've ever thought she would be flying to and from games?" asked her pa-pa.

Not me, I thought; however, there was something else about Mattie that was different and it gave me an uneasy feeling. Maybe it was only my imagination.

Chapter 44

Mattie

As the plane started climbing, I continued to watch my mother until she was only a speck. I settled back in my seat, wondering, why Sam didn't come to watch me play. I had expected him to be there and was looking forward to impressing him. He was probably angry with me for not calling or writing. I had tried on two occasions to reach him on the phone. I didn't have time to sit down and write a letter. A voice in my head whispered, *that's a lie. You didn't want to take the time to write him. You're too busy experiencing the excitement and glory of new found fame. Shame on you for not being honest, even with yourself.* I immediately squashed that voice and moved on to another topic.

It was only three weeks until the Christmas holidays started. I should be looking forward to having time off, but the thought of leaving school and basketball caused me to wish that the holidays were shorter. I had a whole new life now, and it was exciting compared to the old one I'd left behind, which seemed like years ago. I had gone from being a nothing when I graduated from high school to being treated as a princess and feeling like one. Should that bring on guilt? No. I had worked hard and deserved the treatment being doled out to me. Charley, interrupted my thoughts, bringing me back to reality.

"He wasn't there, was he?" she asked.

"No, but it wasn't a big deal?"

"Why do you think he didn't come?" she asked.

"Probably busy," I said, wanting to change the subject.

"With her?"

"I don't know, Charley. I'd rather not talk about it. It was a wonderful day, and I saw Mother and Pa-Pa, plus many of my friends. I'm not going to let him spoil it by not coming. Now, let's talk about something else."

"Are you looking forward to the holidays?" she asked.

"Sorta."

"I am. I love Christmas. I hope it snows. Have you ever had a white Christmas?" she asked.

"I only remember one, a long time ago."

"It's not that unusual for us to have snow. I'm hoping to get a car this Christmas. It probably won't happen since we had another poor cotton crop this year due to the drought. I feel sorry for Flint's family. Christmas is a difficult time for a family that has lost a loved one. So many memories."

When Charley got started, she went on and on. I wasn't in the mood to talk about family or Christmas now, so I lay my head back and pretended to sleep.

Thursday night, December 2, we had a home game with the Arkansas Motor Coaches, a team in the Amateur Athletic Union that was sponsored by an automobile dealership. We played our home games at Plainview High School. Our gym at the college wouldn't seat nearly enough people, and besides, it was old and run down. Many days we had to sweep before we could practice because a dust storm had deposited a layer of sand on the floor.

The game started at 7:00 and the gym was packed, as always. I didn't have one of my better games, but we won easily. Maybe it was a letdown after the excitement of playing at Dyess. Charley, though, had a fantastic night, scoring 16 points. Mr. and Mrs. Norwich, her parents were there, and they took us out to eat after the game. From the time we left the gym until the time we were seated at our table, she talked non-stop. I had discovered that the more excited she was, the more she talked. Her dad finally interrupted her.

"Charley, let Mattie get a few words in."

"I'm sorry. It's just that I'm so excited."

"That's fine. She has a right to be excited after playing such a great game," I said.

"Mattie, I know Charley has told you that we're good friends with the McGowans. They're still having a difficult time getting over the loss of Flint. We had told them earlier about Charley's roommate being friends with Sam Colter. Flint had spoken often of Sam in his letters home. An army chaplain visited them recently and told them about Sam's effort to save Flint. It seems that after he was shot Sam carried him out of harm's way. That was some feat since Flint weighed over 200 pounds. Anyway, what I was getting at is, the McGowans would like to visit with Sam and thank him personally. Would you be willing to relay that message to him?" Mr. Norwich asked.

"Sure, but I haven't been able to reach him lately. I'll probably see him over the Christmas holidays, though. I could tell him then."

"They would appreciate that. Please stress to him how important it is to them. I think they just want to talk to someone who was with him during this time. It's obvious to them that he and Sam were the best of friends. I'm going to give you their phone number in case he's willing to get in touch with them."

I had been trying not to think about Sam and why he didn't come to Dyess. Now, it seemed that everyone wanted to talk about him. I assured Mr. Norwich when they dropped us off at the dorm that I would do my best to get the message to Sam.

It was just two weeks until finals, and I was trying to finish a term paper in English that was due on December 17, which would count as half of the exam. With practice and playing two games a week, my time was limited. I stayed up past midnight on several occasions. Another bigger challenge was a Bible class that Charley and I were taking, along with five other members of the team. The professor, who was a minister, couldn't hide his contempt for us. He would break down occasionally and preach us a sermon on the evils of displaying ourselves in shorts before crowds. I was making a C, which was the highest grade among any of us. Charlie and several others were failing the class. Most of the players on our team were excellent students and it was unheard of for one to fail a class.

We had a game on Saturday the 4th, with Hanes Hosiery in Western Salem, North Carolina. It was one of our longer road trips, and we left at noon on Friday. Sarah had already told me that they were one of the toughest teams we would play. They had won three National Championships during the early '50's.

All the girls who played for Hanes worked in their factory in Winston Salem. The company had built a gym for them to play in which held 2000. When we took the floor Saturday night, it was filled to capacity. I had never played before that many people. I knew from the beginning that we were going to be in for a tough night, and throughout the first half there was never more than a four-point difference. It was the first time I realized how important a hometown crowd was. Virtually everyone in the gym was screaming for Hanes. When we would go to the foul line, the roaring would begin to try and break our concentration.

At the beginning of the third quarter, with the score tied, they shot and missed. I had blocked out and was about to jump for the rebound when one of them came around with an elbow and hit me square in the face. That was the last thing I remember until I woke up on the floor with Coach bending over me, holding something under my nose. Two of my teammates helped me to the bench where I realized blood was gushing from my nose. A person came out of the stands telling Coach he was a doctor.

"Just tilt your head back, Little Lady, and we'll get that stopped in no time," he said. He pinched the bridge of my nose and sure enough in a short time the bleeding had stopped. The game had to be delayed until they could mop the blood from the floor. After that, I was a spectator the remainder of the game. Watching my team play in a close game was enlightening to say the least. They remained calm and confident and by the fourth quarter were pulling away. Sarah was awesome again. It seemed that the tougher the game the tougher she played. As our lead lengthened, the crowd noise decreased, until by the end of the game, the gym was silent. It was humbling to see that they didn't need me to win. In high school if I had gotten hurt, everyone would have panicked. I wasn't missed tonight, in fact, the team did better when I wasn't playing.

That night as I lay in bed, unable to sleep, my thoughts returned to Sam. I had made an effort not to think about him, attempting to put the disappointment of his absence at Dyess out of my mind. I hadn't talked to Sam since Jose died. I should have continued to try and reach him but chose not to. Maybe I was avoiding the sadness that would come with it. Living in a dream world, maybe the thought of facing reality was more than I could handle. I was wrong and sorry for not being there for him. What would his reaction be when I saw him during the holidays? I finally drifted off to sleep sometime after 2:00 in the morning.

Charley and Sarah were already up and dressed before I awoke the next morning. They were sitting on a couch looking at me when I sat up in bed. They immediately began laughing.

"What's so funny?" I asked.

"Go look in the mirror," Sarah said.

I went to the bathroom, and looking at myself, it was obvious what the laughter was about. My two black eyes weren't the least bit humorous to me. Returning to the room, I said, "I thought you two were my friends."

"We are. You just look like a raccoon. We couldn't help it," Charley said.

"It could be worse. Your front teeth could be gone. I've seen that happen," Sarah said. "At least your eyes will return to normal."

"How long will it take?" I asked.

"It's like this. First, they'll be black for several days and then become yellow for several more days. I would guess in about ten days they won't be noticeable," Sarah explained.

"I'm hungry. Let's go eat breakfast. They probably won't even notice you," said Charley.

That was a joke. I drew a crowd immediately when I entered the dining area. There was more laughter, then some sympathy. Wilda came to my rescue, bringing me a pair of large sunglasses that hid my injuries. I immediately felt better and was even able to admit that I did resemble a raccoon.

After finishing breakfast, we went directly to the air field and boarded for our trip home. Sometime experiences that last a lifetime come upon you without warning. After several hours, and flying over Oklahoma, Sarah, who was sitting by the window, said, "Look down there, ladies." Looking down at the snow-covered terrain, with the sun shining brightly was a sight I will never forget. Beautiful is too mild a word to describe it. The snow cover continued until we reached Plainview, where the runaway had been swept clean for our landing.

We played two more games the following week, winning both, and bringing our win streak to 40. Now, the main focus was on final exams. Charley was about to panic, fearing she was going to fail the Bible class. I tried to encourage and reassure her but wasn't successful.

"Mattie, I'm going to fail. I might as well accept it. They'll probably take my scholarship away from me. Professor Dollfuss is going to fail as many of us as he can. Have you noticed how partial he is to Trudy? It's sickening how he smiles at her and talks so sweet to her just because she's pretty. The old codger is a hypocrite deluxe. He preaches to us about wearing shorts and then ogles her. She's probably going to make an A."

"I'll help you study for the final, Charley. You can do it."

"Nope, I'm going to fail. I might as well pack my bags; however, I won't be by myself. Several other girls on the team are in the same situation as me. It could be the end of the Flying Queens if enough of us fail. I'm sorry, Mattie, but it's just not right for one man to be that unfair because we play basketball."

I listened to this for several days until Friday before the start of finals on Monday. Charley came bouncing into the room that afternoon, saying, "Guess what, Mattie?"

"I have no idea."

"We've got the test! Trudy got it for us. She was in the old codger's office, probably buttering him up, and lifted it off his desk. He'd already run off copies so he won't miss it. I can't believe it! I can't say anything bad about Trudy now. She gave it to Mallory, and we're going to meet tomorrow and study together. Isn't it amazing? Somebody up there must me looking after us."

"Charley, I doubt if 'somebody up there' is pleased with Trudy stealing a test and y'all cheating in order to pass."

"Mattie, don't be such a prude! We're not all as smart as you. If it was anybody other than Professor Dollfuss, I wouldn't think about doing it. He's not being fair to us."

"Haven't you ever heard that two wrongs don't make a right?" I asked.

"Oh, Mattie, don't be like that. Be happy for me. I'm going to pass. I can stay in school."

"If that's the way you feel about it, Charley; however, I told you we could study together, and you could pass the test."

"But that's not a sure thing. We have the test and there won't be any doubt."

"Do what you feel is right, Charley. That's all I'll say."

Charley avoided me the remainder of the day. She was gone Saturday morning when I woke up. I assumed she was already with the group studying the stolen exam. Maybe I shouldn't have talked to her the way I did. She was as good or better a person than me. I really didn't have a right to judge her actions. No, that wasn't correct. I wasn't judging her. There was right and wrong and all I did was point that out to her.

I put on my robe, gathered up what I needed for my shower and went to the community bathroom down the hall. I liked to shower early, since most of the girls slept in on Saturday. There were six shower stalls with curtains on each and all were empty this morning. Choosing an end stall, I showered and washed my hair. Afterward, while putting on makeup at the lavatory, I noticed my eyes were beginning to turn yellow, just as Sarah predicted. I had gained weight and actually filled out somewhat. Maybe my high school friend was right and I was going to be a late developer. No one else came in, and satisfied that I had done the best I could to cover up my yellow eyes, returned to my room. I was surprised to find Charley sitting in a chair eating a donut.

"I thought you'd gone to study?" I said.

"Nope, I walked to the shop down the street and bought two dozen donuts. We're not going to be hungry while we study for the Bible exam."

I turned my research paper in a day early and felt good about my other exams. I had noticed that Professor Dollfuss was not always upfront when preparing you for a test. He liked to place a great amount of emphasis on certain areas that made you think it would comprise most of the test. He would vaguely mention other areas as kind of an afterthought, and they would make up the bulk of the exam. I used this strategy when Charley and I studied for the final. We hit all areas, but I emphasized the minor points more. My observation paid off, as Charlie made an 86 and I made a 92 on the exam. I had never seen her so happy, even when she played well.

With finals over, we packed our clothes on Friday, December 17, to leave for home the next day. I had a bus ticket with an arrival time of 1:00 on Saturday. Charley's parents were picking her up. I decided to call Sam late Friday night, hoping to catch him at home. I wanted to be able to tell Charley's parents that I'd relayed the McGowans message to him. I also wanted to tell him what time my bus would arrive. Maybe he would volunteer to pick me up at the station.

No one was in the hallway, so this would be a good time to have privacy. I dialed the number, waiting with change in hand for the operator to tell me how much to deposit. Finally, she said, deposit 45 cents, please. I did so, and the phone rang once, twice, three, four, five times, and I was about to hang up when a soft, female voice said, "Hello." I hung up immediately.

Chapter 45

Sam

After my jail time, Avery came home with me for two weeks but wanted to go home after that. He was no problem and did everything I asked while he was here. I actually enjoyed having him around. I'd heard from his parents several times and he was doing well…back to his old self. My $250 fine was paid, but I never did find out who did it.

Sonia got over being angry with me and was coming over regularly by the time Avery had gone home. It was nice to have someone around, and it wasn't long before she was spending more time at my house than hers. The more she was around, the more demanding she became. I didn't want her to leave altogether, but to just give me some breathing room. I was surprised that her parents weren't concerned about how much time she was spending with me. I actually believe her mother was encouraging her. I'd decided that she had visions of me being in the family permanently. Her brothers had different ideas and treated me with contempt when I was around them. Her dad was nice as always and enjoyable to be with. We always had plenty to talk about. It still hadn't rained, and the drought was about to enter it's fifth year. Every day I was thankful my stock had been sold. I had taken ten of my calves to the sale and was surprised that they brought over $500. They averaged weighing 350 and brought 15 cents a pound. I tried to pay my friend, James, for helping me get started, but he wouldn't take it, saying, I could buy his lunch some day. I still had 16 calves left, but they weren't ready to sale.

I hadn't gone to see Mattie play at Dyess. After Jose died, I expected her to call, but she didn't, and besides that, she didn't write either. I assumed she wanted nothing to do with me so there was no reason to go see her. I went to visit Hollis occasionally and he hadn't said anything about my absence at the game. He had invited me over for Thanksgiving, but I'd already accepted an invitation to the Tollers. Sonia's mother was some kind of cook and eating over there often, I should have been gaining weight. That wasn't the case, in fact, the opposite was true. After Jose died, I started losing again and by Thanksgiving was down to 150. The Levis I purchased after returning home fit again after being too small.

Sonia's mom and dad went to the National Finals Rodeo in December and she talked them into staying home. I don't know whether it was loneliness or the anger at Mattie, but as the old saying goes 'stupid is as stupid does.' She insisted on staying with me the four days they were gone, and I consented. I have a feeling her mother suspected it would happen but her dad had no idea. I knew it was a mistake but didn't realize how big until the third day when she decided to do my washing. It was like she thought we were already married. I went around all day telling myself, *you have messed up big time, Sam Colter.* When the four days were up, I welcomed the loneliness with open arms. Hablo was just as happy to see her drive off as I was, barking until she was out of sight.

It was Saturday, the 18th, and only a week before Christmas. The weather had been milder than usual, and it had been a month since a dust storm. I dreaded Christmas, but there was something positive about the holiday. The Tollers had made plans for the family to spend Christmas in Colorado at a ski resort. No matter how much she pleaded with her parents, Sonia couldn't convince them to leave her home. She begged me to go, but there was no way that was going to happen. They were leaving the first of next week and would be gone ten days. It would be a lonely Christmas, and I would be glad when it was over, but a relief not to have to spend it at the Tollers.

I was out of groceries and needed to make a trip into town. I had put it off since Sonia insisted on going with me everywhere. I checked on my calves, pleased to see that the sick ones were improving. Hablo followed me to my pickup, barking, as if pleading with me to take him. I opened the door and he jumped in, continuing to bark. The weather was beautiful and I decided to go out to James' house to visit him before going to town. He'd asked me several times, but I'd never got around to it. His place was less than two miles northwest of town, and I didn't have any trouble finding it. Turning in, there were several pickups at his arena, and I didn't stop at the house. It was only a hundred yards or so from his house, and seeing me drive up, he came over.

"Sam, good to see you. We're roping some this morning. My brothers and one of my nephews are here. Come with me, and meet them."

James introduced me to his two brothers, SG and Ralph, and his nephew, Jerry. I had a vague memory of Jerry when I was in high school even though I was at least five years older than he was. They were friendly but didn't visit long before they went back to roping calves. They would rotate running the chute and roping. They were all good and seldom missed a calf. James came over and visited after his turn at the loading chute.

"What do you think, Sam?" he asked.

"Y'all are good. Even the young boy," I answered.

"I want you to stay for dinner. I saw my wife kill a chicken a couple of hours ago and you know what that means. Besides, I want you to meet her."

We were interrupted by a loud argument between the other two brothers. "I told you not to jerk on your horse in the box. You don't listen to nothing."

"I don't need advice. I know how to train my horse," the other brother replied.

"The hell you do! You're goin'a ruin him!" the first brother yelled.

"I better get back over there," James said. "It's this way every time we rope."

The arguing continued, going from who had the best horse to how big to build your loop. I had a feeling that even though they argued, if you crossed one of them, you would have all of them to deal with. I would have picked James to be the best roper. He wasn't as fast, but he was consistent and never missed. It was obvious that the nephew had inherited some of the better characteristics of each brother, as well as his dad, and was going to be awesome.

I stayed for dinner and the fried chicken, cream gravy, and mashed potatoes were unbelievable. I thought Mrs. Toller was a good cook but James' wife, Dorothy, was in a class all by herself.

By 1:00 I was in town at the grocery store filling my list. The only checker was Mrs. Quentin. I spoke and asked how she was doing.

"Good, Sam. Mattie should arrive anytime on the bus. I hope it's not late. If you stay around a while you can see her."

Caught off guard, I didn't know how to respond. She saw that I was in a bind and said, "Of course, if you have something to do, you can see her later. She will be here for two weeks."

"I need to get home and check on my calves. Also, Hablo is in the pickup, barking at everyone that comes by."

"It's good to see you, Sam, and we'd like for you to come around more often."

With only two sacks of groceries, I was going to carry them out myself. When I reached the door, someone opened it for me. I turned to thank them, and Mattie was standing there. It was an awkward moment, with neither of us knowing what to say. She looked great and my first thought was how poorly I compared. Finally, I was able to say, "Thank you."

She didn't say anything, but let the door go shut and followed me to the pickup. When Hablo saw her he went crazy, jumping up and down, barking, and wagging not only his tail but his entire body.

I guess that warmed her up a little, because she said, "It looks like someone is glad to see me."

"How've you been, Mattie?"

"Good. You?"

"Fair, I guess. I miss Jose, but it's getting better. Would you like to come out to see Spade and maybe ride him?"

"I don't know. Do you want me to?"

"He's your horse. I shouldn't have anything to say about it."

She hesitated, and then those green eyes blazed as she stared at me and asked, "She there?"

"No. She's going to Colorado Monday morning for a ten day Christmas Vacation."

"I'll come out Monday evening, if that's all right?"

"Sure." I was still holding the two sacks of groceries and she opened the pickup door for me. Hablo was still having a fit and when she reached in to pet him, he jumped into her arms, forcing her backwards. She managed to hang on to him while he gave her kisses. She actually started laughing which relieved some of the tension.

"Why does he like me so much?" she asked.

"Hablo is a good judge of people. He recognizes a good one when he sees them."

"Does Hablo like her?" she asked.

"They haven't gotten along since he peed on her foot. He soaked it good."

"Finally, she smiled, saying, "I'll see you Monday.

I woke up Sunday morning feeling better than I had in a long time. The demons hadn't come during the night, instead, I'd dreamed about Mattie. We were riding and it started raining and we took shelter in an old barn. She was shivering and I had to hold her to get her warm. I realized then that it was cold in the house. We must have had a weather change during the night. I blew a breath of air and it turned to vapor, proving how cold it was in the room. Hablo was buried under the covers and when I got out of bed he didn't move. I went to the kitchen and, opening the back door, a blast of icy wind hit me in the face. It must be well below freezing.

I lit my stoves, noticing an orange flame, which could mean only one thing. I was low on propane. Later in the morning I would call Mina Winter Butane. I hated to call on a Sunday, but they would service my tank as soon as possible. It might be later in the day, because I'm sure that several families woke up this morning to a blue norther realizing they needed fuel. They treated their customers as family and never complained about the hour or day they were called.

I decided to attend church today, something I hadn't done since Jose died. I put the coffee on, and leaving the house, facing a brutal north wind, went to feed the horses. Pouring feed into Spade's trough, I said, "Your girl is home and will be out to see you tomorrow." He raised his head looking at me with those big brown eyes as if he understood. The walk back to the house was easier with the wind at my back. My mood plummeted when I saw the car parked in front of the house. What was she doing over here this early? When I went into the house that question was answered immediately.

"Sam, I want you to go with us to Colorado. I will not take no for an answer. I have looked after you since Jose died and you owe it to me. We're leaving early in the morning. You can get someone to take care of the horses and that dog."

"This is a family vacation and I'm not part of the family. How many times do you need to be told that I'm not going with you?" She started crying, and to make matters worse, Hablo came into the kitchen and started barking at her.

She took a break in her crying to say, "I hate that animal! Get him away from me!"

Hablo stepped it up a notch, moving toward her. "You need to leave, Sonia. I'll see you when you get back. I hope you have a good trip."

Back to squalling, she yelled, "I thought you loved me! You took advantage of me!"

I repeated, "You need to leave, now, please."

"I'm never coming back!" she screamed.

She left with the pedal held to the floor, spinning out until her tires could get traction. I hope she didn't have a wreck before she got home. Again, a voice whispered to me, *you made a huge mistake, Sam, and you're going to be sorry.* Looking at Hablo, he wagged his tail and commenced to speak his happy bark.

Mattie drove up at noon the next day. I had already eaten and was sitting on the porch smoking. Hablo stood beside me until he recognized her and off he went, wagging his tail and barking a welcome. When she got out of the car I thought again how she'd changed. She was more confident, and had gained weight. She was wearing jeans, a pull over sweater, boots, and a cap.

"You look good," I said.

"Thank you. You've lost weight," she said, sitting down on the porch.

"Yeah. Don't have much of an appetite."

"Mother told me about you going to jail. How many times are you going to save Avery?"

"Hope that's the last one."

"I have a message from Flint's parents, the McGowans. They would like to see you. I have their phone number," she said. "A chaplin paid them a visit recently and told them how you tried to save Flint."

"I wasn't successful. Flint died while I was carrying him."

"That wasn't your fault. You tried," she said. "Will you call them?"

"Probably. Are you ready to ride Spade?"

"Yes. Would you mind if I ride by myself today?" she asked.

"No. He's your horse. You can do what you want to. Do you want me to saddle him for you?"

"No. I can do that. I may be gone several hours," she said.

As she got up and walked toward the barn I thought again, how great she looked.

Chapter 46

Mattie

I saddled Spade, with Hablo leading the way and announcing we were coming; I rode into the pasture. The weather had warmed some, but was still chilly, and I was wishing for a coat to go over my sweater. It felt good to be in the saddle for the first time in months. Spade was frisky, having not been ridden much lately. He kept looking for things to spook him, beginning with a jackrabbit that jumped up in front of him. Of course, Hablo took off after the rabbit, with no chance of catching him. He joined me again ten minutes later, with his tongue hanging out, lying down in front of me as if to say, "We need a rest."

My mind went back to Sam. He hadn't touched me, not even a handshake. I guess he was still upset with me for not calling him when Jose died. I intended to and should've kept trying; however, that was when I was moved up to a starting position. After that, the excitement and anticipation of getting to play, along with my studies, caused me to neglect everything else. I have to admit that my thoughts and actions were only centered around basketball and school, neglecting even my mother and pa-pa.

Sam looked bad again. Not so much as when he first returned from Korea and became sick, but still, worse than when I left for college. He had witnessed too much death and loss. Jose was the crowning blow, expanding his loneliness and sorrow to another level. That didn't even take into consideration coming home to a drought and failing at his attempt at ranching. When I came back to earth after floating around in the heavens, basking in my success, it became obvious that Sam was important to me, maybe more than anything else. Now the question was; could he forgive me not being there for him and would I be willing to get by Sonia's fulfilling that role, to a greater extent than I could even think about? I guess time would tell.

I rode for three hours before starting back to the house. Evidence of the drought was everywhere you looked. The grass, what there was of it, was brown, even the rye. Some of the cedars had died, which I'd never seen before. The rabbit Hablo chased was just skin and bone. I had seen several deer in poor condition, with ribs showing and dull coats. Many of them couldn't survive a bad winter. The stock tanks were bone dry and one of the windmills wasn't pumping any water. It was sad and I felt sorry for the farmers, ranchers, and the animals.

Arriving back at the barn, Sam was waiting for me. He'd brought two straight back chairs from the house and built a fire in an open area. I dismounted and started unsaddling Spade.

"I'll do that. Have a seat by the fire. I imagine you got cold with only your sweater. It's almost five and will get colder as the sun goes down."

"Thanks. I should've worn a coat."

"How was your ride?"

"Wonderful. I've missed Spade. He did fine after he settled down. Have you ridden him lately?"

"Just sparingly. My calves stay pretty close to the barn since I feed them every day."

He finished unsaddling Spade, put him in his pen and sat down in the other chair, asking, "Are you hungry?"

"Come to think of it, I am. I ate breakfast but skipped lunch."

"I've got some wieners and buns in the pickup. I could roast you one for a hot dog."

"That sounds good." We sat by the fire, ate two hot dogs each, with the wieners cooked on a green mesquite limb and talked for the next two hours. Occasionally, he would get up and put more wood on the fire. He asked me about college and what it was like to play for the Flying Queens. Once I started, it was difficult to stop. My answer must have taken at least half an hour. He didn't interrupt me and finishing, I felt foolish for taking so long.

"Flying for the first time must have been scary," he observed.

"I was terrified! You've flown, haven't you?"

"Yeah. I flew home when Mother died. Also, I flew to and from Korea, but in a big plane."

I thought of what it must have been like for him to receive word his mother had died, come home to make arrangements and attend the funeral and then go back to a war. At that moment my heart went out to him.

"Would you like to tell me about Jose?" I asked.

"There's not that much to tell, but I did discover information about his past that was fascinating."

He then described Jose's life before he came to the states, including the murder of his family and his relationship with Villa.

"It's amazing, Sam. That little man who was kind and sweet being a part of a rebellion and riding with one of the most famous revolutionaries of all time. Did it surprise you?"

"Totally. I've thought a great deal about it. He never gave any indications of the other life he'd lived."

"I should've called you when he died."

"Let's not talk about that now. It's getting late, and I have to work tomorrow. Let me put some water on the fire, and we'll go to the house."

I needed to use the bathroom before going home. When I was washing my hands, the curiosity over came my manners. Opening the cabinet, her makeup was the first thing I saw. A sinking feeling came over me, then anger consumed me. Going back outside where Sam was waiting, I walked by him, got in my car and left, without saying a word. I drove ten miles before calming down enough to even think reasonably. *What's the deal?* I asked myself. *You knew she stayed with him because she answered the phone late at night. Why react this way, like it was a surprise?* I couldn't help myself. That was all I could come up with that made any sense. By the time I arrived at home, the anger had diminished and been replaced with regret. I shouldn't have ever opened the cabinet, finding what I'd hoped wasn't there. Mother was gone, but Pa-Pa was watching television.

"Mattie, come sit down and tell me about your visit with Sam. Turn off the television, please."

I told him about riding Spade and eating hot dogs beside the fire with Sam. Then I confessed, "I saw her makeup in the bathroom. I left angry, without telling him bye. I feel badly now."

"She's all Sam had after Jose died. She took advantage of his being lonely. I've known the family for years, and Sonia, being the youngest and only girl, was spoiled. She's had everything she ever wanted. Her parents are good people but that's just the way it is."

"Do you think Sam will continue to see her?" I asked.

"Just an old man's opinion. Sam is broken and she can't fix him. No one should have had to go through what he has. I admire him for being able to hold it together."

"What does Sam need, Pa-Pa?"

Smiling, he said, "You asked me a question that you already know the answer to?"

"I just need to hear it from someone else." I said.

"What do you think Sam is feeling at this moment?" he asked.

"Confusion, maybe anger, at me leaving the way I did."

"What should you do?" he asked.

I rose and went to the telephone, dialing his number. He picked up on the second ring. "Sam, I'm sorry. I enjoyed the afternoon."

"No problem, Mattie. It was a good afternoon. Hablo already misses you."

"Will you have a long day tomorrow at the auction?"

"Probably not. The runs have been lighter. Just about everyone has sold their cattle. I should be home by 4:00."

"I noticed you didn't have a Christmas tree. Would you like for me to help you find one and decorate it?" I asked.

"That would be nice. I appreciate it."

"I'll come out early and locate a tree. Hablo can help me. It'll give me a chance to ride Spade again."

After hanging up, I turned around and Pa-Pa was all smiles, asking, "It worked out all right?"

"Yes. I'm surprised he wasn't upset with me. Thanks, Pa-Pa, you always know the right thing to do."

The next morning, I went to see Della, who after finishing six months of cosmetology school, had started working at a beauty shop in town. I was there early before her first customers arrived and we had time to visit. She was living at home and had broken up with her boyfriend. She was doing well and was pleased and surprised that her parents had been supportive. I told her about my college experience and the excitement of playing for the Flying Queens. When I mentioned that I had spent yesterday afternoon with Sam, she seemed surprised, saying, "Really?"

I knew from her reaction that she knew about him and Sonia. Probably everyone in town knew about it. I changed the subject but before we could continue, her first appointment arrived. We made arrangements to get together again after Christmas.

I hadn't taken the time to do any Christmas shopping and that occupied the remainder of the morning. I had spent little of the money earned from my summer job at Taylor Electric and used some of that. Mother was no problem as she always needed clothes. I bought her a Sunday dress at Braggs and while there, bought Pa-Pa two shirts. He didn't have a shirt without holes burned in it by tobacco falling out of his 'roll your own' cigarettes. I wanted to get something for Sam but was at a loss as to what it should be. Last Christmas, I had given him a knife. I wanted to get something for him that he wouldn't buy for himself. Try as I might nothing came to mind. I would ask Pa-Pa for suggestions.

I met Mother at the drug store for lunch, and we were joined by Louise. We ordered sandwiches, and afterwards, I couldn't resist their ice cream. I ordered two scoops of vanilla, which were square, and it was wonderful. It was one thing I had missed while being gone. Mother had told me the first night home about Earnest and their plans to marry after the first of the year. I was pleased for her and told her so. Earnest was nice, and I had no doubt but what they would be happy together.

After lunch, I went to Ben Franklin's Five and Dime. They had a bouquet of artificial flowers which I bought. From there, I went to the cemetery, locating my dad's grave and placing the flowers at the bottom of his headstone. I don't know what caused me to do it. Maybe guilt. It could be I just wanted to do something for him at Christmas. I spoke aloud to him, *we didn't get along and I'm sorry for that. Maybe if I'd tried harder, it would have been different? I'm not angry and don't hate you. I just wanted you to know that.* I left, not feeling better or worse, just knowing that the visit to his grave was the right thing to do.

I was at Sam's ranch in the early afternoon. The weather had warmed up and a long sleeve flannel shirt was enough. I saddled Spade and with Hablo leading the way, rode toward the hills to look for a Christmas tree. I rode for an hour before finding something that would be suitable. It wasn't great but with decorations it would work. I marked my bearings and rode back to the house. I put Spade in his pen, went to the house and into the bathroom, cleaned out the cabinet and put all her stuff in the trash. I felt better.

Chapter 47

Sam

I was right about a light run of cattle on Tuesday. When I arrived and checked at the office we only had about 400 head to sell. That would put us through about 3:00 at the latest. Mattie would have probably already picked out a cedar for a Christmas tree by that time. I should have known she would find something of Sonia's. I kicked myself for not removing all her items. It surprised me that she called back so quickly but it made for a better night's sleep. I didn't know how to talk about Sonia and describe my feelings or lack of feelings for her. I chose the coward's way out by avoiding the subject. I knew after she apologized for not calling when Jose died that she would expect me to talk about Sonia. I simply didn't know how to describe my relationship with her. I do know that it wouldn't bother me if Sonia bowed out of my life. It fact, I was hoping that would happen.

We had a few more cattle come in after I checked, and it was after 4:00 before the sale ended. I was home by 5:00, and two cars were parked at my house. One was Mattie's and the other was the biggest car I'd ever seen. It was white and had to be 30 feet long. Who drove that kind of automobile? It must be somebody important. When I went in, two men were sitting in the living room with Mattie. They stood before speaking and Mattie said, "Sam, these men would like to talk with you." One had on a dark suit and tie. The other one had slacks and a yellow sport coat with a silk scarf around his neck. The man that had on a suit introduced himself as Steven and the other as Timothy. Evidently, they already knew my name, so no other introductions were necessary.

Steven appeared to be the spokesman. "Sam, we've come all the way from California to speak with you. We are in the motion picture industry, and are planning to make a movie about the Korean War. To be more precise, about one of the last battles in which you participated. We've been doing research, but it finally became evident that we needed someone who could give us a first-hand account. Someone that was actually there. We spoke to several of the commanding officers, asking for their help to locate someone. We told them our preference would be a young man. Now, you probably realize why we are here without me going any further."

Here sitting before me, was my worst nightmare; being asked to relive the memories I'd been trying to forget. These guys must be crazy or stupid or both. I didn't speak, trying to find the right words without anger or resentment.

Steven continued, "Of course there would be compensation for you, depending on how much time you spend on the set. I assure you though that it would be considerable."

"I'm trying to forget the war," I said.

"I know it must have been hard on you, being so young. It's over now, and you have an opportunity to make some easy money by describing your experiences," Steven replied.

"I'm not interested," I said.

"Would you think about it for a few days?" he asked.

"No. I want no part of it," I said.

"Don't be hasty, young man. These kind of opportunities don't come along often," Timothy said.

"You heard my answer! It's probably best that you leave before I tell you what I think of you and your movie."

They rose to leave and Steven asked, "We have someone else waiting in the car. Would you talk to him? We've come a long way to see you."

"I guess so. He won't change my mind, though."

They left and a few minutes later a man came in who looked familiar. He was wearing jeans and a flannel shirt. I heard Mattie gasp.

Thank you, Sam, for giving me some of your time. Could we talk alone?"

As Mattie was leaving, he said, "My name is Greg and I apologize for my two friends. They have little tact and no patience. Steven is the money man for the movie and Timothy will direct it. They've offered me a part in the movie, but I haven't accepted. I understand where you're coming from and cannot imagine what you've been through."

"Just within the last few months have I stopped having nightmares about the war. I don't want to go there again. I can't imagine making a movie that would glorify this war," I said.

"If I accept the part in the movie it will not glorify this war. I know enough about what occurred to realize the waste of lives because of decisions that generals and politicians made. I was with Steven when he talked with your commanding officer. He spoke of your courage, bravery, and ferocity. He said that you were a warrior and worth twenty men. I need to hear your story to play the part in the movie. Help me to show the world the mistakes these leaders made that cost the lives of young men. Mistakes that could have been avoided and ended the useless killing on both sides."

Now I was confused. I never once considered the possibility of people being told how useless the final days of this war was, which included the senseless loss of lives for a rocky hill that meant nothing to either side. Flint had died there.

"How do I know you'll keep your word and the movie will portray what actually happened?" I asked.

"You don't Sam; however, you need to understand that I'm not like the other two men that spoke with you. They want me in the movie. If I see the truth is not being told, that will be the end of it. They need me badly enough to follow my wishes."

For whatever reason, I trusted this man. "Can you, give me some time to think about it?"

Smiling, he stood up and offered his hand, "Please consider what I said. I'll give you my personal phone number. Call me collect when you make a decision. The movie will be shot in Arizona and work will start immediately."

"I'll let you know something in a week. If I do accept, whatever money I receive, an equal amount must be given to the family of my friend who was killed. Is that being unreasonable?"

Smiling, he replied, "No, not at all. If your answer is yes, I'll see to it that your wish is carried out."

"Can I ask you a question?"

"Sure. Go ahead," he answered.

"What kind of car is that? I've never seen anything like it."

"It's called a limousine, Sam. I don't particularly like them, but the men I'm with feel a need to look important. I'd much rather ride in your truck. In fact, I envy the life you have on your ranch. It's quiet and peaceful. It would be nice to go outside in the morning without facing a crowd stopping you everywhere you go, wanting to make conversation. I'm not complaining, only saying sometimes it's not easy."

"Will you and your friends drive back to California?"

"No. Just to Abilene. We have a chartered plane waiting for us there. I better be going. As you could see, my companions don't have much patience. I look forward to hearing from you."

I walked with him to the car, noticing they had a driver and both of the other men were sitting in one of the back seats. Hablo wasn't even doing his usual barking at strangers. I guess he was impressed with the car. When I went back inside Mattie was jumping up and down, trying to talk. Finally, words came out that made sense.

"Sam! Do you know who that was?"

"Sure, it was Greg. He did look familiar, but I couldn't place him."

"Oh, Sam! Surely you recognized him!" she said, continuing to fan herself with a newspaper she was holding.

She then told me his name and I was surprised and a little shocked that he would come to my house. "He was really nice," I said.

"Nice! Nice! He's famous, Sam! Aren't you impressed he would come all this way to see you?"

"I guess so. He did come a long way."

"Are you going to do it?" she asked.

"I don't know. He gave me his word the movie would reflect the truth and not be a glamorized war movie. I'd have trouble reliving that again. The movie will be about the battle in which Flint was killed. I just don't know if I can go through it again even if it's not real. I trust Greg. I believe he'll keep his word."

"Believe me, Sam, they'll do whatever he tells them to. As Pa-Pa's saying goes, if he says froggie, they'll just ask how high he wants them to jump."

"I'm going to have to think about it before I make a decision. Now, what about the Christmas tree. Did you find one?"

"Yes, but I'm so excited, I probably can't find it. I can't wait to tell everyone who came to see you."

"Please don't do that, Mattie. Nothing may come of it, and I'd rather no one else knows. Now, let's go find that tree before it gets dark."

We were together every day for the next week. We climbed Castle Peak, went to the movies in Abilene, rode horses, and spent Christmas Day with her mother, pa-pa, and Earnest. She gave me a new black hat for Christmas which was a perfect fit that she had bought at Lusky's. Her gift was a tiny gold cross on a chain that I found at Wilson's Jewelry. We enjoyed each day, but the best part was sitting by a fire outside in the evenings roasting marshmallows and talking. We stayed away from the sensitive topics until the Tuesday after Christmas when we were sitting by our fire. I assume she had been counting the days and knew Sonia would be home tomorrow.

"What're you going to do when she gets home?" she asked.

"She was mad because I wouldn't go with them to Colorado and said she wasn't coming back over here."

"I don't believe that," she said.

"Me either, I guess. I'm going to stop seeing her. Her parents have been good to me, and I hope we can continue to be friends."

"Are you talking about her or her parents, because if you're referring to Sonia, you can forget it. She'll never be your friend."

"I know. I was talking about her mom and dad."

"It's best that I not come back out here until it's settled. I don't want to be around when she shows up," she stated.

"When do you have to go back to school?"

"I have to be back for practice on January 4, so next Sunday is when I'll be leaving."

"Do you want me to take you back?" I asked.

"Yes. I would like that. Have you decided what to do about the movie? It's been over a week since they were here," she said.

"I can't decide. On one hand, I'd like to be a part of showing what a waste of lives the war was, but what difference does it make now? Flint is dead. It won't bring him back. I would just have to go through hell again just to make a point that doesn't matter."

"That's one way to look at it. Another is, you would be doing something for everyone that suffered a loss. You would be a part of something that spoke for thousands that had family and friends killed in a useless war, especially those that died in that particular battle."

"That's right. You can't imagine how much hate I had for the people that kept the war going when peace was being negotiated. They should've gone to prison."

"Sam, it's your decision. Whatever you decide won't be wrong. It's understandable why you're reluctant."

"I'll decide before you go back to school."

The next morning, I was on my way back to the house after feeding the horses when a car came speeding up my lane toward the house. When it was close enough to identify, I breathed a sigh of relief, seeing it wasn't Sonia. When close enough to identify the occupants, I realized Sonia would have been a blessing compared to the two men who got out of the car. Her brothers met me before I reached the house.

Jake, the older one, said, "We need to talk to you."

"Sure. You want to come inside for some coffee," I offered.

"No. This isn't a social visit. We're here about our sister," he said.

"Yeah," said the other brother who was standing with his feet spread and clinched fists.

"Look, I don't need any trouble. Tell me what you're here for," I said.

"First, you ruined Sonia's Christmas. She cried most of the time we were gone. She told us that you took advantage of her, saying that you planned on marrying her. What are you going to do?"

"What do you mean?" I asked.

"We know she stayed over here the four days Mom and Dad were gone to Oklahoma for the National Finals. Are you going to deny that?"

"No. That's true. I made a mistake for allowing her to stay, and I've regretted it ever since. I'd lost a friend and was lonely but that doesn't justify it. I certainly didn't say anything about marrying her."

"We believe her and that she stayed with you, thinking you would marry her."

"No. That's not true. I think it's best if we don't see one another again," I said.

"You leave us no choice then," Jake said, moving closer.

Chapter 48

Gladys

I found the lump the day after Christmas when taking my bath. It was on my left breast, about the size of a marble, and a feeling of panic engulfed me. My mother had died of breast cancer just short of her 60th birthday. It had been my one great health fear for as long as I could remember. It was Sunday, and I continued to get ready for church. Earnest was coming by to pick me up to accompany him to the Methodist Church where he was a member. I took several deep breaths trying to remain calm, telling myself, *it's probably nothing to worry about and may be gone by tomorrow. If not, I can go to the doctor and get it checked out.*

After getting ready, I went into the living room and sat down. I tried to think of something that would get my mind off the discovery. Mattie had gone to Sam's early this morning and would attend church with him at the Pioneer Methodist Church in the Canyon. She was back to her old self after being with Sam. Her Pa-Pa had reminded me that she needed Sam in her life almost as much as he needed her. Christmas had been wonderful with Sam and Earnest eating dinner here and spending the day with us. Then the thought came out of nowhere; I couldn't marry Earnest until I found out. If the diagnosis was bad, he shouldn't have to go through with me what he did with his first wife. We had agreed to get married next Friday before Mattie left for school on Sunday. My thoughts were interrupted by the sound of a car driving up. I opened the door before Earnest knocked.

"Morning, Gladys. You look great this morning."

"Thank you, Earnest. Let me get my purse and I'll be ready to go."

On the short-drive to the church, Earnest asked, "Are you feeling all right? You aren't talking much."

"Oh, yes. It was a wonderful Christmas. I enjoyed it."

"Family at Christmas. That's the way it should be," he said. "Next Friday's a big day for us."

When I didn't respond, he asked, "You're not getting cold feet or you?"

"No. I keep thinking about leaving Hollis by himself when I move in with you. I'm not sure he can take care of himself. He insists that it won't be a problem."

"I've told you, Gladys. He's welcome to stay with us."

"He'd never do that," I said.

We arrived at the church before he could respond. It was a nice day with sunshine and little wind. Attendance was down since a number of families were visiting out of town during the holidays. People were friendly and several congratulated us on our plans to get married. We had already made arrangements to get married at the Pioneer Methodist since I knew the pastor there. Only a handful of people would be present including, Mattie, Sam, Hollis, Louise, and a few of Earnest's friends. Earnest was so agreeable, he let me decide where we would get married and who would perform the ceremony.

The sermon was good, and as always, toward the end of the service, prayers were offered for those who were ill or grieving from the loss of a loved one. I wondered if in a few weeks I would be on that prayer list.

Monday morning the lump was still there, and maybe it was my imagination, but it seemed larger. Before leaving for work, I called the hospital. Hollis was gone to coffee with a friend and Mattie was still in bed. I was hoping they would be open and sure enough the nurse answered. I explained my situation, asking if it would be possible to come in during my lunch break to see the doctor. She agreed, saying it wouldn't be a problem.

The morning dragged by, and I made several mistakes, either over-or-under charging people for certain items, which was not typical. At 11:45, I asked Mr. Wilson if I could leave early for a doctor's appointment. He said it would be okay and not to worry if I was late returning.

Upon arrival, I was taken to a waiting room immediately. Within a few minutes Dr. Sadler came in, asking, "What's the problem, Gladys?"

I explained about the lump and he left, returning a few minutes later with his nurse. He then examined the lump and said, "Gladys, we're going to need to do a biopsy. That's the only way to tell if we have a problem. It's a simple procedure and can be done without a hospital stay. It'll be a week or ten days before we get the results back."

"When do we need to do the biopsy?" I asked.

"Right away. I can work you in Wednesday."

"Will anyone need to come with me?" I asked.

"A local will be all you need for the procedure, but I would feel better if someone came with you. You're going to be uncomfortable for a day or two. Mattie's home, isn't she. By the way, everyone's proud of her."

"Yes, she's home. I was hoping to do this without anyone knowing."

"Don't do that, honey. I know you're going to worry. Lean on your family. We'll set you up with an appointment Wednesday," he said, leaving.

I left in a daze after making an appointment for Wednesday morning, at 7:30. I actually still had a few minutes to go by the drug store. I caught Louise before she went back to work.

"Do you have a few minutes?" I asked.

"Sure."

We found a vacant booth, and I told her about my doctor's visit and appointment for Wednesday, asking her if she could go with me.

"Of course, Gladys. Are you going to tell anyone else?"

"I can't decide. I'll not put Earnest through another episode like he had with his first wife. I guess it'll be necessary to tell him. The results won't be back for at least a week. The wedding is scheduled for Friday. Maybe I'm just not ready to talk about it. Everything happened too quickly. After the biopsy, I'll probably tell Mattie and Earnest. At that time, I can tell him the wedding is off until I know something for sure."

"I'll meet you at the hospital Wednesday morning, Gladys. It's going to be all right. Now, it's time for me to get back to work. Why don't you come over to the house tonight and we can talk some more?"

I went through the afternoon and the next day in a daze, doing my job, and remembering little of what happened. Wednesday morning, I was at the hospital early and waited in the car until they opened. Louise arrived and we went inside.

Within an hour, the procedure was over and Louise followed me home. I had taken off work for the day but planned on returning tomorrow. Louise went in with me and Hollis and Mattie were at the breakfast table. I went to the living room and called Earnest, asking him to come over.

When I sat down at the kitchen table, Mattie asked, "What's going on, Mother?"

"Let's wait on Earnest. He should be here shortly."

Within a few minutes, Earnest arrived, and I explained the events of the last three days.

"You should have told us, Mother."

"I know, Mattie, but I couldn't talk about it for a few days. You wouldn't have done anything but worry. Now we have to wait for the results. There's something else we need to talk about. I don't want to get married until after we find out the results."

"It doesn't matter about the results, Gladys. I still want to get married. Let's go ahead with the wedding this Friday. We can go through this together."

"No. I've made up my mind. I won't discuss it further."

Nothing else was said, with Mattie coming over and hugging me, after which, I said, "I'm going to lie down for awhile. I didn't sleep well last night."

In my room, I knew that sleep would be impossible, but was hoping everyone would leave. I wanted to be left alone, at least for today. Everything had been going so well. I was happy, more so than in years, and now this happens. If the test came back positive, it would mean surgery. I had heard enough to know that the treatment was removal of the breast as well as outlaying lymp nodes. Could I endure that? I had never considered myself a strong person. I was 55 and my mother had died when she was 59. I had seen her wither away for a year before she was gone. I would go over to Louise's tonight and talk to her. I needed someone to listen and it would be easier with her than Mattie. It would even be all right to cry.

Did I do the right thing by calling off the wedding? After all, Earnest would stay with me through it all if the test was positive. Maybe I wasn't thinking clearly. I could see his disappointment when I said the wedding would be delayed. I'd ask Louise her opinion. I had lived with Leon for 30 years and never stood up to him. In fact, I don't ever remember standing up to anyone. I needed strength in meeting this challenge. I rose from the bed, went to the dresser, opened the drawer, and took out my Bible.

Chapter 49

Mattie

I was shocked and then alarmed at what Mother had told us. I didn't know what to do. I wanted to reassure her, comfort her, tell her we would be here for her, and then she went to her room. I assume she wanted to be left alone to deal with it in her own way. She had led a difficult life for the past 30 years with my dad and had a chance for happiness and now this happens. I couldn't help but believe it would turn out all right for her. Suddenly, I wanted to see Sam and tell him. He didn't expect me today because Sonia was home, but maybe she wouldn't be there this early. I tried to call, but he didn't pick up. He was probably at the barn, doctoring his calves.

I left immediately and was at his entrance by 10:00. Driving up his lane, I noticed a car parked by his house and two men between the house and barn. What was going on? What were they doing? Suddenly, the scene became clear. Screaming and baling out of the pickup, I ran with everything in me to where two men were kicking a figure on the ground, who had to be Sam. They were completely absorbed in their anger and didn't pay any attention to me. I reached them, never slowing down, and ran into one of the men, jumping on his back and clawing at his face. He stumbled and fell to the ground.

"Get this bitch off me!" he yelled as I continued scratching at his face.

Feeling hands grab me and pull me backward, I grabbed a handful of hair and took it with me. All the time, I continued screaming at the top of my voice. The one who held me, kicking and struggling said, "Let's get out of here," and dropped me. I moved over to Sam who was doubled up in a ball with his hands over his head. I knelt down beside him and turned him over, gasping at the sight of his face which was bloody from cuts on his cheek and his forehead. He wasn't conscious. I ran back to Pa-Pa's pickup, driving it as close to Sam as possible. I opened the passenger door and picking him up, put him inside. He fell over in the seat, still unconscious. Driving away, I noticed Hablo for the first time. He was lying motionless a few yards away from where Sam was. No doubt, he was dead.

I stopped at the house and running inside found a wash rag and wet it with cold water. Returning, I bathed Sam's face with it and cleaned off some of the blood, saying, "Sam, Sam, it's me! Wake up, please! Talk to me!"

He opened his eyes and mumbled, "Thank you, Mattie. Are they gone?"

Placing the rag on his face I said, "Yes, I need to get you to the doctor."

"No, please, I'll be all right. Just let me lie here a few minutes and then you can help me in the house."

"Sam! You need to see Dr. Sadler."

"I've spent enough time in the hospital. I feel better already. I'm going to sit up until my head clears and then you can help me get into the house. Would you clean up my cuts and determine if stitches or needed?"

"Yes, but I still think you need to see a doctor." He sat up but I could tell his eyes were still not focused, and he hadn't regained his balance. We sat in the pickup for another fifteen minutes, with me bathing his face and then started into the house. He was wobbly, but we made it without him falling. He lay down on the couch, and with a rag and pan of warm water, I cleaned the cuts on his face. They weren't deep enough to require stitches and the blood caused them to look worse than they were. I helped him out of his shirt, and the abrasions on his side and back would look bad tomorrow. He complained about his side, and when I touched it, he flinched.

"I must have some bruised ribs. That really hurt," he said.

"Sam Colter, you're one stubborn man. You need to be examined."

"You're a good nurse. I feel better already," he said, trying to sit up and falling back on the couch. "It's a good thing you found me when you did or I might not be feeling anything."

"What happened, Sam?"

"Sonia's brothers never cared for me. They thought I wasn't good enough for her and were jealous because her parents did a lot for me. Sonia added to their hate by telling them I took advantage of her. When I told them I wasn't going to see her anymore they jumped me. I didn't fight back. Being on probation, I would've gone to jail for six months, besides I don't want any more fighting. They knocked me down and then started kicking me. That's all I remember until you called my name. Then it's still fuzzy. Did you see Hablo?"

I nodded, unable to stop the tears. "He was lying a little way from you...not moving."

He started to say something and his voice broke. "No," is all that came out.

We sat in silence for several minutes before he said, "I'm losing everyone, Mattie. Why?"

I moved over and sat beside him on the couch, putting both arms around him. "No, Sam, not me. I'm here with you."

"Mattie, will you do something for me?" he asked.

"Anything."

"Bury Hablo. The coyotes will come tonight."

"Sure."

I left immediately, going out the door, alternating between crying about Hablo and thinking about how much Sam had been through. First his mother, then his best friend, next the illness, and now, his beloved dog. Add to that the drought and being put in jail. Now, he takes a terrible beating.

The closer I got to the barn, the more Hablo came into my thoughts. He was such a sweet dog. Not too smart but loyal and that's probably what got him killed. I'm sure he was defending Sam. Maybe I could find another dog for him. I arrived at the spot where I left Hablo. He wasn't there! Maybe I had the location wrong. I looked all around the area and he wasn't there! Oh no! Had the coyotes already gotten him? Then I heard the bark, coming from behind the barn. He was trotting toward me and I burst out sobbing, "Hablo, Hablo, you're alive." I knelt down, and he came right into my arms giving me kisses. I rubbed his head, finding a large bump. Evidently, they had hit him with something and knocked him out. I felt all over him and found no other injuries.

I went back to the house immediately, with Hablo beside me. *What a day*, I said aloud, as my thoughts returned to my mother. It was already afternoon, and after seeing about Sam, I needed to get home. Hopefully, she would be willing to talk, and maybe I could provide some comfort and encouragement. I opened the door and let Hablo in, waiting a few moments before entering. He barked several times and I heard Sam say, Hablo! I gave them a few minutes and went inside, seeing Sam trying to dry his eyes. Hablo was up on the couch with him.

"What happened, Mattie? I thought he was dead."

"He has a bump on his head as big as a hen egg. I assume they kicked him or hit him with something that knocked him out. He seems to be fine." He immediately started barking as if to verify my statement.

I then told him about my mother. "I don't know what to do, Sam. It seems anything I say or do will be too little."

"Your mother is a wonderful person. It doesn't seem fair for her to be facing this. It will be a long week waiting on the results.

Just knowing you care and being there for her is about all you can do."

"But, I'm leaving in less than a week and I won't be here for her. I'm thinking about not going back to Plainview."

"That would be the worst thing you could do for your mother, Mattie. Her dream is for you to get a college education. Don't even consider that."

Hablo didn't like being left out of the conversation and he started barking.

"It's after 4:00, Mattie. You better check on your mother."

"Will you be all right by yourself?" I asked.

"Sure. Thank you again, Mattie."

Mother wasn't at home when I arrived. Pa-Pa said she'd gone to visit Louise. I asked Pa-Pa how she was doing.

"As good as you could expect. I'm surprised you were gone so long. We were worried about you."

I told him about Sam, leaving out the part about my attack on the Tollers. "I should've called, but I was stressed out over Sam."

"Sam has gone through a lot. I don't know how he does it. I'm glad you were there to help him."

We visited for a few more minutes and then I headed back to the ranch. I needed to get back in time to help Sam with his supper. When I arrived her car was there. By the time I was in the house, steam was probably coming out of my ears. Sonia was sitting on the side of his couch holding his hand.

"What're you doing here?" I growled.

"I came to apologize to Sam."

"Well, Sonia, I don't believe Sam wants you here so you get your big boobs and big ass out of here or I'm going to put you out."

"You hurt my brother! He may lose his eye. You're terrible. How could you do something like that?"

"Because I was defending the man I love."

Chapter 50

Sam

I was miserable the first two days after my injuries. The least amount of exertion caused a shooting pain in my side. I wouldn't accept the consequence of trying to complete a few tasks but paid the price each time. I had notified the auction of my predicament that would keep me from working for at least the next two weeks.

Mattie was at the ranch by 7:00 each morning. She would cook my breakfast, make up my bed, and do whatever else needed to be done. The weather was mild for mid-winter and after finishing the chores she would saddle Spade and ride for a couple of hours. After lunch we drove around the area; Thursday visiting my parents' graves at White Church Cemetery and Friday driving up a mountain pass and through one of the larger ranches that had a public road. We would return to the ranch and sit on the porch and talk. Most of the time the conversation was trivial but occasionally would turn serious. That was the case late Friday evening when she caught me looking at her.

"What are you staring at, Sam Colter?"

"You have the smoothest face?"

"You mean my complexion?"

"Yes. That's what I mean. You always smell good, too."

"Well now, Sam Colter, that's a compliment and could be interpreted as slightly romantic."

"You're making fun of me now. I want to express my feelings to you but it's hard. My face looks terrible, with the swelling and bruises."

"Oh, Sam. I wouldn't ever make fun of you. Your face is not what's important. It's what's on the inside that counts and you're beautiful there. Something else, I wonder about; you avoid touching me, like you're afraid."

"I'm sorta. You might get the wrong idea."

"You mean that I might think you want me to sleep with you?"

"Yeah."

"No, Sam. I don't think that at all. Besides no matter what you might want, I'm not going to jump into bed with you like someone else we know. I might want to but that will come later. Now, do we have that cleared up?"

"I guess. You told Sonia that you loved me. Is that true?"

"I've come to that conclusion, Sam Colter. Is that all right with you?"

"Sure. Am I supposed to say I love you, too?"

"Only if you mean it. If you don't, it's no big deal. You like me, don't you?"

"Yeah, a lot. More than anyone else in this world."

"Even Hablo?" she asked.

"Even Hablo," I said.

"Well, since we've settled all that, it's time for me to start home. Come over here and kiss me like you care more about me than you do Hablo."

We left early Sunday morning for Plainview with Mattie driving her mother's car. She had insisted we take it since it would be a more comfortable ride for me. I'd brought both horses in to Hollis's pens, which had been spared by the fire that destroyed his house. Hollis would feed them while I was gone. One of his friends would take him in the morning and Mrs. Quentin would take him in the afternoon. It was obvious that it gave him a good feeling to be useful. Hablo went with us, riding in the back seat and barking at every car that came close.

The car had a radio and we picked up a Lubbock station at Post. They gave a weather report that was anything but encouraging. A winter storm was approaching the Texas Panhandle and would begin affecting the area by late afternoon. The report called for a drastic drop in temperature and freezing rain, sleet, and snow for the next several days. Roads were expected to be iced over by nightfall and could be impassable by morning.

"It's 9:00 now and we should be in Plainview by noon. I'll have to start back immediately and try to get ahead of the storm. We should've paid more attention to the weather reports at home. I can't get stranded up here with nobody at home to look after my calves."

"I should have taken the bus then you wouldn't be in this situation," she said.

"No. I wanted to take you back. It's going to be several months before I see you again. At least, we get to spend some time together. I can get ahead of the storm."

"I'm going to call once a week and write at least every two weeks," she said.

"You need to call collect. It's easier for you that way."

We talked the remainder of the way about everything from her basketball and class schedule to my friendship with James and my work at the auction. Sonia was not mentioned. We spent a good part of the trip discussing her mother and the anticipated test results. She kept insisting that if the results came back positive she was coming home to be with her mother. I didn't try to argue, knowing that it would be useless.

We were at the dorm by 12:30, and you would never know by the sunshine and pleasant temperature that a storm was on the way. She insisted that I go with her into the dorm so she could introduce me to Charley and Sarah. I waited for her in the lobby while she checked to see if they were there. She returned in a few minutes with a girl who I assumed was her roommate, based on her earlier description.

"Sam, this is Charley, my roommate. I told her you had some injuries and not to be surprised."

"Charley, nice to meet you," I said extending my hand. "Mattie has told me some nice things about you. She's mentioned several times how fortunate she is to have you for a roommate and friend."

"Believe me, Sam, the feeling is mutual. I just got off the phone with my parents and the wind and cold has already arrived in Spearman. That means it will be here within a couple of hours. Are you going back today?"

"Right away," I answered.

"I'm sure Mattie gave you my message about contacting the McGowans."

"She did. Eventually I'll get in touch with them," I said.

"Please do. You're a hero to them and they want to thank you. Now, I'll let you have a few minutes alone. Be careful on your drive back," she said.

After she left, both of us were silent. I didn't know what to say, and it seemed she didn't either. Finally, I said, "I better get on the road. I'll miss you. I hope you don't forget me."

She moved over into my arms, kissing me, and saying, "I love you, Sam Colter. You take care of yourself." Then, before I could respond, she was gone.

When I left town, looking to the north I could already see the low lying black clouds. I had half a tank of gas and stopped in Tulia to fill up, thinking that would get me home. After paying the attendant, I returned to the car and pushed the starter button. The motor turned over but didn't start. I tried again and nothing. I got out and raised the hood looking for something that was out of place. I checked the coil wire and it was intact. My knowledge was limited, unlike some of my high school classmates who were enthusiastic about cars. I tried again, and it still wouldn't start. The attendant came out and asked if he might help.

"It won't start. I have no idea what the problem is. Would you see if you can tell what's wrong?" The attendant looked under the hood and came to the window, shaking his head.

"I have no idea. You might try Tulia Automotive, down the street a ways. Not but a couple of blocks. I'll help you push your car out of the driveway."

I walked the three blocks to the automotive shop and asked the person behind the counter if he could help with my car.

"Nope. Sorry, but weather is coming in and we're closing in fifteen minutes. Got to get home and drain the pipes then go to the grocery store to stock up. Bad storm coming."

Dejected, I left, not having any idea what to do. The attendant asked me if I was able to get help.

"No. They're closing because of the storm."

"Tell you what. There's a Negro man that works on cars. In fact, I take my car to him. Of course, the shops won't hire him, but he knows his business. I'll pull your car down to his house. Maybe he can help you."

We hooked a chain to the bumper and he pulled me down to the west part of town, which was composed mostly of shacks that were on the verge of collapse. We stopped in front of one of the worst. An old man with a gray beard and a limp came out.

"Whatch all doin'? Don't you know a storms a-comin'?"

"This boy's got problems, Zeb. No one is willing to help him. His car won't start."

"Let's have a look-see. I luv these little Fords."

The station attendant left, with me thanking him for his trouble. No sooner was he gone than Zeb asked me, while he was working under the hood, "Boy, what happened to you? Yur face looks like it got in a grinder."

I dodged the question, telling him that it was a long story and not worth telling."

"You a solider, boy. I can spot them a mile away. Don't lie to ole Zeb."

"Yeah, Korea."

"My boy went to Korea and never came back," he said.

"I'm sorry."

"I miss him. He was a good boy," he said.

"Where was he in Korea?"

"He was killed trying to take that God-forsaken hill toward the end of the war. I understand it meant nothing."

"Yes sir, you're correct. It meant nothing."

"Nobody knows that. They still praise the war for them generals and politicians. I lost my son."

"I know. I lost my best friend in that battle."

"Bless you, son. We share a common sorrow. Now I think you fixed up and good to go. Hit that starter and see what happens."

It kicked right off and was purring like a kitten. "That's great, Zeb. How much do I owe you?"

"Just go on your way. It was no problem."

I gave him $10 and was on my way with the wind and sand chasing me. It was already after 3:00 and was going to be touch and go for me to get ahead of the storm. At least the north wind was pushing me toward home. Driving gives one time to think. Was it only a coincidence that my car broke down and a man who lost a son on that same damn hill fixed it for me? How could that be possible? What are the chances of that happening? Maybe one in a million. Zeb felt the same way I did. What a waste and a tragedy, with most people never knowing the truth. A voice in my head kept repeating, *you were meant to come in touch with that old man.* I'd always doubted religious people who spoke of 'Godly' acts. Much of that doubt had been erased the last three hours.

I didn't stop again until Sweetwater. I'd gone as far as possible without a bathroom break. After stopping in Sweetwater, I drove into my lane just as it was getting dark. I parked, got out of the car, went into the house, picked up the phone and gave the operator Greg's telephone number.

Chapter 51

Gladys

It was Monday, January 10, and I hadn't been at work but an hour when told I had a phone call. Answering, it was the nurse at the hospital informing me that my test results were in. Ten minutes later I was at the hospital waiting to talk with the doctor. It was half an hour before I was taken to one of the examination rooms. I waited for another 20 minutes before Dr. Sadler came in.

"Gladys, your test results came in this morning. The test was positive. I'm sorry to bring bad news, but the sooner we get you scheduled for treatment the better."

"I expected the results to be bad. In a way it's a relief not to have to wonder any more. What should I do?"

"I'll make you an appointment with a specialist in Abilene, and after you are examined by him, he'll make a recommendation for treatment. I'll get you in as soon as possible."

I thanked him and left in a daze, with all kinds of thoughts running through my head. *Who should I tell first? Maybe I should wait until after I see the specialist to share the information with anyone. After all, the only thing I knew for sure was that the test was positive. Mattie would be upset and want to come home. Earnest, of course, would be alarmed, after what happened to his first wife. Mr. Quentin and Louise would be supportive and encouraging, as would be my other friends. I didn't want sympathy and would prefer to keep it to myself, but that wasn't possible. It had already been two weeks since the biopsy and Louise was already expressing frustration about it taking so long for the results to come back.*

Somehow, I made it back to work without giving any attention to my driving. The last thing I wanted to do was go home and think about it. Work and distraction was what I needed. I stayed as busy as possible the remainder of the morning. If I had a period with no customers, I would stock shelves. When 12:00 came, I walked around to the drug store to meet Louise. When she met me coming in the door the first words out of her mouth were, "You found out, didn't you?"

Well, so much for my secret. "How did you know?" I asked.

"The look on your face, Gladys. You're my best friend, and I know that look."

"Can we go somewhere private and talk?" I asked.

"My house. I have leftovers."

On the drive to Louise's, I told her about the test results and Dr. Sadler scheduling me an appointment with a specialist. She didn't respond until we were in her house eating lunch.

"When're you going to tell Mattie?" she asked.

"Probably after my appointment with the specialist."

"That might be several days or even a week. You know she's worried about you, anxious to find out something," she said.

"I know, Louise. I just want to stick my head in the sand and hide from everybody. That's not right, but I don't want to give people I care about the bad news."

"They want to be there for you, Gladys. You should call Mattie tonight."

"I know you're right. Maybe I just needed to hear it. That's what makes you such a good friend, Louise. You tell me the truth, not what I want to hear."

We finished eating, and I went back to work feeling better.

I called Mattie that night. They had a pay phone in the hall and whoever answered would notify the girl who was getting the call. I went straight to the point, telling her the result was positive and what the next step was.

"Mother, I can come home."

That was my expected response, and I was ready for it. "Mattie, don't even think about it. You couldn't do any more here than you can at school. I'll keep you informed. My dream is for you to get a college education. Please don't destroy my dream."

"You promise to let me know what's going on?" she asked.

"I give you my word." We visited a few more minutes about her school and then ended the call.

It was still early and Mr. Quentin was watching television. I told him the results of my test, and he did his best to be optimistic and encouraging, just like I thought.

Now all that was left was Earnest and my other friends at work. It wouldn't take long for word to get around. Before I could call Earnest, my phone rang, and it was Dr. Sadler informing me that I had an appointment with a specialist Wednesday, the 10th, at 9:00. I called Earnest immediately afterward and told him about the results and my appointment with the specialist. He was kind and sweet. I realized that we needed to go ahead with the wedding. That's what he wanted and it was the right thing to do.

It was amazing how much better I felt after sharing the news with my loved ones. Louise was right, and I was fortunate to have her for a friend. I actually slept better than I had since my first visit to the doctor.

I was at the doctor's office in Abilene at 8:30 on Wednesday. It took me at least 15 minutes to fill out the information sheet. I didn't get to see the doctor until 9:30. Dr. Shultz was an older man, probably in his seventies. He had my test results and after an examination he informed me in a matter of fact voice that I needed a radical mastectomy.

"That's the only route to go. We remove your breast and all the lymph nodes around it and under your arm. We'll do our best to get it all." I guess it was routine for him to inform patients of this procedure and he showed no emotion, not offering any encouragement. I left disappointed and cried off and on during the drive home. I went directly to the hospital to talk with Dr. Sadler. The nurse was able to get me in to see him immediately. I told him about my visit and being disappointed with the doctor.

"I tell you what, Gladys. Let's see if I can get you an appointment in Houston where MD Anderson has recently opened. I have a friend who is a doctor there and we stay in touch. They are on the cutting edge of cancer care with the most effective treatments available. I'll call him today. Did you make an appointment in Abilene to have the surgery done?"

"No. I was so disappointed that I left."

Leaving the hospital and going to work, I felt a little better. I hadn't expected the visit in Abilene to be so depressing. I'd heard about the radical mastectomy and had been hoping there would be another option.

Three days later, I was in Houston at MD Anderson for my appointment with Dr. Wrotham. Dr. Sadler had wasted no time getting me an appointment after we had talked. Louise took off work and went with me, making the seven-hour drive much easier. The traffic was terrible, but we were able to locate the hospital.

We had to wait an hour before I was notified that the doctor would see me. I was surprised at how young Dr. Wrotham was. He was probably in his mid-thirties and totally different from Dr. Shultz. He introduced himself, asking about my family. When I told him about Mattie playing for the Flying Queens he seemed impressed.

He did an examination, and after completing a series of tests involving X-rays, I was back in the room. An hour later he came in and explained the procedure that would be used.

"Gladys, the most common surgery used today is a radical mastectomy. We feel strongly here at MD Anderson that it is no more effective than a simple mastectomy and radiation treatment afterward. I believe, after looking at your test and X-rays, that we have a good chance of a successful outcome. I would like to schedule you for surgery next week. You would need to come in a day early for pre-op and we would perform the operation the next day. Of course, all of this depends on what you wish to do. Some women prefer the other procedure because it is the most common treatment."

"I want you to do the surgery, Dr. Wrotham."

"Good, my receptionist will give you the day and time," he said, smiling.

I left, feeling much better, and wondering how there could be so much difference in doctors. The drive home seemed easier.

I called Mattie that night, explaining the type of surgery I would have and telling her it would be next Monday, the 17th, at 7:00 in the morning. I also informed Earnest and Mr. Quentin.

It would also be necessary to take off work. The next day, when I told Mr. Wilson, he was understanding and told me to take whatever time I needed and that my job would be waiting for me. Living in a small town had many advantages; however, one of them was not how quickly information spread. A number of people who came into the store would express their concern about my illness. I didn't know how to respond and usually just thanked them.

The week crawled by until I thought Saturday would never get here. More people wanted to talk about my surgery and several would tell me about a relative who had gone through treatment and been cured. Occasionally, one would tell me about losing someone to breast cancer, not understanding about the effect it had on me. Finally, Saturday evening came, and Mr. Wilson brought me my check. I noticed it was too much and told him so.

"Gladys, I added an extra week's pay to your check. You'll probably need it and I wanted to do something for you."

"Thank you," was all I could get out, leaving and trying to stop the tears.

I left early Sunday morning, since my check-in time was 2:00 that afternoon. No way could Louise take off work for ten days, the allotted time for my recovery. Earnest wanted to go with me, but I insisted that he stay to look after Hollis. I admit it would have been nice to have someone with me, but that couldn't be helped. Traffic was lighter since it was Sunday, and I arrived at the hospital by noon. I was directed to the check-in-station, and after filling out paper work, taken to a room. After X-rays and blood tests, which took two hours, I was taken to a room for the night. I was given a sleeping pill around 9:00 and didn't wake up until early the next morning. Groggy from such a deep sleep, I realized someone was in the room with me. It was still dark, and I couldn't make out who was standing by my bed and then a familiar voice spoke.

"Good morning, Mother."

Chapter 52

Mattie

"Mattie! What're you doing here?"

"I came to be with you."

"You shouldn't have. What about school and basketball?"

"They're not as important as you are, besides they can do without me for a couple of days."

"How did you get here?"

"I came with the Hutchersons. Wilda insisted that she wanted to go shopping in Houston. I know that's not true. When they heard about your surgery and my concern, they fabricated a reason to come to Houston. Of course, they invited me, saying I might as well go with them. I've never known people so caring and generous. Now, how do you feel?"

"Good. The doctor is nice, and I have confidence in him. I want you to meet him. He'll be in shortly since my surgery is scheduled at 7:00. What time is it now?"

"It's 6:45. What time is breakfast?"

"I can't have anything to eat or drink until after the surgery. My fast started at midnight."

I then told my mother about talking to Sam this week. He'd accepted the offer to help with the movie about the Korean War. He would be leaving for Arizona next week. I hadn't told her about the visit by the group from Hollywood, so it was necessary to go back and explain what happened. I became excited again when telling her about Greg. I still couldn't believe he came to Sam's house. I told her what changed Sam's mind. The car trouble in Tulia and the Black man repairing his car who had lost a son in Korea. Sam thought it was too much of a coincidence and it was meant for him to tell the truth. Had it not been for that, I doubt if he would've accepted the offer.

"Can Sam do it, Mattie? I mean, can he hold up to going through those memories again?"

"Yes, I believe he can. In fact, it might be good for him to let it all out. I certainly don't think it will hurt him any more than he already suffers."

"Changing the subject, Mattie, but Ernest and I are going ahead with the wedding when I get home."

"That's great. Ernest is a good person and I know y'all will be happy."

"It was selfish of me to put it off. I realize that now."

We were interrupted by the doctor coming in and saying, "Good morning, ladies."

"Dr. Wrotham, this is my daughter, Mattie."

"The basketball star?" he stated, in the form of a question.

"I'm glad to meet you, Dr. Wrotham. Mom has been telling me how nice you are. I thought at one time 'star' might be appropriate, but after arriving at Plainview and meeting the Flying Queens, that description didn't fit."

"Just the same, I would like to hear about your Flying Queens before you leave," he said.

"How about it, Gladys? Are you ready to fix that little problem?" he asked.

"Yes. How long will the surgery take?"

"Approximately, two hours from the time you leave the room until you are in recovery. I'll send someone to get you," he said. "Mattie, it was nice to meet you, and I still believe you are a star."

After he was gone, Mother said, "See, I told you he was nice. He reminds me of one of those doctors on TV."

We talked about our upcoming basketball games until two men with a bed on wheels came to get her. "Love you, Mother," I said, as they rolled her out of the room.

There was a large room with chairs and couches just inside the entrance to the hospital where I spent the next several hours. I tried looking at magazines but couldn't concentrate, with my thoughts returning to my mother. It was going to be difficult to leave her here alone and return to school. Wilda had said that we'd have to return to Plainview tomorrow. I'd only been back from the holidays for two weeks, which included a week of school, with basketball workouts each day, except on Sunday. Maybe I could stay the rest of the week and catch the bus back to Plainview this weekend. Mother should be almost recovered from her surgery by then. That's not being realistic, I thought. I have to go back with them tomorrow. It's obvious that she is in good hands. A nurse interrupted my thoughts.

"The doctor would like to see you now. Your mother is out of surgery. If you'll come with me."

I followed her through a series of doors to a small lounge close to the operating room where Dr. Wrotham was waiting.

"Mattie, everything went well. Your mother did great and is in recovery. As soon as she wakes you can go in and stay with her. We'll keep her there for at least a couple of hours before moving her back to a room. Do you have any questions?"

I hadn't considered him taking the time to visit with me and answer questions. "At the moment, I can't think of anything to ask," I said.

"Let me answer a few of the most common that patients have. Your mom will be in the hospital for about ten days. By then, she should be able to do almost anything she wishes. As far as returning to work, I would recommend adding a week to that. She will need to return in three months for a check-up. I feel good about the surgery, but, of course, we do not know anything for sure. Your mother is young and in good heath and I believe the chances of a recovery are good."

"Will you tell her these things?"

"Yes, tomorrow. She may have additional questions," he said.

"Thank you, Dr. Wrotham. I have to leave tomorrow, but I know she'll be well taken care of."

"If you will leave me a phone number, I will get in touch, if anything comes up" he said.

"I appreciate it."

I stayed the afternoon and night with Mother. When she woke up I gave her the information Dr. Wrotham shared with me, even though she would hear it again tomorrow. When she became fully alert, her spirits were good, and by supper she was hungry. She had a good night and the next morning you would not have known she had gone through surgery.

"Mattie, I'm glad you came. I admit it thrilled me to see you. Would you thank the Hutchersons for me?"

"Sure. I have to meet them back at their hotel at noon. The flight takes us four hours so we'll be home by late evening."

We visited the remainder of the morning, with an interruption by Dr. Wrotham who came by to see how the patient was doing. He told her almost word for word what he had said to me the day before. Of course, it meant more coming from him than from me when I told her. After talking to her, he turned to me.

"Mattie, I have allowed myself a 15-minute break. I want to hear about this basketball team."

I spent the next few minutes describing the Flying Queens, including players, our coach, and the Hutchersons. I had no problem expressing my excitement and relating stories of our success. I finally stopped, afraid I'd gone overtime.

"You travel by plane to all road games?" he asked.

"Occasionally, we go by bus if it's only a few hours. That doesn't happen often."

"Amazing. This gives me hope. I have a ten-year-old girl that loves athletics; however, opportunity is limited in our public schools for girls. I am going to give you a number where you can reach me. If you ever have a game in this area, let me know. My little girl would be thrilled to attend and so would I. Now, back to work."

It was hard to leave, but at 11:00, I hugged Mother, telling her I loved her, and left the hospital. I gave myself an hour to get a taxi back to the hotel.

Two hours after I arrived back at the hotel, we were speeding down the runway, becoming airborne and headed west. On the flight, I thought of Sam and what he was about to endure. I'd told Mother he could hold up going through those memories, but I wasn't so sure. He had been through so much even after getting home. His stay in Arizona would be for at least two weeks and maybe more. He had moved his horse and Spade to Pa-Pa's place in town and Avery was going to care for them while he was gone. I didn't see how, but he was taking Hablo with him. With his barking, he would disrupt the entire movie set.

The flight was long, but due to lack of sleep the night before, I was able to doze off for an hour. We landed at dusk and were greeted by a bitter cold north wind that seemed to go right through you. The Hutchersons drove me to the dorm, and I thanked them over and over for taking me to Houston.

We won our next two games, and the layoff didn't seem to bother me, as I played well in both games. We now had a 42 game winning streak and were already talking, in a whisper, about a National Championship.

I called Sam again Sunday night before going to bed. He was leaving the next day for Arizona. The phone only rang once before he picked up.

"I was hoping that would be you," he said.

"Are you packed and ready to go?"

"Yeah. I'm probably forgetting something, though."

"Did you talk to your boss about being gone?"

"He said it would be fine. People have about sold all their cattle due to the drought. The runs are small."

"How long a drive is it?" I asked.

"It's going to take me two days. Long days," he answered.

"Are you really taking Hablo?"

"Yep. Can't leave him here. He's good company anyway."

"I miss you, Sam."

"I miss you too, Mattie. I'm coming to see you when I get back if it's all right."

"Sure. That would be awesome. Maybe you can see a game while you're here."

"Do you think I can do it, Mattie? Tell them what it was like over there? I couldn't even talk about it with you."

"Yes, you can, Sam. Just think, you are representing all the soldiers who didn't come home, plus those that came with terrible memories. You can do it," I repeated.

After we hung up, I stood there in the hall, saying a prayer, *Please, God, be with Sam and give him the strength to tell his story so that others may know the truth.* I went back to my room, put on my night clothes, and crawled into bed. I lay there, staring at the ceiling, suddenly smiling, and saying to myself, *Sam Colter, I love you and will marry you, even though you don't know that yet.*

Chapter 53

Sam

I left Sunday morning, January 23, for Patagonia, Arizona. I'd taken the remainder of my calves to the Thursday sale, and with the horses in town at Hollis' place, nothing was left on the ranch. Hablo let loose a series of barks as we were pulling on to the highway, as if saying, "Goodbye, we're on our way." It was approximately 800 miles, and my plans were to drive to El Paso, spend the night and be at my destination by late tomorrow afternoon. It was a small town, according to a map, but I assume the terrain was similar to that of Korea.

The weather was good for mid-winter, and I drove to Odessa before stopping for gas. I let Hablo out for his break, and once back on the road didn't stop until Pecos at a little drive-in for a late lunch. At dusk, I was entering the city limits of El Paso, bringing back a host of memories of my first trip here to begin my basic training at Fort Bliss. I found a small motel on the west side of the city from where I could see the lights of houses across the border in Mexico. I paid the $5 for the room, sneaking Hablo in and giving him instructions to stay quiet. When it was dark, I walked down to a small grocery store and bought bread, lunch meat, and chips for our supper.

I was on the road at daylight the next morning, only stopping twice for gas as I drove across southern New Mexico and into Arizona. I was in Patagonia by 5:00 in the afternoon, and following Greg's directions, easily found the site of the filming. I immediately saw the reason for the location, as the hills in the distance had a striking resemblance to those in Korea. A number of small low-lying buildings which I assume were to be bunkers made up most of the set. I parked and walked up to a roped off area. I was about to step over the rope when someone asked, "Where do you think you're going?"

"I'm here to see Greg," I answered.

Laughing, he replied, "So is everyone else within a hundred miles of this god-forsaken country. Now you just remove yourself from this area."

Evidently, he was the security officer, and I wasn't going to get anywhere with him. "He's expecting me. Would you please tell him that Sam Colter is here?"

"Look, buddy, the last guy that tried to see him told me that he was Greg's brother. You need to leave, now!"

I went back to my pickup, not knowing what to do. Within a short period of time, I saw him coming, walking fast. I didn't realize he was that tall. I got out of the pickup to meet him.

"Sam, I'm sorry. Security didn't know you, and I failed to tell them you were coming. I'm glad to see you. We haven't started filming yet but plan to in a few days. You're just in time. Of course, I have gone over the script, but I'm anxious to hear your story of what happened. If you'll come with me, I'll show you where you're staying."

"I brought my dog,"

Laughing, he replied, "That's not a problem. If anyone objects, tell them to see me."

I left Hablo and followed him to the other side of the site where several trailers were parked. He went to one of the smaller ones, saying, "This will be your living quarters while you're here. It's small but has running water, a fridge, and a television. It has a bathroom, but it's tiny. I stocked you up with some eats, but we have a cafeteria set up where you will be welcome. Thank you again for coming, Sam. I know it wasn't an easy decision. I have to go now, but will see you in the morning. You can drive your truck around here."

"Thanks, Greg. Will we start right away?"

"As soon as possible," he said, walking away.

I went back to where my truck was parked, meeting the security guard on the way.

"I'm sorry for the misunderstanding. It's really hard to keep people away from Greg. These locals all want to meet him. I'm Rodney Flowers, but everyone calls me Rod," he said, extending his hand.

"Sam Colter," I said, accepting the handshake. "That's all right, you were doing your job. Do you have any idea how long you'll be here?"

"They're saying the filming should be done in three months. I hope so. This is a desolate place and there's not much in the way of entertainment. I saw where Greg took you, and my trailer is next to yours. I know my way around, and if you need anything, just ask me."

"I appreciate it. I'm sure that questions will come up."

Continuing to my pickup I thought, it was great to have someone close by that I could rely on. I was a little nervous but felt better after meeting Rod. Hablo welcomed me back. I drove around to the trailer and went inside to inspect it, which didn't take long. It was small by any standard. I stepped into the kitchen which did have a small refrigerator, a stove with two burners, a table with a bench and a small television. I was amazed at the height of the antenna that was attached outside for the TV. It must have been thirty feet high, which was probably necessary in this remote area. The bedroom was just that. Big enough for a bed and nothing else. I could barely turn around in the bathroom. It still was roomy compared to the bunker where I spent the winter in Korea.

I found a dish in the refrigerator composed of meat and vegetables which probably came from the cafeteria. I heated it and found it to be tasty. After finishing and leaving Hablo, I walked around the area, surprised at the number of people. I counted fifteen trailers, with mine being the smallest. The largest was at least forty feet and probably was Greg's quarters. I didn't know if he was married or not. I returned to my trailer, and after going to bed, lay there wondering if I could do this.

The next morning, sitting outside my trailer drinking my second cup of coffee, Rod came walking up from the direction of the set.

"Morning, Sam. Sleep well?"

"Fair. My sleeping partner has a tendency to want more than his share of the bed," I replied.

"Greg sent me to tell you that a meeting will be held after breakfast. If you would like, we can eat in the cafeteria, and I can show you where the meeting will take place."

"Sounds good. Let me tie my dog outside."

The cafeteria was one of the buildings located in the middle of the set. Long tables and benches had been set up, with the cooking being done in an adjoining room. We went through a serve yourself line, that included, bacon, sausage, eggs, potatoes, pancakes, and all kinds of cereal.

"One thing about it, we eat good. I don't know where they got their cook but he's amazing," said Rod.

Rod's statement proved to be true. If I ate like this three times a day maybe I would gain weight. After we finished, he escorted me to a small building. Going inside, it resembled a bunker. There were a dozen chairs around a large table. Three of the chairs were already occupied. Rod introduced me and left, saying, he had to get to work. Within a short time, four more men appeared. No introductions were made, and they talked among themselves, laughing and joking. I was left out of the conversation, which was fine with me. Greg came in and everyone became quiet.

"Good morning. Ready to go to work?" he asked, prompting a nod of heads around the table. "Have all of you met Sam?"

One of the last men to come in, said, "Some of us haven't."

Greg asked each of the men to introduce themselves. Their expressions told me that some wanted to be here, but several didn't.

"I need to tell you a little about Sam. He was drafted right out of high school, did his basic training in El Paso and was sent to Korea in 1951. There was a rotation system at that time, where troops were changed out every few months or so. For some reason which I wasn't able to find out, Sam was an exception. He was on the front lines for 18 months. I'm sure some of you are wondering what he is doing here. There's a simple explanation; he's going to tell us first-hand what it was like. It's important to me that this movie script is accurate and doesn't mislead the audience. I don't trust what the writers have had to say, and Sam is going to help me understand if the role I'm playing is the truth or a lie to glorify this war. Do you have any questions about why you're here?"

One of the men who I had identified as not wanting to be here, asked, "What does this have to do with us? I understand what you're saying, that you need to hear his version of what happened, but it seems that our presence is a waste of time."

For the first time, I saw a different side of Greg. I hope that he never gives me the look directed at the man asking the question. When he spoke, his voice was low, coming from somewhere deep inside him. It wasn't angry and certainly not soft.

"We're not just making a war movie. It will be a look into a conflict and especially a battle that was a waste of American lives. I want you to hear first-hand what it was like to be in that war and battle. You each have a role in the movie, and to be able to play the part, it is necessary to know how that solider thinks and feels. I don't believe all of you realize how important this is to me. If this script doesn't reflect what this boy tells me, I'm walking out. That means you may be out of a job also. Is that understood?"

Again, a nodding of heads. I was nervous not knowing where to start, but Greg helped me out.

"We're going to start out by allowing you to ask questions of Sam? We'll just go around the table. If you don't have a question, we'll skip you."

"What kind of weapon did you have?" asked the first one.

"BAR 30 caliber M1918A2 and a .45 pistol. I trained with them in basic and they were the only guns I carried throughout the war. In my opinion the BAR was the best weapon used in the Korean war. Many of the soldiers in my company were from the city and knew nothing about guns. Training was done too quickly, and the result were men who were not familiar with their weapons. That's not being critical. It's just a fact. They were brave men and learned quickly once we were engaged in battle, but they needed more training before being sent into combat. Virtually all the weapons we used were from World War II. Most of the men were issued M1s. It was never suspected that we would be in another war so soon, and improvements in WWII weapons were not made. It's a well-known fact that we never expected to be in another ground war with the development of nuclear weapons."

"How did you feel before, during, and after your first battle?" asked the next man.

"It was in the spring after the snow melted. We were defending ground that the North Koreans and communists were determined to take. Before it started, I was nervous, frightened, unsure. During it, I reacted to my training, blanking everything else from my mind. After it, I was drained, sad, becoming emotional and crying. Later, I realized my ammunition belt had only one magazine left. Each magazine held only 20 shells. I had a belt with twelve magazines. For the remainder of the war, I never felt I had enough ammunition. My friend carried ammunition for me as did some of the other men."

I answered a dozen or more questions until Greg stopped the meeting, saying, "We've been here two hours. That's enough for today. We'll get together again in the morning. Thank you, Sam. You did well."

Several of the men, before leaving, came and shook hands with me, saying they appreciated my help in understanding the war. The man who had objected to having to stay and listen to me was not one of them.

It wasn't time for lunch, so I made my way back to the trailer. Hablo had a visitor. A cute little Cocker Spaniel was laying beside him. Hablo didn't usually take to other dogs, but I assumed this was a female. He barked at me and then turned his attention to his friend, like he was saying, "Look what came to see me." I unleased him and opened the door, but he wouldn't follow me inside, even after offering him a slice of lunch meat. I leashed him again and tied him to the trailer. "You can just stay out here and be hungry. Some friend you are," I said.

A short time later, Hablo started barking, and there was a knock on my door. Opening it, a young lady was standing there.

"I'm sorry to bother you, but I came after my dog. She got loose and I've been looking everywhere. You're Sam, aren't you?"

"Yes ma'am. This is Hablo," I said, pointing to him.

"I'm Julia, Greg's wife, and my dog's name is Bitsy. She's spoiled rotten."

Laughing, I said, "Hablo seems to think she's special."

"Greg told me about you. He was pleased that you came. How did the meeting go this morning?"

"Much better than I expected."

"Swell. I'll take Bitsy off your hands. I'll know where to find her now when she disappears."

"Nice to meet you," I said as she was leaving.

Hablo spoke his threatening bark but followed me into the trailer when they were out of sight. He accepted the lunch meat this time when it was offered. I still had some time before going to the cafeteria, thinking, I told the truth to Greg's wife about the meeting. I was pleasantly surprised that it was easier than expected. Maybe the difference was that it was for a good cause, and important to Greg, who I admired more each time we were together. Anyway, maybe the next one would go as well.

Chapter 54

Gladys

The first few days after Mattie left I was depressed from the physical discomfort brought about by the surgery. I could barely move my arms which meant I couldn't go to the bathroom alone. Of course, I needed help to put on my clothes. I was weak, it seemed all the strength had been sapped out of my body. I couldn't lie on my stomach, which had always been my sleeping position. I couldn't even sit up in bed without help. I had never thought about the limitations that would be placed on me, not understanding why someone didn't warn me.

On the fourth day after the surgery, when I got up enough nerve to look at myself in the mirror, the world came crashing down on me. I have no idea why the sight of my upper body would have that effect on me. I had a mastectomy which was a breast removal. What did I expect to see? They had cut out a part of my body and I would be disfigured the remainder of my life. It was done to save my life. Shouldn't that make me accept the sacrifice?

I tried to rationalize my thinking and depression. Self-worth had always been a problem for me since I could remember. I had felt better about myself the last year than I ever had. I had even begun to feel attractive and more sure of myself. My confidence had increased dramatically. I was more outgoing and social, believing myself to be on an equal with my peers. I dressed better, applied makeup, had my hair done, and thoroughly enjoyed the compliments that were received. Now this. When told about the cancer and surgery, I never considered the effect it would have on my self-value. If informed, would I have gone ahead with the surgery? *"Of course, dummy, you want to live,"* said a voice inside my head. Would I be able to overcome the insecurity and fading self-image that was surely in my future?

I did have a phone in my room and Earnest had called each day. He was planning to come to Houston, but Mr. Quentin had come down with the flu and was in the hospital. I hadn't told Mattie about her pa-pa when she called yesterday. There was no use putting any additional worry on her. I begged Earnest to stay and look after her pa-pa until he was better. He agreed but said as soon as Mr. Quentin's fever broke he was coming. I know that part of my reluctance about seeing Earnest was a fear that he would realize I wasn't the same woman he wanted to marry. I didn't see how any man wouldn't be troubled with the thought of marrying a disfigured woman.

The fifth day after my surgery a social worker came in, introducing herself as Lindsey and asked me how I was doing.

"I feel stronger and the soreness is better," I replied.

"How do you feel mentally?" she asked.

"Depressed. Looking in the mirror brought me back to reality," I said.

"That's not unusual for women who go through this operation. Would you like to talk about it?" she asked.

"Do most of the women recover emotionally?"

"Yes, I would say so," she answered.

"How long does it usually take?"

"That depends on the individual."

"I don't feel like a whole person anymore. I'm afraid others will see me that way, also."

"I assure you...that's not true. Your family and friends will love and respect you even more after what you've gone through. Are you married?"

"No. I'm a widow. I had plans to marry again soon after getting home. Now, I don't know."

"Tell me about him."

"His name is Earnest. He lost his wife several years ago. He's a nice man, and we enjoy one another's company. He's a good friend and has been wanting to get married for some time."

"And you think he might feel differently, now?" she asked.

"Maybe. I don't know. My first husband would have."

"Is Earnest anything like your first husband?" she asked.

"No. Not in any way."

"So, you're basing your doubt on your first husband, who I assume was not good to you. I imagine he abused you and destroyed your self-image. I see that a lot in my kind of work. Now, you have a good man who is kind and will treat you good. Don't think for a minute that your surgery will have any effect on how he feels about you. You're fortunate to have someone who will support you during your physical and emotional recovery. What a pretty lady you are. He's a fortunate man, also"

"Thank you. I needed to hear that. The doctor told me that my chances of a full recovery are good. I need to be thankful for that," I said.

"Yes. It's helpful to concentrate on the positive and that is good news compared to what many patients receive. I have to be going now, but I'll be by tomorrow to check on you."

For the next four days I went to physical therapy in the morning and afternoon. The soreness was still there but not nearly so bad. I could dress myself, go to the bathroom, and even bathe without help. Lindsey came by each day and talking with her, I began to feel like a whole person again. The doctor came in every day to check the incision for signs of an infection. On my ninth day in the hospital he had some good news.

"Gladys, everything looks good. I don't see any reason why we can't get you out of here tomorrow. I would like to see you again in three months. I'm going to make arrangements for you to receive radiation treatments in Abilene. If any problems arise call my office and we'll get you in. Do you have any questions?"

"What are the chances of the cancer returning?" I asked.

"Unfortunately, I can't say for sure. I believe we caught it early, and it may not come back. I feel good about your prognosis but with cancer there are no guarantees."

"Thank you, Dr. Wrotham, for everything."

"I'll see you in three months, Gladys," he said, leaving.

The remainder of the day dragged by, and I had to request a sleeping pill at 11:00 that night. I was awake by 5:00 the next morning, but it was noon before finally being dismissed. I prayed all the way to my car that it would start after sitting for ten days. It started immediately.

On the drive home, I had plenty of time to think. Earnest had not been able to come. Mr. Quentin had developed pneumonia and was still in the hospital. When I talked with Earnest yesterday, he had shown some improvement. The drive home was more difficult than I expected, with the pain in my chest and arms causing me to stop several times. It was 9:00 that evening before I drove up in front of my house, seeing Earnest's car parked in my driveway.

Earnest and I were married on Saturday, February 5, one week after I came home. The ceremony, which was attended only by Louise, and several of Earnest's close friends was held at the Methodist Church. Earnest had given me a choice, but I insisted on using his church and pastor. I changed my mind about wanting it at Pioneer Methodist.

Earnest had been wonderful, with encouraging words and sincere affection since coming home. It was hard to believe; I was marrying such a different man than Leon. I'd never truly loved my first husband, but sincerely believed that it would be different with Earnest. Of course, Mattie didn't attend the wedding, nor her pa-pa. He was still in the hospital and it looked as if a decision was forthcoming to decide where he would live. He insisted that his next residence would be the nursing home. Of course, the problem with that would be Mattie.

I moved my personal belongings into Earnest's place, leaving the furniture and appliances intact. In the future, if Mattie's pa-pa did make enough improvement, he could move into my house. I insisted that Earnest leave the pictures of his first wife in place, that it would not bother me in the least. We were going to start a new life together, but he should have the right to remember the past.

I talked with Mr. Wilson and we agreed that one more week should be enough time for me to rest before returning to work. He was kind and understanding, saying that if I needed more time, to take it.

Chapter 55

Sam

I spent the next morning wandering around the set. They had begun shooting some scenes and Greg asked me to observe the uniforms and weapons to check for authenticity. It was fascinating to watch them shoot a scene over and over. I had never thought about the challenge of getting everything just right. I was so intent on watching that she spoke before seeing her.

"It's interesting, especially the first time you see it."

I turned and saw it was Julie, Greg's wife. "Yes ma'am. I never would've thought about being present at the filming of a movie."

"You don't have to say ma'am. It's makes me feel old. Greg is quite taken with you and that's unusual. He's not impressed easily, which the director can verify. Of course, I'm not impressed with the director either. Greg doesn't appear until fifteen minutes into the movie. By the way, Bitsy is gone. I assume she is at your trailer. She's a purebred Cocker Spaniel and I have her papers. What breed is your dog?"

"I guess you would call him a mixed breed. He does have good taste. Your little dog is cute."

"Has your dog been, you know… fixed?"

"No. He's all boy."

"I have to be going," she said, getting up and leaving.

During a break, Greg came over and asked me if I saw anything that was a problem.

"The BAR that one of the guys was carrying had a bayonet attached. They didn't have a place to fasten a bayonet. I kept wondering if they glued it on. Also, if you carried a BAR, you had suspenders, to hold up your ammunition belt. The twelve magazines that the belt carried made it heavy. I didn't carry any grenades, even though I could have, because of the additional weight; however, I did carry a knife. Your men are clean. We were filthy most of the time."

"Thanks, Sam for the information. I saw my wife talking with you."

"Yeah. She's nice."

"Sometimes," he said, smiling. "You have a lady friend, don't you?"

"I think so. She's at college in Plainview, Texas."

"Have you talked with her since your arrival?" he asked.

"No. I don't have a phone in my trailer."

"We'll fix that in the next day or two. In the meantime, come over to my trailer tonight and use mine. Now, it's back to work."

I was about to leave and go back to my trailer when Rod appeared, asking, "How's it going, Sam?"

"Good. It's fun watching the filming."

"After you've been here awhile it gets boring, watching them do a scene over and over. You catch yourself saying, 'just get on with it'."

"Do you ever get any time off?" I asked.

"Occasionally, every two weeks or so. If it wasn't for the locals trying to get a glimpse of Greg, I could take off more. They're a persistent bunch."

We visited a few minutes longer and then went to lunch. The food was great and there was plenty of it. Two kinds of meat, bowls of vegetables, salads, several kinds of potatoes, rolls, and numerous desserts. Most everyone was friendly, since Rod was well known. Greg came over to where we were eating, saying that we were meeting this afternoon at 5:00.

When I returned to my trailer, Hablo was gone. He had slipped out of his collar which was lying on the ground. I had a pretty good idea about where he was. I started toward Greg's trailer and met Julia, who wasn't too happy.

"Bitsy is gone. I imagine she is with your dog. I came to get her."

"Hablo isn't at the trailer, either," I said.

"I've got to find her. Her groom will be here anytime. She is scheduled for a trim and manicure today."

"Where does she usually go when she runs off?" I asked, meekly.

"She didn't run off until she met your dog. She would stay right at the trailer."

We looked in vain for the next hour, but there was no sign of them. The only explanation had to be that they had left the area. "I'm going to drive back toward town. You're welcome to go with me," I offered.

She mumbled something I didn't understand which was probably good. She did accompany me to my pickup. We hadn't driven but a few hundred yards toward town when I noticed the dam of a stock tank. Hablo loves water, I thought. It's worth checking out. The tank wasn't far from the road, and I opened my door, yelling, "Hablo! Come here! Hablo!" Immediately, he appeared, trotting over the dam. He was a mud ball and right behind him came a smaller mud ball. Suddenly, Julie started laughing, and my first thought was, *she's hysterical*. She continued to laugh so hard she had tears running down her face.

"Are you all right?" I asked.

It took her a minute to be able to respond, "Yes, I'm sorry. The groom is going to earn her money today."

I will never understand women. I thought she would be furious but her response was exactly the opposite. We put Hablo and Bitsy in the back of my pickup for the ride back. Both of them had a huge smile and Hablo spoke his happy bark. I volunteered to hose them down from a facet by the cafeteria. We drew a crowd of curious onlookers. I wasn't that successful since the mud had dried and was matted in their hair. Bitsy didn't look at all like a pure breed with papers, but she was a happy little girl wagging her tail the entire time. I apologize to Julie before she left with Bitsy.

"Don't worry about it, Sam. We socialites like to get down and dirty sometime."

The meeting at 5:00 included the same group, but this time Greg had a large stack of papers which I assume was the script. He started the meeting by asking if I had anything else to add after watching the scenes this morning.

"No, only what I mentioned earlier."

"We will follow the same procedure today, giving everyone that wishes a chance to ask you questions. I will start the ball rolling today. What was morale like among the men?"

"When I first arrived in January of 1951 it wasn't that bad. As time passed, it grew worse, and by the time the war ended it was bad. Dissertations increased and there was constant grumbling. You have to understand, it was bitter cold in the winter, almost unbearable. There was less combat, but the weather was also the enemy. Our guns would freeze up. At times, I could only fire one shot at a time with my BAR.

"There was general confusion among the men as to why we were there in the first place. Of course, we understood the political viewpoint, insisting that we had to stop the spread of communism in Asia. To the men, that was not a reason to fight and die for. Many of them couldn't even tell you what communism was. The men I fought with were brave and followed orders. The ones I felt sorry for were the blacks. They were fighting for their country and at home the KKK was still active. Many places in the United States still had signs up stating, 'Whites Only'. Most of the men went out of their way to encourage them and show support. After all, skin color meant nothing when you were fighting side by side for your life."

Sam, the script doesn't portray men having low morale. I'm going to make some notes and address it with the director tomorrow. Now we'll move on to the next question.

One of the men asked, "Other countries representing the United Nations were involved in the war. Did one country stand out to you as being superior to others?"

"Definitely. That's a great question and one I will gladly answer. No one could touch the Ethiopians. They were tough, disciplined fighters. They never received the publicity or respect they deserved."

"Was there a low point of morale?" asked the next man.

"The last several months of the war. It was well-known that a peace was being negotiated, and because of this, the fighting escalated. You would wonder why it was this way. The answer was simple. Whoever had the upper hand on the battle field would have the advantages in the negotiations. Men on both sides were being sacrificed to allow a more favorable bargaining. We knew that and no one wanted to be the last to die... please understand, we followed the orders, and our soldiers fought bravely, but the morale was at a low point."

The next question made me flinch. "What was the low point for you?"

I hesitated, looking at Greg, who said, "Sam, it's up to you. Stop anytime you want."

"We were ordered to take a Godforsaken piece of ground. They called it Hill 255. Of course, our offensive movements were at night, with our colonel telling us we had to be on top by daylight. Any man carrying a BAR was a prime target for snipers. The reason was simple. Any time a machine gun nest or sniper was located the BAR was a far superior weapon to the M1. One BAR was equal to at least six M1s to take out a sniper. As I told you, the BAR went through ammunition quickly. Flint, my best friend since basic, carried extra magazines for me. We started up the hill, taking heavy fire, with flares lighting up the sky. About halfway up, a sniper fired not 50 yards above us, with a flame shooting from his gun. I immediately emptied a magazine at the spot, spacing shots to include a small area. I turned and Flint was lying on his back. 'I'm hit, Sam'. I dropped my weapon and picked him up, carrying him over my shoulder. All the way down the hill he kept saying, 'Don't let me die, Sam.' I-I-I'm sorry," I said, breaking into tears.

"Thank you, Sam. That's all for today," said Greg.

"No, please, I need to finish," I said, taking a few deep breaths. "I reached the bottom, but of course, when I put him down, he was dead. A medic came, knelt down, examined him and said, "Go join your unit. You can't do nothing for him. I'll see to it that his body gets back to camp. I walked back up the hill found my gun, and joined the rest of the men. We didn't reach the top, but 25 of us out of the 135 that started up the hill managed to dig in near the top. Of that 25, several were wounded. We were supposed to get reinforcements, but they didn't come. Our colonel, through the radio operator, asked for water, plasma, and ammunition. We were totally exhausted, taking shelter in a bunker. The Chinese still held two-thirds of the hill. Our request for supplies and reinforcements by radio and messenger were not fulfilled."

"Sam, this script said that your commanders didn't realize how bad the situation was, thinking the men were only fatigued and could hold the hill," Greg explained, holding up a page of the script.

"That's a lie. I heard our colonel plead for ammunition and supplies, saying, 'If we didn't receive help, we can't hold our positon'. We knew if it didn't come, in a matter of hours we were all going to die. Finally, the reinforcements came. I assume the high command thought the hill was worth holding. Only 14 of us out of the original 135 walked down Hill 255 the morning of April 18."

"It looks like me and the director are going to need to have a serious talk before we continue shooting this movie. That's all for today."

I was surprised when the man who earlier felt the meetings were a waste of his time came by and put his hand on my shoulder, squeezing it and saying, "Thank you, Sam. I'm sorry about your friend."

Greg stayed until everyone was gone, coming over and sitting down by me. "Sam, I really appreciate it. I'm sorry it's so tough on you."

"I feel like a load has been lifted from me. I needed to talk about it and tell someone. Will they change the script to reflect the truth?"

"It depends on how badly they want me to play the leading role. We'll have to wait and see. I'm not going to glamorize this war or excuse the conduct of the commanders or politicians. My goal is to show the American people how brave our soldiers were and the sacrifices they made. This war is called the 'Forgotten War'. I want to change that for the families of those who died and for men like yourself who gave so much. I don't think that is asking too much.

"Come over tonight and have a drink with me. You can call your lady friend. I would invite you for dinner, but I eat in the cafeteria. Julie is a terrible cook."

"I usually wait until 9:00 or so to call. Mattie's in the dorm by that time and usually studying."

"No problem. I'll see you later," he said.

After he left, I sat there thinking about the afternoon. I had finally been able to get through it. I was telling the truth to Greg. I felt better after talking about it.

Chapter 56

Mattie

It was Saturday, February 5, and Mother was getting married today. In fact, it had already happened. I had wished all day that it would have been possible for me to be present. She deserved the happiness that was going to come with being married to Earnest. Talking with her this morning, she sounded good and very optimistic about her surgery. We had talked a number of times on the phone, and each time she had sounded more upbeat.

It had been a month since Sam brought me back to school. I'd talked with him three times since then, but not since he'd gone to Arizona. After spending time with him Christmas, my school and basketball didn't seem as important. Going back home to my family and friends had the effect of bringing me back to reality and what was important. I still loved school and basketball but realized that would end one of these days, and my future would be elsewhere. We had played six games since Christmas and increased our winning streak to 46. We were getting national publicity now, with articles appearing in some of the big city newspapers. I was playing well but becoming more aware all the time that my contribution was no greater, maybe even less, than the other players. The team effort was what made us successful and individuals took a back seat.

I still hadn't gotten used to the weather in the Panhandle. It was cold most days, and even with the sun shining, I had to wear my heavy coat. We had received a big ice storm with snow, the day after returning from the holidays. For two days we hadn't ventured out of the dorm except for meals. We didn't even practice because our gym was too cold due to the wind that came through the cracks in the walls. Today was an exception with no wind, sunshine, and a temperature in the 50s. When Charley and I went to supper we didn't need our coats. With Charley, there was never a lack of conversation. I was amazed that she could eat and talk at the same time, usually finishing her meal before I did.

"Have you heard from Sam?" she asked, with a mouthful of spaghetti.

"It's been over a week."

"Better call him. Sonia's lurking just around the corner, waiting to pounce."

I hadn't told her about Sam being in Arizona since he'd asked me not to tell anyone about his famous friend who asked him to help with a movie. I really didn't see how it could hurt if I told Charley. Maybe he only meant people in his home town."

"Sam's not home. He's in Arizona."

"What's he doing there?"

"Working."

"At what?" she asked, putting half a piece of bread in her mouth. How could she be so small and eat like that?

"Will you not tell anyone?"

"A secret! I love secrets, Mattie. I promise… cross my heart and hope to die."

"There's a movie being made about the Korean War, and he was asked to be on the set to see that it was accurate," I explained.

"Mattie! With movie stars? You're kidding!" she exclaimed.

"No. It's true."

"Who's playing the leading role? You gotta tell me!"

I leaned over and whispered in her ear which was a mistake. She started choking, and I thought she was going to pass out. People all around stopped eating, with one guy coming over and asking if he should call a doctor. I was beginning to wonder that myself when she caught her breath and started fanning herself.

Clearing her throat and taking a sip of water she said, "Oh my, oh my. I get dizzy just thinking of him."

I then told her of the day he came to Sam's ranch and walked right into the house and asked for Sam's help with the movie. She actually stopped eating.

"What did you do? What was he wearing? Is he as good looking in person? Did you shake his hand? Does he really talk that way, in that deep voice that goes right through you? Is he really that tall?"

"What questions do you want answered first?" I asked.

"Is he as good looking in person as on the screen?" she asked, still not eating.

"Better. He had on jeans and a flannel shirt. He had to duck coming through the door he's so tall. I gasped when he came in, thinking I must be hallucinating."

"I can't believe it! What did Sam do?"

"Nothing. Acted like he was just another visitor," I answered.

She went back to eating, still talking. "I would of fainted. I guarantee you. I couldn't have taken it. Why did you wait so long to tell me?"

"Sam didn't want people to know. Sam avoids attention."

"So he sees him every day and talks with him?" she asked.

"I guess so."

"Amazing," she said, reaching for her dessert.

The next three weeks we played three more games, increasing our winning streak to 49. Our regular schedule had ended, but of course, we received an invitation to play in the National AAU Tournament, which was held in St. Joseph, Missouri the 4th and 5th of March. We were feeling a lot of pressure, not only because of our winning streak, but we were the defending National Champions. One of Coach's favorite sayings was that we were like the old western gunslingers…everyone wanted to take us down. Neither Charley or I were starting, but we were getting a lot of playing time. It was exciting, sometimes a little too much so. On a flight to Kansas City, the wings on our Beechcraft Bonanza iced over and we had to land. We drew good crowds, whether at home or on the road. Sarah still roomed with us on road trips and had become a good friend to both Charley and me.

We left for St Joseph on Thursday, March 3, for the AAU Tournament. We had a semi-final game with Hanes Hosiery the next night. After we arrived and checked into the hotel, we were taken to the gym for a short practice session. I was surprised at the size of the gym, which they said had a seating capacity of 4000. After our workout, we returned to the hotel and were met in the lobby by Wilda Hutcherson.

"I need a few minutes with you girls," she said.

We followed her to several chairs and a couch in the corner of the lobby, wondering what was going on.

"How was workout?" she asked.

"Good," we answered, together.

"I wanted to give you some news in order to prepare you. There's going to be enough excitement without any additional surprises. Claude started a tradition at last year's AAU tournament of flying some of the parents to the tournament. This year, Charley, your mom and dad will be here. Mattie, Claude is flying your mom and granddad here, also. They will arrive sometime around noon tomorrow and will stay here with us."

First, I was stunned, then when it soaked in, I began crying. How could people be this nice? I couldn't talk, so instead, I hugged her. Charley didn't have any trouble expressing herself.

"That's wonderful! That's awesome! Thank you! Thank you!"

"You need to thank Claude. It was his idea. After all these years of marriage, he still amazes me."

I could talk by the time we were back in our room. "Charley, can you believe it? We play a game at Dyess so they can see me play now he's flying them here. I never thought anyone could be that thoughtful and generous."

Before she could respond, Sarah came in, saying, "I heard about Claude bringing your families. He flew mine in last year, and it had to be one of the biggest thrills of their lifetime."

She continued, "This tournament is a big deal. They have several activities, including a beauty contest and a free throw contest. Mattie, several of the girls have already informed the coach that they want you to be our beauty contestant."

"Me? Why me?" I asked, confused.

"Because you have the best chance of winning," she answered.

"But… But," I stammered.

"Awe, come on Mattie. Just look in the mirror," said Charley.

Rather than make more of a fool of myself, I remained quiet. I couldn't believe all of this was happening to me. I went around in a trance the rest of the day, but that evening, at supper, I did get a chance to tell Claude how much I appreciated him bringing my mother and pa-pa to the game.

"I'm glad to be able to do it," he replied. Has Coach told you about representing the Flying Queens in the beauty contest?"

"No. Not yet."

"He will. I guess it has slipped his mind."

The next morning, after a sleepless night, I was busy. Dressed in my traveling clothes, I was taken to the gym where the beauty contest was being held. There were twelve of us competing with a panel of three judges, all male. Most of the girls were attractive with several being beautiful. I kept repeating to myself, *what am I doing here?* We were interviewed individually and asked questions by the judges including; where we were from, what our goals were, and how basketball had influenced our lives? The interview didn't last over five minutes. The girls were dressed nice but none with any finer clothes than my traveling uniform. After the questions, we had to walk single file by the judges, several times. It reminded me of our county stock show in high school when animals were paraded before the judge.

I was glad to get back to the hotel where Charley met me at the door asking, "How was it?" I bet you were the prettiest. Did you take long strides like a model?"

"Charley, we need to get our minds on basketball. I'm not a beauty queen, for crying out loud. Let's go to our room and talk about the game tonight."

"Fine, but I still bet you were the prettiest."

We spent the remainder of the morning in our rooms. I was even able to take a short nap after lunch. We were in the lobby when Charley's parents arrived. It was a contest to see who could get the most words in, Charley or her mother. Now, I understood where she got her gift. Two hours later my mom came through the door, pushing my Pa-Pa in a wheelchair. I choked up but held back the tears as we hugged. Pa-Pa was all smiles.

"Mattie, I'm so proud of you. What a plane ride. It was something," he said, still holding my hand.

"This is exciting, Mattie! I never dreamed we would get to see you play again. I thought I must be dreaming when Mr. Hutcherson called and offered us a ride to the tournament."

"Mother, you look great!"

"I feel good, Mattie."

We sat in the lobby and visited for the next hour. A bellboy showed them to their room and I left with the team to get ready for the game.

When we took the floor for our warmup, the gym was about a third full. When we came back out to start the game it was packed. I had never seen so many people in one place. Charley and I didn't start but by the second quarter both of us were in the game. The game was close the first half, but by the third quarter we were pulling away. I was satisfied with my play, scoring eight points and stealing the ball several times. By the beginning of the fourth quarter, we had a 15-point lead, with the final score being 58-40.

The next morning, Mother and I had a chance to visit alone in the lobby. She assured me again she was doing well. She had been taking radiation treatments in Abilene and had gone back to work. She told me she was feeling fine and her strength had returned. I asked her about Pa-Pa.

"One thing about your pa-pa...he's a fighter. After being released from the hospital, he's been able to stay at our old house by himself. I go by in the morning and fix his breakfast and Earnest checks on him during the day. He is slow moving, but with our help he's able to stay out of the nursing home. He can get around with a walker, but the wheelchair was easier when we arrived here."

She continued, "What about Sam, have you heard from him?"

"Yes. When I talked with Sam he seemed like a different person. He was able to describe his experiences in Korea, even the death of his friend. He has stayed longer than expected in Arizona, but said he was in no hurry to get home. He actually was talkative, with our calls lasting 15 or 20 minutes. Each time we talk he tells me that he's looking forward to when we can be together."

"I'm glad to hear that, Mattie. Sam is a special person, and it's good to know he's been able to talk about his horrible experiences in the war. I've always believed that the two of you belonged together."

Me too, I said to myself.

It was a wonderful weekend. Before the final game, the winner of the beauty contest was announced. I was first-runner up, which shocked me. Of course Charley was irate, announcing to everyone in hearing distance that the winner was chosen because she was busty and that the panel of judges should include at least one female.

I don't know why, but I started the final game. Maybe it was because my mother and Pa-Pa were there. We played Omaha Commercial Extension and they were tough. Their strategy from the beginning of the game was evident. They slowed it down to a crawl and played fearless defense. We led at the half, 12-10. Coach reminded us that we had to be patient and take care of the ball, making our shots count. They became careless in the third quarter and lost the ball several times. We took advantage and scored six points, increasing our lead to 18-10. After that, they panicked and abandoned their game plan. We ended up winning 31-20, and once again the Flying Queens were the National

Champions. We received our trophy at mid-court celebrating with hugs and high fives. There was a piece of tape across the bottom of the trophy covering up the sponsor for the tournament...Budweiser. Our picture was taken with the trophy and would appear in many of the large newspapers across the country the next day.

Pa-Pa told me the next morning at breakfast that yesterday was the best day of his life.

Chapter 57

Sam

I had stayed in Arizona much longer than anticipated. January ended, and February, with only 28 days, came and went. It was the second week in March, and I knew that it would be necessary to leave soon. I talked with Mattie at least once a week. She had called Sunday night when she was back in Plainview, excited about winning the AAU Tournament and the National Championship. I didn't tell her, but my plans were to go home, check on everything, and drive to Spearman. I was confident that it would now be possible to visit with them about Flint and our time together in Korea. From there, I would go on to Plainview. It had been two and a half months since I'd seen Mattie and that was long enough.

We had given up trying to keep Hablo and Bitsy separated. He was either over at their trailer or she was over here. At least twice a week they visited their swimming hole. We stopped going after them, just waiting until they decided to return, covered with mud. They could be seen throughout the day roaming around the set, receiving handouts. By dark they would show up at mine or Greg's trailer.

I had gained weight from eating three good meals a day, and my clothes were too small. When Rod invited me to go into Tombstone with him, I accepted. It was only 50 miles and would give me a chance to purchase clothes that fit. I'd spent none of my money that I brought with me, since my room and board were free. We went on a Saturday and decided to make a day of it.

Upon arriving, our first stop was at a dry goods store, where I bought three pair of jeans and four shirts. Our next stop was the OK Corral where the legendary gunfight had occurred. There wasn't much to see except a lot of bullet holes in the fences and buildings. They did have a sign describing the famous incident.

After lunch, we decided to check out the movie theater. *Rear Window* was showing, and we were in time to catch the start. Entering the theater and finding a seat, the newsreel had already started. Pictures of President Eisenhower flashed across the screen of him playing golf, followed by Nikolai Bulganin becomes Soviet Premier and then the pictures of girls playing basketball and a voice saying, *"The Flying Queens of Wayland Baptist College have again won the National Championship of women's basketball and you thought it was a man's game. The ladies now have a 52 game winning streak,"* and then there she was, dribbling down the court, for all the world to see. My heart was pounding and when the newsreel moved to another subject, I got up and left. Going outside, I lit a Camel, and my first thought was, I'm ready to go home. I finished the cigarette and went back inside; however, my mind was not on the movie.

The next day, March 13, after a sleepless night, I went to Greg's trailer asking if he had time to talk with me.

"Sure, come in, I have the coffee on. What's on your mind?"

"It's time for me to leave. I've stayed longer than I intended. Is that all right with you?"

Laughing, he replied, "Certainly, Sam. You've been everything and more than I expected. I have a much better understanding of the war after our meetings. I knew that the information from an enlisted man would be more accurate than from an officer. I owe you some money though."

"Could you mail it? I'd like to leave today."

"I can do that. If I remember, your friend's parents were to receive the same amount as yourself."

"That's correct," I said.

"I've seen a change in you, Sam, and it's for the best. I'm hoping that we can take a little credit for that."

"Yes, sir. After being able to describe my experiences in Korea, even talking about Flint, I felt as if a load had been lifted from me. I want to thank you for being patient and understanding."

"Good. Now, maybe you can get on with your life. You have been helpful with the information you provided about the battle-field. I would like to tell you a few things about the domestic war here at home against communism. It might help you understand why we became involved in Korea. The motion picture industry was caught in the middle of it. Of course, we are a liberal minded group and when McCarthy started broadcasting that the United States was being infiltrated by communists, we were one of the first targets. As you probably know, it became know as the 'Red Scare'. The movement, which began in the late 40s was successful in the sense that many people believed it. I spoke out against it and fortunately wasn't blacklisted, as many of my peers were. When North Korea invaded South Korea, the stage was set for political pressure for US intervention. McCarthy deserves his share of the blame for inciting the public. He lied and created fear in people. I hope and pray we never have another politician like him."

He hesitated and then continued, "I voted for Truman but like all politicians, he wasn't perfect. After he fired McArthur for wanting to invade China, he was dubbed as being soft on communism. Of course, McArthur was a hero to the American people for his role in World War II. I really believe that it made the President less flexible in seeking an end to the war. Maybe, I'm wrong, but that's what I think.

"Sam, maybe it will help you understand that several different circumstances were responsible for the war. Hopefully, we learned something from Korea and the next time pressure is placed on us to fight in a foreign country because we disagree as to their type of government we will be more cautious. Now, I have a small problem that you might help me with. Julie left yesterday, going back to California. She had all of this camping out in a desolate country she could take. I was surprised she stayed this long. Julie didn't take Bitsy, and she's not here, so I assume she's at your place. Is that correct?"

"They were still in bed when I left this morning."

"I can't look after her without Julie. Would you be willing to take her with you?" he asked.

I couldn't say no to Greg. He'd been good to me. "Sure. Hablo would like that."

"If Julie throws a fit, I'll send someone to get Bitsy. Thanks, Sam."

We shook hands and I left, returning to my trailer to pack. Hablo and Bitsy were up and wanting out, but I knew better than let them loose. I packed my few belongings, and putting them in the pickup, was on the road, not wanting to go through any emotional goodbyes. As I drove away, an inner voice spoke, *you made a good choice in deciding to come to Arizona. You're leaving in much better shape than when you arrived.*

Late the next day, after many potty stops for my two passengers, I drove through the gate of the Colter Ranch. Everything seemed to be fine, but the house was musty, being shut up for three months. I opened up some windows and unloaded my pickup before calling Gladys. I couldn't call her Mrs. Quentin any longer so maybe it was all right to just use her first name.

"Sam, I'm glad to have you home. Is everything all right at your place?"

"Looks good, except still dry," I replied.

"Have you talked with Mattie?" she asked.

"Yeah, after they won the AAU Tournament."

"Did she tell you they were going to Mexico City to play in an international tournament the last of this month?" she asked.

"No, she didn't mention that. She was pretty excited about winning the National Championship and y'all being able to come."

We talked another several minutes with me promising to see them when I came to town. Going, outside, Hablo and Bitsy were not in sight. They had been cramped up yesterday and today on the 800-mile drive and were enjoying their freedom. Today was March 14, and since Mattie was going to the tournament in Mexico the last of this month, I could go to Spearman next week. I could then surprise her by being in Plainview when they returned from Mexico. I felt good about my decision, realizing how much I was looking forward to seeing Mattie.

I walked down to the barn and found Hablo and Bitsy. Hablo was prancing around carrying a big rat in his mouth that he had killed. Bitsy didn't seem impressed, moving away from him when he came close. I took the rat away from the mighty hunter and deposited it in a trash barrel kept at the barn for that purpose. "I don't think she's that impressed, Hablo."

Later that evening, sitting on my couch watching "I Love Lucy" with a dog on each side of me, I was as content and relaxed as I had been since before the war.

I received a registered letter from Greg on Friday, March 18, before I left for Spearman on the following Monday. The letter contained two cashier's checks for $6,000 each. One was made to me the other was to the McGowans. I went straight from the post office to the bank and paid off my loan. I had paid the loan down to $1,500 which still left me $4,500 to deposit in my account. I had no idea that my payment would be that much. Greg had included a note with the checks.

I hope you're doing well. I want to thank you again for sharing your experience with us. If I can help you in any way, please let me know. We are almost finished shooting the movie; however, due to circumstances beyond my control, it may not be released this year.

Your friend,
Greg

There was plenty of time to think on the drive to Spearman. I had experienced several low points in the last three years, including: the death of my mother and afterwards, having to return to Korea; the death of my friend, Flint; the illness that came at a time when I was suffering with the demons; the death of my lifelong friend and companion, Jose; and to a somewhat lesser degree, the drought, jail time, and beating I took from Sonia's brothers. Now, here I was, driving down Highway 83, with no debt and money in the bank, able to complete a task that was long overdue. Maybe, from now on my life would have high points. I felt good…better than good.

Earnest and Gladys had agreed to keep my dogs. I assumed Bitsy was my dog now because Greg hadn't mentioned her in the letter. Besides, she was pregnant and wouldn't have been able to make the trip back to California. Avery was still looking after the horses. I was planning on spending a week with the McGowans, who were expecting me, and at least another week in Plainview.

I stopped for lunch in Canadian, a beautiful little town on the river from which it received its name. I continued on Highway 83 for another 20 miles and turned back west and drove into Spearman in the early afternoon. The only directions given to me by the McGowans were to turn north in Spearman and go five miles. I would come to a brick house located on the right side of the road. I followed their instructions, checking my odometer for the correct mileage. I came to the brick house and seeing the two John Deere tractors parked behind the house knew this was the McGowan Farm.

They had been watching for me because they were out the door before I came to a complete stop. The mother grabbed and hugged me, crying and not letting go. I relaxed and let her hold me, realizing what it meant for me to come and regretting putting it off this long. She finally let go and his dad stepped forward. I put out my hand expecting a handshake but instead he hugged me, also, crying softly. It was an awkward few minutes but ended quickly when he stepped back, saying, "Welcome, Sam. Thank you for coming."

From that time on, there was not a difficult moment. We went into the house, sat down in the living room, and talked for three hours. I told them about mine and Flint's relationship, from basic training to Korea, going into detail about the bitter cold and the miserable conditions. I told them about our conversations to pass the time. I left out the combat stories, but touched on everything else, even telling them about the terrible rations that we had to endure.

They, in turn, told me about Flint's childhood and growing up on the farm. They talked about his girlfriend who had married this summer but still came to visit them. Flint's sister had married a rancher in Oklahoma, but they hadn't been blessed with grandchildren yet. I was surprised at how young they were, probably in their mid to late forties. Flint resembled his dad, being short and heavy set. His mother was also larger than most women. After the initial greeting, it was evident that they were jolly, and fun loving people, much like their son.

Flint had never mentioned them by name, only Mom and Dad. I discovered that his name was Lloyd and her name was Trudy. As the evening wore on Lloyd said, "Sam, let me drive you around and show you the farm while Trudy puts something together for supper."

I discovered, as we rode around, that his farm included half a section, or 320 acres, and had been in the family for three generations. There were no fences separating the fields since he didn't run any livestock. He described his crops at each of the fields.

"We didn't make any wheat this year. It wouldn't have even paid the combining. We had several snows in January and February so we have a little moisture that might be enough to get up the cotton. I left the wheat stubble to keep the soil from blowing away. We've had some terrible dust storms. Flint was a big help on the farm. He would run one tractor and me the other. The years have been too lean for hiring someone to plow.

It was obvious that the land was good and fertile but without moisture, impossible to grow crops that were profitable. I mentioned that to Lloyd.

"It's a good farm, Sam. We did fine here until the drought and now we're struggling to make ends meet. If it doesn't start raining soon, we're going to be in a world of trouble."

The supper was delicious, with fresh squash and okra from the garden which they could water from their well, and baked chicken, with cherry cobbler for dessert. We visited after supper, and before they showed me to my room, we stopped by Flint's. They hadn't changed it since he left for basic training. All of his pictures were up, including one in his band uniform.

I stayed a week with the McGowans and enjoyed every minute of it. I volunteered to help with the plowing and was on a tractor from sunup until late in the evening, only taking off for lunch. There was something about tilling the soil that was wholesome and invigorating. I understand now how someone could love this lifestyle and never want any other. In the evening before retiring for the night, we would visit, sometimes about Flint, other times about myself. I told them of my adventure in Arizona and its purpose, emphasizing that it was not only for me but for Flint as well. I didn't tell them about the money. It was the last day before leaving that I would come to a decision as to how I would handle it. I wrote the letter the night I was to leave the next morning.

The only way I would agree to offer information on the war was if whatever I was paid Flint's parents would receive an equal amount. They agreed to my demand, and I received a check for this amount, also. After being with you a week, I can now understand why the goodness in Flint was beyond measure.

Love,
Sam Colter

I left the letter with the check on the dresser by my bed. I was afraid that saying goodbye would be emotional, but after promising them a return visit, it was only hugs and well wishes.

It was Monday, March 28, and Mattie was due back into Plainview around 3:00 that afternoon. Her mother had given me the information in a conversation we had earlier in the week. I was at the airport two hours early. The two-hour wait seemed forever, but finally the planes appeared. They landed, and I waited anxiously to see Mattie exit one of the planes. When she didn't appear, I asked one of the players where Mattie Quentin was. The girl told me to wait and went over to one of the pilots. He came over and explained Mattie's absence.

"Mattie became really ill last night in Mexico. She was running a high fever, and throwing up. We didn't want to take her to a doctor over there but waited until we could take her to Amarillo. Coach Redin took her right on to the emergency room at Northwest Hospital. They should be just about there by now. I can give you directions if you like?"

Within minutes I was on the road to Amarillo, thinking, *why did I feel so good. I should've known something bad was going to happen. How can I be this stupid? I'm destined for sadness and loss. Please God, don't let anything happen to Mattie.*

I found the hospital due to the good directions and went directly to the emergency room. I was directed to a waiting room where a nurse informed me that tests were being made. After what seemed like hours, a doctor came out and introduced himself as Dr. Pate.

"Are you a relative?" he asked.

"No, she's my girlfriend."

"Can you get in touch with her parents?" he asked.

"Yes. I have her mother's phone number."

"You better contact them. This is a sick young lady. I believe she has meningitis and it may be one of the worst kinds. We are going to make more tests, and I'll keep you informed," he said, turning and walking away.

The next three days were terrible, with the reports only getting worse. I'd called Mattie's mom and she was there with Earnest. They got a motel, but I stayed in the lobby outside her room. They wouldn't allow me to see her because the disease was contagious. I slept in a soft chair and ate out of the vending machine. I prayed day and night that the next report would be good.

The doctor came out the evening of the fourth day and gave us the worst report yet. We stood around him as he explained. "She is not responding to antibiotics and her condition is worsening by the hour. We have done all we can. I'm sorry".

Gladys broke down, and after two hours of grieving, Earnest convinced her they should go back to the motel. I stayed, wondering why this was happening. Surely, there had to be a reason. I lose everything that is important to me. I don't understand. I sat there for the next four hours, saying the same prayer over and over, *please God, don't let her die.* I finally leaned back in the chair and closed my eyes. I wasn't asleep when I heard someone call my name.

"Sam. Sam."

Opening my eyes, a figure was standing in front of me, who said, "Sam, it's ole Zeb, who fixed your Ford. Member me?"

"Sure. What're you doing here?"

"Oh, I comes by here sometimes. How's the little one?"

"Bad. I'm afraid she's going to die. I love her. I can't stand to lose her."

"Let's go in, Sam, and sees her," he said.

"We can't. It's contagious and we aren't allowed."

"Well, ole Zeb's's been known to break a few rules."

We went into the room, and I saw her for the first time. She looked terrible and her breathing was labored. Zeb stood by the other side of the bed.

"Sam, we need to pray over this little girl." He took her hand and began to pray.

"Lord, this is ole Zeb. We been friends a long time. I's need your help now. This boy has lost so much and he needs this little girl in his life. Please heal her, I begs You, Lord. You knows, today would be my son's twenty-third birthday if he had come home from the

war. I knows what it's like to lose someone you love. This boy has lost too much and he needs this girl in his life. Please heal her."

I had closed my eyes for the prayer and when I opened them, Zeb was gone. I didn't even get to thank him for coming. It was strange that he knew about Mattie. My thinking was interrupted by the nurse who came in.

"What're you doing in here? You leave immediately."

I followed her order, going back to my chair in the lobby. For some reason, I felt better. I lay back and dozed off, until someone was shaking me. It was the same nurse who had run me out of the room.

"The doctor is here and would like to speak to you," she said.

"Finally, I have a better report for you. She is responding to the antibiotics and her fever has broken. We can't get our hopes up too much. She is still in danger but at least she is improving."

After that, all the reports were good. Mattie was released from the hospital five days later. She was still weak, but there was no evidence of permanent damage. She rode with me back to Plainview and received a royal welcome from her teammates. It was only six weeks until the end of school, and she wanted to finish the semester. Charley assured me she would be there for her.

I confessed to her in an emotional goodbye that I did love her and left to return home. No way was I going through Tulia without stopping and expressing my appreciation to Zeb for what he had done. I didn't find anyone at home so I went to the station, reminding the owner who I was and asking about Zeb.

"Sure, I remember you. You came through here right before the ice storm in January. I'm sorry to tell you but old Zeb died in January, two weeks after he fixed your car. He's been gone nearly 3 months."

Epilogue

Mattie didn't return to school in the fall of 1955. The Flying Queens still had a rule that prohibited girls on the team from marrying, and she became ineligible on August 18 of that year. The wedding was held in the Pioneer Methodist Church, and the honeymoon to San Angelo was short since there were now five additional puppies to look after. Also, she had to get back and enroll in McMurry College.

Her mother had received a good report on her last trip to Houston, and her pa pa was still living by himself with help from the family.

In January of 1957, a prayer meeting asking for rain was held at the church. One of the ranchers brought his raincoat and others chuckled at his being so sure their prayers would be answered. Leaving the church that day, everyone but the believer, received a good soaking. That day signaled the end of the seven-year drought with the stock tanks filling to capacity. Farmers, once again made good crops, and ranches were restocked with cattle and sheep. She also became pregnant with their first child that year. Sam was ecstatic, asking if they could name him Flint if it was a boy.

A package had come in the mail which contained a poster for the movie, *Pork Chop Hill*, with a picture of Gregory Peck and a list of cast members. Each one of them had signed the poster. She put it up in their bedroom, but wasn't sure if they would ever see the movie.